John Louis William Thudichum

A Treatise on Wines

Their Origin Nature and Varieties with Practical Directions for Viticulture and

Vinification

John Louis William Thudichum

A Treatise on Wines

Their Origin Nature and Varieties with Practical Directions for Viticulture and Vinification

ISBN/EAN: 9783337023911

Printed in Europe, USA, Canada, Australia, Japan

Cover: Foto ©Andreas Hilbeck / pixelio.de

More available books at **www.hansebooks.com**

A TREATISE ON WINES.

GEORGE BELL & SONS

LONDON: YORK ST., COVENT GARDEN

NEW YORK : 66, FIFTH AVENUE, AND

BOMBAY : 53, ESPLANADE ROAD

CAMBRIDGE : DEIGHTON, BELL & CO.

A TREATISE

ON

WINES

THEIR ORIGIN NATURE AND VARIETIES
WITH PRACTICAL DIRECTIONS
FOR VITICULTURE AND
VINIFICATION

BY

J. L. W. THUDICHUM, M.D.

F.R.C.P. LOND.

LONDON
GEORGE BELL AND SONS
1896

First published December 1893.

Reprinted in Bohn's Scientific Library 1896.

PREFACE.

THE publishers of this treatise had intended to arrange a new issue of the work on wines of the late Mr. Cyrus Redding,[1] which had been so well received by the public that it went through several editions. But it was found on approximating the proposition to execution, that not only had time enlarged and altered many parts of the subject, but that as Mr. Redding's work had been written mainly for a political economical object, which had been fully attained by the legislation of 1860, its argument was exhausted and its cycle of life complete. Such a work could not practically be revived by rearrangement to meet the demands of the present time, and the publishers therefore desired me to compose a new and independent treatise of similar dimensions. In view of the exhaustive treatise[2] which I had published jointly with Dr. August Dupré, and of the studies which I had instituted subsequently, and communicated in part in my Cantor Lectures,[3] delivered before the Society of Arts in 1873, I was glad to have an opportunity of treating the subject in an abridged and more accessible form, for the

[1] "A History and Description of Modern Wines." Third Edition. London, 1860.
[2] "A Treatise on the Origin, Nature, and Varieties of Wine, being a complete Manual of Viticulture and Œnology." London, 1872.
[3] "On Wines : their Production, Treatment, and Use." Six Lectures. Reprinted from the Journal of the Society. London, 1873.

cognizance of the public as well as the use of traders, of medical practitioners, and of that part of the inhabitants of naturally favoured colonies and other English-speaking countries, who have begun to look to viticulture as a legitimate and permanent branch of agronomy. The work is strictly scientific as far as it reaches, but by the exclusion of ultimate technical details concerning viticultural, or œno-poetic, or chemical analytical processes, and of statistical accounts of production and trade, it is more adapted for reading than for decisive reference. Savants, traders and other specialists, who desire final information, should consult the treatise quoted above, which it may be confidently asserted rivals any treatise in any language, either as regards fulness and originality of information, or as concerns correct-ness and effect of technical elaboration. The present treatise, within the limits ordained for it, can make a similar claim to confidence, as no accessible means for imparting the utmost value to its contents have been left without con-sideration by the author.

In the history of the culture of the most important nations wine takes a significant place, and is eminent over all other beverages, as well in its daily trivial as in its festive and solemn use. It rouses the higher faculties of thought, memory, and imagination, the poetical forms of all phases of the mind ; it increases the zest of life and its duration. Subordinate, but of similar significance in the given cases, are its powers to remove pain and cheer and strengthen the heart in processes of recovery from fatigue, injury, or illness. Compared to the benefits which wine confers, the harm produced by its misuse is truly insignificant ; even its sym-bolic role has protected its physiological mission, and ought to increase and secure that protection for all time to come.

In the work of my late father, " Grapes and Wine in the

History of Culture,"[1] will be found an almost poetical appreciation of this part of the history of civilization, clothed in diction reminding of Tacitus by brevity and significance. It presents one of the pleasing aspects of the process of culture, as it does not include the record of any conflict of opinions concerning the practice of past centuries. Sixty-seven authors of antiquity, arranged alphabetically from Ælian to Xenophon, contribute the materials for this appreciation, and sixty-seven modern writers, from Anton to Welles, treat the subject either expressly or *passim*, and thus accumulate an amount of ethical testimony for which we moderns have to be highly grateful.

The technical literature, on the other hand, comprises some hundreds of volumes, of which I have scrutinized all that are of any importance or originality, and those in my possession occupy several yards of shelves. To a number of these works reference will be made in the text, *e.g.*, to the works of Guyot, p. 195; of Bronner, *ibid.*; to Dr. Batt's, Von Babo's and Metzger's publications. But it is incompatible with the proportions of this treatise that I should give a bibliography, still less an account of the contents of the works alluded to, much as I should like, and well able as I should be to perform the task. I therefore confine myself to a few short indications of the most prominent writings, in order to aid active minds who should like to institute independent inquiries.

French œnological literature in general is voluminous, and includes many works of interest and importance. Amongst these are the "Universal Ampelography" of Count Odart,

---

[1] Thudichum, Dr. Georg, "Traube und Wein in der Kultur-geschichte." Tübingen, 1881. Published after the death of the author as "the last graceful bequest of his always active Muse," by Professor Dr. F. von Thudichum, of Tübingen.

the "Ampélographie Française" of Victor Rendu, works
which mainly treat of the natural history and cultivation of
vines. Amongst the best known works on the art of making
wine are those of Count Chaptal, peer and minister under
the Bourbon dynasty, who treated the subject from the
chemical standpoint. The work of B. A. Lenoir consists of
a first viticultural and a second œnopoetic part. The work
of M. C. Ladrey (1857), like that of Chaptal, embodies
mainly the application of chemical principles and is the best
French work of the middle of our century ; it represents the
practice of the Bourgogne, in a town of which, Dijon, the
author was professor of chemistry: to it is appended a useful bibliography. The work of Maumené, "Sur le Travail
des Vins," is also chemical, but treats also with great detail
of the physical conditions called into play in the production
of effervescent wines. The works of Pasteur led to great
developments in the knowledge of the nature of the diseases
of wine, which were recognized to be the result of the invasion
of fungi, and of the means for their destruction by the skilful application of heat. The vineyards and wines of the
Médoc were described at length by W. Franck, by
D'Armailhac, and by Ch. Cocks, re-edited by E. Fêret
(1868). This latter contains many sketches of habitations
called "châteaux," and thereby approaches to an illustrated
traveller's guide, for which indeed Cocks had originally intended it ; other parts of France have not been so explicitly
treated, and on some important areas, e.g., the Moselle valley
of Alsace-Lorraine, the French vine-crowned muse has
remained silent.

Spain counts only few œnological publications; first
amongst them is the work of Clemente, "On the Vines of
Andalusia." Useful encyclopædic works are those of Morales,
who was formerly secretary to the Spanish Board of Agri-

culture; of Tablada, an author of merit, almost the only one who gives original information on Spanish wines in general. A work by Arago opens with an extensive description of Spanish vines; to the œnological part is appended a discourse on cider and on beer. Of special monographs one by Barreto, a physician of Madrid, on the wines of Jerez deserves special notice.

Of Portuguese works we have to notice a series of exhaustive "Reports on the Viticulture and Wines of Lusitania," published by its government in 1867, which fill a large octavo volume, but owing to the want of systematic arrangement and of indices are difficult to peruse. Another Portuguese official publication was ornamented with colour-printed plates representing the principal vines and their fruit in the elegant style of the modern French Duhamel, but the costly enterprise was not completed. Amongst Portuguese monographs on special subjects, that of Oliveira, jun., "On the Phylloxera" (Porto, 1872), is meritorious and well illustrated.

Concerning Italian wines the period of the Renaissance had more and better authors than the present time. An authoritative summary description of Italian wines was published in 1869 as a result of their exhibition in Paris.

Many British authors have left us works of interest and value. One of the earliest was Sir Edward Barry, a physician at Bath, and afterwards state-physician to the Viceroy of Ireland. Dr. Henderson's "History of Wines" was published in 1824, that of Redding in 1836; the works of M'Culloch ("Commercial Dictionary") and of Busby ("Travels") gave much useful information. Forrester, "On Port Wine," appeared in 1854, Tovey's work in 1862. The sale of the contents of the cellar of this scientific and accomplished wine merchant, which took place after his death, a few years ago, at Bristol, realised remarkably high prices. The work of Mr. T. G. Shaw was distinguished by original information, and by the endeavour to lighten what he thought a heavy subject by the buoyancy of much poetry. Sheen's work also was a creditable performance, though, like most authors who attempt to treat didactic scientific subjects in what I may be allowed to call a belletristic manner, its writer rather diluted his essence by the introduction of anecdote for the diversion of the reader, as Shaw imported poetry. The late Dr. Druitt's writings were intended to popularize cheap wines, and in this direction they have had a certain amount of success, particularly by making the public better acquainted with the effervescent wines of the valley of the Loire. Sir J. Emerson Tennent's essay, "On Wine, Its Use and Taxation," 1855, was mainly directed against the reduction of the import tax on wine; it was an able diplomatic and economical memorial, and much of its argument has been borne out by modern developments of the wine trade.

Wines of Australia were for the first time scientifically described by the Rev. John I. Bleasdale, in one of the so-called "International Exhibition (Melbourne, 1872-73) Essays."

Much useful information was at one time collected by the Parliamentary Committee on the Wine Duties, which is embodied in two volumes of Reports of Evidence. The annual reports of our consuls are also valuable sources of information, particularly on statistics of commerce and production.

It is to be hoped that the political movement for the expansion of the wine trade which was begun in 1860 may be continued in the future, and obtain the hygienic results which its promoters endeavoured to secure. The art of making wine must include as an integral part the art and science of *preventing its diseases*, those remarkable parasitisms by the agency of which great volumes of originally excellent material are ceaselessly and irrecoverably spoiled and lost. When this art and science shall have found systematic application, the present insecurity of viticulturists and traders will disappear, and the public will be able to obtain excellent wines, such as at present are beyond the reach of most people. When wine on its field shall be as good and cheap and accessible as bread now universally is in this country, the striving of politicians and men of science will have been rewarded by the success, which will add another pillar to the great edifice of modern freedom and civilization.

CONTENTS.

A TREATISE ON WINES.

CHAPTER I.

ORIGIN, GEOGRAPHY, AND HISTORY OF VINES.

§ 1. DEFINITION AND ETYMOLOGY OF WINE.

WINE is a beverage obtained from the juice of grapes by fermentation, composed of alcohol, ethers, acids, water, and peculiar agreeably-smelling ingredients, which some term aroma, others, with more reason, bouquet. Fermented beverages are obtained from many other materials besides grape juice, such are the sap of different palms, the Mexican *pulque*, from the stem of an agave, the sap of the maple, birch, the Homeric lotos,[1] and all kinds of sugar-containing fruit and berries, honey, corn, rice, vegetable roots, including manioc.[2] Such drinks have also been termed wine, but generally distinguished by prefixing the name of the vegetable from which their main character was derived, *e.g.*, gooseberry-wine.[3] The name wine comes from the Indo-German orient ; in Hebrew it occurs as *jaïn*, in Ethiopian as *waïn*, in Greek as *oinos*, not improbably pronounced *woinos* in Homeric times,[4] Georgian Caucasian *ghwins*, Latin, *vinum ;* this last name is repeated in the Romanic languages with only a modification of the terminal syllable. From these names, which are only a selection out of many,

---

[1] Hom., "Od.," ix. 94 ; Herodot., iv. 177 ; Virgil, " Georg.,"ii. 84.
[2] Humboldt, "Reisen in den Æquinoctialgegenden," vi. 119.
[3] Plin., "Hist. N.," xiv. 16, gives a list of made wines.
[4] Plato gave a humorous derivation of the word, which pointed to delusions of intoxication. (Plutarch, "Sympos." vii. 10.)

B

it has been concluded, and with no small degree of certainty, that viticulture and the preparation of wine have been introduced to western nations from the orient. The Greek *mythos* of the migration from India to Hellas of the wine-god Dionysos point to the same conclusion.

§ 2. ORIGIN AND DESCENT OF VINES.

The vine is older than all history, and indeed older than humanity itself, as is evident from the occurrence of its fruit and leaves in deposits formed during geologically so-called tertiary times, which are far anterior to any trace of human existence. It grows in a so-called wild or uncultivated state in many parts of the old and new world, in the valley of the Rhine, of the Danube, as well as that of the Orontes in central Asia, and that of the Amoor at its eastern end, in Italy, Sicily, and Portugal, in central and northern America. Many wild vines bear no fruit at all, others bear uneatable and useless fruit, others again, sour or sweet and eatable berries.[1] The assumption therefore that cultivated vines were derived from one particular species, the *vitis vinifera*, and that wild vines were degenerated offsprings of this native of Asia is not tenable. Candolle,[2] who has made such a deep study of the origin and distribution of plants, particularly those which are cultivated by man, does not think it practical to derive a distinction between vines from the fact of their being "cultivated" or "spontaneous," but he declares Armenia to be the land in which the species originated.[3] As a reason for this opinion he adduces the fact that in Armenia the most gigantic vines, with stems of the thickness of the human body and the height and expanse of large trees, produce without cultivation grapes of good taste.[4] But vines of similar size are known to have grown in Campania, on the Caspian Sea, in Cashmir, on the Lebanon, where in the last century there were yet vines

---

[1] Meyen, "Grundr. d. Pflanzengeographie."
[2] Alph. de Candolle, "Geogr. botanique raisonnée," p. 872.
[3] "Patrie originaire de l'espèce," *l. c.*
[4] Cf. Gervinus, "Histor. Schriften," Bd. vii., § 177.

with trunks six inches in diameter, bearing bunches of the weight of twelve pounds.[1] Meyen on the other hand believes Cyrenaica to be the fatherland of the vine. In the presence of the theory of evolution it would not be difficult to comprehend a derivation from one original species, or from several varieties. But the discussion is not likely to be conducted to an acceptable conclusion, as the scientific data for its consideration are too scarce and too imperfect.

We find in viticultural literature many allusions to, or even descriptions of, wild vines. Thus Crescentius, who lived in the thirteenth century at Bologna, and wrote a compendium[2] on agriculture, mainly after the ancient Latin authors, Palladius and Columella, stated that he had met with many varieties of wild vines in Italy, which appeared to him to be peculiar sorts; and Clemente[3] recognized the peculiar character of the wild vines of his country, and believed them to be indigenous to it, and consequently to have existed there previous to the introduction or origination of the cultivated species. He expresses himself as opposed to the limitation of botanists who assume the original existence of only one *vitis vinifera* and refer all other varieties to a play of nature. He describes different kinds of wild vines, perfectly characterized, as growing in the Algaida, a sandy district near San Lucar de Barrameda, mainly grown over with sea-pines. Of this district and its vines, the so-called *garañones*, the reader will find a special description under the chapter referring to Andalusia, entitled " The Algaida and its Indigenous Vines," in which the author has embodied the results of a special visit made to the locality.

In the southern parts of France, in Provence, Languedoc and Guyenne, wild vines are met with on hedges, in jungles, or in woods and forests. According to Duhamel[4]

[1] Schulz, "Diary of 1754," ed. Volz., "Beiträge zur Kulturgessch," 1852, § 52.

[2] Petrus de Crescentiis, "Opus ruralium commodorum," Augsburg, 1471, Louvain, 1474, and many other editions in various languages.

[3] Simon Roxas Clemente, Director of the Botanical Garden, Madrid, in his work, " The Vines of Andalusia."

[4] Duhamel de Monceau, " Traité des Arbres fruitiers," p. 212.

they differ from the cultivated varieties by their leaves being in general smaller, and more cottony on the surface, and particularly by their fruit being much smaller, and of a less soft and sugary taste. These wild vines, to which the ancients had given the name of *Labrusca*,[1] are yet known in the present day in the south of France under the name of *Lambrusco* and *Lambresquiero*.

With Gmelin begins the scientific diagnosis of wild vines. In elaborating the *Flora Badensis* he observed that the wild vine frequently occurred in the dioic state, that is to say, that some plants were male, and bore no fruit, while others were female, and bore fruit provided they stood in the neighbourhood of male plants. He described such plants botanically and gave them a separate place in his treatise, under the title of *vitis sylvestris*. In most botanical works which appeared subsequently to Gmelin, the *vitis sylvestris* is quoted after him, but the discovery is mostly neutralized by the observation that the *vitis sylvestris* was nothing but a degenerated *vitis vinifera*. Other botanists, including Reichenbach, fell into the error of confounding the American *vitis labrusca*, as accepted by Linné, with the *vitis sylvestris*. These errors were removed, and the observations of Gmelin were re-established and expanded by the distinguished œnologist, J. P. Bronner, of Wiesloch near Heidelberg. He studied these children of the forest in their natural haunts, the woods which border the marshy shores of the Rhine between Mannheim and Rastadt, where they grow by thousands; he visited them in early summer-time, and selected from innumerable individuals the types of inflorescence, and multifarious forms of leaves; he marked the places of their abode, and returning in the fall, saw and tasted the grapes, which had then come to maturity. After devoting years to the observation of the several constant varieties, he took cuttings from them and planted them in his garden at Wiesloch, in order to observe their bearing in

---

[1] Linné does not seem to have been acquainted with wild vines of Europe, for he applied this ancient name or adjective of theirs to an American indigenous vine, the first variety which he admitted by the side of the *vinifera*.

the state of cultivation.   (I visited this vineyard in 1866, and examined a considerable number of these children of the Rhine marshes.[1])   Bronner had thus planted thirty-six varieties, when in the year 1842, a very favourable wine-year, most of his plants bore very perfect fruit, and brought it to the utmost maturity.   None of these plants had changed their original character by cultivation.   He caused accurate pictorial representations of their fruit to be made.   Already, during the time of blossoming, he had obtained faithful portraits of the flowers, leaves, and branches, partly by a kind of nature-printing, and when these were coloured by an artist, the whole formed a complete botanical atlas of the wild vines of the Upper Rhine valley.[2]   At the same time Bronner made an accurate botanical diagnosis of, and attributed a suitable Latin name to each variety, and arranged the whole as a special system, based upon the construction of the flowers, and the formation of the fruit.

The inflorescence of these wild vines shows three distinct forms.   A considerable number of plants exhibit only a male inflorescence without any umbilicus capable of fructification; in the place where there should be a beginning of a berry there is a yellow receptacle filled with honey.   The plants showing this peculiarity produce an enormous number of blossoms, each of which is several inches in length, and with its long yellow stamina and terminal pollen bags resembles a brush such as is used for cleaning bottles.   The flowers distribute a most agreeable odour around the plant.[3]

A certain number of the other vines have exactly the same inflorescence as the cultivated vines, they are hermaphrodite, with long projecting yellow stamina and pollen bags, and an umbilicus capable of impregnation.   The leaves of these vines differ but little from those of the cultivated varieties, but the fruit has a different shape, and a different chemical nature, being often very acid and sometimes quite inedible.

[1] Cf. Thudichum and Dupré, *l. c.*, p. 4, footnote.
[2] This atlas is now in the Library and Museum of the Œconomical and Agricultural Society of Baden, at Karlsruhe.
[3] Compare with this description the account which Pliny gives of the "Œnanth."

But the great majority of individuals as well as species of wild vine have a most peculiar inflorescence, differing con-

Fig. 1.—Inflorescence of hermaphrodite wild and cultivated vines. (Magnified.)

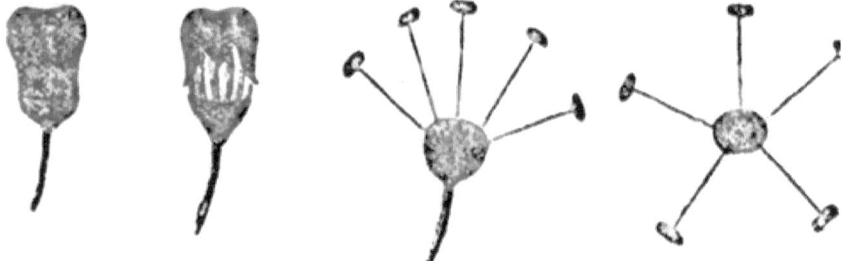

Fig. 2.—Inflorescence of male or sterile wild vines, with open honey cup in place of fruit. (Magnified.)

Fig. 3.—Inflorescence of female or fructiferous wild vines, with recurved stamina.

siderably from the two forms just described. On close examination of an active blossom of this class it is seen that the ordinary so-called crown or cap, which the cultivated vine always sheds completely, is actually detached, but remains hanging upon the flower, while the stamina are bent downwards below the basis of the future fruit. The stamina become, as botanists technically term them, *stamina recurvata*, and thus greatly differ in appearance from the *stamina erecta* of the wild unproductive variety above described, and of the hermaphrodite wild and cultivated plants.

Bronner surmised that the plants which show the *stamina recurvata* were unable to fructify themselves, but required the male plants with *stamina erecta* for impregnation. The transfer of the pollen from the male to the female individuals, which are mostly standing at a distance from each other, is very probably effected by the agency of insects.

American vines also occur in the polygamic as well as in the dioic state. Monographers do not admit this to be a characteristic feature, but hold it to be an accident to which any variety of vine may be subject.

In some vineyards of the department of the Ain, in France, a variety of vine is cultivated which is termed the *mescle*. It has long bunches of oval grapes and deeply lobated leaves, mostly with five divisions. Each of these divisions or lobes is provided with a considerable expanse of vegetable membrane on both sides of the principal so-called nerve in every case in which the plant is fertile; but a leaf with a narrow strip of membrane on both sides of the nerve indicates a sterile plant; such a leaf resembles that of a Virginia creeper. By these peculiarities the plants can be easily distinguished from each other, even at a distance.

The absolutely and always sterile plants of the *mescle* vine are termed by the vine dressers *plants craputs*. They grow luxuriant branches, and the apparently crippled character of their leaves is no indication of any general want of vigour. Their cuttings and pro-vines are as sterile as the parent stocks. The French imperialist viticultural author, Guyot,[1] was as unable to account for these phenomena as were the vine-dressers; but these latter did not dare to

---

[1] "Rapport sur la Viticulture de l'Ain," pp. 137.

totally extirpate the sterile mescle from the vineyard, although they abstained from increasing the number of individuals. The sterile mescle is no doubt the male, and the
fertile its female variety, with probably hermaphrodite plants
intermixed.

Bronner classified the hermaphrodite indigenous wild
vines of the Rhine valley; his list comprises twenty-eight
varieties, of which the details may be consulted in his
original work.[1] Not a single bunch of grapes was met with
which could be said to be similar to or identical with any
variety of the cultivated grapes of the Rhine valley. The
grapes were mostly *black*, and amongst many thousands of
plants only three were found bearing *white* fruit. Of these
latter one had *acid*, the other moderately *sweet* fruit; the
third bore delicious *orange-flavoured* grapes. The bunches
of the two first white varieties were loose, pendulous, and
carried long small berries; the orange-flavoured vine had
bunches with densely placed grapes. Among the black
varieties some bore very small bunches, others reached
from two to five inches in length; most common were the
black grapes of *oval* shape. The shapes of the leaves
differed greatly.

In Upper and Lower Austria, particularly between Vienna
and Pressburg, there grow many wild vines on the shores of
the Danube, as well as on the islands of the river.[2] Similar
vines appear below Buda, and extend to Transylvania. The
borders of the Theiss are enlivened by their presence; the
Save, where it issues from Croatia, waters many plants of
this kind. On the Adige, in the Tyrol, there are some
jungles formed by wild vines creeping over low shrubs of
Rhus cotinus and wild fig-trees; the wild vines accompany
the Adige into the low marshy country.

From the foregoing it is evident that all those European
countries which possess the climatic conditions have in their
flora many species of the genus *Vitis* in a wild state, with
such botanical characters as leave no doubt that the plants
are indigenous, produced by natural selection from proto-

[1] Cf. also Thudichum and Dupré, *l. c.*, pp. 8 and 9.
[2] Jaquin in an article in the Austrian "Annals of Agriculture."

types, and not derived from imported cultivated races of vines, or degenerated by the struggle for existence from previously cultivated races, the products of artificial crossing or human selection.

§ 3. ORIGIN OF CULTIVATED VINES.

In the appreciation of the nature of the different wines produced in the world, it must be borne in mind that each particular district producing a particular kind of well-charac-terized wine does so by means of particular well-characterized varieties of vines. These vines must be considered as having been either indigenous to these districts, or as having been produced in them by natural or artificial selec-tion from indigenous varieties; for when transplanted to other districts they change their character more or less so as to produce a different wine; or they lose their peculiarities so completely as to be worthless for making wine; or they cease to be fructiferous; or lastly, they do not succeed at all, and pine and die out.

The *Aramont* is a vine commonly grown about Montpellier on account of its extraordinary fertility; transplanted to the south of Germany it begins to bear in the fourth year and produces many and large bunches of grapes, but year by year its fertility decreases, its originally large berries become smaller, until the viticulturist is obliged to remove the barren plants. Bronner[1] who had become acquainted with the extraordinary fertility of some vines of Upper Austria—the *Rothgipfler, green Muscateller, the white one of Grinzing* (a village near Vienna) and the *red Zierifandler of Vöslau*—planted numerous samples of all four varieties in his vine-yard at Wiesloch. During ten years he did not obtain a single grape from any of them, and after ten further years all the vines had died out.

The vines of Europe transplanted to North America do not succeed. Viticulture in that country has hitherto only succeeded with indigenous varieties or their crosses. Even the wine made from the celebrated Catawba is so flavourless

---

[1] Bronner " Die wilden Trauben," etc. p. 32.

that the best which we could obtain from St. Louis was strongly flavoured with elder-flower.

Invariably American vines which yield yet drinkable wine in the United States, when grown in the Gironde degenerate and yield no drinkable wine.[1]

Vines transplanted from more northern to southern latitudes do not succeed any better than those which have made the inverse migration. We dismiss as unproved the often repeated statement, that the Portuguese *Bucellas* wine was made from the "hock-grape;" but we reject as entirely fabulous the statement that the vine called *Pedro Ximenes* had been brought to Spain from the banks of the Moselle by the man whose name it bears. As a French author[2] wittily said, "If he took any he took all; for no such vine grows nowadays north of the Pyrenees."

The vines of the Alto Douro differ in specific botanical character from all other vines, as port wine differs from other wine. The Gironde produces the peculiar red wines by means of its Carbenet, Carmenère, Malbec, and Verdot. Transplanted to Spain, these vines do not produce claret any longer; in a climate less moist and less warm, these vines so lose their fertility as to cease to be remunerative objects of agriculture.

We might greatly increase the number of data, all pointing to the same conclusion, but those above given are sufficient to prove a general law, namely, that every uniform climatic region has its peculiarly adapted varieties of wild and cultivated vines, which cannot be so successfully cultivated in other regions, or cannot be cultivated at all anywhere else.

§ 4. FOSSIL VINES AND GRAPES.

The vine existed certainly in Germany, and perhaps also in Bohemia and Tuscany,[3] during the tertiary and before

---

[1] We learned this from the late M. Boucherot of Carbonnieux near Bordeaux, who planted American vines on a large scale.

[2] Count Odart, "Traité des Cepages."

[3] Cf. Gaudin, "Mém. sur quelques Gisements des Feuilles fossiles de la Toscane."

the basaltic outbreaks which succeeded the tertiary deposits. In the relative situations there existed jungles close to lakes or morasses, in which latter the decaying vegetation of the neighbourhood became imbedded, and by commixture of clay, preserved. Thus deposits of lignite, or brown-coal were formed, which now supply the neighbourhood with fuel. In this lignite the preserved parts of vines are found in our time. But these deposits have been preserved from ulterior changes, from being washed away by rain, or the combined effects of the agencies which produce what in geology is termed *denudation*, by having been covered over by basaltic lava, which in the particular case of Salzhausen in Hesse, is no less than 180 feet thick.[1]

These lignites contain a great variety of impressions of leaves, such as oak leaves resembling the Mexican evergreen varieties, species of smilax and anona, leaves of a walnut-like tree called carya, and its nuts, the small fruit of a pistachia, and the broad leaves of a fig-tree, with here and there the impression of a half-grown fig. Interspersed with these, or in separate layers, are found the impressions of the leaves of the fossil vine, *vitis teutonica*,[2] and large quantities of the seeds of its fruit, " regular fossil raisin-stones," in the shape of regular cakes of " murk," or compressed masses of kernels and membranes, the residues of husks.

§ 5. Geographical Distribution of Vines on the Northern Hemisphere.

The vine meets with the climatic conditions of its growth, and the perfection of its fruit, on the northern hemisphere, in a belt of territory which is enclosed between two lines, a northern one on the polar limit and a southern or equatorial

---

[1] For details concerning this deposit cf. Thudichum and Dupré, " Treatise," etc., p. 14-16 ; also Tasché, in the " Transactions of the Imperial Caroline Academy of Sciences."

[2] They were formerly believed to be derived from a species of acer, but correctly diagnosed by A. Brown. Cf. F. Unger, " Sylloge Plantarum Fossilium," in the Sitz. Ber. d. K. Acad. d. W. ; Wien, 1861, vol. xix.

limit. Commencing north of the Azores, the *polar limit*
passes through the Channel south of England, excluding
that country, enters France in the Brétagne at Vannes, and
runs by Mazières, Alençon and Beauvais. It then takes
a more northern turn, includes a portion of Rhenish
Prussia, passes to the north of Thuringia, the valley of the
Saale, Saxony, and then crosses the Carpathians, to pass
through South Russia, almost in a straight line to the northern
end of the Caspian Sea. Thence it proceeds to the river
Amoor, and somewhat to the north of the southern bend of
that river ends in the Pacific Ocean. The *equatorial limit*
passes south of the Canary Islands, including them and all
the islands near the African and Spanish coast. It enters
Africa about the 30th degree of northern latitude, and,
running near that degree, leaves Africa at the middle of the
Isthmus of Suez; runs across Arabia and the Persian Sea,
enters India near the 25th degree of northern latitude, runs
down into Hindostan with a loop, nearly parallel to its
sea-borders, so that the whole interior of Hindostan is comprised in it while the whole seaboard is excluded. It
then passes again to the north, enters China and forms a
loop southwards similar to that in Hindostan, to terminate at the eastern end of it, on the 27th degree of northern
latitude.

These limits are really those of the *culture* of the vine; for
some varieties will grow to the north of the limit, though its
fruit never ripens unless with the aid of exceptional protection: to the south of the equatorial limit the vine becomes an
evergreen on which all stages of growth are represented at
the same time; and under these circumstances it does not
mature its fruit with the same perfection as when it is subject to the rotation of the seasons.

The vine requires for the ripening of its fruit not a certain
high average temperature of the year, but a maximum of
summer heat, without which the fruit does not ripen. In
accordance with this general law England does not produce
wine, for although its average temperature is very high, its
maximum summer heat is not high enough, owing to the
large masses of water vapour which constantly pervade the

air over Britain, and prevent the sun's rays from influencing the vegetation with the required energy.

The cultivation of the vine in America is apparently included between limits similar to those prevailing in Europe. Even the indigenous American vines cannot be cultivated north of 50 degrees north latitude. The scuppernong does not succeed north of the Potomac, and the indigenous vines apparently do not pass south of the centre of Mexico.

On the southern hemisphere, Peru, South Africa (at least the Cape of Good Hope), and Australia produce wine. The extent of the cultivation in these districts is at present not exactly known, but it seems somewhat to increase in Australia.

§ 6. Viticulture in England in Mediæval Times.

In apparent contradiction to the foregoing and apparently unexplained, but supported by documentary evidence, stands the assertion that during some centuries, beginning somewhat before the Norman Conquest, wine was grown in many parts of the south of England. We take the following data from Redding's work,[1] premising that in the scrutiny of ancient documents a doubt must be allowed, whether the Latin word, which has been read as *vinarium*, whether it mean a vineyard or a wine-cellar, may not have signified, and therefore must not necessarily be read as *vivarium*, meaning a pond in which fish were reared or kept for use in a living state.

Doomsday Book proves that wine was made in Essex, six acres producing 160 gallons. Rabelais, who was born in 1483, makes an allusion in his works to wine of Britain— not Bretagne, but England. William of Malmesbury, in his book, "De Pontificibus," says that the Vale of Gloucester used to produce, in the twelfth century, as good wine as many of the provinces of France. Near Tewkesbury is a field still called the "Vineyard." A messuage and land in Twyning were held of the lord of Tewkesbury on certain conditions, one of which was the "finding a man for sixteen

[1] *L. c.* p. 33, *et seq.*

days in digging in the vineyard, and gathering the grapes for three days." *Ing. ad.* q. d. 39, Ed. III.—Fosbr. Glouc., ii. 293. In the counties of Worcester, Hereford, Somerset, Cambridge, and Essex, there are lands which bear the name of vineyards, many of them having been attached to particular church establishments, whose ruins are yet in their vicinity. Raleigh, in Essex, was valued, in the time of King Edward, at ten pounds, *propter vinum.* In regard to the Vale of Gloucester, William of Malmesbury says, "There is no province in England which has so many and good vineyards, neither on account of their fertility nor the sweetness of the grape." The tithes of the vines of Lincombe, near Bath, were confirmed to the abbey there in 1150, by Archbishop Theobald. The village of Winnal, or Wynall, near Winchester, was so named from a vineyard, and not from any saint, as some pretend. Besides the counties above mentioned, Hertford, Middlesex, Norfolk, Suffolk, Kent, Hants, Dorset, and Wilts, had vine cultivation, as appears from Doomsday Book; but no county north of Cambridge is said to have borne vines. Hence it may be concluded that the vine did not yield any profit if it grew northward of that place. The etymology of Winnal is said to be the Welsh "gwinllan," a vineyard. Vines are distinguished in old writings as "portantes" or "non portantes." The terms, "Vinea nova," "Vinea noviter," and "Nuperrime plantata," occur about the date of the Norman conquest. Six "arpens" of land were then said, if the vines turned out well—*si benè procedit*—to produce, by one author, 160 gallons—by another, 120. In seeming opposition to this, it is recorded, in "Mémoires pour la Vie de Petrarch," p. 337, tome i., in an extract from one of Petrarch's own letters to a friend, A.D. 1337, that "in England they drink nothing but beer and cyder. The drink of Flanders is hydromel; and as wine cannot be sent to those countries but at great expense, few persons can afford to drink it." Petrarch, however, must have spoken from hearsay alone. More recently, M. Arago, of the French Institute, has commented on the changes in the climate of France. He says that at Mâcon, in the department of the Saone and Loire—ancient Burgundy—

wine, in 1553, was made of the Muscat grape, which it is not now possible to ripen there. The vineyards of Etampes and Beauvais were at one time celebrated. Their wines, if now made, are unworthy of notice. According to a report compiled in 1830, no wine can be made in the whole department of the Somme. M. Arago instances a similar change of climate in England, proved by old chronicles as above quoted, and, inquiring into the causes of this change, thinks that a very marked alteration of climate has taken place both in France and England. "The cause," he says, "is certainly not connected with the sun—a proof of which is given in the steadiness of the temperature of Palestine."

CHAPTER II.

CHEMICAL CONSTITUENTS OF SOIL AND VINES.

§ 7. MINERAL CONSTITUENTS OF THE VINE AND THEIR RELATION TO THOSE OF THE SOIL.

AN exact knowledge of the mineral constituents of the vine enables the viticulturist to adapt his soil to the necessities of the plant in the most perfect and economical manner, and thus to furnish one of the most important elementary conditions of the greatest possible production of grapes and wine. The mode of obtaining this knowledge is part of the science of analytical chemistry, and as such is without the limits of the present treatise. We therefore deal only with the great features of the results as far as they are necessary to the reader to enable him to appreciate facts and processes which have to be alluded to summarily in the later chapters.

The mineral constituents of vines, like those of all organized living beings, are obtained as ashes by the combustion of their several parts. A part of the ash is soluble in water, and comprises the alkali metals, potassium and sodium, combined with carbonic and sulphuric acid and chlorine; while another portion is insoluble in water, and consists of calcium, magnesium, iron and manganese, combined with carbonic, phosphoric, and silicic acid. The proportions of alkalies to earths are about equal: and again, the united weight of the bases is about equal to the half of the weight of the entire ash. Different vines yield different proportions of ash, but vines of the same kind and the same period of vegetation yield very similar proportions of ash. The ashes of the various parts of the vine, of leaves, branches, wood, and roots, differ from each other in a very striking manner.[1]

The *ripe woody* canes at the end of the year's growth contain from 20 % to 25 % of moisture, and from 2·2 % to 4·2 % of ash. *Old wood* and *roots* contain a little more; *capillary roots* with 63 % moisture, 6 % ash; *pith* with 86 % moisture, 7·5 % ash. These large quantities of moisture in pith and capillary roots explain partly why they are more easily killed by frost.

Leaves yield the greatest amount of ash, and *ripe grapes* the smallest. The less mineral matter a part contains the greater is in its ash the proportion of soluble salts; inversely with the rise of the total ash falls the proportion of soluble salts, so that the percentage of soluble ash in leaves is the lowest among all specimens of ash examined. Half-ripe grapes contain a very low percentage of ash, and in this the maximum percentage of soluble salts.

As canes and grapes are mostly removed from vineyards, while the leaves are left on the ground, it is economically important to consider what *kind and amount of ash* is removed annually from a vineyard. This inquiry was instituted by the celebrated French philosopher Boussingault at his estate in Alsatia, and led to the following remarkable results.

The *canes* yielded 2·44 % of ash; the *murk* after the must had been pressed out, air-dry, 6·65 %; the *wine* gave 0·19 %. The ash of canes contains less potash and more lime than that of the murk, and the proportion of potash to lime is highest in the wine. Thus we get per cent. of

---

[1] Analytical details, the results of many thousands of analyses, tables showing the per cent. composition of ashes, and references to the literature of the subject are given by Thudichum and Dupré, *l. c.* pp. 19-30.

potash contained in ash of canes 18·0, murk 36·9, wine 45·0; per cent. of lime contained in ash of canes 27·3, murk 10·7, wine 4·9. The percentage of magnesia contained in the ash of canes is 6·1, murk 2·2, wine 9·2. The wine yields a very small percentage of ash compared to the other parts, and in consequence its percentage of alkalies is smaller than that of any other part of the vine; but as it has lost much mineral matter during fermentation, the quantity of its ash is not the measure of the quantity of mineral matter removed by it from the soil; for ascertaining this latter amount the murk before fermentation, or must and yeast with accompanying matters, have to be examined.

Berthier [1] analysed a fruit-bearing one year's branch, cut from a Gamay vine at Nemours, in October, 1850, at the time of the vintage, and the grapes attached to it. The branch and leaves contained nine times as much inorganic matter, four times as much alkaline salts, fourteen times as much earthy salts, and six to seven times as much phosphates as the grapes.

Raisin stones contain about 2 % of ash, and of this quantity one half is phosphate of calcium.

The leaves in full vegetation contain about 75 % of water, and 2·1 % of ash; therefore, ash in the dry residue 8·4 %. Of this ash one half is carbonate of calcium, or 51 %, and 15·3 % is phosphate of calcium. The soluble potassium salts obtained, as sulphate and carbonate, amount to 15 % of the ash.

Leaves at the time of the fall contain only 66 % of moisture and 11·34 % of ash in about 34·02 % of dry residue. In this ash the carbonate of calcium is increased to 62·62 %, the phosphate decreased to 13·27 %, and the soluble potassium salts are diminished to 8·82 % of the ash.

The mineral matters of ripe grapes are so distributed that if the stalks contain one part, the murk contains about two parts, and the juice from three to four parts; an entire bunch of grapes yields from 0·364 to 0·468 % ash.

[1] See details of analysis in "Treatise," etc., p. 22.

Many other analyses by Vergnette, Bouchardat, Crasso, Walz, Hrushauer, Levi, which have yielded results closely corresponding to the foregoing data may be seen in the "Treatise," pp. 23-26.

Of 100 parts of grape bunches, about 4 parts are stalks, 22 parts are murk, *i.e.* husks and stones and 74 (filtered) juice.

§ 8. Influence of the Soil on the Mineral Constituents of the Vine.

The quantations of the proportions between the bases, or alkalies and alkaline earths in the vine, have taught us that the vine is in this particular respect influenced by the soil on which it is located. Of course it grows best where all the bases are ready at hand in excess, or the necessary quantities for a season's growth; but when the vine cannot find a particular kind of base which it ordinarily wants for its development, it takes another instead; it does not take a random and uncertain quantity, but substitutes for the one which it cannot have *a chemical equivalent* of that which happens to be available, and by this means accomplishes the cycle of its functions. These data have manifested the existence of *a law of nature*, which has been chemically expressed thus:—*The ashes of the vine may contain very variable quantities of potash, soda, lime, and magnesia; but the sum of the quantities of oxygen contained in these bases is always the same, showing that the substitution of one base for another takes place in equivalent proportions.*

§ 9. Functions of Mineral Ingredients of the Vine.

The ash of the vine is obtained by the combustion of its parts; during this process the organic matters with which the bases or salts were in combination are destroyed. Instead of malates, tartrates, and tannates, we obtain in the ash carbonates of potash, soda, and lime; the carbonate of the latter again yields its acid in high temperature and appears as caustic lime. Organic phosphorus compounds, *e.g.* of seeds, and cell nuclei yield phosphoric acid, which expels some of the more volatile acids.   Against this latter emergency no sufficient precaution has hitherto been taken in ash analysis by incineration, and all analyses affected by this error are faulty, and have to be repeated.

To appreciate the part which the bases take in the organic life of the vine, we must therefore consider them in their combinations, just as they occur in the natural tissues and juices.   In these their main function seems to be the fixing and neutralizing of acid nuclei, which, under the reducing influence of light, and in the presence of the elements of vegetable nutrition, water, carbonic acid, ammonia, and nitric acid (from which these nuclei themselves have just been formed) are gradually developed to more complex bodies.   If these bases are not present in the soil in an accessible form, the vine cannot grow at all; if they are present in insufficient amount the growth of the vine is stunted, and its fertility is impaired or suppressed; if they are present in the soil in false proportions the vine effects a substitution, and is able to accomplish the cycle of its changes.   But at the same time this necessity affects, in various ways, its growth, durability, fertility, and the nature of its product; it is very probable that a large amount of failure in viticulture is engendered by such a disproportion in the necessary mineral constituents of the soil.   Lastly, in soils where the vine finds all the mineral ingredients in proper proportion, quantity, and condition, it grows and bears with the greatest perfection.   In this argument it is implied that the position, exposure, watering, and mechanical conditions of the soil are equal in every case, and that the sole variation refers to the mineral ingredients.

§ 10. AMOUNT OF MINERAL MATTER WHICH VITICULTURE ABSTRACTS FROM THE SOIL.

Boussingault obtained from his vineyard, an inclosed property of 170 acres surface, called Schmalzberg, near Lampertsloch, Alsatia. in 1848, 55·05 hectolitres of wine; the murk weighed, air-dry, 492 kilos., and left, at 6·65 %,

32·72 kilos. of ash.　The cutting of the vines in the spring of 1849 yielded 2,624 kilos. of canes, which at 2·44 % left 64·03 % kilos. of ash.　A litre of wine left 1·870 gramme of ash, or 102·94 kilos. for the 55·05 hectolitres.

Calculated for an hectare all available data seem to show an annual exportation by a crop of *mixed canes* of more than 40 kilos. of mineral matter, of which 6 are potash, 7·28 phosphoric acid.　If during the progress of viticulture green branches with leaves are removed from the vineyards, as is not rarely done in viticultural districts for the purpose of feeding domestic herbivorous animals, greater quantities of mineral matters are exported.

Vergnette calculated that on the Côte d'Or an hectare of land supports about 25,700 vines ; these produce annually about 11,462 kilos. of *wood, leaves,* and *grapes,* which burnt together would leave 356 kilos. of ash, containing 69·40 kilos. of soluble and 286·60 kilos. of insoluble salts.

§ 11. Organic Ingredients and Chemical Development of the Vine.

The ingredients of the seed are *lignine,* which builds up its woody structure, then *starch, tannic acid, fatty oil,* several *albuminous and phosphorised substances,* and the *mineral salts* already referred to.　As soon as with the aid of these substances the young plant, consisting of a root with fibrils and spongioles, and a little stalk with leaves, has been constructed, it becomes independent of the nourishment from the seed, and draws its supplies from earth and air.　These it transforms by the elimination of oxygen and the combination of the more carbonized products with the elements of water.　Thereby a series of *acids* are formed, which from the beginning are combined with the *bases* above described. Carbonic acid is first transformed into *oxalic acid ;* by the combination of two of its particles, and the substitution of some oxygen by hydrogen, *malic acid,* the acid contained in apples, berries of the mountain ash, and unripe grapes, is formed.　This malic acid, by a small addition of oxygen, is easily transformed into tartaric acid.　Tartaric acid again, by the union of three of its particles, and the addition of hydrogen from decomposed water, may easily be transformed into *grape sugar*, or similar carbo-hydrates, just as, inversely, tartaric acid can be obtained by oxydizing agents from carbo-hydrates such as sugar of milk.

The various chemical processes in the plant are effected by the vegetable cells, particularly of the leaves, under the influence of the rays of the sun; and the green colouring matter, or *chlorophyll*, and the yellow ingredient, *luteine*, have an important mediating share in these processes.

Three entire seasons are mostly required for the development of the roots and wood of the plant to such a size as to enable it to produce ripe fruit. During these various stages the following chemical compounds are met with in the various parts and juices of the plant.

The Sap.—The first fluid which rises in the canes at the beginning of spring is called *sap*. As it runs in drops from a cut surface of canes it is called " tears," and the act of its effusion is called " weeping " of the vine. It contains 2·5 per mille of solid matter, being a little *acid potassium tartrate*, and *gum* and *soluble starch*, together 1·9 per mille, while the remaining 0·6 per mille are *bases* with a trace of *phosphoric acid*; it also contains *ammonia* and *nitric acid*, but probably not any albuminous matter.

The *rising of the sap* in the vine takes place with an enormous force, which was first measured by Stephen Hales, more than a century ago; he found it equal to the pressure of a column of mercury 22 inches in height, while the German professor, Mohr, of Bonn, found it to rise to a maximum of $19\frac{3}{12}$ inches.

The *young shoots* of the vine contain acid tartrate of potash in much larger quantities than the sap; cellulose and chlorophyll in constantly increasing quantities are deposited within their structure and that of the leaves. The expressed juice of *entire branches* deposits *vegetable fibrine* and *chlorophyll* as a green sediment; it contains in solution *tannin*, recognized by its astringent taste, its inky reaction with iron salts, and its precipitate with gelatine; *vegetable albumin* is precipitated from it by boiling; *acid tartrates* of *potash and lime* can be obtained from it by evaporation and crystallization ; *starch* is recognizable by its assuming a blue colour with iodine ; *gum* is precipitated from it by alcohol ; *mineral salts* remain as ash. The part remaining insoluble consists of *lignin* or *cellulose*, the substances of which all wood, young and old, is composed. In the cell-cavities of the wood there is deposited in autumn a quantity of *starch*, which can be extracted from the rasped wood by boiling water. The *tendrils* taste like, and have the composition of, unripe fruit. Unripe *grapes* contain **malates** and *tartrates*, mainly of potassium in varying proportions, changing with each period of development. Before the appearance of any sugar, *malates* prevail ; when the grapes become sugary *tartrates* prevail, of which a certain portion remains in the fully ripe grapes. The grapes then also contains fibrine, albumin, gum, pectin, tannin, and in largest quantity the sugar peculiar to fruit ; the tannin is not at first in solution in the juice, but deposited in the husks and seeds, and requires maceration for its extraction. The husks of the blue and black grapes contain the *blue colouring matter*, also deposited in the insoluble state along with the tannin, and extractable only by alcohol and acid, or by wine, and then assuming a red colour in dilute solution. The amount of acid in the grapes increases during their growth, and decreases again during ripening.

The proportion of juice to husks, or husks and stalks combined, varies in different vines, and in the same vines in different years ; thus fine *white Chasselas* grapes contained only 3 % of husks and seeds, with 97 % of must; *black Fineau* grapes, from which Champagne and Burgundy are made, yielded juice 94·8 %, and murk (no stalks) 5·2 %; another sample pressed with stalks, as in the Champagne, gave juice 91·8 % and murk 8·2 %. Again, *black Pineau*, which had been allowed to ferment with husks and stalks, as in the preparation of Burgundy wine, gave wine 69·6 %, and murk 30·4 %.

In the "Treatise," pp. 36-45, will be found the records of a number of original observations on the relation of acid and sugar in grapes, grown on the Rhine or in France, made by A. Dupré, Rendu,[1] and Pasteur.[2] They show that, at least as regards black grapes, there are two kinds of ripening, one peculiar to the grape which is not yet black, consisting in an augmentation of sugar; the other, a process mostly accomplished in the black grape, consisting in a diminution of acidity.

CHAPTER III.

PRINCIPLES OF VITICULTURE, GENERAL AND SPECIAL.

§ 12. SOIL FAVOURABLE TO VITICULTURE.

THE vine requires a territory which must not be clogged with water, but pervious to it, and admit air at frequent intervals. But at the same time it requires a constant supply of water within easy reach of the roots. Thus in the fertile paludal districts of the Gironde the ground-water is within a few feet of the surface, while the vines of the Médoc are placed upon little hillocks of gravelly soil, and receive rain at frequent intervals from the clouds which come landwards from the Atlantic.

The vine grows on chalky, silicious, aluminous, and magnesian soil, on granitic mountains, on formations of transition, such as the Devonian slate of the Alto Douro, on tertiary formations such as the hills of Jerez, on volcanic and alluvial territory. In all it requires the presence of decaying matter called *humus*; of considerable quantities of chalk and potash and of the other mineral ingredients. Our English gardeners have considerable experience in the production of an *empirically* prepared soil, in which they grow the vines which

---

[1] " Ampelographie française," p. 255.
[2] " Maladies du Vin," pp. 202 and 209.

produce the beautiful grapes of English conservatories
Thomson[1] says that the best is a fibry calcareous loam,
taken not more than three inches deep from an old sheep
or deer-pasture.   Such soil should consist of 65 % of
sand, 33 % of clay, and 5 % of chalk, with an abundance of
vegetable fibre.   This is next mixed with old plaster with
hair in it, charred wood and wood-ashes, horse-droppings,
broken bone and horn-shavings.   Of such soil a full-grown
vine under glass requires from 120 to 150 cubic feet, but of
an ideal soil it would only require 27 cubic feet.

§ 13. MANURING AND IMPROVEMENT OF THE SOIL IN VINEYARDS.

Most natural soils admit of being improved in their composition, and for such improvements no general rules can be
given.   But as all crops remove certain mineral constituents,
they exhaust the land more or less rapidly ;   the material
abstracted must therefore be restored to the land, and this
is done by manure.   Such manure may be of two kinds,
stable manure and *mineral manure.*   Of the latter *potash
salts* are the most important ingredient, and amply supplied
by the German potash mines.   The manuring and improvement of the soil of vineyards in all their aspects are fully
described in Thudichum and Dupré's " Treatise," &c., pp.
49-57, and to this we must refer the reader for further and
more detailed data.

§ 14. METHODS OF PROPAGATING AND MULTIPLYING THE VINE.

As it takes from five to six years before *a seedling vine*
begins to bear, propagation by seed is not frequently employed.
Frequently seedlings do not fulfil the expectation with which
they were reared, and have to be torn out.   If the viticulturist
take care to properly impregnate the flowers from which he
wishes to grow seed, beautiful and interesting varieties of
vines are produced.   But no vine of extended applicability
for wine-making has ever been reared in that way.   Among

---

[1] " Cultivation of the Grape Vine," 1867, p. 14.

noted vines obtained by crossing of races and growing from seed are several American varieties, *e.g.* Norton's Seedling, and the largest and finest grape which grows in France in the open air, known at Thoméry under the name of Chasselas Napoleon. A seedling can be made to bear fruit in the third year by grafting it upon an old stem.

§ 15. PROPAGATION BY MEANS OF EYES, OR BUDS.

Eyes with the node of wood attached may be cut from vines and planted in open beds and vineyards. Such will, in one season, form a small vine with particularly great development of roots.

A specifically English method of propagating vines, when practised in forcing-houses, yields in one year a strong vine, capable of bearing twelve bunches of grapes the next year. The eyes to be " struck " are cut right across the cane, about half-an-inch above and below the node, and then a slice is taken off the side longitudinally opposite the eye.

English viticulturists place these buds or eyes in pots filled with light turfy loam and a small proportion of decayed leafmould. These are placed in tan, in vineries or peach-houses, and forced at temperatures between 55° F. at night, and 90° F. in the daytime. At the end of the season each plant is an enormous ripe cane with closely set buds ; each will bear in the next year from eight to twelve bunches of grapes. Whereas by the ordinary method it takes at least six years to bring a vineyard to bearing, by this method a vineyard can be established in two years, and will bring four harvests, amongst them three full ones, before a vineyard planted with cut canes will bring one, and will thereby not only repay the first outlay on the forcing-houses, and the interest of the cost of the land, but also leave a large profit.

§ 16. PROPAGATION BY MEANS OF CUT CANES.

The most common and, as to outlay, cheapest method of multiplying vines is by the planting of *cut canes* (French, *boutures*, German, *Blindholz*). The canes are obtained at the time when the vines are cut, and in bundles of from

eighteen inches to two feet in length form an article of trade.
During winter-time they are kept deep under ground; in
May they are placed with their lower ends in water, and
when the buds have swelled the canes are planted in the
ground in the order in which the future vines are to stand.

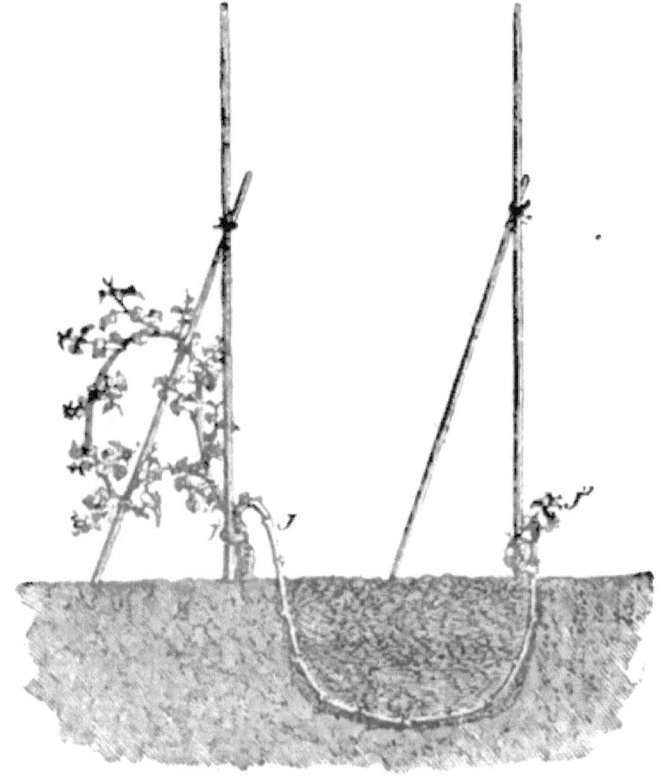

Fig. 4.—Mode of propagating vine by layer or buried slip. J, point
where the slip is severed, a year after interment, J', growing branch
of the new vine.

A vineyard planted with such canes will require six years
before bearing a crop.

§ 17. PROPAGATION BY MEANS OF LAYERS OR SLIPS.

A long cane, left in connection with the vine on which it
grew, is partly buried in the earth, but allowed to project into
the air with its cut end.   It forms roots and branches, and

then its connection with the parent plant may be severed, and it may be transplanted. Such a layer the French term *marcotte*, the German, *Senkrebe*, English *slip* (fig. 4).

Another kind of layer is the reverse (fig. 5), produced by

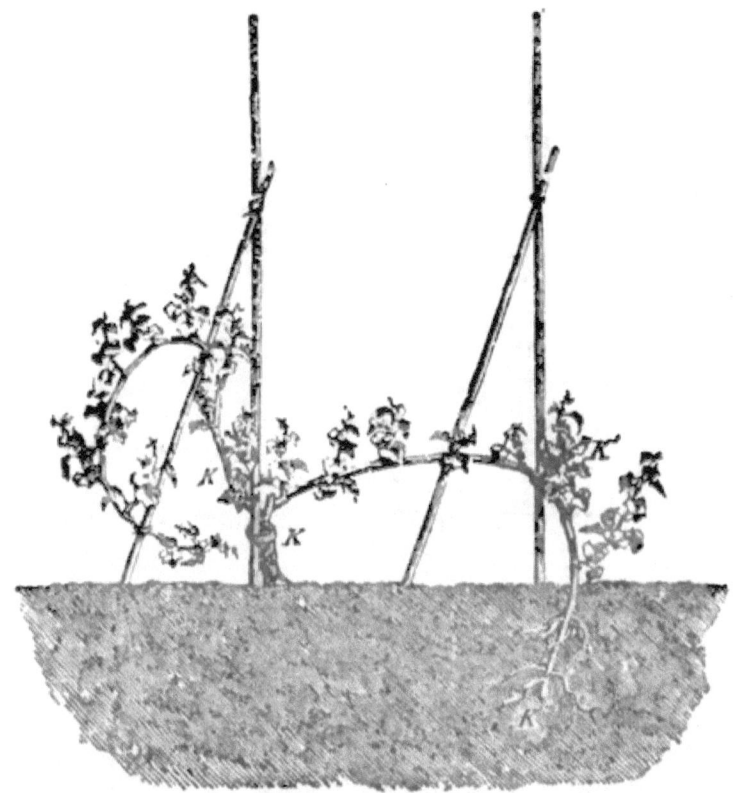

Fig. 5.—Mode of propagating vine by inverted slip. K, point where the fruit arch on the left will be severed, K, point where the slip will be severed from stock, K', point where the new vine will develop, after the horizontal slip is suppressed.

burying the end of a long cane in the earth. In this case the growth of the cane becomes inversed after separation.

§ 18. Grafting of Vines.

Of late years grafting has been employed much more frequently than formerly for the following reason. The phylloxera was found to destroy the roots of European vines, while it left those of American vines relatively untouched. But American vines grown in Europe gave no saleable wine. Viticulturists therefore planted American vines, and, when these had attained a certain size, grafted European vines upon them, and by this means obtained saleable wines. Grafting of vines may be done by the process of *eye* or *bud-grafting*, the same as that commonly used for the propagation of superior roses ; or by *simple inarching*, a process by which two vines previously distinct are united, and when this has been effected, the foot of the one and the top of the other vine is removed or suppressed ; a somewhat more complicated process is called *compound inarching*. *Grafting in grooves* is very suitable for use with rootless canes, or one year's vines ; it should be resorted to in all cases in which the top and branches of a vine have perished by frost, or wind, or disease, and the stem and roots are strong and healthy. Grafting may be resorted to in conservatories when it is decided to change a vine which yields grapes of undesirable quality for another with preferable fruit.

§ 19. GENERAL PRINCIPLES OF THE CULTIVATION OF THE VINE.

The soil having been prepared by deep digging and the admixture of any new ingredients deemed necessary, it is to be planted with canes or rooted plants. The latter must be transferred in March, but canes swelled in water may be planted during the period from March to June. All vines should be placed in parallel lines, distant from each other a little more than a yard, and the single vines to be removed from each other by the same interval. The quincunx may be employed where manual labour is relied upon, and short, small vines are reared. The young vine is not cut or interfered with in any way during the first three years, but the ground is freed from all weeds. The vine is pruned for the first time in the fourth year of its growth ; the pruning is then mainly directed to the training of the future stock, and the production of a first harvest must be a subordinate consideration.   The particular principles of the many methods of training the vine are generally the same.   It is required that every plant should grow every year *at least* two long branches ; of these, one is to produce fruit in the next year, and no long branches or wood ; while the other is to reproduce the two long branches by means of which fruit and wood are to be reproduced in the following year.

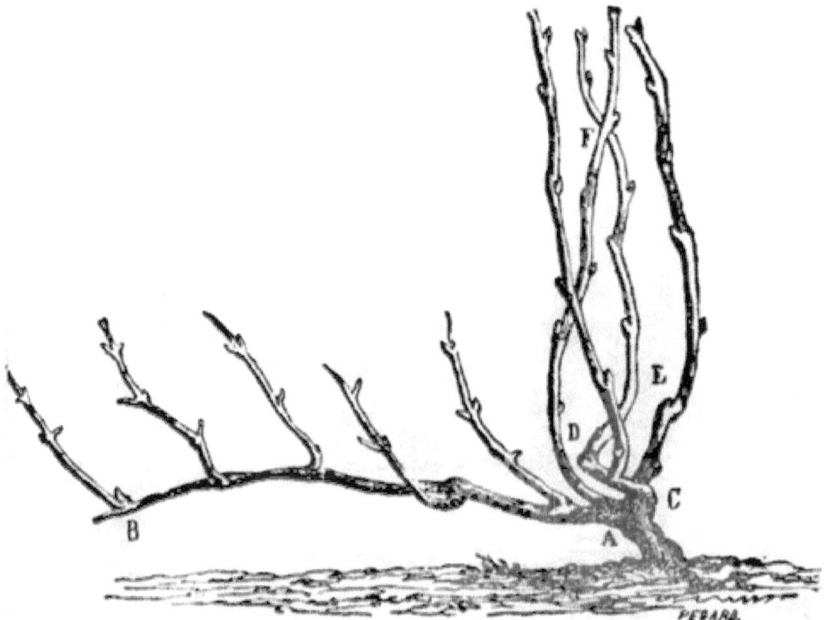

Fig. 6.—Vine after the fall of the leaves.   A B, the year's fruit branch,
C D E F, branches to be trimmed for the next season.

The branch which has borne fruit is cut off entirely in the spring following the harvest.   Suppose the viticulturist has before him the young stock from which everything has been cut away except the two principal canes, he should select the strongest for fruit, and cut it down to a length not exceeding a yard, and not less than half a yard, in direct proportion to the strength of the vine.   This fruit-branch he should now attach horizontally, near to the earth, to a stretched wire,

or to a couple of stakes; the other branch he should cut
back to a spur of three eyes. When the fruit-branch has
formed its shoots, and the buds of flowers are seen, all
shoots without flower-buds should be broken off absolutely,
while all those with buds should be stopped by pinching off
their tops above the sixth leaf. The shoots of the wood spur
must never be pinched or cut back under any circumstances;
they produce but few grapes, must be kept in a vertical

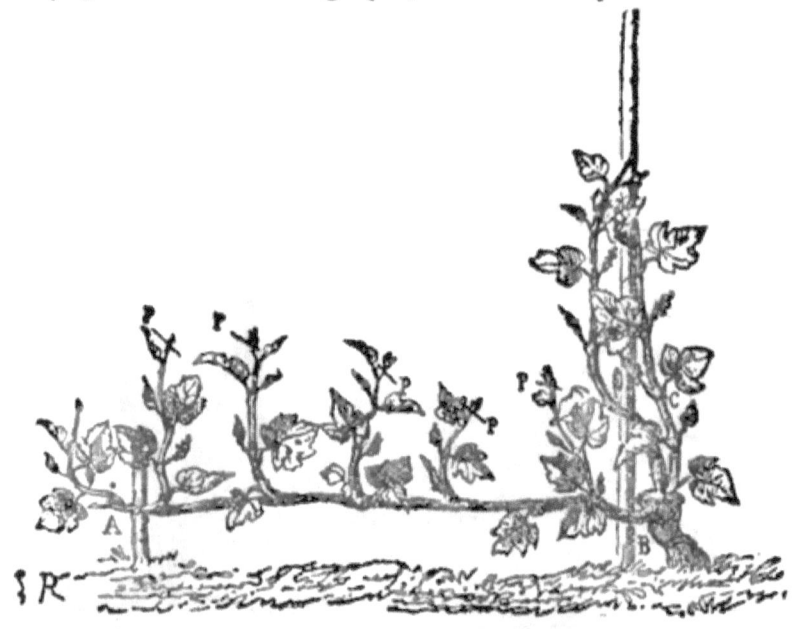

Fig. 7.—Vine in spring, just growing. A B, the fruit-branch, C, growing fruit-branch and spur-branch for the next year, P P P P, points
where the new fruit-branches are stopped (cut off or pinched off).

position, and tied in a bundle to a stake. This simple vine,
consisting, after pruning in spring, of a stem or foot rooted
in the ground, a longer cane for fruit-bearing, and a short
spur for wood-bearing, may be said to carry *one viticultural
element.* In practice, a single foot may be made to carry
several such elements. Thus in the Rhenish so-called
basket cultivation a foot carries from three to five such
elements—that is, older branches—on each of which, at the
time of cutting, a fruit spur with three buds, and a wood spur,

with two buds, or eyes, are left. The Médoc vines have regularly two elements, but the spreading large vines on espaliers in the paludal districts of the Gironde, or those grown anywhere on walls and in conservatories, may have any number of such elements up to several hundred. The greater the number of elements on a single trunk, the greater must be the region for the development of its roots. It is therefore necessary to give to vines which are to grow on the extension system a greater amount of wood under ground at the time

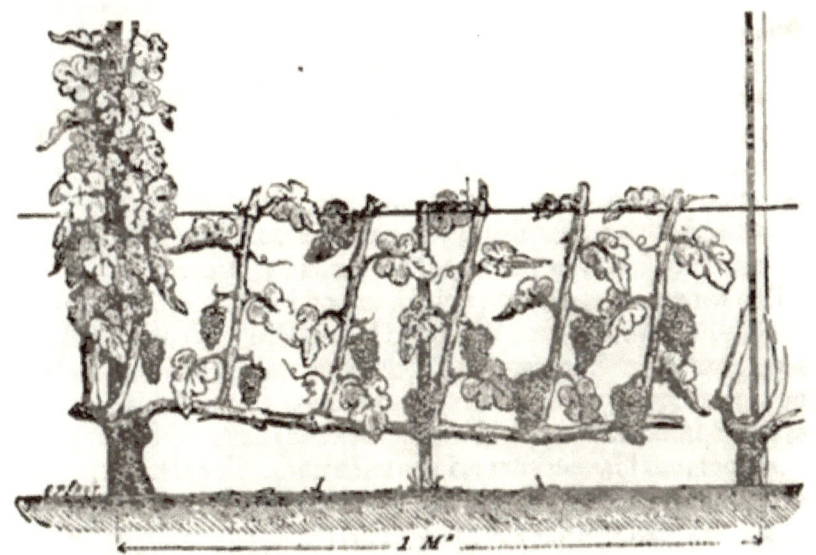

Fig. 8.—Vine in bearing, autumn.

of planting. The system is, however, not well suited for the growth of the vine in open vineyards, where to ripen grapes they have to be kept near the ground. Every vine with a proper element, or number of elements, and which occupies the required square yard of land, and receives sufficient nourishment, ought to be able, without exhausting itself, and without interfering with the growth of neighbouring vines, to produce sixteen bunches of grapes on the fruit-branch, and four bunches on the wood-branch, altogether twenty bunches, weighing on an average fifty grammes per bunch (of small-graped, small-bunched vines), or one kilo.

per vine. Middle and large-sized grapes and their bunches (such as are produced by the vines of Alto Douro, or those of Jerez) attain a greater weight, and a Jerez vine may produce from five to thirty kilos. of grapes. During the growth of the vine all the branches must be tied up and fixed to stakes and wires to maintain the lines. All unnecessary shoots and all weeds must be removed. The soil must be repeatedly loosened by means of the hoe or plough, but deep cultivation is to be reserved for spring and autumn. In vineyards where the oidium has appeared, flowers or dry milk of sulphur must be dusted over the vines, either with bellows or fumigating machines. Manure should be carried to the vineyard in autumn, and never be placed in contact with the vines, but in the earth around them. In dry situations, vines have to be irrigated during the summer months. Where that is not feasible, the soil has to be saturated with water during the rainy season, by collecting it in excavated hollows near each vine, as at Jerez.

The foregoing general principles of viticulture have been specially elucidated in Chapter III. of the "Treatise," etc., as regards the Rhenish, and South Spanish, and Portuguese countries from personal experience, and as regards France, on the information of the best French authors,[1] as well as from personal inspection and examination. For the purposes of the present work the manner in which vines are cultivated has been stated under the chapter referring to each particular kind of wine. In this manner the information of interest to particular classes of readers will be kept closer together, and be easier available.

[1] Guyot, "Viticulture;" R. Charmeux, "Culture du Chasselas;" Lenoir, "Traité de la Culture de la Vigne;" Odart, Comte de, "Ampélographie Universelle ou Traité des Cepages."

CHAPTER IV.

VINES AND VINTAGE.

§ 20. VARIETIES OF VINES TO BE SELECTED FOR CULTIVATION.

EACH variety of vine generally preserves its main characters wherever the climatic conditions allow it to be cultivated so as to produce fruit. Exposure, territory, and climate may make a vine poor or rich, or extinguish it altogether, but it will never transform it into anything else; the Muscat will not become Carbenet, the Pineau will never become Gamay, the Riessling will never become Chardenay or Tokay. But although it is thus unquestionable that the vine dictates the quality of the wine, this fact, that the specificity of the plant governs the nature of the product has always been applied only to the so-called great growths. In these vineyards the races of vines are kept select and pure. Indeed, if the vineyards of Chateau Lafitte were planted with Gamay, or Gouais, they would produce only detestable wine. If the old Pineau vines of the Clos Vougeot were substituted by Gamays, the value of the wine of that vineyard would sink to one-tenth its present figure. Take the Carbenet Sauvignon from the Haut Médoc, or the Franc Pineau from the Bourgogne, and plant it at Madeira, at the Cape, in Spain, or in Algeria, and everywhere you will obtain wines, which will at least recall the wines of the countries from which the plants have been taken. The exposure, the climate, the mode of cultivation of the vine, and the mode of making the wine will of course influence the lightness, richness, taste, and bouquet of the ultimate product; but the Pineau, wherever grown, will reproduce the main qualities of the Burgundy wine, and the Carbenet, wherever grown will recall that of the Médoc. The Riessling, whether grown on the Rhine, in the Tyrol, in

D

Croatia, or at the Cape, will always recall the qualities of
the wine of the Rhine.   But the quality of the transferred
vines is not preserved for any very long time, and they either
deteriorate, or degenerate and die out.   This has been the
case absolutely with European vines transplanted to America.
In Australia, vines have preserved more of their original
character, but it remains to be seen whether this adaptation
will be permanent.   Not all bad results of new plantations
must be placed to the account of the vines, much depends
upon the culture of the vine, and upon the vinification.
Thus the Duke de la Vittoria, Espartero, caused Bordeaux
grape-vines to be planted in his vineyards in Navarre, and
they produced a wine resembling Bordeaux, so far as
taste and body were concerned, but it had a sour and bad
after-taste, found in many Spanish wines from other kinds of
grapes, which is not due to the grapes, but is produced
by the methods of preparation and keeping adopted
throughout Spain.

For this reason it ought to be a demand of trade that
each wine, no matter from what country it comes, should
bear the name or names of the grapes from which it is made.
Thus " wine of Burgundy " is an incomplete, deceptive name ;
it should be stated whether the wine comes from Pineau or
Gamais, or other grapes.   Bordeaux wine should always be
distinguished as " wine of Carbenet from Bordeaux," or
" wine of Verdot."   One should speak of " wine of fine
plants of Champagne," and not of Champagne simply.   In
the Bourgogne there are produced, side by side on one and
the same slope, excellent wines from good varieties of grapes,
and very bad wines from bad varieties of grapes.   These
varieties are frequently mixed in the vineyard for purposes
which may be very justifiable in the eyes of the producer,
but are sure to deteriorate the wine by the time that it comes
on the table of the consumer.   The Germans, in practical
recognition of our contention, call their wine made from
Riessling grapes " Riessling," that from the Traminer by its
name also ; and we may rely upon it that these are pure
wines, because their characters are so striking, and an admixture of other grapes would produce so infallible a de-

terioration in the quality, that no prudent person would think
of effecting such a mixture. All great "growths" were
originally produced by intelligent persons who planted
favourably-situated vineyards with excellent vines. The
excellence of the produce was gradually ascribed to the
situation only, and the effect of the particular cultivation and
of the species of vine was forgotten. But the great law is,
that the variety of the vine governs the quality of the wine,
and no inferior vine will ever in the best situation and the
best seasons produce wine equal in quality and value to that
of the higher class vines. The finest varieties will not give
less produce than the coarsest if they are cultivated in a
manner adapted to their nature.

The ampelographic school of the garden of the Palace of
the Luxembourg, at Paris, founded in 1819 by the then Duc
Decaze, under the direction of M. Hardy failed in exercising
any influence on viticulture anywhere : it was the same with
the collection of vines made at Baden, and another at
Heidelberg, in which Metzger, the botanist, took so distinguished a part, and which has served as the basis of the
monograph on vines by Von Babo, of Weinheim : and
another at Gratz made under the direction of the late Archduke John, the quondam German *Reichsverweser ;* another
at Kloster Neuburg, which serves as the botanical school of
the Agricultural Institute of that convent. All these have
augmented the knowledge of vines in general, but vinification has not thereby been improved in any appreciable
manner. The Luxembourg collection was displaced to
Algiers under Napoleon III. before 1870, and will there
also continue to be an interesting botanical collection ; it
comprised more than 500 varieties of vines.

The "Ampélographie" of Count Odart is a highly in-
structive and entertaining work for all those who appreciate
the subject of vines in connection with wine. The count
had formed an extensive collection of vines from all parts of
the world, studied their physiology, and formed vineyards
by hundreds of vines of all those which promised a good
yield. The collection was near La Hardellière, Cormery,
(Indre-et-Loire), and was left by the count to his gardener, as

the departmental council refused to undertake its guardianship, which had been offered to it by the count on liberal terms.

In the introduction to his work he proves at length that, contrary to what had been maintained by some authors, *e.g.*, Chaptal, vines transplanted from one country to another, provided they find the required climatic conditions, do not change in character. On p. 37 he gives the interesting information from Auguste Saint-Hilaire, that grapes and all other fruit such as is common and excellent in France, remain of very mediocre quality in Brazil. This is ascribed to the humidity of the climate, and the absence of the cold nights which arrest the circulation of the sap at the end of the vegetative period. He discusses the information and names for vines of the authors, and denies that those vines, which could be recognized from the description, such as the *Aminea* of Columella, now Pineau, had altered in character since ancient times. When vines or vineyards had degenerated as it was termed, that is to say become old or barren or exhausted, the vines could always be recalled to their pristine character, either by amelioration of the land, or by transfer of the vine to new land.

In the chapter "On Vines reared from Seeds," Odart proves that most allegations of new good varieties of vines having been obtained from seeds, even seeds derived from the best varieties of vines, were fables; most seedlings which bore fruit stood to their parent vines in the relation of "crabs;" they generally were made to bear fruit only after ten to fourteen years, and wine, if at all, after twenty years; and no wine was ever produced from seedlings which has become a staple article or a desirable object of commerce. This experience does not exclude the occasional success of seedlings produced with selected pollen as well as receptacles; but even of such no wine has ever been made.

§ 21. Selection of Suitable Species of Vines for Wine-Making.

How great the problem of the selection of vines may appear when it is considered without reference to locality, will appear from the fact, that in the whole of France no less than thirty-eight principal varieties of vines are cultivated on a large scale. Of these about one-fifth are used for the production of raisins, liqueur-wines, or for the distillation of best brandy, the other four-fifths serve for the production of wine in the true sense of the word. We will first enumerate the vines best suited to the south and south-east of France. They are, for box-raisins, the *Mayorquin*, or *Bourmen*, and the *Panses*; for liqueur-wines, that is to say, grape-must, the fermentation of which has been prevented by the addition of spirit, the *Furmint, Grenache, Maccabeo, Malvoisie, Muscat blanc*, and *Muscat noir*. All these are large-berried and large-bunched vines, requiring for the whole of their vegetative period a very hot climate. For good wines are used in the south-east of France the following vines: *Carignane, Clarette, Marsanne, Petite-Schiraz, Picpoule, Roussane, Rousselet, Rousette Ugni, Vionnier*. In the south-west of France only medium and small-berried small-bunched vines prevail; these are used for the best wines, the *Carbenet, Carbenet gris*, and *Carmenère*, these prevailing in the Médoc: the *Cruchinet, Muscadelle, Sauvignon, Semillon*, these latter two yielding the white Sauterne, and the *Verdot*, yielding the best ordinary Bordeaux wine; the best brandies in the district of the Charente extending in a circle round the town of Cognac are obtained from a vine called *La Folle blanche*. In the east, the central, and the western districts, the following vines are grown for good wines: *Epinette* and *Blanc Fumé, Fromentés Rose, blanc* or *gris, Meslier, Pineau blanc*, or *Chardenay, Pineau gris* or *Beuret, Pineau of the Loire* or *Vouvray, Pineau noir* or *Noirien, Plant Doré, vert* or *gris, Riessling*, or *Savagner*.

We shall have to refer to the vines again, when we shall treat of each particular district of cultivation. Bronner was right when he said that the vine made the wine, and that, *e.g.*, in the must of Carbenet one could taste the full bouquet of fine Médoc wine.

§ 22. VINTAGE AND VINIFICATION.

The principles of the most common methods of vinification are easily stated, but the details to be noted are so numerous, depending as they do upon different vines, customs and countries, that they are better reserved for the chapters treating of the viticulture of each œnopoetic district. White grapes are generally crushed and pressed, and the juice, freed from stalks and husks, is put into barrels and allowed to ferment in a cellar or other temperate place. In some districts, however, the juice is allowed to ferment while the husks and stalks are immersed in it, *e.g.*, in the Alto Douro, as regards white wine as well as red. Black grapes which are to yield red wine are crushed and put into vats, not rarely, as in the south, consisting of masonry, and allowed to ferment until the wine has extracted the colouring matter. The wine is then drawn off, the must pressed, and the united products are put into barrels or great vats to complete their fermentation or have it arrested by the addition of brandy.

§ 23. TIME OF VINTAGE.

The first condition of the vintage is that the grapes should be ripe. In many parts of the south of Europe it is considered that the grapes should be vintaged when they have attained their greatest volume. But must from such grapes is quite unfit for the production of good natural wine; this can be seen in the product of the vineyard of San Lucar de Barrameda, which owing to its bitterness is called Manzanilla; but here the early vintage is probably a necessity produced by the climate, which by its early rains in September is liable to deteriorate or destroy the vintage.

In the most celebrated districts for the production of white wine the grapes are allowed to hang on the vines until they have attained the maximum of sweetness and maturity, and are commencing to decay on their outside. Thus in the Sauterne district the best berries of every bunch are cut out at intervals and carried to the press. In the finest situations of the Rhinegau the grapes are collected only when rain or frost of the latest autumn necessitate the vintage. At Tokay the best grapes are allowed to passulate, *i.e.*, to become shrivelled to raisins, and are then extracted with must from plump grapes; but the result is here not wine in the true sense of the word, but a sweet liqueur which contains only little alcohol formed in the liquid or added thereto.

Black grapes are never allowed to attain the same degree of maturity as white ones, except at a few places such as Rota, in Spain; for the colour of red wines required by the traders can only be obtained from grapes at a certain stage of maturity, and that stage does not coincide with, but precedes the stage of maximum maturity which the grapes can attain on the vine. Consequently, much of the quality of the wine is abandoned in favour of a conventional dye; and the unripe wine has to remain years in barrels and bottles before it acquires the qualities which fit it for use. The Champagne grapes, on the other hand, are not permitted to attain the stage of highest maturity, because it is conventional that the effervescent wines of that country shall be as pale as possible, and not have the slightest tint of redness. But whereas the fully ripe Pineau always yields a rosy or partridge-eye coloured juice, the stage of fullest ripeness is not awaited, but the grapes are gathered at the time of their greatest volume, when they yield a perfectly colourless juice and wine. In Burgundy again, where red wines are produced, the same time is chosen, but for another reason: fully ripe Pineau, when fermented with the husks, yields wine which has a tawny red colour, and not the lively bluish red of elder-berry juice; but as traders prefer the latter, the grapes, with few exceptions, are collected at a time when the husks produce the deepest colour.

Viticulturists intent upon producing the best wine possible allow their grapes to hang on the vine as long as is compatible with the safety of the harvest. The proprietors of large vineyards make sample trials from time to time to ascertain the progress of the formation of sugar in the grapes, by pressing samples of grapes and testing the must by special instruments for its specific gravity. Some of these gravimeters or glucometers are so arranged as to indicate by one degree of their scale a quantity of fruit-sugar, which after fermentation would yield a volume (per cent. of the must) of absolute alcohol, or, in other words, each degree would indicate the presence in one hectolitre of must of 1,500 grammes of sugar. Now as must which would only yield from 6 to 8 per cent. of alcohol would give inferior wine, grapes showing only as much sugar as would yield that amount of alcohol should not be harvested; the harvest should be contemplated only when the samples of must show above 8 per cent. of future alcohol, but it should even then be delayed if possible as long as by repeated trials any increase in the quantity of sugar is observable. Even when the sugar has attained its maximum the grapes will still, if the season be favourable, particularly if the soil be dry, undergo beneficial changes by hanging upon the vine.

It is an important fact that fully ripe grapes in all viti-cultural districts contain about the same amount of sugar, *i.e.*, a little more than 16 per cent. of the must. When the must is much richer in sugar this result has been attained by passulation of the grapes on the vines, by twisting the stalks, or by drying of the cut bunches on mats, on straw, in the sun or sheltered places. In many of these rich musts, *e.g.*, the Sauternes, fermentation ceases long before even a great part of the sugar has been consumed, or even the high degree of alcoholicity, at which all fermentation is absolutely arrested, namely, 16 per cent. of alcohol, has been attained. Musts of a saccharine strength of less than 16 per cent. of fruit-sugar, should be raised to this strength by the addition of fruit-sugar produced from cane-sugar; each kilogram and a half of such sugar added to a hectolitre of must will raise its alcoholicity by 1 per cent. of alcohol after fermentation.

§ 24. MODES OF VINTAGE.

The mechanical operation of cutting off all the grapes and carrying them to the press can be performed by children and adults of both sexes. All labourers are required to remain in line, the work being of course equally distributed to equal agents. These cut the bunches off with scissors or knives, and place them in little baskets. Every full basket is replaced by an empty one and carried away by a collector, who thus attends to the wants of from four to six labourers. The vintagers may be taught to cut out of every bunch all unripe, corroded, or spoiled berries, long stalks and tendrils,

Fig. 9.—Mode of separating stalks from grapes, by stirring with a trident. *A.* The trident. *B.* Pail with grapes in course of being stirred.

and put them aside. But it is preferable to intrust this work to particularly instructed labourers located at the place where the contents of the primary baskets are deposited. The cleaned grapes should then be placed in vessels of known capacity, such as a hectolitre, so that the vintage is immediately measured and the amount of work done ascertained. A butt of the capacity of a hectolitre will hold fifty kilos. of grapes, and with its own weight of ten to fifteen kilos. can be lifted and carried by a single man.

§ 25. SEPARATION OF STALKS.

When the grapes are very ripe, the stalks are woody and do not easily yield juice to any pressure, however strong. But when the grapes are less ripe, the stalks are green and suc-culent, and yield some harsh astringent juice on pressure. In the case of white wines the stalks are not often separated from the grapes; in Sauternes, *e.g.*, only the first grapes, which yield only the "head-wine," or *tête*, are so separated; the "middle" and "tail" are pressed with the stalks; as a

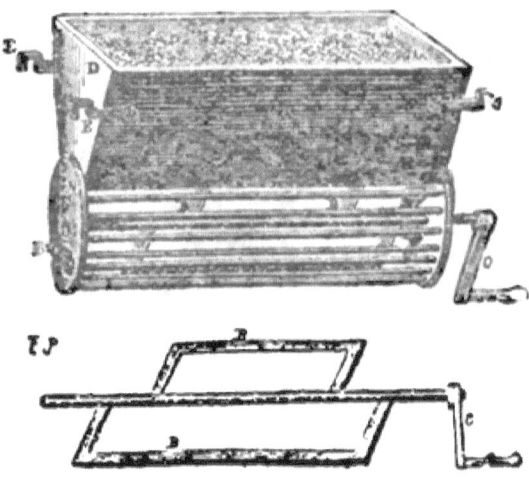

Fig. 10.—Machine for separating grapes from stalks. The funnel-shaped top *D* is taken from the stand on which it rests by means of the hooks *E* to show the cylindrical box of parallel wires and stirrer *B B* within. *C.* Handle of stirrer. One thirtieth of actual size.

rule, must of white grapes is pressed immediately and not left in contact with the murk for any length of time. The black Champagne grapes are also pressed with the stalks, and the juice of the latter causes the last third of the must which flows from the press to be harsh and of less value than the first two-thirds. All black grapes which are to yield red wine, on the other hand, have to remain in contact with their juice during fermentation until the red colouring matter is extracted. If then the must be very astringent a harsh wine is produced, while the same grapes, without the stalks, yield a milder, better maturing wine. The stalks are therefore separated before the grapes are mashed. This separation, called in France *égrappage*, in Germany *Abrappen*, can be effected either by stirring the bunches in a tub with a trident of wood (as shown in fig. 9) or with the aid of specially constructed machines, such as that represented in fig. 10. The bunches enter above by a funnel, the berries

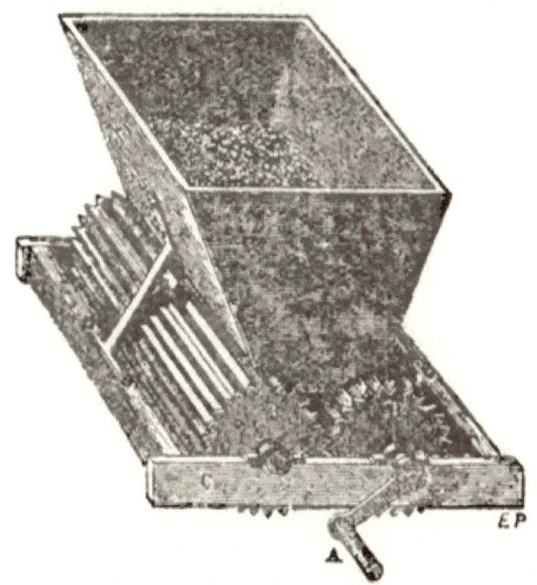

Fig. 11.—Grape mill for crushing grapes, with grooved rollers. *A.* Handle for turning. *B.* Grooved Rollers. *C.* Frame supporting funnel and rollers. One-thirtieth of actual size.

are detached by the stirrer, which is put into a rotatory motion, and then drop through the interstices of the wires of the cage; the latter at last contains only stalks, which are removed through a side door. Ripe Verdot of the Gironde will drop its grapes like hail when it is merely shaken, while ripe Pineau of Burgundy is less easily separated.

§ 26. MASHING AND CRUSHING.

. The grapes, whether they have been separated from the stalks or not, have to be crushed, with the precaution not to comminute any stones and stalks if they remain. From ancient times to the present this has been most commonly effected by means of the feet of men. This treading of grapes is a very excellent method; it is done on a wide wooden platform, or in a large vat, and the juice which is pressed out simultaneously is allowed to flow off into a separate receptacle. Another mode of crushing the grapes is by crushing machines, or grape-mills, consisting of grooved wooden rollers working against each other, as in fig. 11 on p. 43. Such rollers should be covered with felt or vulcanized caoutchouc.

CHAPTER V.

PRESSING AND VINIFICATION.

′§ 27. WINE-PRESSES AND PRESSING.

IN the preparation of Champagne wine the grapes are not crushed at all in detail previously to their being put into the press, and the only crushing which they receive is in the press itself. We have already explained that this is done to keep the must of the black grapes perfectly colourless. It is for this reason that the presses in the Champagne are the most powerful of any known. In the preparation of other white wines, however, the must is separated from the murk as much as possible before the latter is pressed, so that the volume of the matter to be pressed may be as small as possible.

In the preparation of red wine on the other hand, the juice which flows off the treading platform, together with all the husks and the stalks, if they have not been removed, are put into the fermentation vat; when the stalks have been isolated they are placed in a heap on the top of the murk about to be fermented. Fermentation is now allowed to complete itself under various modalities, of which we

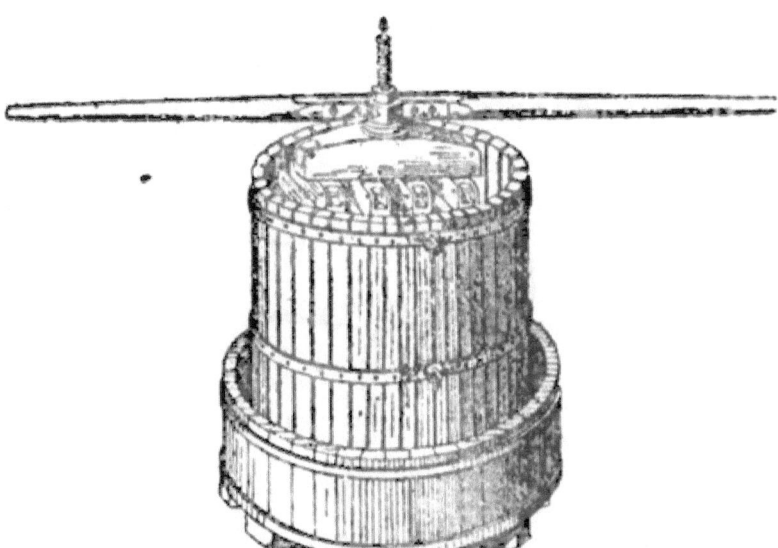

Fig. 12.—Wine-press for pressing the murk of red wine after
fermentation.

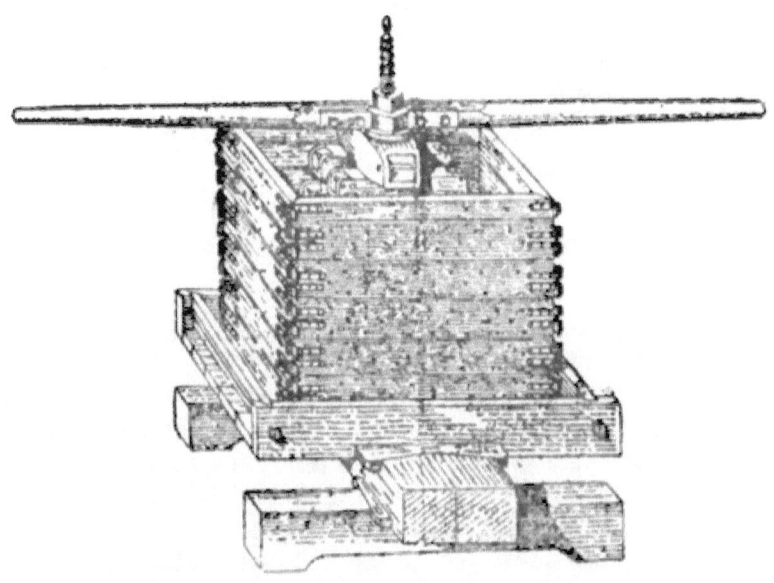

Fig. 13.—Wine-press for pressing white grapes before fermentation.
The box consists of six horizontal sections.

shall give details lower down under each viticultural region.
When the fermentation is finished the wine is stirred
energetically with the husks—which are mostly collected as
a hard cake on the top of the wine—so as to extract the
utmost amount of colouring matter ; all the wine which will
run off by itself is drawn from the taps ; the murk, removed
by a manhole at the bottom or side of the vat, is placed into

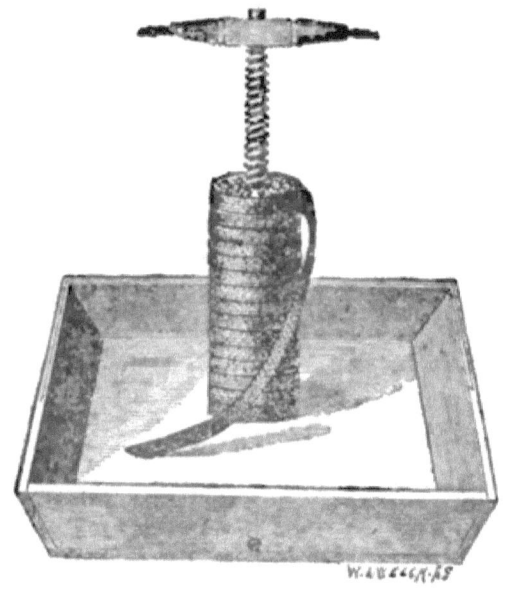

Fig. 14.—Wine-press as used in Spain (Jerez).   Grapes in bandaged
cylinder.

the press, and the wine flowing from it is added to the other,
if it be already in barrels, equally distributed amongst them.

The science of the wine-presses is so extensive that it
would admit of being represented in a separate treatise.
Most of these machines reflect the tendency to squeeze the
utmost amount of juice out of the murk, but some are so
powerful as to force the juice out of the stalks ; the application of this maximum of pressure should be under all
circumstances avoided, or the juice so expressed at the end
of an operation should be put aside and not mixed with the

must. The most suitable presses appear to be those common in the Gironde, which have an iron screw in the centre of a round receptacle made of perpendicular or horizontal boards, such as are represented in the engravings. In fig. 12 as the murk sinks the screw-nut has to be raised from time to time by interposed logs of wood; in fig. 13 the screw-nut need never be loosened, as when it sinks over the murk,

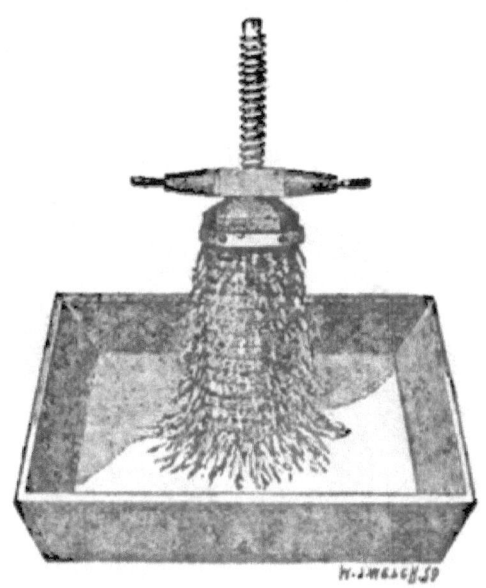

Fig. 15.—The press in action. Juice flowing.

the lateral filtering boards can be removed in tiers and allow free play to the screw lever handles.

Figs. 14 and 15 represent wine-presses as used in Spain (Jerez). Fig. 16 represents a beam or lever press of the Alto Douro.

It is probable that presses will soon have to compete with centrifugal machines, which perform in two hours, with the aid of three men, what presses working upon the same amount of material can only perform in seventeen hours, with the aid of seven men.

§ 28. FERMENTATION OF THE WINE-MUST.

Must for white wine is generally fermented in barrels with only the ordinary bunghole at the top open for the escape of the carbonic acid gas. The white wines of the Gironde are all fermented in *barriques*, which in this country are called hogsheads. New casks are always taken; they are not completely filled with must, so that no yeast or scum can escape from the bung, but all is retained in the wine. This therefore differs from the mode in which fermentation

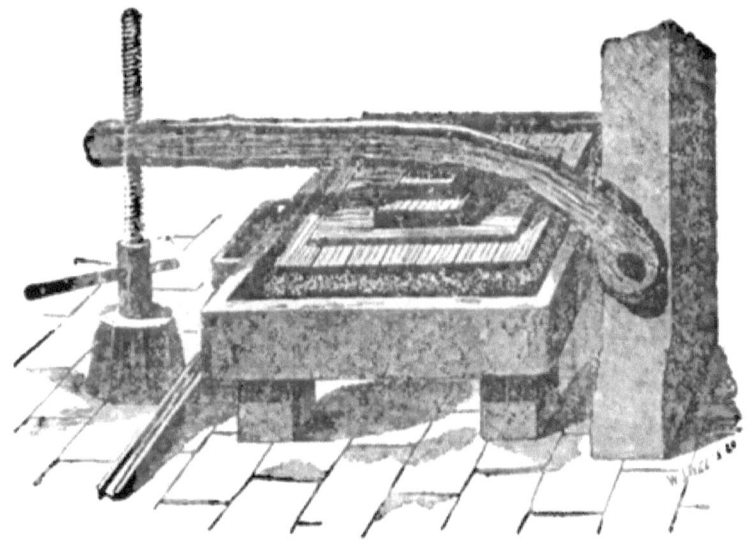

Fig. 16.—Ancient beam or lever wine-press as used in Alto Douro and other wine-producing countries.

is allowed at least to complete itself in the production of beer, according to the Burton-on-Trent method, where the beer clarifies itself by the expulsion of the yeast through the bunghole with the rising froth. The white wines of the Rhine are mostly fermented in large casks, containing 1,200 litres each, and called "piece," German *Stück*. Sherries are fermented now mostly in butts, rarely in vats of wood or masonry. The Champagne musts, after having been cleared of scum and deposit, are also fermented in small casks of 220 litres each.

The mash of black grapes for red wine is generally fermented in vats, being conical wooden casks open at the top ; this is a mechanical necessity resulting from the complications introduced into the preparation of red wine by the bulk of the husks and the necessity for stirring. The Portuguese also ferment some of their red wines in large closed barrels, with manholes for the removal of the murk. Port wine is fermented in flat receptacles built of masonry. In the south-west of France the vats are filled to a certain point ; if the stalks have been separated they are placed on the top of the murk, the house is shut, and fermentation is allowed to complete itself. The heap of stalks on the top, called "hat" or *chapeau*, is now taken off, together with the outer layer of murk which is mostly somewhat decomposed. The bulk of the murk is now submerged and vigorously stirred with the new wine, so that its colour may be fully extracted. At last the wine is drawn off, and the murk put in the press. In other parts of France the husks of black grapes are kept submerged in the fluid by a wooden cover fixed some distance below the level of the fluid, and pierced with holes to allow the gas to escape. In other parts, again, the vats are covered, but opened daily, and the murk is submerged with wooden instruments. In parts of Burgundy the vats are not covered, nor is the murk stirred before fermentation is complete ; it used then to be agitated by men in a state of nudity, but this practice, we hope, has been abandoned.

In all cases when the fermentation of red wine is complete the liquid is put into barrels and allowed to settle. It clears much quicker than the white wine, which remains thick for weeks when fermenting in the temperate atmosphere of northern climates. In the south the white wine ferments with great violence, and becomes clear very rapidly. It is probable that the red wine is ready more quickly because, fermenting in larger bulk, it attains a higher temperature, and therefore is finished in a shorter period.

By the time that the wine has completed its fermentation and become clear, all the yeast and impurity are deposited at the bottom of the cask. From this deposit the wine has to

be separated by *racking*.   This can be done by drawing the
wine through a syphon placed in the bunghole and causing
it to flow over either by gravity or by air pressure produced
in the cask by bellows, or by simply running it off through
a tap-hole or tap fixed in the most suitable place.   The clear
wine is put into a clean, not new, but wine-green cask, *i.e.*,
a cask in which, when it was new, at least one charge of
must has been fermented to wine ; the cask just emptied is
freed of its lees, washed and rinsed, and is immediately
ready to receive the clear wine from another cask to be
racked.   By this operation the wine generally becomes
disturbed a little, or it was not yet quite clear, but in any
case requires fining.   This is mostly done, in the case of
white natural wine, with isinglass; in the case of brandied
wines and of red wines with white of egg.   All casks thus
treated are made bung-full, closed, and allowed to rest for six
weeks.   After this period the wine is mostly quite clear and
bright, and, being racked another time, mostly remains so,
and is ready for the spring sales or other purposes.

§ 29. Various Modes of Correcting the Composition of Must before Fermentation.

There are produced, particularly in bad seasons, quantities of must which are either too deficient in sugar, or too
abundantly provided with acid to give good wine.   These
faults require to be corrected.   In some parts, *e.g.*, Portugal,
must which is too watery is concentrated by evaporation in
a cauldron.   But in France such must is now corrected by
the addition of sugar or of sugar solution.   The sugar to
be employed should always be the so-called grape sugar,
technically called "invert sugar," or saccharine made from
cane sugar.   When the must is only thin, and not excessively acid, it has to be improved by the addition of sugar,
until its concentration is equal to that of normal must, *i.e.*,
until it contain at least 18 and not more than 23 per cent.
of sugar.   If however the must be too acid, it has to be
reduced to the normal standard of acidity by the addition of
sugar solution of from 18 to 23 per cent. strength.   These

processes were first applied on the large scale by French chemists who happened to be also proprietors of vineyards, namely, Pétiot, Thénard (father and son), Ladrey (of Douay in Burgundy), and introduced into Germany by Thilmany, and particularly by Dr. L. Gall, of Trèves. Pétiot and the Thénards also produced second wines by fermenting the murk repeatedly with sugar solution. It was the French cabinet minister, Chaptal, who first improved wine-must by the mere addition of sugar (at that time cane sugar) but he did not diminish the acid; this removal of excess of acid was generally effected by the addition of chalk or of plaster of Paris containing chalk. The addition of sugar and of sugar solution to faulty must was therefore an improvement, and it kept the wine pure and homogeneous, and did not introduce any foreign element into its composition. Maumené [1] relates how the celebrated chemist Macquer, already in 1777, made from unripe and hard grapes an agreeably tasting, fiery wine like that from ripe grapes. All these wines prepared by the processes of Pétiot, Gall and others retain the bouquet of the natural wines. The amount of acidity or of tartrate of potash is less than in normal wine, so that they do not deposit any; they are, therefore, more like old, long-kept wines, which gradually deposit their redundant tartar. There is little doubt that although these processes have been and may be applied with perfect success by scientific chemists, they will not be useful to the ordinary agricultural wine producer, just because they require too much practical scientific attention and knowledge. Those, therefore, who object to them may rest assured that they are not likely to meet in trade with such products. In fact, their production would be more expensive than that of natural wines is, and they could not, therefore, unless they were very much better, enter into commercial competition with the ordinary products.

It should, however, be remembered in this connection that the process of Gall was only an extension to wine-must of a practice which for a very great length of time had been

[1] "Sur le Travail des Vins."

commonly applied in all countries to fruit wine. In all old cookery books will be found numbers of prescriptions for making gooseberry, currant, and other sorts of fruit wine, and in all of them water is added to the fruit juice to reduce the acidity, and then sugar is added in its turn to bring the sweetness up to the standard of at least 18 per cent., in order to furnish the material for the production of that amount of alcohol which will make the product an alcoholic beverage of the nature and strength of wine. It should be remembered that wine with more than five per mille of acid, considered as tartaric, is not drinkable, or at least not agreeable, or not useful even after dilution with water; and that the best unbrandied wines contain even less acid, namely, from 3 to 4 per mille, and from 8 to 11 per cent. of alcohol.

§ 30. PLASTERING OF WINE AND MUST.

In Spain and the south of France plaster of Paris, in the shape of powder, is added to the grape juice in the process of wine-making. The plaster is either thrown upon the grapes before they are crushed, or it is added after fermentation has commenced, and is applied as well to white as to red grape-must. The reason generally given in favour of such addition of plaster is this, that gypsum (sulphate of lime) by uniting with some of the water of the grape juice, rendered the remaining juice richer in sugar and therefore more valuable. If such were really the intention, the desired effect would not be obtained to any degree worth noticing, because even perfectly pure and anhydrous plaster of Paris unites with only about one-fourth of its weight of water, while the gypsum thus formed takes up mechanically some of the must and reduces the yield.[1] The effect is not altered if the gypsum be allowed to ferment with the must, for in that case the mineral retains a little wine, which can be as little recovered by pressure as the sugar. We have, therefore, to set aside this attempted explanation as unsatisfactory.

[1] See the experimental proofs in Thudichum and Dupré, "Treatise," p. 119, et seq.

The addition of gypsum to must or wine has a chemical effect which is of a somewhat complicated nature. The sulphate of lime decomposes the tartrate of potassium present in the juice, insoluble tartrate of calcium being formed, and sulphate of potassium going into solution. At the same time the carbonate of calcium, which is always present in larger or smaller quantities in plaster of Paris, precipitates the free tartaric acid. It neutralizes some of the other free acids of the juice, and, if present in sufficient quantity, it neutralizes them completely, in which case the phosphates of the juice will also be precipitated. Thus malic acid, which grapes have in common with all other sour fruit, is also partially neutralized, but remains in solution. The place of cream of tartar, however, is taken by sulphate of potassium, a salt having a perceptibly bitter taste, and acting as a purgative in even moderate doses.

§ 31. PROBABLE OBJECT OF THE PRACTICE OF PLASTERING.

As the amount of tartaric acid increases with the increasing ripeness of the grape, while the malic acid diminishes, the plastering virtually reduces the juice of even the ripest grapes to a state of unripeness, at least as regards the nature of the acids. From all these considerations we have come to the conclusion that the object of the practice as ordinarily stated, namely that it withdraws water, and thereby effects a condensation of the must, is not the real object.

In view of the fact that southern wines are much more liable to diseases, that is to say, decomposition by minute fungi (microzymes) than the wines of more northern countries (where plastering is never practised), and considering that such diseases are counteracted by sulphurous acid, and by sulphates; and considering further that such fungi absorb and decompose tartrate of potassium, and leave acetic or other acids instead, and do not thrive so well without tartar as with it, we have thought it not impossible that this process of plastering might have been directed against these diseases and have acted as a double precaution; the fungi had less chance to develop at all in the absence of tartar, and in case they did nevertheless develop, the result of their action could not spoil the wine by the development of that peculiar acidity which just gives the wine an acetous flavour and depresses its value. From our observations it seems certain that the presence of tartar favours the development of the viscosity fungus, and we have even observed the reappearance of the fungus in old originally plastered wine of natural strength after the sulphate had been removed and substituted by tartrate. But it must not be supposed that the viscosity fungus is killed or removed entirely from wine by plastering; it still exists in even plastered and somewhat brandied wine, and does not die in wine of less than 34 per cent. alcohol. Therefore, even if the object of plastering were the protection of the wine from the worst effects of this viscosity fungus or scud, it would be but partially attained, and there would still be room for the better prevention and curing of this bane of the southern wine-growers.

CHAPTER VI.

CHEMICAL CONSTITUENTS OF WINE.

§ 32. ETHYLIC ALCOHOL.

THE principal constituent of wine is *alcohol*, a colourless very mobile liquid, of a peculiar spirituous smell and extremely burning taste and poisonous qualities, of a specific gravity of 0·79319 at 15·5° centigrade, water at 4° centigrade being 1·0. It does not solidify at the temperature of 150° centigrade, though it becomes somewhat viscid. It is readily inflammable and burns with a blue non-luminous flame. It is miscible with water in every proportion. Its admixture with water is attended with evolution of heat and contraction of volume ; the mixture has a higher temperature and occupies a smaller space than water and alcohol separately.

The contraction is greatest when 53·939 volumes of alcohol are mixed with 49·836 volumes of water, when it amounts to 3·638 per cent.; the 103 775 volumes of water and alcohol become reduced, after cooling of the mixture to the original temperature, to 100 ; or 100 volumes become 96·362 volumes. In these mixtures the specific gravity, the boiling point and the capillary attraction fall, the rate of expansion and vapour tension rise with the increasing percentage of alcohol ; and hence these properties may be made use of for estimating the amount of alcohol present in a mixture of alcohol and water.

The bearing of alcohol towards animal membrane is of importance for the explanation of its physiological action. If an animal membrane, such as pig's bladder, be made by a suitable arrangement to separate alcohol from water, or a stronger from a weaker spirit, an interchange of liquids will take place through such membrane until the composition of the mixture on both sides is equal, the alcohol, or stronger mixture, losing alcohol, but gaining in bulk by the accession of water ; the water, or weaker spirit, on the other hand, gaining in alcohol, but losing in bulk by loss of water ; the exchange takes place, generally, the more rapidly the greater the difference in alcoholic strength on the two sides of the diaphragm. If the liquid on one side of the membrane be always pure water, kept pure by renewal, all the alcohol will find its way out into it, and the interchange will only cease when nothing but pure water remains on both sides of the membranous diaphragm.

The German anatomist, Soemmering, discovered a method for producing strong alcohol which was based upon these relations of alcohol and water to animal membrane, and had some practical value a century ago. It consists in putting a weak spirit into a bladder from a calf or ox and hanging it up in a warm place for a certain time. Both alcohol and water pass through the bladder and evaporate on the outside, but more than four times the amount of water passes through in the time during which one part of alcohol passes, consequently the alcoholic strength of the liquid in the bladder increases, and it is said even absolute alcohol may thus be obtained, particularly if the bladder before use be covered inside and out with a thin coating of isinglass.

§ 33. ALCOHOLS HOMOLOGOUS TO ETHYLIC OR COMMON ALCOHOL.

When sugar ferments, alcohol and carbonic acid are the principal products as regards quantity : but besides these, of which carbonic acid, or as it is called in modern chemistry, carbonic anhydride, passes into the air, some other alcohols and some acids are formed. It is possible that these other alcohols are formed by peculiar ferments ; they are glycerine, or *glycerol*, and *propylic, butylic, amylic* and *caproic* alcohols. They are mostly present in very small quantities only, glycerol in the largest, next to ethylic alcohol. When these alcohols occur in higher proportions they influence the taste of the wine unfavourably, and sometimes spoil it altogether. But on the whole the relation of these alcohols to the various qualities of wine are not yet sufficiently investigated.

§ 34. ALDEHYDES.

When some of the hydrogen of the alcohol is removed by combination with oxygen from the air, a new body, *aldehyde*, is formed (*alcohol dehydrogenatus*) ; to each alcohol corresponds a particular aldehyde. Of the several aldehydes, the *ethylic* and *propylic* are occasionally found in wine, the former particularly as an intermediate product of the acetous fermentation.

§ 35. ACIDS FORMED FROM ALCOHOLS IN WINE.

When aldehyde is remaining under the influence of the acetous ferment in the presence of oxygen, it is transformed into *acetic acid*. This transformation of ethylic alcohol into aldehyde, and ultimately acetic acid, constitutes the process known as the *acetous fermentation*, the final product of which is *vinegar* (*vin aigre*, sour wine). It is remarkable that wine contains some *formic acid*, although it has never been known to contain any methylic alcohol; the formation of this formic acid is therefore due to another process, and not to a derivation from this alcohol through the intermediate stage of methylic aldehyde; *propylic acid* also occurs in wine.

§ 36. COMPOUND ETHERS.

All the foregoing alcohols and acids, and all the other acids of the wine may combine with each other to form *compound ethers* in which an alcoholic and an acid radicle are joined together. These ethers are the main agents in forming the bouquet of the wine.

CHAPTER VII.

ANALYSIS OF WINES.

§ 37. MODE OF ASCERTAINING THE STRENGTH OF WINE BY THE SPECIFIC GRAVITY OF THE DISTILLATE FROM IT.

THERE are various methods for finding the strength of wine and other alcoholic mixtures; these mainly rely upon specific gravity, or boiling point, vapour tension, or rate of expansion; all these methods were devised for the purpose of saving the trouble connected with the process of distillation. But they are liable to be affected by many sources of error arising, *e.g.*, from imperfect instruments, and therefore the process of distillation and ascertaining the alcoholicity of the distillate by its specific gravity are almost universally preferred; to this process no objections have ever been raised on the score of want of accuracy.

§ 38. DISTILLATION.

The quantity of wine to be subjected to distillation should amount to from 200 to 300 cubic centimetres. It may be weighed, in which case the experiment becomes independent of temperature, and therefore most accurate ; or it may be measured, when the temperature of the sample has to be ascertained. The weighed or measured quantity of wine is introduced into a flask or retort, rendered slightly alkaline by caustic soda, mixed with a small quantity of tannin to prevent frothing, and then carefully distilled by driving the alcoholic vapours, by means of heat applied underneath the flask, into a tube surrounded with cold water, a so-called condenser. It is well to drive over from one-half to two-thirds of the liquid in the flask. Strong and heavy wines may advantageously be diluted with water before distillation. The flask and condenser should be connected air-tight, and the receiver should be closed with a little mercury valve, so as to prevent the evaporation of any portion of alcohol.

As soon as the necessary quantity is distilled, the distillate is mixed with so much water as may be required to raise it to the exact weight or measure of the wine originally taken for distillation. In the case of filling up to measure, the mixture must be brought to the same temperature as the original wine, and must be well agitated before being employed for the purpose of determining its specific gravity. The latter may be ascertained by a floating hydrometer, or the balance and specific gravity bottle. The specific gravity bottle should have a capacity of from 20 to 60 cubic centimetres, or a thousand grains. Its contents should have the temperature of $15.5°$ C. or $60°$ F., the temperature for which most alcohol tables are constructed ; in case it should be either higher or lower, it should be cooled down or warmed up to the desired point. When the contents of the specific gravity bottle have been weighed, and compared with the weight of the amount of pure water which fills the bottle, considered as 1, the specific gravity of the distillate is found. In order from this datum of specific gravity to find the amount of pure or absolute alcohol contained in the distillate, it is necessary to consult tables which have been empirically constructed by experiments on all kinds of mixtures of alcohol and water, so-called *alcohol tables*. On such tables we first find the specific gravity which our experiment has yielded; next, the temperature at which it has been weighed, and opposite this we find the amount of alcohol in per cents. The reader should bear in mind that there are several modes of stating the percentage of alcohol, one being per cent. by volume in volume of wine; a second, per cent. by weight in weight of wine; and a third, per cent. by weight in volume of wine.

The method of expressing the alcoholic strength of a wine in per cent. by weight in volume seems, on the whole, the preferable one. If in this case the decimal point is moved one figure to the right, the number of grammes of alcohol contained in one litre of wine is obtained; and if this figure is further multiplied by seven, the number of grains of absolute alcohol in one gallon (six bottles) of wine is given.

In England the government department which collects the taxes on alcoholic liquids, etc., called the Excise, has adopted a mode of giving the alcoholic strength of wines and spirits differing from those of all other nations; namely, in volume per cent. of proof-spirit, indicated as degrees by a hydrometer, called, after its constructor, that of Sikes.

§ 39. QUANTATION OF ALCOHOL IN WINES BY INDIRECT MEANS.

We here merely indicate the nature of these processes, without any description of their details; these latter and the mathematical formulæ of their application can be seen in Thudichum and Dupré, "Treatise," pp. 139-158.

The first method was proposed by Tabarie, and much used and recommended by Balling and Mulder. A quantity of wine of known specific gravity is measured or weighed off (100 c.c.), carefully evaporated in a water bath to about a quarter of its bulk; it is then cooled and mixed with sufficient distilled water to bring up its weight or bulk to the original weight or bulk. Balling preferred the use of weighed quantities; we employed Tabarie's measuring process, as the former gives the alcohol a trifle too high, but with sherries Tabarie's method gives the alcohol too low; in neither case does the error exceed 0·25 per cent. either way. From our experiments it follows that the results obtainable by this process are sufficiently accurate for all practical purposes, whilst as regards rapidity and facility of execution, no other proceeding is comparable to it, particularly when large numbers of samples have to be examined.

In other methods for the quantation of alcohol the boiling point of the mixture is used as the test of strength. A number of instruments, to which the name of *ebullioscope* has been given, have been devised by Brossard, Vidal, Pohl, Ure, Conatz, and others. In a metal boiler containing the wine a delicate thermometer is sunk, which latter is provided with a converted scale, *i.e.*, an indicator which shows not the temperature of the boiling liquid or vapour, but at once the percentage of alcohol in the boiling fluid. We have found that the presence of sugar in wine produces an error in this method, which raises the percentage of alcohol by about 1 per cent. for every 5·95 per cent of sugar.

A third method of alcohol quantation is based upon the vapour tension of alcoholic liquids; it is applied by means of an instrument termed a *vaporimeter*, invented and constructed by the late philosophers' mechanician, Geissler of Bonn; it was studied by Professor Plücker, and others, *e.g.*, Mohr. Wine is made to boil in the complicated apparatus; its vapour is made to force mercury from the bottle into a tube, until the height of this column of mercury exactly counteracts the pressure of the vapour rising from the wine at the temperature of boiling water. This height of the mercurial column is the measure of the alcoholic strength of the wine. This process offers difficulties by the presence of gases in wine, by the changes of boiling point with elevation above the sea-level; it also does not actually show the strength of wine, but only the proportion of wine to water.

A fourth method of alcohol quantation is based upon the expansibility of alcoholic mixtures by heat, measured by an instrument called a *dilatometer* (Silbermann). In this process it is found that the presence of sugar increases the rate of expansion beyond that of a mixture of alcohol and water of equal strength.

With light wines or natural wines of low alcoholicity, and without any admixture, all the above methods give tolerable results; the process of distillation and Balling's plan give however the best results; the other methods, while requiring much care and skill in their application, are liable to considerable errors from even slight inattention to minute points in the manipulation or in the character of the wine. With strong, heavy, sweet wines no process except that of Balling or distillation deserves any consideration.

§ 40. STATE IN WHICH ALCOHOL IS CONTAINED IN WINE.

It has frequently been asked whether alcohol is present in wine as free alcohol, or is only produced and liberated during distillation, and this question has been answered sometimes in the negative, and sometimes in the affirmative. What gave rise to this question was the observation that pure wine differs in taste from wine to which alcohol has been added. Most persons of moderate experience in tasting wine are able to detect the addition of a few per cent. of alcohol to a wine, even if its strength after this addition is not greater than the strength of many pure wines in which the spirit cannot be detected by the taste. A practised wine-taster will detect the addition of even a few per milles of alcohol to a pure wine. From these facts, namely, that no alcohol can be tasted in pure wine, while the addition of even a few per milles of alcohol to pure wine is instantly detected by the taste, it has been argued that no free alcohol is contained in wine, but that what appears as alcohol by distillation exists in some kind of combination, and that the application of heat breaks up the compound, alcohol distilling over, the other constituents of the compound remaining behind. We have, however, not found a single physical or chemical property possessed by wine which is not in perfect harmony with the assumption that it contains the alcohol as a simple admixture and not in any sort of combination. When wine is freed from all its alcohol by distillation, and the distilled spirit is again returned to the residue in the still, a compound is made which no doubt tastes differently from the original wine, but is identical with it in all its physical features, such as specific gravity, boiling point, vapour tension at high and low temperature, effects of freezing, facility with which the alcohol can be separated, endosmotic equivalent, capillary attraction and specific heat. Some of these physical qualities, such as endosmotic equivalent and specific heat, would certainly have manifested even slight differences in the physical or chemical character of the two liquids had there been any, but all the eight tests prove identity. We have therefore to account for the change in taste by the process of distillation by hypotheses other than that which assumes the alcohol in natural wine to be in combination. The alcohol or spirit from fermented liquids is always accompanied by matters not being ethylic alcohol, but being, like this, products of fermentation, or being products of the action of heat on certain ingredients of the fermented liquid. Some of these products remain mixed with the alcohol with great pertinacity, are hardly separable by practical means, and impart to it a peculiar pungent taste, differing from that of pure alcohol. What tastes disagreeably in newly distilled spirit is not the alcohol, but these admixtures produced by the influence of heat. The by-taste can be diminished or removed by purifying the alcohol, distilling it over caustic lime, diluting it to a strength of 20 or 30 per cent., and filtering it repeatedly through fresh animal charcoal; gradually the taste becomes less pungent, and, as the purification proceeds, the mixture will appear less strong to the taste than a mixture of equal strength which has remained unpurified. It is owing to the admixture of these heat products, which have been termed empyreumatic, that new whiskey is harsh and objectionable, and requires the influence of air admitted gradually through the pores of the wood of the barrels, and of time to become mellow and fit for use. Alcohol which has been entirely freed from these admixtures is called *silent spirit;* but this in its turn never acquires any flavour of any kind, and remains always unfit for use as a beverage in dilution; to be drinkable it must have a flavour imparted to it, such as that of juniper, which makes it gin, or must itself be mixed with large volumes of flavoured alcoholic liquids, such as Andalusian wine, which makes it sherry.

Of the matters which give a peculiar flavour to spirit distilled from wine *aldehyde* is not rarely one. Mostly such wines are condemned to the still which are not fit for being drunk in their natural state; and are undergoing progressive deterioration by the viscous or acetous ferment. To this rule only the wines of the Charente and of Languedoc are exceptions, which are grown for being distilled soon after their fermentation is complete, and which have no time allowed to them for becoming spoiled; they are not good wines for drinking, but their spirit is precious as Cognac brandy or as Trois-six. The presence of aldehyde is readily detected by the peculiar smell and flavour; it may be removed from the wine, neutralized by an alkali, by distillation, and collected in a well-cooled condenser; it then maintains its smell and flavour on the tongue, reduces silver salts, and is easily converted into acetic acid.

Chapter VIII.

¡ACIDS IN WINE.

§ 41. Varieties of Acids in Wine.

The acids which have hitherto been distinctly recognized as present in wine are of two kinds, namely, such as are already found in the grape, *tartaric, malic,* and *tannic acid,* and such as are produced during fermentation, namely, *acetic, formic, succinic,* and *carbonic* acid. In addition to these wine nearly always contains traces of some of the more complicated members of the fatty acid series, as *propionic*, *butyric*, and particularly *œnanthic* acid; from the latter some philosophers have derived the peculiarly agreeable flavour common to all wine apart from any special bouquet.

Tartaric acid.—This is the most characteristic acid of wine; it occurs in it as acid potash salt, so-called *tartar*, in trade also *argol*, which is deposited from wine when it is kept long in barrels. Of the acid six varieties are known, all of which have the chemical composition expressed by the formula, $C_4 H_6 O_6$; they are all dibasic and form therefore two classes of salts and ethers, neutral and acid. Of the six varieties of tartaric acid only two have been found in wine, namely, *ordinary tartaric acid*, which as it turns the plane of polarized light, as seen in an instrument called a *polarimeter*, to the right, is characterized as *dextro-tartaric acid*; and *paratartaric* or *racemic* acid, which has no influence on polarized light. This latter acid is found in small quantities in nearly all crude tartar, but more particularly in tartar from Italy. By various chemical proceedings it can be split up into two equivalent parts, one being the ordinary dextro-tartaric acid, the other being an acid of the same chemical composition and almost identical chemical properties, but having upon polarized light the opposite effect to that of the ordinary acid, namely, a turning to the left, and hence being called *laevo-tartaric acid*. The ordinary acid turns polarized light just as much to the right as laevo-tartaric acid turns it to the left; when the two are combined to racemic acid one optical effect neutralizes the opposite one, and the twin acid shows no polarity effect at all. With these optical characters of the two simple acids and of their conjugation product other physical and chemical properties are combined, which are, so to say, oppositionally symmetrical, the left and right turning acid being in the same relation to each other as a body before a mirror is to its reflected image. These relations are of great crystallographical interest, but we must leave their further consideration to more specifically chemical works. In wine we have practically to deal with ordinary tartaric acid, its salts and ethers. In the same form it is a regular constituent of the juice of the fruit of many plants, as tamarinds, mountain ash, mulberries, pine-apples, and others.

Tartaric acid ether ($C_2 H_6$, $C_4 H_4 O_6$), a compound consisting of the acid and alcohol, is analogous to the salts, and is gradually formed in all wines, very slowly in the cold, more rapidly in higher temperatures. It contributes not to the bouquet, but to the rich taste of the wine. Wines which as must or as wines have been treated with gypsum or plaster of Paris have thereby lost all tartaric acid present in the must, consequently do not develop the rich taste of natural wine, but exhibit a bitter metallic taste of Glauber's salts, or sulphate of potash.

Malic acid ($C_4 H_6 O_5$) is found either free or in combination with alkalies and earths, in the juices, particularly those of the fruit of many plants, as apples (from which it bears the name), cherries, plums, grapes, the berries of the mountain ash, etc.; the latter, containing it in great quantity, are generally employed for its preparation. Malic acid is also obtainable from *asparagin*, a body present in the young shoots of many plants, *e.g.*, vetches, asparagus, and in edible roots, *e.g.*, salsifis. Malic, like tartaric acid, is a dibasic acid, and therefore forms two series of salts and ethers, neutral and acid ones. As regards the formation of ethers, it behaves like tartaric acid.

Succinic acid ($C_4 H_6 O_4$) derives its name from its formation during the destructive distillation of amber, the fossil resin used for ornaments. It is found in some parts of the animal organism, *e.g.*, the brain, of which it is a regular constituent. It is a frequent product of the oxydation of organic substances, more particularly the fats and the fatty acids. It is also produced during the decomposition by ferment of various substances, as asparagin, malic acid, sugar, etc., and is therefore always found in small quantities in wines. Grape sugar during its fermentation by yeast yields about 0·5 per cent. of its weight of succinic acid. Malic and tartaric acid may also be transformed into succinic acid by the abstraction of some of their oxygen. Commercial succinic acid is prepared by the fermentation of malate of lime in water with some cheese. Upon every

two parts of succinic one part of acetic acid is simultaneously formed, and it is not improbable that some of the
acetic acid formed in even plastered wine by the viscosity
fungus is produced from malic along with succinic acid.   It
is a very stable body, and is sublimable without change ; it
is dibasic, and forms two series of salts and ethers.   Succinic acid is extracted from the dry residue of wine by ether-
alcohol, combined with lime, and separated as calcium salt
from the glycerol simultaneously extracted.   One litre of
wine contains from 1 to 1·5 gramme of succinic acid, equal to
one-fourth or one-fifth of the whole of its acidity considered
as tartaric.

The relation of the three acids of wine described in the
foregoing are chemically very conspicuous; they all three
contain the same number of atoms of carbon, C_4, and hydrogen, H_6, but differ as regards the oxygen, of which tartaric
acid contains six, O_6, malic five, O_5, and succinic four, O_4;
and that this difference in the quantities of oxygen is the only
constitutional difference is proved by the fact that by abstraction of oxygen, tartaric acid can be transformed into
malic, and this into succinic acid, while inversely succinic
acid by the addition of oxygen can be promoted to malic,
and this, by a further addition, to tartaric acid.

Acetic acid.—Acetic acid ($C_2 H_4 O_2$) is found in the juices
of some plants and animals, either free or in combination,
but only in extremely small quantities.   The chief sources
of its production for use as vinegar are the oxydation of
ordinary alcohol under the influence of a particular ferment called the vinegar plant (*mycoderma aceti*), and the
destructive distillation of wood.   The manner in which
the plant acts is not known, but it transfers oxygen to
alcohol, forming first aldehyde, afterwards acetic acid.   The
mycoderma cannot live in strong alcohol, and converts only
weak spirit, not much exceeding ten per cent. alcoholic
strength, such as is common to natural wine, into vinegar.
The temperature most favourable to the formation of vinegar
is between 22° and 37° C.

Must after partial fermentation contains many of the
elements favourable to the production of vinegar.   Where

the must ferments in open vats, as in many parts of the south, it exposes a large surface to the atmosphere, which is further increased by the thick froth covering it, or, as is often the case with red wines, by the skins and stalks of the grapes which float on the top. Much wine in southern countries is lost by a beginning of acetous fermentation, and its value is partially recovered only by distilling off the main bulk of the alcohol. In more northern wine-producing countries, however, the temperature prevailing during the time of fermentation is not high enough to favour acetous fermentation; and, moreover, during the greater part of such fermentation the carbonic acid constantly produced and escaping at the surface prevents the free access of air. In all moderately warm countries it requires, therefore, but slight attention to prevent an excessive production of acetic acid, and in the wines produced there the quantity of this acid usually ranges from between 0·5 to 1·5 per mille. In warm countries and seasons, however, and in all cases where the husks are allowed to remain in the fermenting must, great care is requisite to prevent the formation of vinegar, and sometimes the fermentation of the must has to be stopped by the addition of alcohol, in order to limit as much as possible the time during which the wine has to be kept in open vats. For just as in the manufacture of vinegar from wine it is found that the rapidity with which wine is converted into vinegar increases to a certain extent with the increasing amount of acetic acid, so in vinification it is observed that if once the quantity of acetic acid present has reached a certain amount, its further production will go on at a greatly increased rate, and the wine can no longer be kept in vessels to which air has access without turning sour entirely. If the oxydation of alcohol takes place under conditions when there is but a limited supply of oxygen, it often stops short at aldehyde; in many wines of Sauternes, and in Greek wines which had been kept in barrels, we have found aldehyde and acetic acid simultaneously. Many Australian wines imported into London, red as well as white, are acetous, and some lots of wine in barrels from that country we found almost entirely transformed into vinegar. The highest amount of acetic acid found in more than a hundred samples of French and German wines amounted to 1·78 pro mille, the lowest being 0·36 pro mille; while in a number of samples of Greek wines the acetic acid varied between 1·53 and 3·63 pro mille.

If the acetic acid, as is the case in wine, is mixed with a great many other substances, and it is desired to test it and estimate its quantity, it should be separated from them by distillation, and the tests should be applied to the distillate, neutralized, if necessary, by potash or ammonia. That the volatile acid of wine is almost all acetic acid is readily proved by estimating its atomic weight This is done by combining the acid, once purified by re-distillation from its soda salt, after addition of sulphuric acid, with baryta; the pure acetate of baryum contains 53·54 per cent. of baryum; the volatile acid from many wines we have found to contain, as baryum salt, from 53·3 to 53·9 per cent of baryum. The estimation of the baryum in the salt produced by the whole of the volatile acid, is not, however, in itself a perfectly reliable criterion of the purity of the acetic acid contained in it.

Formic and other acids of the acetic or fatty series.—The series of these acids runs parallel to the series of alcohols which we have enumerated; they are *formic, propionic, butyric, valerianic, caproic,* etc., acids. The only acid of this series, besides acetic acid, which has been recognized as certainly present in many wines is *formic acid;* of the others we only know that they are represented in wine by one or more of their number, though we cannot certainly say by which. Formic acid is recognized in the distillate by appropriate tests, particularly that when heated with silver nitrate it causes a black deposit of silver. When only little formic acid is mixed with much acetic it must be separated first by a process of fractional distillation. By the same kind of fractionation the heavier acids may be isolated, and their atomic weights may be fixed by baryta. In all cases in which the acids distilled from large quantities of wine were examined, the salt of the first fraction contained less baryum than corresponds to an acetate; the intermediate portions contained almost the exact proportion required by pure acetate; the last fraction contained perceptibly more. Formiate contains 60·18 per cent. baryum, acetate 53·54, propionate 48·22, and butyrate 43·87 per cent. To carry, analytically, the separation of the volatile acids of wine to perfection would require the distillation of very large amounts of wine.

Œnanthic acid.—This acid does not occur in wine in its isolated condition, but only combined with alcohol as *œnanthic ether*. Of this ether we shall again speak in the chapter on ethers. Here it may suffice to state that it was obtained by Liebig and Pelouze in the course of an examination of the ether in question. Its formula is $C_{14} H_{26} O_3$, and it forms an oil solidifying below 13° C. Its origin and mode of formation are unknown. It is curious that by itself the acid is quite inodorous, and that the characteristic smell of its ether should not be foreshadowed in it. It is insoluble in water, and therefore could scarcely be contained in must before fermentation; it is therefore probably formed during fermentation and in *statu nascendi* at once combines with alcohol to form ether.

§ 42. CHEMICAL ESTIMATION OF THE QUANTITY OF ACIDS IN WINE.[1]

We must only indicate the general principle of the processes by which the quantities of acids in wines may be ascertained. For the purpose of ordinary analysis it is sufficient to estimate the whole of the *volatile acids* as *acetic*. The *fixed acids* may be treated as if they were *tartaric* and *malic only*. The entire acidity in wine is ascertained by adding an alkaline test solution of known strength, and using freshly prepared tincture of logwood as an indicator; when the acid has all been neutralized, the colour of the logwood changes from yellow to brown or red. In some wines this change from yellow to red takes place at once,

[1] For full details of the processes cf. Thudichum and Dupré, "Treatise," pp. 189-197.

and can be easily observed ; in others, however, the colour passes gradually through brown, blue, green, etc., and never becomes actually red.   In these cases it is impossible to accurately fix the point where sufficient alkali has been added, and then the process has to be modified by testing a small portion of the mixture with logwood tincture a second time.   The mixture remains brown while it is neutral, and becomes red the moment it is alkaline.

The total amount of volatile acid in wine may be estimated not only by the acidity of any distillate, but more conveniently by deducting the amount of permanent acidity, after evaporation of the wine, from that which the fresh wine showed.   This proceeding has the advantage that it can be carried out on as small a quantity of wine as 20 cub. centimetres, and thus taking much less time than an experiment on the larger quantities required by other methods.

It is almost impossible to estimate accurately the volatile acid by distillation and quantation of the acidity of the distillate, because a part of the acid is obstinately retained by the residue, even when fresh water is added and the distillation is prolonged.   On the other hand, evaporation and drying in an open dish expels all the volatile acid.

In good sound wines the total amount of free acid ranges from 0·3 to 0·7 per cent. ; wines with more than the latter amount of free acid are neither pleasant nor wholesome.   Of the total acidity not more than an amount of 0·15 per cent. of the wine should be due to volatile acid.

§ 43. ESTIMATION OF TARTARIC ACID AND BITARTRATE OF POTASH IN WINE.

This quantation is mostly effected by a process elaborated by the French chemist Berthelot, and is based upon the insolubility of the bitartrate in a mixture of strong alcohol and ether.   Any free acid is soluble, and can be precipitated by caustic potash.   In a process elaborated by the German chemist Nessler, absolute alcohol only is used to precipitate the tartar.   Both methods give accurate results if the amount of tartaric acid present does not fall short of 0·05 per cent. ; if it be below this amount the results are of less accuracy, because the alkalimetric liquids fail to be applicable. To increase the accuracy of the method we recommend that the operator should use double the quantity of wine prescribed for the test by both Berthelot and Nessler. These authors probably had to deal with wines rich in tartaric acid, while the wines which we examined were less endowed with that ingredient.

In the majority of wines all the tartaric acid is present as bitartrate, that is to say, there is a sufficient amount of potash present to enable the whole of the tartaric acid to be precipitated in this form by the addition of ether and alcohol ; the wines, in fact, frequently correspond to a solution of bitartrate, saturated at the lowest temperature to which the wine may have been exposed for a certain length of time.

All pure natural wines contain more or less of tartaric acid, and the quantity is probably the higher the riper are the grapes from which it is produced. There is not, however, any apparent connection between the amount of tartaric acid present, and the quality of the wine; the excess of acidity perceptible to the taste depends not upon the quantity of the tartaric, but that of the malic, succinic, and the volatile acids present ; we have also occasionally observed lactic acid as a cause of excessive acidity of wines. All wines in the course of the preparation of which plaster of Paris, gypsum, sulphate of lime has been used are nearly free from tartaric acid.

In the majority of unplastered wines, if not in all, the amount of *tartaric acid* corresponds to only a fraction of the total free fixed acid present ; the rest of the acid consists mainly of *malic*, with some *succinic acid*. In the course of the analytical proceedings for the isolation and quantation of these acids, particularly of the tartaric, it has to be borne in mind, that the wine contains sulphate and chloride of potassium, which are decomposed by free tartaric acid in the presence of large quantities of alcohol and ether, as used in the Nessler and Berthelot processes.

The quantation and isolation of malic acid is based upon the insolubility of its calcium salt in absolute alcohol.

The presence of any considerable amount of acetic acid shows the wine, even when yet of good taste, to be unsound; the presence of much malic acid shows the must from which the wine was made to have proceeded from somewhat under-ripe grapes; the absence of tartaric acid proves that the wine has been plastered; any excess of tartrate of potash is easily removed by exposing the wine to a wintry temperature.

CHAPTER IX.

ETHERS OR BOUQUET OF WINES.

§ 44. VARIETIES OF ETHERS IN WINE.

THE ethers in wine are compounds of the fixed and volatile acids with alcohols, and are formed after fermentation, with the exception perhaps of œnanthic ether, which seems to be formed during fermentation. They are formed very slowly, and as wine owes to them much of its flavour it has to remain long in barrels or bottles to allow of the etherification to be effected.

Aceto-Ethylic Ether.—By far the greater part of the volatile ethers found in wine is acetic ether; it is volatile and possesses a very decided smell, of an agreeable kind; and thereby no doubt contributes much to the general flavour of wine, although neither the characteristic wine-flavour, nor the peculiar bouquet of wine is due to it. It serves rather as a background to these, and its excess is detrimental to the specific flavours. It can easily be produced by combining acetic acid and alcohol in the presence of sulphuric acid; in wine it is formed by the interaction of acetic acid and alcohol under the influence of the other acids, but its quantity is kept within certain limits by the great bulk of water contained in wine. Its formation in wine is gradual, and thus the amount of it present in wine at a given time can be used as a measure of the age of the wine.

Aceto-Propylic, Butylic, Amylic, Caproylic, etc., Ethers.—
The place of ethyl in the acetic ether just described may be
taken by any of the radicles of the other alcohols present in
wine, when the ethers enumerated in the heading result.
They correspond in their general characters to acetic ether,
and are all volatile; they all have an agreeable smell, greatly
resembling the smell of certain qualities of fruit, more particularly when much diluted; thus acetate of amyl has the
odour of pears. Minute quantities of these ethers are present, particularly in old wine, and contribute to its flavour
and bouquet.

*Butyro-Ethylic, Caprylo-Ethylic, Capro-Ethylic, and Pe-
largo-Ethylic Ethers.*—Just as acetic acid forms a series of
ethers with the radicles of the alcohol series described in the
foregoing, so the other acids form each a series of ethers with
the same series of alcohol radicles. In wine we may expect
these acids always to combine with the prevailing, namely,
ethylic alcohol. The etherification is apparently facilitated
by the presence of tartaric acid. Many of these ethers have
a very powerful and characteristic odour. Very frequently
the odour of the concentrated pure ethers is rather disagreeable, but becomes agreeable, and resembles the flavour of
fruit, when it is greatly diluted. Thus dilute butyric ether
resembles in its smell that of pine-apples; caprylic ether has
a similar smell; caproic ether has the odour of melons, and
to pelargonic ether probably a portion of the characteristic
wine-flavour is due.

§ 45. ŒNANTHIC ETHER.

At the end of the distillation of large volumes of wine,
such as are used in the south of France, a small quantity of
an oily liquid passes over, which is the crude ether here in
question. Forty thousand parts of wine yield about one
part of the oil. The ether is also contained in wine yeast,
and removed from it by distillation with water. The ether
as first obtained contains also acid as an admixture which
has to be removed by alkali and re-distillation. The pure
ether is a colourless, thin, oily liquid, with an overpowering

vinous smell and a sharp, disagreeable taste. Its composition is expressed by the formula C_{18} H_{36} O_3; it contains
two ethyle radicles. It is very soluble in even diluted spirit,
but insoluble in water. It is generally admitted that the
characteristic vinous smell, which distinguishes all kinds of
wine from every other fermented liquid, is due to the
presence of this œnanthic ether. The particular flavour or
bouquet, however, by which the wines of different vineyards
and vines are distinguishable from each other, is produced
by substances of a different nature and composition. Much
so-called œnanthic ether is synthetically produced in manu-
factories and used in the transformation of silent spirit into
so-called British brandy.

§ 46. TARTARIC ETHER.

Tartaric acid being dibasic may be made to form two
varieties of ethers, namely, neutral and acid ones. Only the
latter kind is met with in wine, tartro-ethylic ether, C_6 H_{10} O_8.
It is a crystallizable, but deliquescent, solid body, and
behaves like an acid, as it even forms salts with bases. It
cannot be distilled, but under the influence of higher temperatures breaks up into various products.

By the interaction of the alcohols and ethers present in
wine a great number of compound ethers may be formed.
Thus, assuming the presence of five acids and five alcohols,
they might form twenty-five compound ethers, any or all of
which might be present and contribute their share to the
flavour ; and the flavour would alter with the predominance
of the one or the other of these ethers. In the manufacture of
brandy very large quantities of wine are distilled, and a considerable amount of so-called fusel or fousel-oil is obtained,
in which a number of the above-named volatile acids and
ethers, as well as several different alcohols have been detected.
The more volatile ethers of course remain with the distilled
brandy.

§ 47. QUANTATION OF ETHERS IN WINE.

Berthelot estimated the ethers in wine by destroying them
with baryta and ascertaining the quantity of acid which had

entered into combination with the earth.   But we have found
that the presence of sugar makes the process inapplicable.
We have therefore used another method ; [1] the *volatile ethers*
are separated by distillation, and decomposed by alkali, and
in the salt the quantity of *acid* is estimated ; the fixed ethers
are decomposed in the residue by alkali ; and the *alcohol*
separated is estimated.   Wine may be distilled from a retort
with the usual precaution of a water or sand-bath, without
any of the ethers undergoing decomposition.   The dry
residue of wine by long heating loses its acidity, but not its
fixed ethers ; by careful experiment it has been ascertained
that tartaric ether in the presence of tartaric acid is not decomposed by being heated in an open dish on a water-bath.
All the volatile ethers are expelled from wine, together with
the alcohol, by a concentration of the wine to one-fifth.   The
foregoing process of separate quantation of volatile and
fixed ethers is as applicable to dry natural as to sweet or
sugared wines.

§ 48. Theory of the Limitation of Ethers in Wine.

It has been maintained by Berthelot that the amount of
ethers found in any mixture of alcohols and acids is after a
certain time a constant quantity, independent of the nature
of the alcohols and acids present, and a function only of
their relative amount.   He has given a formula for calculating the amount of alcohol contained in the compound ethers
of one litre of a mixture of acids, alcohol, and water, such as
wine essentially is when etherification is complete.   The
formula is available for any alcoholic strength up to 25 per
cent.   As by far the greatest proportion of alcohol present is
ethylic alcohol, the other alcohols may for the present purpose be left out of consideration.   We have found that the
data obtained by the application of Berthelot's formula agree
very well with those obtained by direct analysis ; the only
exceptions to the rule are very young wines, in which etherification is incomplete, and wines to which alcohol has been

[1] Thudichum and Dupré, " Treatise," pp. 203-216.

added just before they come under observation, and in which therefore etherification has not yet re-attained its equilibrium.

The estimation of ethers in wines thus affords a valuable means of judging of their age and genuineness. A natural wine should during the first few years contain somewhat less ether than required by the formula; the amount should gradually augment with age, until after from four to six years the maximum would be reached. If then an appreciable amount of alcohol be added, the wine be fortified, etherification will begin afresh, and again reach a maximum after a number of years. On the other hand, wine prepared artificially, with addition of ethers, will probably at once show a maximum of ethers, or will even exceed this, and will then, instead of increasing in richness, remain stationary, or show a diminution of ethers with increasing age. Thus sherries, on arrival from Spain in wood, are always out of equilibrium, because they have been brandied just before their departure, and require some years in bottle before they acquire the limit of etherification.

Although the total amount of alcohol present as ether in wines which we have examined expressly generally agrees closely with that required by theory, yet the amount present in fixed ether on the one, and volatile ether on the other hand bears no regular relation to the amount of fixed and volatile acids present. The amount of alcohol present as volatile ether is almost always greater than the amount present in fixed ether, in spite of the circumstance that the amount of volatile acid present is almost always much smaller than the amount of fixed acid. The proportion between the volatile and fixed ethers bears no proportionate relation to the amounts of volatile and fixed acids present. All the fixed acids are present already in the grape juice, and their etherification can therefore begin as soon as alcohol begins to be formed during fermentation, and continue simultaneously with its production. Moreover, the amount of fixed acids is greatest at the beginning of fermentation, decreasing as the amount of alcohol increases, on account of the lesser solubility of acid tartrate of potassium in alcoholic liquids. It is therefore evident that the amount of fixed ethers formed in a given time is greatest in quite young, or still fermenting wine.

The volatile acids, on the other hand, are all formed during or after fermentation. If therefore fermentation has taken place under circumstances unfavourable to the production of volatile acids, say acetic acid, as is the case when must ferments at a low temperature, or in carefully closed vessels, little or no volatile acid will be present at first, but the amount will increase gradually with the age of the wine, provided it be kept in well-ullaged casks. In such a wine, therefore, the production of fixed ethers begins before that of the volatile ethers. But the continually increasing amount of volatile acids, aided by their greater tendency to etherification, and the gradual decrease in the amount of fixed acids, aided further by the circumstance that the volatile acids are in presence of alcohol in *statu nascendi*, when this combining tendency is at its maximum, soon reverses the conditions, and causes the volatile ethers to preponderate.

In judging of the relative quantity of free, fixed and volatile acids present it should be borne in mind that the volatile ethers being neutral ethers, neutralize their acid completely, while the fixed ethers being acid ethers, have only half their acidity neutralized. It is therefore necessary, in order to find the quantity of that part of fixed acid which is really free and uncombined, to subtract an amount of acid equal to that found neutralized in the fixed ethers from the total amount of free fixed acid found. And from this the acid present as bitartrate should perhaps also be deducted in order to obtain data by which the amount of etherification due to fixed and volatile acids respectively may be accurately determined.

§ 49. SMELL, BOUQUET OR AROMA OF WINE.

There are odoriferous constituents common to all wines which we have seen are essentially compound ethers, and these produce the truly vinous smell; this can hardly be called either aroma or bouquet with much propriety: indeed

the word aroma indicates *spice*, and wine to become *aromatic*,
in the language of past pharmacy *aromatites*, has to be
mixed with spice; of such spice myrrh is used in the
present day at Naples to give a flavour to the flavourless
white wine; *crocus* or *saffron* was extracted with Canary
wine and this tincture went by the name of *aroph*, a contraction of *aroma philosophorum*. But pure wine was never
termed, and is not aromatic in the true sense of the word.
Odoriferous constituents which are characteristic of particular kinds of wine, being always mixed with the more or
less prominent flavour of the œnanthic principles, may
properly be termed bouquet. The substances producing
the bouquet and peculiar characteristic flavour of special
wines are of two kinds; namely, such as are already present
in the grape, and are unaltered during fermentation, *e.g.*, the
smell of the muscatel, or Isabella grape; and, secondly, such
as are formed during and after fermentation, partly out of
substances already present in the grape, partly from matters
formed during or after fermentation. Some of the substances
present in the grape are formed apparently in greater quantity with their increasing ripeness, and have probably the
characters of essential oils. On the other hand the
substances yielding the bouquet are sometimes contained in
greater quantity in unripe than in ripe grapes. The fruit,
blossoms, or other parts of certain plants, when steeped in a
liquid undergoing alcoholic fermentation, produce or yield
a small quantity of essential oil, termed ferment oil, which
possesses a characteristic smell, not rarely resembling the
bouquet of certain kinds of wine. Thus the flowers of elder
when allowed to ferment with the must, or extracted with
spirit, impart to the solvents a flavour not unlike that of
muscatel grapes; while the flowers of any vine, more particularly the wild vine, yield to alcohol the Rhine wine
bouquet.

It has been attempted to separate the odoriferous constituents of wine by means of ether, but their extremely
unstable character under the influence of heat and air, and
their small amount made these attempts abortive. The
extracted bouquetted matter of a litre of wine was entirely

destroyed when fifty cubic centimetres of air were left in contact with it. This explains the manner in which very old wines gradually lose their bouquet; the air penetrates both wood and corks. On the other hand in young wines the limited access of air is essential to their development as regards bouquet; and as the access of air is much more rapid in casks than in bottles, it is a part of the art and knowledge and skill of the wine-maker to mature the wine in cask until it has attained its maximum of bouquet, and then to bottle it to maintain the bouquet, and effect the rest of the changes which demand exclusion of air.

CHAPTER X.

SUGARS IN GRAPES AND WINE.

§ 50. VARIETIES OF SUGAR OCCURRING IN GRAPES AND WINE.

THE sweetness of grapes is due to the presence of a considerable amount of sugar in their juice, which is probably a mixture in atomic proportions of two different kinds of sugar, called respectively fruit-sugar and grape-sugar. The same mixture is produced by the action of dilute acids upon cane-sugar, and is then termed invert sugar.

Cane-sugar has never been found in grapes; it is however sometimes added to must or to wine, for example to the sweet kinds of Champagne and other effervescent vinous products, and in large quantities to British wines. But when thus dissolved in wine cane-sugar is soon changed into invert sugar, so that, after the lapse of a few weeks, cane-sugar is no longer found in the wine to which it has been added.

During the fermentation of the must, the fruit and grape-sugars are decomposed so as to yield chiefly alcohol and carbonic acid, besides small quantities of glycerol and succinic acid. The grape-sugar is decomposed more quickly than the fruit-sugar, so that at the end of the fermentation generally more fruit-sugar than grape-sugar is left. The sugar which remains permanently in wine consists mainly of fruit-sugar, with only a small proportion of grape-sugar. The proportion between them differs in different kinds of wine, and seems to depend in some sort on the mode of fermentation; in wines which retain much sugar the grape-sugar sometimes predominates, while all the fruit-sugar is decomposed. The sugar, whether fruit or grape-sugar, left undecomposed at the end of the fermentation, in pure natural wines, rarely amounts to more than 0·5 per cent., and is generally much less in quantity. Even this small amount is confined chiefly to young wines, and disappears with progressing age of the wine, generally after a second fermentation in the spring following the first fermentation. In wines to which alcohol is added to check fermentation, or in liqueur wines made from sun-dried grapes or raisins, the so-called *dulce* of the south of France and Spain, the sugar ranges from 2 or 3 per cent. to upwards of 20 per cent.

§ 51. GRAPE-SUGAR, DEXTROSE, OR RIGHT-TURNING GLUCOSE.

Grape-sugar has the composition expressed by the formula $C_6 H_{12} O_6$, and is found in many kinds of fruit, and in bees' honey, mixed or combined with fruit-sugar. It is produced by the action of warm diluted sulphuric acid on starch or cellulose, is excreted in large quantities by the kidneys in a disease termed diabetes, and is obtained by the decomposition of substances, products of organic nature, which from this fact are termed *glucosides*. It is also formed by the action of ferment, *e.g.*, yeast or cane-sugar; this change takes place instantaneously when two parts of finely-powdered white cane-sugar are mixed in a mortar with one part by weight of solid yeast, and the mixture becomes fluid. Dextrose, as we shall hereafter term this sugar, crystallizes from a moderately concentrated solution in granular masses containing a molecle of water of crystallization, which they lose at a temperature of 60° C. If the solution be evaporated to a thick syrup, so as not to contain this necessary water, it will crystallize only after having attracted sufficient water from the atmosphere to form the hydrated crystals. From alcohol of 95 per cent. strength it crystallizes in fine needles containing no water of crystallization. It is soluble in its own weight of water, but slightly soluble in alcohol, scarcely soluble in ether. Its most remarkable and useful chemical reaction is that when a salt of copper is mixed with it, and caustic alkali is added to the mixture a deep blue solution, without any precipitate, is formed ; when this mixture is allowed to stand, after a lapse of time, or when it is heated immediately, a yellowish-red precipitate of hydrate of suboxide of copper, or cuprous oxide, or a red precipitate of the anhydrous suboxide is formed and deposited. As one molecle of grape-sugar thus reduces ten molecles of oxide of copper to suboxide, by withdrawing the oxygen from the copper, this reaction may be used as a means for estimating the amount of dextrose present in a solution. The reaction was discovered by Trommer, and bears his name ; its quantitative application was elaborated by Fehling, and the fluid of known strength used in it bears the name of the later chemist. The test is so delicate that the presence of even a thousandth part of dextrose in a solution may be detected by it. The name of dextrose is derived from the fact that solutions of the sugar turn the plane of a beam of polarized light to the right, as seen in an apparatus called a polarimeter, or saccharometer. The actual rotating power is 56° of the circle to the right ; this power is but little affected by differences in temperature.

§ 52. Fruit-Sugar, Levulose or left-turning Glucose.

Fruit-sugar is found and formed in conjunction with dextrose in all the cases above described. It can be separated from the latter by combination with lime, and from the lime by oxalic or sulphuric acid. It forms an uncrystallizable syrup, soluble in water in every proportion, soluble in alcohol, slightly soluble in ether. Like dextrose it decomposes an alkaline solution of copper salt, and in exactly the same proportions. Its solutions turn the plane of polarized light to the left, its molecular rotating power being 106° of a circle at 14° C. This power is much affected by temperature, and at 90° C. is reduced to 53°.

§ 53. INVERT SUGAR.

As cane-sugar turns the plane of polarization to the right, but after decomposition by acids turns it to the left, it was said to have become inverted, and this gave rise to the name of inverted or, abbreviated, invert sugar. It behaves like a mixture of levulose and dextrose, and either of these sugars can be extracted from it. On adding to a solution of cane-sugar in strong alcohol much hydrochloric acid, pure dextrose crystallizes in time, while levulose remains in solution ; the levulose in its turn is separated by lime as already stated. Invert sugar turns the plane of polarization to the left, its molecular rotating power being 26° at 15° C.; as the temperature rises above 15° C. the rotation diminishes by 0·37° for each degree of temperature, while a sinking temperature increases the rotation by the same amount for each degree below 15° C.

§ 54. INOSITE OR PHASEOMANNITE.

It has been stated that the syrupy wines of Sauternes, and some Rhine wines of the best years, which retain permanently up to 4 per cent. of sugar contain, besides dextrose and levulose, a kind of sugar which was first discovered in green beans, and hence received the second name of the above title. It was discovered as an ingredient of the flesh of many animals, and therefore termed inosite ; it is also present in considerable amount in the brain of man and of the ox. Some have supposed that the presence of this sugar in the wines named might explain in part their strongly intoxicating quality, which is also peculiar in its kind, and termed by the French *heady*. But there is no record of inosite, though it is an alcohol, having any narcotic effect. Inosite is particularly liable to the lactic acid fermentation, and it is to lactic acid formed in the barrels that many medium sweet wines of the Gironde owe their acidity, which forms so striking a contrast to their sweetness ; this makes them undrinkable to an accomplished palate.

§ 55. TESTING WINES FOR SUGAR.

For details regarding the preparation and application of the several tests to wine we must refer to p. 226 of the great "Treatise." As wine must be colourless for the application of either the chemical or optical test, red and dark-coloured varieties have to be decolorized by agitation with charcoal ; very concentrated wines have to be diluted. Some extractive matters which are not sugar, but affect the copper test, can be removed by lead acetate, so-called sugar of lead ; this reagent also removes the brownish matters from wines coloured with caramels, such as sherry and Marsala. If any cane-sugar be present in the wine to be examined it has to be transformed into invert sugar by boiling with dilute sulphuric acid. Cane-sugar, $C_{12} H_{22} O_{11}$, by taking up a molecle of water, $H_2 O$, becomes by this process, called hydrolysis, $2 \times C_6 H_{12} O_6$, or 342 parts of cane-sugar become 360 parts of invert sugar.

As regards the *optical test*, a full explanation of the theory of polarization, and description of some of the best apparatus for its application, will be found in the "Treatise," *l. c.*, pp. 231-252. The wine to be subjected to the optical test is made colourless by the application of lead acetate, and afterwards a little animal charcoal, and the bright colourless liquid is placed into the tube of the polarimeter. As wine contains a mixture of dextrose and levulose in proportions which are not those of invert sugar, the amount of polarization which it shows depends upon the proportion of the two sugars present. As one part of dextrose turns about as much to the right as half a part of levulose turns to the left a mixture of the two in these proportions would show no polarization at all; a prevalence of either sugar would cause the polarization to turn in its peculiar direction; but whatever might be the proportion between them, half a part of levulose would always neutralize the optical effect of one part of dextrose, and the visible optical effect would be due only to the excess of either sugar over the stated proportion. The optical test, therefore, is unable to estimate the amount of sugar present; it can only estimate the non-neutralized excess of either. But if to the data obtained by this test be added the datum obtained by the chemical test, the quantity of each variety of sugar present is easily calculated.

A number of specimens of wine from the Rhine and the Gironde contained about 1·057 per cent. of sugar by chemical test; of this, 0·802 per cent. were levulose, 0·252 per cent. dextrose, or upon one part of the latter 3·19 parts of the former. A fine old Madeira showed 1·024 per cent. of sugar, of which dextrose placed as 1 part the levulose amounted to 3·43 parts. Six high-class port wines showed 1·179 per cent. sugar: in this, dextrose 1 part, levulose 2·57 parts.

A sample of cheap port contained 1·971 per cent. of sugar; in this 1 part of dextrose corresponded to 1·35 part of levulose.

A high-class sherry, fifty years old, contained 2·11 per cent. sugar, in this 1 part dextrose was present besides 1·26 part levulose.

A commercial Marsala showed 4·329 per cent. sugar; here 1 part dextrose was by the side of 0·84 part of levulose.

A cheap sherry contained 4·617 per cent. sugar; in this dextrose as 1 was to levulose 0·81 part.

A sample of Elbe sherry (Greek wine mixed with sugar and spirit at Hamburg) contained 6·512 per cent. of sugar; in this dextrose = 1 was counterbalanced by levulose = 0·37 part.

In the cases of the last three wines so-called saccharine (matter) mainly dextrose, had no doubt been added.

In a sample of port chemical tests showed the presence of 0·177 per cent. of sugar, while not a trace of polarization was perceptible in a saccharometer which will yet indicate 0·01 per cent., or one-seventeenth the quantity found chemically in the wine. In this case the sugars were in the proportion in which one neutralized the other, or one dextrose upon one-half part levulose. When the proportion of levulose sinks still lower the wine begins to turn to the right. It is usually assumed that this condition indicates an addition of dextrose to the wine; we have, however, met with several wines which turned to the right, although, as we had been credibly assured, no addition of dextrose or any other sugar had been made. These wines were young, and had undergone a second fermentation in bottle. One specimen before fermentation turned to the left, after it to the right, so that more levulose than dextrose had been destroyed. Another contained 0·144 per cent. of dextrose and 0·010 per cent. of levulose, which is equivalent to an almost total disappearance of the levulose.

Thus while in the above seven and more samples the residual sugar was mainly levulose, and while these cases represent the ordinary result of fermentation, under special conditions dextrose mainly may be preserved, and its presence in wine in excess of the equivalent of levulose must not be assumed to necessarily indicate any adulteration or illegitimate addition.

The sugar contained in champagne is chiefly invert sugar, formed by the action of the acids in the wine on the cane-sugar added in the liqueur. Thus the sugar found in a sample of champagne was found chemically to be 2·935 per cent.; and the optical test showed it to be almost pure invert sugar.

Should cane-sugar be suspected in wine, it may be found by destroying the dextrose and levulose by boiling with caustic alkali, and then transforming the cane-sugar, proved by its right-handed polarization, into invert sugar, by boiling with 10 per cent. of strong hydrochloric acid, and finding in the product the amount of polarization now directed to the left.

It is thus proved that neither the optical nor the chemical test can by itself give information on the quality and proportion of the sugars; the chemical test alone can give the total sugar; both tests conjointly are alone able to furnish complete qualitative and quantitative results.

CHAPTER XI.

COLOURING, ASTRINGENT, EXTRACTIVE AND MINERAL CONSTITUENTS OF WINE.

§ 56. GLYCEROL.

GLYCEROL, $C_3 H_8 O_3$ formerly termed glycerine, but now marked as an alcohol by the terminal syllable, one of the constituents of animal and vegetable fats, and of those peculiar substances contained in the brain known as phosphorised matters, may be prepared by saponification or decomposition of fats with superheated steam. For our present purpose it is of importance as a product of the fermentation of sugar, and contributes, in a limited manner, to the agreeably sweetish taste of wine. It is a colourless, syrupy, sweet liquid at ordinary temperatures, but crystallizes when subject to temperatures much below the freezing point of water. Owing to its being a tridynamic alcohol it forms three series of ethers and other compounds, and undergoes a variety of interesting chemical transformations.

In the process of fermentation 100 parts of cane-sugar, or 105·26 parts of dextrose, yield 3·64 parts of glycerol. It should, therefore, always be present in wine in the proportion of about one-fourteenth part of the alcohol, and thus contribute the more sweetness to the taste the richer the wine is in natural alcohol. It is separated from the residue of wine obtained by evaporation by extraction with a mixture of alcohol and ether, but then is always mixed with a little dextrose. But with all care the methods of Pasteur and of Pohl for the quantation of glycerol in wine do not exclude other extractives besides this dextrose, and thus it cannot be said that our means of ascertaining its quantity in wine are very accurate at present. Nevertheless wines are empirically adjusted to taste by the addition of glycerol, and it is as legitimate to add glycerol to wines which have been strengthened with alcohol, as to add this alcohol itself. When so added it should always be in the proportion of one part to fourteen parts of alcohol considered as absolute.

§ 57. COLOURING MATTERS.

French, German and Spanish wines in their youth are almost colourless, so much so that this state was at one time made a test of genuineness, a colour obtained by age only being easily imparted by art. It is therefore important to be able to distinguish natural from artificial tints, for a good wine matured by age cannot be colourless. Other wines are purely yellow, like old Sauternes. Other wines have all varieties of shade of colour up to dark brown; the darker shades are all artificially produced by the addition of boiled must, either to the fresh must before the fermentation, or to the made wine before sale. The colour of the boiled must is due to the browned, dehydrated or so-called burnt sugar, technically called caramel, and used in all kitchens for browning soups, sauces, and other accompaniments of solid productions of culinary art, e.g., custards. In consequence of this knowledge many wine-makers colour their products with culinary caramel, i.e., cane-sugar boiled to the desired colour; but every caramel, be it of dextrose in must or of cane-sugar, introduces an element of bitterness in the wine, which we hold not to be to its advantage. Some kinds of Marsala and Madeira, otherwise excellent cheap wines, are not rarely overcoloured, and thereby prejudiced in their taste and quality.

The natural colorations assumed by wines originally colourless, or white, as they are popularly termed, are produced by the oxidizing effect of the air upon certain matters contained in smaller or larger quantities in grapes, viz., the so-called extractives, being bodies not yet known in an isolated form, and the tannic acid which is extracted by the juice or wine from the husks, kernels and stalks. The wine during fermentation and rest in the cask also extracts tannin from the oak. Now just as raisins, and other kinds of fruit, during drying assume a brown colour, which becomes a light yellowish brown in any dilute, watery or alcoholic extract, so the wine during ripening becomes darker in colour, and in many cases sheds a brown deposit, being the fully oxydized extractive matter and tannin which is incapable of remaining in solution.

Amongst the colorations of white wine which are due to abnormal agencies there is one which, in the opinion of Pasteur, is due to the presence or preliminary action of decomposing fungi. It is observed occasionally upon all kinds of white wines, upon Graves, Barsac, Haut Sauternes, Rhenish, Hungarian and Italian wines, upon Champagne, and effervescent wines of the Loire, Saumur, and Vouvray. When the bottle is opened, and some wine is poured into the glass, the liquid is white or nearly so, but when it is allowed to stand a short time. it becomes somewhat coloured so as to attract attention. When such wine is filled into a white glass bottle and allowed to stand open, it will become brown on the surface, and the coloration will gradually descend to the bottom of the flask. The upper layers will, after some days or weeks, be actually blackish brown ; ultimately a dark deposit falls. During this process some of the alcohol is oxydized to acetic acid, probably by a collateral action of acetous ferment. Wine showing this phenomenon of quick darkening on exposure to air is unquestionably unsound, or sick, and requires appropriate treatment for its recovery.

The tints of all kinds of red wine, whether they are slightly rose-coloured, or almost black and impenetrable to light, are produced by peculiar colouring matters contained originally either in the pulp or the husk of the grape. The *soluble colouring matter* contained in the pulp of the grapes produced by such varieties of vines as the *teinturier*, or dyer, which is extensively grown in France and Spain for the purpose of producing wine of deep colour, which may be used to dye white wines, in quantity up to eight times the volume of the red, differs greatly from the colouring matter deposited in the husks of grapes, particularly by the evident fact of its *solubility* in the juice of the grapes, in which the pigment of the husk is *insoluble*. This soluble colouring matter is more closely related to that contained in the juice of elderberries and black currants. It enters into the composition of many Spanish, Portuguese, south and central French red wines. It has not, that we are aware of, been chemically examined with the desirable method and degree of accuracy. But the colouring matter from the husks of blue and black grapes has been examined by Mulder and others, so that we know a little more about it. It is precipitated from wine by lead acetate, and this precipitate is decomposed by sulphuretted hydrogen. From the purified sulphide the pigment is extracted by alcohol and acetic acid. This alcoholic acetic solution is now evaporated, when it at first becomes red like wine; as the alcohol evaporates further it becomes violet; and lastly, when only little acetic acid remains, beautifully *blue*. The residue is dried completely, freed from a little fat by ether, and is then pure pigment. It is in the dry state bluish-black, like black lead (graphite); it is amorphous, insoluble in alcohol, water, ether, chloroform, bisulphide of carbon, oil of turpentine and of olives. It is soluble in alcohol containing a trace of acetic acid, and the saturated solution has a blue colour; more acetic acid makes the solution red. In alcohol and tartaric acid it is also soluble with a red colour. The same acids do not make it soluble in ether or chloroform. A red solution in alcohol and tartaric acid will, after neutralization with ammonia or any other alkali, become blue; acids restore the red colour. If a slight excess of ammonia be added to the acid alcoholic solution, the colouring matter becomes *green*. If an acid be now quickly added, the red colour is restored, but not with the same intensity as before; and if the ammonia is allowed to act upon it for a few moments, or an excess has been used, the subsequent addition of an acid does not any longer restore the red colour, but produces only a brown tint; the colouring matter has been decomposed. This decomposition also ensues when large volumes of its acetic acid and alcohol solution are heated for a long time; it is necessary to effect the evaporation on small volumes in shallow vessels at the lowest possible temperature. Almost the same reaction is observed upon all red vegetable juices, particularly of fruit. Fixed caustic alkalies effect the destruction as certainly as and quicker than ammonia. Strong acids do not much affect the pigment, but hot nitric acid destroys it. Chlorine destroys it, and leaves a brown liquid; excess of chlorine makes the solution yellow. Light has a double effect upon the pigment, it bleaches it in part and makes another part insoluble.

The colour of wine depends upon two factors, the amount of blue colouring matter present, and the quantity of free acid which acts upon it. The more free acid is present, the more red will the wine appear; and with the decrease of the acidity, the colour will approach towards the violet.

The colouring matters of Burgundy, Bordeaux and Oporto wine behave essentially in the same manner when subjected to the above proceeding, although port wine generally contains some of the soluble pigments of the *teinturier* grapes. This requires a little modification of the process of analysis. The crust which port wine forms in bottles contains oxydized tannin in an insoluble state, and colouring matter probably also in a changed state. The changed tannin combines with the colouring matter like the lead oxide. The colouring matter when once precipitated seems to be rather stable, for it can be prepared with all its characteristic properties from crude red tartar.

There are added to wines in many parts of the wine countries other natural dyes; some red wine is made of white wine coloured with vegetable pigment not being the product of any vine at all. Black cherries are a favourite dye. Next come elderberries, the production of which for this purpose is very considerable. Bilberries are used in some parts; logwood is said to be used in others, but we have not been able to obtain any proof of this. Some British wines made on a certain scale are coloured with cochineal, which is also used largely in confectionery and culinary proceedings. All these pigments are in themselves quite wholesome. The great bulk of red wines contains so much natural pigment that no addition is needed.

§ 58. Ammonia.

The grape juice, like all vegetable juices, contains small quantities of ammonia; a little more is formed during fermentation from nitrogenized matters not defined. The greater part of this ammonia is precipitated during the progress of fermentation as ammonio-magnesic phosphate. An extremely small quantity however remains in solution in the wine, and can be isolated and estimated by the usual chemical proceedings. In some wines, and particularly in the syrupy liqueur wines, such as Tokay and Tintilla de Rota (Rota Tent) the ammonia is accompanied with traces of trimethylamine.

§ 59. Albuminous Matters.

Grapes contain albuminous substances, of which some curdle like the fibrine of the blood of animals after the juice is expressed; others are made insoluble during fermentation. When exposed to the air on the top of fermenting vats they are liable to be oxydized as well as decomposed; and it is necessary to guard against the contamination of wine by such products. Properly fermented white wines contain very little of this albuminous substance, and are but little liable to further change. In imperfectly fermented wines, on the other hand, particularly wines made from underripe grapes, some of this albuminous substance remains dissolved, and renders them liable to further change. All red wines contain, when young, much albuminous substance, which is preserved from change by the tannin present. In the course of time the greater part of it is thrown down with the colouring matter and tannin.

When testing wines, particularly sherries, Marsalas, Canaries, Madeiras, and red wines of the Gironde and Burgundy for albumen, it must be remembered that these are habitually clarified, or as it is technically termed, fined, by the addition of considerable quantities of white of egg. In some sherries we have found enormous quantities of albumen, which could be removed by ferrocyanide of potassium; the precipitate is bluish-black, from admixture of some iron salt, but leaves the wine perfectly clear and potable. Indeed sherries which refuse to be clarified by white of egg alone, can be perfectly clarified by the combination of albumen and ferrocyanide.

The amount of albuminous matter found in wines varies between four parts per thousand of wine, or a quantity equalling that of the free acid, and five in ten thousand; the latter quantity we found in port wine, made by ourselves in the Alto Douro, which had never been fined with albumen but had been clarified by filtration. Some natural wines deposit albumen when they are heated according to the process of Pasteur; but all the albumen is not deposited; in the case of an excellent young Palatinate wine we found that the heating diminished the albumen from 0·3550 per cent. to 0·2448 per cent. In the forms of apparatus working with tubes for Pasteurizing wine special arrangements are necessary to clear the tubes from time to time of the albumen and other matter deposited on their inner surface during the heating.

§ 60. TANNIN.

The astringent principles, which give precipitates with solutions of gelatine and of albumen, and produce a deep bluish-black precipitate or coloration with persalts of iron (so called ink), are termed tannins from their use in the production of leather. There are many varieties of these substances, occurring in different plants, from which they derive their surnames. They are all glucosides, that is, bodies which under chemical decomposition break up into at least two substances, of which one is a sugar.

The juice of most grapes is perfectly free from tannin; the skins and stalks, however, contain a considerable quantity of a substance, which though it be not ordinary tannin of the oak or its galls, yet closely resembles it in properties. While ordinary tannin breaks up by means of the influence of acids, or of a special kind of fermentation into glucose and gallic acid, the tannin of grapes, under the like circumstances, breaks up into glucose and an acid which is not gallic acid.

White wines, in the preparation of which the must is at once separated from the murk, contain little tannin; while red wines, being allowed to ferment with the murk, are rich in tannin, which imparts to them the well-known astringent taste. The tannin of white wines, as of brandies, is sometimes derived from the oaken casks in which the wine or spirit is kept; their colour, at first very pale yellow, increases in depth in the course of years. The tannin contained in them absorbs oxygen and is converted into a yellow, or brown humus-like substance, which, though much less soluble in wine than the tannin, is yet sufficiently so to impart a strong colour to it. Red wines, on the other hand, gradually lose their dark colour by the agency of the tannin they contain. In these wines so much tannin is present that more of the humus-like substance is gradually formed than can remain dissolved; it is then thrown down as a precipitate, and carries the colouring matter with it.

The presence of tannin in white wines may be detected by the inky coloration produced on the addition of a ferric salt and acetate of potash, and by the precipitate produced by the addition of gelatine.

Tannin is supposed to render wines more durable by its preservative action upon the albuminous substances. The addition of tannin to wines liable to turn has also, on this account, frequently been proposed, and seems to act beneficially. Thus to white Champagne wines it has been systematically added to prevent viscosity. It would be advisable to use for this addition a tannin extracted from the skins, stalks, or kernels of the grapes, or even the green parts of the vine, instead of the ordinary tannin extracted from galls or other sources.

§ 61. EXTRACTIVES.

By the side of the matters which we have described there are contained in wine certain matters the chemical characters of which are at present unknown. As they remain in the treacly state of vegetable extracts as they appear in pharmacy, they have been termed extractives. They are never absent from, but, on the contrary, generally constitute the greater part of the total solids in all genuine wines which contain little or no sugar.

Many factitious wines contain only small proportions of these extractives, or none at all, and it is therefore frequently possible to distinguish such wines, or diluted wines, by a quantation of the extractives. Inversely, in genuine wines, the extractive matter frequently stands in a direct relation to the value of the wine, the higher class wines containing generally more extractive than the lower class ones.

§ 62. MINERAL CONSTITUENTS.

The residue which remains after the liquids of the wine have been evaporated, when subjected to combustion, leaves the mineral constituents in the form of ash. This consists chiefly of potassium in the form of carbonate, chloride, sulphate and phosphate, sodium as chloride, calcium as phosphate and carbonate, with traces of magnesia, iron, silica, and sometimes alumina and manganese. The carbonates of potassium and calcium are not as such contained in the wine, but are produced by the combustion of the tartrate or malate of potassium or calcium. From the ash of pure natural wines carbonates and chlorides are scarcely ever absent; sometimes, however, if the wine has been subjected to much sulphuring, either as must to prevent false fermentation, or as wine, it may contain an excess of sulphuric acid, which, during the evaporation and incineration, drives out all the volatile acids; the ash, in such a case, consists exclusively of sulphates and phosphates. The ash of wines made from must, to which, as to sherries, plaster of Paris has been added, scarcely ever contains carbonates, and is very frequently free from chlorides, on account of its containing an excess of sulphuric acid formed by double decomposition from the calcium sulphate and potassium bitartrate.

The amount and nature of the ash left by a wine is a very

valuable means of judging of its genuineness. The analysis
to be used for that purpose has been described at length in
the "Treatise" at pp. 267-272. Some mineral constituents,
such as chlorine, are expelled during combustion, and these
must be sought for in the wine itself, and the disarrangement
in the proportion of other acids must be rectified by
similar experiments made on the wine without combustion
of its residue. Sulphuric acid in particular must always be
precipitated from the wine itself, as, in case it were free, it
would be expelled or expel other acids from the mixture of
salts in the ash.

Iron is generally present in wines in minute quantity,
larger in red wines. It is maintained that the blue colouring
matter of grapes contains iron in organic combination, like
the colouring matter of the blood, but of this there is no
acceptable scientific proof at present to be found in œnological records. It is said that alum is sometimes added to
flat red wine to heighten its colour and improve its taste; but
this is probably a very rare adulteration, as we have never
met with a single instance of it, or encountered a judicially
proved case of that kind.

The amount of mineral matter contained in different
wines varies considerably; in pure natural wines it amounts
generally to from 0·15 to 0·30 per cent.; in wines which
have been plastered the ash rises to 0·5 per cent. and upwards;
and in all wines in which any excessive acidity has been neutralized by an alkali or an earth, the ash may rise considerably
above that amount.

§ 63. TOTAL SOLID CONSTITUENTS OF WINE.

We have experimentally ascertained that the complicated
mixture of substances constituting the solid residue left after
the evaporation of wine, cannot be completely dried even at
the temperature of boiling water, 100° C., without suffering
decomposition. This is proved by the great diminution of
the free fixed acid, and the insolubility of a portion of the
dried matter, which previously was quite soluble; by long
drying the residue becomes dark brown, semi-charred, de-

composed; much matter is volatilized, and the residue may weigh less than the mere dextrose, which, as shown by tests on the wine itself was originally contained in it. The total solids can therefore not be estimated by drying and weighing the residue.

Balling has endeavoured to estimate the quantity of solids in wine by means of the specific gravity of their solution. Extract of malt has been taken as the standard of comparison. But as the mineral constituents of wine differ from sugar as regards specific gravity of their solutions in this, that for a given specific gravity the amount of mineral matter is about double that required for a sugar solution of the same gravity, it is necessary to subtract from the percentage of extract thus estimated the percentage of ash found in the same wine; or if the amount of extract without the ash be required, the percentage of ash multiplied by two has to be subtracted from the percentage found according to the specific gravity. In wines containing but little ash this correction is not very important; but as in some wines the ash amounts to 0·5 per cent. and upwards a serious error would be committed without it.

In our experiments a Marsala contained 5·780 per cent. total solids; a Spanish red wine called port 6·909 per cent ; a Greek Lachrymæ Christi 32·022 per cent.

CHAPTER XII.

WINES OF THE GIRONDE.

§ 64. DIVISIONS OF THE GIRONDE.

THE wines of the department of the Gironde, in which definition are comprised seven viticultural provinces situated to the south and north of the Gironde and Garonne, namely, Médoc, Graves, Sauternes, Entre deux Mers, Libournais, Fronsadais, and Blayais, are celebrated for their variety, their remarkable perfection or roundness, the low prices of their common qualities, the high prices of their first qualities, and the remarkable trade to all parts of the world to which they give rise. The department possesses about 140,000 hectares of vineyards, which produce an annual average of 250,000 tonneaux, or 2,280,000 hectolitres of wine. The estimated average value of two-sixths of the annual produce is 50 francs the barrique; two-sixths 125 francs; one-sixth is 250 francs, and the last sixth 500 francs the barrique, immediately after the spring racking. This gives a gross production of 280 millions of francs, and if we deduct from that sum an average expenditure of 500 francs per hectare, we find that the Gironde raises an annual clear value of 180 millions of francs in the shape of wine alone.

The Médoc.—The Médoc geographically so-called, is the tongue of land which, bordered on the Atlantic side by the Gulf of Gascony, forms on the north-east the left border of the Garonne after its union with the Dordogne (the two combined rivers forming the estuary called the Gironde), and extends on this border from Blanquefort, a little town about fifteen kilometres west of Bordeaux, to the sea. But the Médoc of the œnophilist begins only west of Ludon, in the commune of Macau. It produces the wines of Labarde and Cantenac; in its very heart those of Margaux. Further on are the growths of Saint Julien and Pauillac. Still further west it produces the St. Estèphe, and at its western limits the wines of Saint Saurin-de-Cadourne. The districts just mentioned form the Haut-Médoc, which is about forty-five kilometres in length, and from eight to twenty kilometres in width. In its main features it is a plain, falling somewhat towards the Gironde. Its soil is gravel, or rolled quartz, or flint, covering a subsoil which is sometimes clayey, but most frequently formed of sand, or of sand which by an infiltration of hydrated iron oxide has been concreted partly into a soft, friable pudding-stone, partly into a very hard rock-like material, both being known under the name of the *alios.* This variation of the soil causes a great diversity in its products, so that very good and inferior wines grow often side by side.

H

§ 65. VINES CULTIVATED IN THE MÉDOC.

The vines cultivated in the Médoc, although not very numerous, are designated by various names, so that their identification is a matter of difficulty. The most common vine is the *Carbenet Sauvignon*, (as spelt by Guyot, *Cabernet*, Rendu, and known as *Petite Vidure* in the neighbourhood of Bordeaux). *Sauvignon* is a mere surname derived from a similarity to another vine bearing that name exclusively. It has small, rugged, light green leaves, the lower side of which is woolly ; the bunch of grapes is less than middle-sized, pyramidal, longish, generally bearing two somewhat detached wings. The berries are small, of even size, bluish-black, very bloomy, with a thin husk. They are very juicy, and have not the sweet astringent taste of the Burgundy grape, but a more acidulous, refreshing, and most agreeable taste, giving the impression, says Bronner, as if one had the ready-made wine in one's mouth. It is the best and most fertile of all the fine black grapes of the Gironde, ripens the earliest and spoils the last. It is the most esteemed in the great growths of Pauillac, Saint Julien, and Margaux; it makes up five-eighths of the plantations of Lafitte, Mouton, Latour, Léoville, Margaux, Rozan, and others. It is regular, but never abundant in production, and carries all grapes to an equal degree of maturity at the same time, without showing on the same stalk black, red, and green grapes. It yields wine of a fine colour, full of delicacy and possessing great bouquet. The wine during the first years is a little harsh, and in order to acquire its perfection must be kept up to four years in wood, and two years in bottle. It increases a little in bouquet up to the fifteenth year, if bottled at the right time. After the twentieth year of its age it loses its soft fulness and becomes drier. The Carbenet Sauvignon stands to the great wines of the Médoc in the same relation as the Pineau or Noirien to the great wines of the Côte d'Or, as the Riessling to the great wines of the Rheingau ; they would not exist without it.

A variety of the former, and only second to it in importance in the Gironde, is the *Franc Carbenet*, also termed *Carbenet gris ;* its leaves are of a darker green colour, its berries are smaller and less deeply coloured than those of the previously described variety. It prospers in lighter soil (*graves douces*); its wine is excellent.

The *Merlot*, or *gros doux*, is stated by Paguierre to bear its name from *merle*, a thrush, because this bird was particularly fond of the grapes of that vine. As these plagues of the vineyard eat all kinds of grapes, and destroy much, their alleged preference for the Merlot is probably due to the fact that this vine ripens its grapes a little earlier than do the Carbenets, and when once ripe become easily rotten ; they are a little flabby when the vine stands on dry soil, for the vine cannot bear drought, and grows best on moist inclines, or so-called *graves fraiches en côteaux*. Its wine is lighter and earlier ready than that of the Carbenet, and has much less juiciness (*sève*) than the latter; it also lacks body and durability, but it is soft and tender.

The *Malbec* bears many other names in the Gironde, amongst them *Noir de Pressac, Gourdoux, Ertrangey, Côt rouge, Pied de Perdrix*. In central Germany it passes as *blaue Jacobstraube* (blue James or Jacobin). It is an abundant producer and thrives in consistent or in gravelly soil; its grape is very precocious, very sweet and tasty, much inclined to rottenness when once ripe, and gives a light wine without qualities, particularly when grown on fat land. In the Médoc it is allowed only on low grounds, where its precocity is neutralized by the situation, and its grape is admitted only as material for second-rate wines. Count Odart ascribes to the wine made from this grape alone, purity, a dark colour, and much body. This property, says the great œnologist, enables the wine merchant to mix this wine with white wine, and thus to impart to it the spirit which it wants. In this manner most of the white wines of the north side of the Gironde are transformed into red and exported. The variety of Malbec with red grapes and stalklets is the *Pied de Perdrix*, from the colour of the feet of the red-legged partridge of the south ; another variety has green berries and stalklets. In its general character the Malbec is closely related to the Pineau of Burgundy, and in systematic classification is always placed by its side.

The *Verdot* vine occurs in the Médoc only as an auxiliary, but in the "Palus" or marshes, it is the vine of the first importance. The wines of Queyrier and Montferrand owe their reputation to this vine. Its grapes are small, soft, uneven, round, reddish-black, strongly bloomed, with a thin skin and an acidulous taste, ripening late, latest of any in the Gironde. The vine prospers the better the moister is the subsoil on which it grows; and of such position it requires the best, just on account of its ripening its grapes so late. Its wine has much juiciness, fulness and vinosity, and combines well with that of the Carbenet; it gives durability to wines with which it is mixed. The Verdot is therefore found amongst the best growths of the Médoc, in Pauillac, St. Julien, and Margaux.

The *Cruchinet*, sometimes also specified as *Cruchinet rouge*, as if it had to be distinguished from a white variety, has a large bunch with closely packed, and hence somewhat elongated grapes. Its five-lobed leaf is but slightly woolly. It gives a remarkably agreeable bouquet to wine, and for this reason has for some years been somewhat multiplied at Château Lafitte.

The *Carmenère* is cultivated amongst other vines at Margaux and Cantenac; it thrives in light, sandy soil, and is not injured by drought. It sprouts early in spring, and thus makes sure of a long vegetative period; it yields a sweet and tasty grape with black skin. Its wine has more body and colour than that of the Carbenet Sauvignon. The Carmenère develops its full bearing powers only seven or eight years after plantation, and is never very fertile, yielding about half the crop which the Carbenet vines yield on the same area. It is therefore cultivated solely for its peculiar qualities in particular situations, and not rarely mixed with the Cruchinet. The mixed wine of these two plants is of excellent quality.

Besides these principal or dominant vines of the Médoc others are cultivated in mediocre situations solely for their producing quantities of wine. Among these are the *Brasac*, with a small grape; the *Mareye*, with very large grape; and the *Enrachet*, with sour grapes and red woolly leaves. All these offer certain advantages in certain localities.

§ 66. MODES OF CULTIVATING THE VINE IN THE MÉDOC.

The more valuable the situation the more care is bestowed upon the preparation of the land by levelling and draining by tile-tubes ; in the marshy land, or "Palus," ditches are cut round the vineyards, and at certain seasons kept full of water by sluices, which at others are opened to let the water flow out at low tide. In parts where the *alios* is not far from the surface it is broken up, however hard it may be, but if it lies deeper than one metre it is left untouched.

The canes are planted in holes made with an iron rod, surrounded with a little loose sand, or placed into holes made with a bidented hoe. In the second year any canes which have failed to grow are replaced by rooted canes or *barbeaux.*

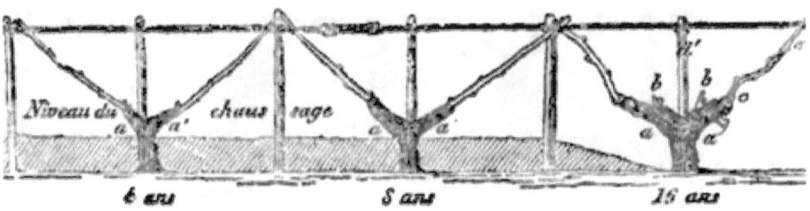

Fig. 17.—Training of vines in the Haut Médoc. Vines four, eight, and sixteen years old. *a a'*, branches rising from foot ; *b b'*, wood spurs ; *c c'*, bearing or fruit-branches.

Two eyes are left above ground, and the young plant is protected by a stake. The vines of the same line stand at a distance of a little more than one metre apart ; the lines are one metre from each other. The hectare generally carries 9,000 vines. Weeding of the land is most assiduously attended to. In the third year the vine-dresser commences to form the two arms which constitute the peculiarity of the Médoc cultivation. In addition to the "tutor" close to its stem (*carasson*), a second stake is placed equidistant from each two vines, and their tops are united horizontally by a single line of lath (*latte*). To these the vines are fixed in the manner illustrated by the figures. The whole of the vines of the Haut-Médoc are thus cultivated. As the vines begin to bear they are manured with rotten stable-dung, so-called *consommé*, a cubic metre to every fifty vines. The pruning of the vines takes place between November and January, and is called *taille à l'aste*. This word *aste* in the Médoc has the specific meaning of "fruit-branch," and reminds us of the German *Ast*, a branch in general. There are several words referring to the cultivation of the vine, derived from German roots, used in the Gironde, which do not occur in any other part of France. Possibly the transplantation of vines from the Moselle to the Bordelais, related by Ausonius, was the occasion of the transfer of these terms. The *aste*, strictly so-called, is the strongest cane of the one year's wood, grown from the stationary arm, cut to a length of from six to eight eyes; it is always kept fixed to the lath, in such a manner that the bunches of grapes which it bears hang downwards

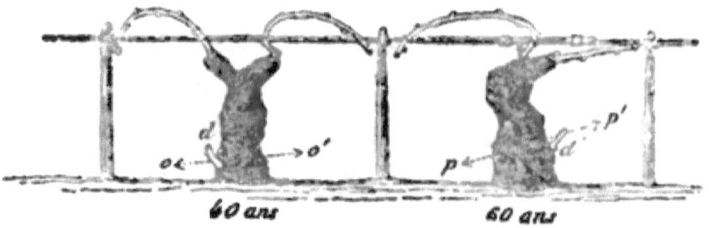

Fig. 18.—Vines forty and sixty years old, trained for season. *d d'*, low wood spurs ("cots"); *o o'*, and *p p'*, line where stem may be cut off, in case of the top perishing.

towards the earth. By the side of the aste is left a cane-stump of two eyes, intended to produce the canes from which the next year's aste is selected. Each arm, therefore, carries one aste, and one two-eyed stump, that is to say a viticultural element as defined in the general part of this treatise. As each fruit-bearing branch may carry from six to eight bunches, and each stump three to four, each vine may bear from eighteen to twenty-four bunches of grapes.

Attempts to cultivate the Médoc vines in different modalities have mostly failed. Some vines, however, are treated a little differently from the above. The *Carbenet gris*, or *Franc Carbenet*, must have at least eight eyes to the aste; if it is cut shorter it runs into wood and sheds its blossoms. The Carbenet Sauvignon, on the other hand, should not have more than six or seven eyes to the aste. The Malbec and Merlot are also cut upon *aste, tiret*, and *côt* (an auxiliary stump, to be called into action in case the principal one fail) but there are one or two tirets left in addition which produce a few grapes more. The Verdot is cut shorter than the other vines. The soil is either ploughed or turned with the hoe ; the earth is removed from the vine, to allow the water to collect in the furrows during the winter period ; during the vegetative period the earth is again heaped up around the vines, and the draining furrows are established between the lines. Most vineyards are now ploughed with the improved instruments of Portal of Moux, and of Goëthals and Scawinsky of Giscours ; each plough is drawn by one horse or ox. The first ploughing takes place in March and is called opening the vine (*ouvrir la vigne*), and removes the earth from the plants, which are now cleared of visible high roots, day-roots ; the second ploughing is performed in April, with the apparatus attached to the plough called *la courbe ;* this pushes the earth back to the vine, and transforms the intervals between the rows into furrows, through which the rain-water can flow towards the terminal ditches. In May the vines are again unearthed as at the first ploughing, and at a fourth and last ploughing, in July or beginning of August, they are again covered at their base.

The vine in the Médoc blossoms during the period from the 10th to the 15th of June. Immediately after it has passed that critical period, the superfluous shoots are cut off with a knife (in other parts they are broken off). The shortening of the principal green canes, *rognage*, is only effected towards the approach of the vintage.

During the hundred days which generally elapse between the blossoming of the vine and the maturity of the grape, the plants have to be cleared of any vermin which may settle upon them, such as several kinds of endemic caterpillars, *altise*, and *attelabe*, called *crabe* by the country people ; slugs, and snails of the *helix* tribe, *H. hortensis, nemoralis* and *arbustorum ;* most commonly, and in some years forming a veritable plague, the *helix aspersa*, or *escargeot*, which may ruin entire vineyards. The vine-beetle (*Curculio Bacchus*, should be *anti-Bacchus*) which pierces green canes and causes them to pine or die, also causes much damage in some years.

The cultivated vine lives long, in some places up to seventy years, while in others its vitality is quickly exhausted, so that Margaux and Cantenac have to re-plant every twenty or thirty years.

§ 67. VINTAGE IN THE MÉDOC.

In exceptionally good years the vintage commences in August; in ordinary years between September 20th, and October 1st. Years in which the vintage can only take place in the first fortnight of October are said to be bad. All the other vintages of red wine in the Gironde are a fortnight later than those of the Médoc; the vintage in the white wine district of Sauternes is a full month later. There is no vintage-ban in the Gironde, and every proprietor harvests whenever he chooses.

The vintage is performed by labourers who congregate for the occasion from the south of France; most of them are given food and shelter, and the women and children receive from fivepence a day to eightpence, men tenpence; the labourers in the press-house, who must possess some little skill, receive a gratuity in addition to the wages and keep. The vintagers are organized in gangs, consisting of women and children who cut the grapes; of a superintendent (*rangeur*); a basket-emptier (*vide-panier*), who puts the grapes from the cutter's basket into a large pail, called *baste;* when a baste is full, a porter (there are two porters to every eight ranges of vines) carries it to the waggon, when the two attendants, one the driver of the horses or oxen, and the other the attendant of the vat fixed upon the waggon, empty the contents of the baste into the vat (*douil* or *douillat*) and stamp them down. A commandant directs the whole of the operation from the cutting and cleaning, including the removal of green, rotten, or otherwise spoiled grapes, to the moment when the vat, being full, is drawn to the *cuvier*, or place where the grapes are converted into wine.

This building mostly contains the presses (*pressoirs* or

fouloirs) on the one side, and the vats or *cuves* on the other; in the term presses are included platforms on which the grapes are trodden, and apparatus for removing berries from stalks. The true presses, with screws for the application of power to murk, are now mostly made of wood, but there were up to a late date also some presses of stone, *e.g.*, at Lafitte, Calon Ségur, and Château Margaux.

The square press has the advantage that any quantity of grapes, large or small, may be pressed at any time. If the vintager desires to add fresh pulp to the murk already in the press, he need only add a tier of boards all round, and thus raising the height of the receptacle of the press, increase its capacity. On the other hand, as the pulp is being pressed dry, the upper boards may be removed, and thus give free scope to the levers by which the screw-nut is turned. Some of these presses measure three metres a side; those of smaller dimensions have only one metre a side. They may be fixed, or movable on wheels, so as to be easily transportable to each fermentation vat. In one of the largest cuviers of the Gironde we saw two presses which were moved backwards and forwards on railways running in front of the two rows of fermentation vats. Red wine murk is pressed only after fermentation, and requires less power than the murk of white grapes, or of red Champagne grapes which are pressed before fermentation.

When the berries are pulled from the stalks by any of the many contrivances invented for that purpose, they are placed on a platform and trodden by men. This process is frequently described in books in a spirit of poetical exaltation; the sound of music produced by clarionet and violin, to which the vintagers keep time in forms resembling a *contredanse*, is heard here and there, but this has merely the object and effect of mitigating with the vintagers the sense of fatigue and tedium which is produced by the long-continued daily work; for the vintage must be hurried to bring all the vats into fermentation within as short a compass of time as possible, in order to be able to close the cuvier, and preserve the temperature most favourable to a quick and perfect fermentation.

This method of crushing the berries is falling into desuetude, and at the present time more than half the proprietors in the Médoc do not crush their grapes at all. The wine produced is of the same quality whether the grapes are crushed or not. The stalks are not cast aside, but put into the fermentation vat either partly or wholly. Many rake them out of the murk, and place them as a thick layer on the top of the murk, where they increase the bulk of the top solids or so-called *chapeau* (hat) ; this is not rarely weighted with stones, to keep the rising husks submerged.

The fermentation vats, being thoroughly cleaned and sponged with brandy, are filled with the mixture of juice, stalks, skins, and kernels ; each vat is, if possible, filled in one day, and then left at absolute rest until the wine be formed. The time required for the vinification varies somewhat according to the quality of the vintage and the temperature of the season ; in good years it is not more than four or five days. If the vatting is continued longer the wine becomes fuller, but loses a little in taste, softness, and delicacy ; these latter qualities are preferred to body in the good parts of the Médoc, where also deep colour is rather avoided. When the must has lost its sweetness, and assumed a vinous flavour, it is drawn off by means of an instrument called a *griffon* into a large wooden vessel, and is thence transferred by means of cans into the barriques or hogsheads, so that each barrique receives an equal number of cans of each running from the vat, and at the end of the operation all the barriques of the storehouse (*chais*) contain wine of the same quality. This wine, which runs spontaneously, *i.e.*, without pressure, from the vats, and runs clear, is termed *the first wine*. In this operation a so-called *second wine* is not produced by itself, although, curiously enough, there is a *third wine* made from the contents of the same vat which yields the first, thus :—When all the clear first wine has run off, and the run becomes thick, this *fond the cuve*, or bottoms, which flows yet spontaneously, is put aside ; it is put with the whole of the wine made from grapes which are grown in inferior situations of the estate, and this mixture constitutes the second wine. When all liquid which will spontaneously flow has left the murk, this is put into the press ; a very dark " thick " wine is obtained, which by cautious operators is never mixed with the first wine. It is more commonly used for blending with white wine, whereby it loses much of its hardness and alcoholicity ; for the pulp retains much alcohol by a peculiar affinity, and the wine pressed from it is from 3 to 5 per cent. stronger in alcohol than the first wine.

The filling of the hogshead with wine must be completed in three days at the utmost, in order to preserve to the wine all its qualities. The barriques are then closed. During the first month they are ullaged, that is to say, the amount of wine which they have lost by evaporation is supplied every four or five days ; during the second month every eight days ; and subsequently every fortnight : this is always effected with wine of the same quality. In January the wine is drawn from the lees, or racked, a first time ; a second time in June ; and a third time in September. In subsequent years it is racked but twice. It remains in the barriques for four years before it is put into bottles, and may be drunk when six years old. But in these respects each vintage has its peculiarities. Some, like that of 1825, produce wines which require twenty years to allow the wine to reach its full perfection ; that of 1828 required seven or eight years ; the wines of 1831 were late, those of 1839 and 1847 precocious. The wines of 1846 were hardly ready ten years later.

§ 68. VARIOUS QUALITIES OF THE WINES OF THE MÉDOC.

There is no viticultural district in which so many distinctions are made between different wines as in the Médoc. The vineyards occupy an area of 20,000 hectares, of which each produces 2 tonneaux, or 18 hectolitres and 24 litres of wine ; on an average, the whole Médoc consequently produces about 40,000 tonneaux. Of these 4,500 are wines of high quality, and termed *classified* because they are again sub-divided into five *classes*, or great divisions, or *growths* (*crus*), as they are technically termed. Another 4,500 tonneaux are simply fine wines, and are not, in the trade, classified. Actually, therefore, only about 9,000 tonneaux (or

82,000 hectolitres) out of the 40,000 tonneaux are choice wines, the other 31,000 tonneaux, although sold under the name of Médoc, and frequently more choice names, are of ordinary quality. The 9,000 tonneaux of fine wines of the Médoc, yielding about ten millions of ordinary wine-bottles full of wine (six bottles making a gallon), may be arranged in three categories. (1) The *classified wines* coming from certain vineyards in the arrondissement of Bordeaux and Lesparre. (2) The "citizen" or *bourgeois* wines, which are again sub-divided into higher, good, and ordinary citizens, or *bourgeois supérieur, bon bourgeois* and *bourgeois ordinaire.* (3) The "peasants" or *paysans,* or wines of the small proprietors. Whatever the category to which they may belong, all wines of the Médoc are distinguished and recognized by certain general characters, which exclude all confusion with other wines. They have a certain slight, peculiar roughness, are fine, juicy, marrowy in the mouth, and after having been in bottle for some years they have a very beautiful bouquet. They possess the hygienic quality, that they can be drunk in larger quantities than other wines, without, as the French say, "fatiguing" either head or stomach. The Médoc wines also endure transportation better than other French wines, and by long sea voyages are greatly improved.

§ 69. CLASSIFIED GROWTHS.

The commercial specialists of Bordeaux recognize as classified the wines from about 200 estates, or small districts. They may be conveniently sub-divided, after M. Frank, the author of a monograph concerning them, into five great divisions or growths.

First growths.—This division includes only three vineyards, called the three first growths (*les trois premiers crus*) out of the whole classified sixty of the Médoc. They are the following, their names being derived from the dominating country-house of the district.

Château Margaux produces annually from 100 to 110 tonneaux of wine. As at Johannisberg and Steinberg, a great farm is attached to the wine-producing establishments, on which a very great number of cattle yield the manure by means of which the vines later on luxuriate. The *cuvier* or fermenting shed contains eighteen vats, all in one line; opposite to these are six *pressoirs*, all built in stone, upon which the grapes are separated from the stalks and trodden into pulp. The *chais* or cellar, is an enormous hall of great height, its ceiling supported by eighteen columns. The vinification has been unchanged from time immemorial. The vats are filled up to within a foot of the upper margin, and the contents allowed to ferment without covering or limitation of

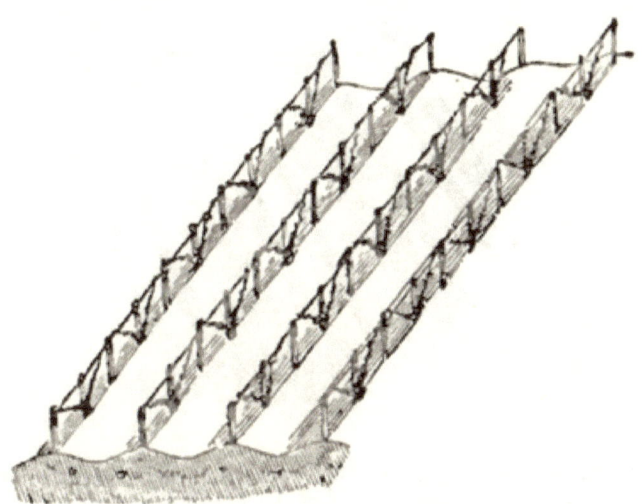

Fig. 19.—Normal Cultivation of the Haut Médoc.

air. The *chapeau* rises, sometimes to the extent of an entire foot, above the margin of the vat, its upper half is always taken off; and no part of it is left that has not a purely vinous smell, without admixture of acetic or putrid odours. No selection of grapes is made, and the whole of the vintage of all the vineyards of the estate furnishes but one quality of wine. Notwithstanding, the wine is nearly always the best of the whole Médoc. In good or great years it is absolutely the best, but in middling years Lafitte and Latour are superior to it. As compared to St. Julien and Pauillac, the wine of Château Margaux has more *finesse* and juiciness, but less

body.   The vineyards of the Château are about 80 hectares
in extent.   Their soil is a grey-coloured, heavy material
(*grave*), with a substratum of clayey pudding-stone, often
containing sand and veins of iron oxide.   The principal slopes
are towards east and west, but the best part of the vineyards, the Sampeyre, slopes towards the north and the south,
and nevertheless yields the best wine.   One half of the entire
surface is planted with the Carbenet Sauvignon.

Château Lafitte has 67 hectares of vine plantation ; its soil
is very variable, being a strong *grave* or clay-gravel, with all

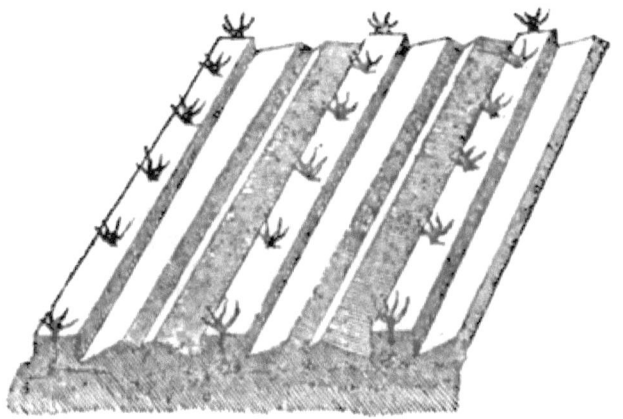

Fig. 20.—Lines of vines, the earth in course of being dressed with the
plough.   Department of the Haute Garonne.

directions of slopes, amongst which those toward the north
predominate.   The subsoil is very uniformly made of quartzy
rolled stones mixed with sand and clay.   Five-eighths of
the vineyards are planted with the Carbenet Sauvignon, the
other parts mostly with the Carbenet gris and the Merlot.
The wine of Château Lafitte has all the qualities of Château
Margaux except alone its *finesse* ; it has, however, more body
and a distinguished taste.

Château Latour is surrounded by 42 hectares of vineyards.
The vines are planted in heavy clay-gravel, with a compact
subsoil of much rolled stone.   The surface is more regular
than that of Lafitte, and inclined uniformly one-half towards

the north, and the other towards the south. Two-thirds of the vines are Carbenet Sauvignon; there are also Carbenet gris, and Malbec prevails in the low situations. The wine of this Château has the most body amongst the three great growths of the Médoc, but less *finesse* and bouquet.

Second, third, and fourth growths.—These comprise about 130 separate properties, half of them, and amongst them compact large areas belonging to the fourth growth. We

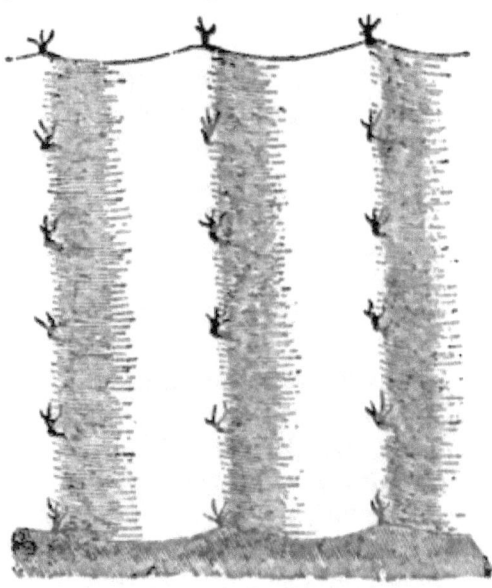

Fig. 21.—Vines in lines on ridges, the earth being thrown up around the stems (*chaussées*). Department of the Haute Garonne.

abstain from giving a detailed list of them, it may be found in Thudichum and Dupré's "Treatise," etc., pp. 329, 330. The yield of the whole of these growths may be estimated to be about five millions of bottles. The excess of 220,000 bottles, which might be calculated from the sum of the numbers of tonneaux raised, would be quite absorbed by filling up, racking, and loss in bottling operations and transmission. When these five millions of bottles are distributed amongst the wealthy consumers of the whole world, it becomes apparent how small a quantity each can obtain, particularly if he insists upon having the product of good years only, and how enormous must be the substitutions which the traders of Bordeaux and other places make of unclassed, and, indeed, of any kind of wine, whether from Bordeaux or other parts of France, for Médoc.

From a careful consideration of many data at our disposal concerning the money value of these wines we have derived the following scale of prices for average growths of classified wines of the Médoc:

1st class	2,000 to 5,000 francs per tonneau.
2nd do.	1,200 to 1,400 do.	do.
3rd do.	800 to 900 do.	do.
4th do.	700 to 900 do.	do.
5th do.	600 to 700 do.	do.
Bourgois supérieur .	400 to 500 do.	do.
do. ordinaire .	350 to 400 do.	do.
Paysans	300 to 325 do.	do.

The prices of the latter wines are curiously alike in all villages of the Médoc. As the travelling brokers cross the country, a uniformity of price is established, at least so far as the price demanded is concerned, which astonishes those who do not know the machinery by which it is brought about. These brokers effect most of the sales; they know the districts and all their varieties and accidents; they visit the cellars, taste the wines, and arrange them in order of value. They sometimes raise or reduce the rank of a certain growth according to the care which has been bestowed upon the cultivation of the vine, and upon vinification. The merchants of Bordeaux mostly rely upon the judgment of these brokers, but the growers are often dissatisfied with it.

§ 70. CONSUMPTION OF MÉDOC WINES.

Of the first growths only a very small proportion is consumed in France, the bulk goes to foreign parts. England is the principal consumer of the best qualities of Médoc; lower classes go to Holland, Russia, and particularly the north of Germany. There is a tradition that fine wines destined for exportation to England were mixed with red Hermitage, in order to please better the palates accustomed to ports and other strong alcoholic drinks. Such wines obtained thereby a warmth and spirituosity which is by no means natural to them, and lost much of their juicy softness and *finesse*. Persons of taste would recognize such wines at once and put them in their proper places. We are, however, assured that at the present time most fine wines are not any

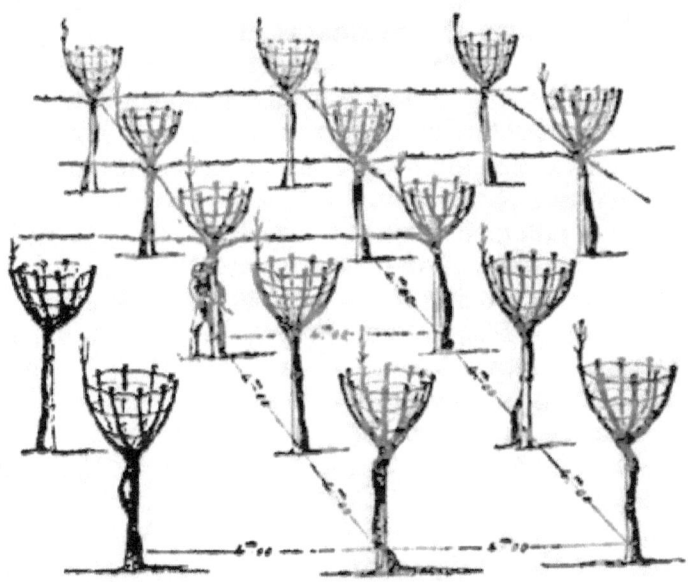

Fig. 22.—Vines trained upon trees, "goblet-shape," as seen at St. Gaudens near Toulouse. Department of the Haute Garonne.

longer mixed with Hermitage. Common sorts of Médoc wines going to England are sometimes—and were formerly more frequently than at present—prepared, especially before exportation, by being mixed with wine from the east or centre of France, or with brandy. The amount of mixing carried on at Bordeaux is enormous; for its exports are twelve times as great as the production of the entire Médoc, and one-half of these exports sells as Bordeaux wine, so that it is quite fair to assume that the Gironde wine is multiplied

several·times by the addition or substitution of other wines
of France, the Gard furnishing alcohol and colour, the
flat land of the Mâconnais, on which formerly wheat was
grown, producing the acidity, and all other parts of France
the special subordinate needed ingredients.

We have ourselves witnessed on the quay at Bordeaux
the addition of brandy to red wines of ordinary quality
destined for exportation to England. The admixture is by
no means uncommon, but is not carried to the same amount
as with Portuguese red wines. Bordeaux wines rarely exceed
in their alcoholicity the maximum of 10 per cent., while
ports have double that amount, namely from 19 to 20 per cent.
of absolute alcohol. According to the statements of the
exporters the addition of spirit to red wines at Bordeaux is
made to suit the English palate, and is by no means required
as a preservative of the wine.

In Thudichum and Dupré's "Treatise," pp. 334-348 can
be seen the statistics of viticultural property and production
in the Médoc, according to districts, of which the following
are the names :—Blanquefort, Ludon, Le Taillan, Le Pian,
Parempuyre, Palus, Arsac, Macau, Labarde, Cantenac,
Margaux, Sousans, Avensan, Castelnau, Moulis, Listrac,
Arcins, Lamarque, Cussac, St. Julien de Reignac, Pauillac
and St. Lambert, St. Estèphe, St. Seurin de Cadourne,
St. Laurent, St. Sauveur, Cissac, Vertheuil, St. Germain
d'Esteuil, St. Christoly et Couqueques, Valeyrac, Iau,
Lesparre and Uch, Prignac, St. Trélody, Potensac, Blaignan,
St. Yzans, Ordonnac, Bégadan, Gaillan, Civrac, Queyrac,
St. Vivien.

§ 71. THE GRAVES.

The district immediately surrounding Bordeaux on the
south side of the Garonne is called *the Graves*, from the
territory, which consists of sand and gravel, mixed here and
there with more or less clay and marl. The same soil occurs
also at the confluence of the Garonne and Dordogne; it is
based in most places upon limestone, in others, however, it
overlies the *alios*, the peculiar concrete-like siliceous layer,

which has mostly to be pierced in many places to give to the rainwater access to the subsoil; if such ditches be not made, the *alios* causes the land in the hollow parts to be swampy.

The red wines grown on the Graves have greater body, deeper colour and a little more spirit than those of the Médoc, and resemble thereby more to the wines of Burgundy, but yet have an altogether particular taste and quality. The bouquet is not great, and they require some as much as six,

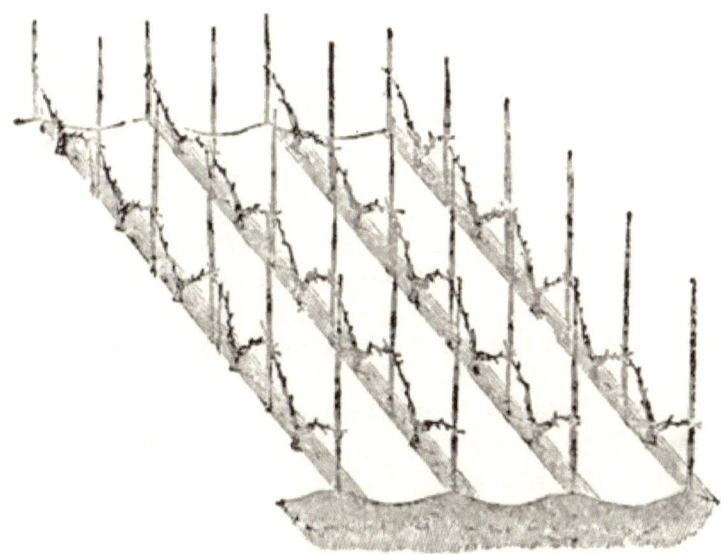

Fig. 23.—Normal Cultivation of the Graves.

others eight years in barrel before they can usefully be put into bottles. After that they remain of excellent quality. But the production of white wine prevails in the Graves over that of red, because the latter are too unlike the Médoc wines to be sold with them, while the white ones resemble those of the Sauternes district, and can be sold as such; neither white nor red wines are of sufficiently distinguished quality to make a name for themselves. Many of the white wines have a peculiar taste, called "of the pebble," which seems to us to arise from bad management. Higher up the

Garonne, in the whole district of Sauternes, the white wines, which should properly be called yellow, prevail, and no red wines are produced.

§ 72. RED WINES OF THE GRAVES.

The leading quality, classed immediately after those of the Châteaux Margaux, Lafitte and Latour, is that of Château Haut-Brion, distant about six kilometres from Bordeaux, and situated in the community of Pessac. The vineyards have forty-four hectares of surface; the mode of cultivating the vine is peculiar to the district, and differs from that of the Médoc. The principal vines cultivated here are the *Grosse Vidure* and the *Vidure Sauvignone*, together with the *Malbec* and *Cruchinet*. The vines stand in rows; the earth is worked by the plough. Each vine is generally trained upon two arms, and after that upon three branches, of which each is supported by a stake. To each arm there is left a cane of six or seven eyes in length, and a spur of four eyes: the rest of the operations and the vinification are as in the Médoc.

At some distance from Haut-Brion is an estate which was owned by a well-known vinologist, M. Boucherot. This gentleman had a collection of vines from all the world on his estate, amounting to upwards of six hundred varieties. With many of them he had made experiments of plantation and vinification on a large scale. All the American vines failed in these experiments. The German and other European vines gave indifferent results, and it was established that the only vines which succeed well in the district are those which are peculiar to it. We ourselves had the pleasure many years ago of seeing the whole estate and all its varieties of viticulture, and of deriving much information from the kindness of M. Boucherot.

§ 73. WHITE WINES OF THE GRAVES OR SAUTERNES DISTRICT.

This district is situated to the south-east of Bordeaux, on

the left bank of the Loire.   The centre is Bazas, its eastern termination Captieux. A little west of Podensac, on the Loire, it passes into the Graves of Bordeaux, already described.   It consists of a series of easy hills, rising gradually from the Loire towards the south and west, mostly with western exposure, some with all kinds of orientation.   They are interspersed with woods and a little cultivated meadow-land. The gravelly soil is easily worked. The vines bear, almost exclusively, white grapes ; they are mainly of two varieties, the *Sémillon* and the *Sauvignone*, mixed here and there with a little *Muscatel*. It is calculated that the Sémillon occupies two-thirds of the surface, the

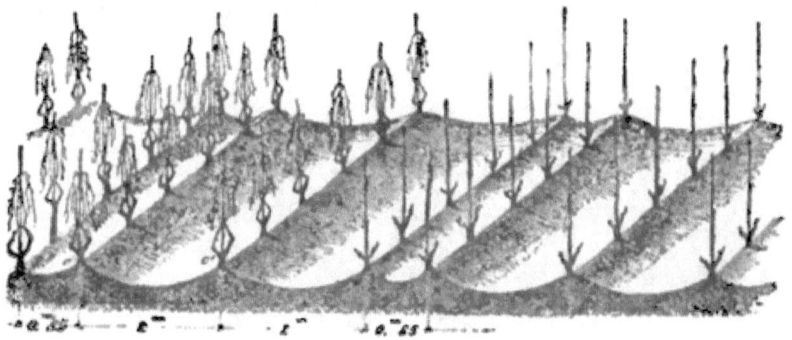

Fig. 24.—Normal Cultivation of the Sauternes District.

other third is occupied by the Sauvignone. The soil is worked partly by the plough, partly by hand ; the pruning is done between December and February. The canes are left with three eyes, and the spurs with two eyes only, the Sauvignone generally gets an eye on each cane or spur more than the Semillon.

§ 74. VINTAGE.

The vintage in these districts is altogether different from the vintage in any other part of the world ; for the grapes are allowed to hang until they are ripe and begin to decay, and then they are collected berry by berry, only such berries being taken as fully answer to the description, "ripe and rotten." The definition of "rottenness," however, requires a qualification, which is also well-known on the Rhine, namely, it must be "sweet." The decay applies in reality only to the husk, or a portion of it, while the flesh of the grape remains sound underneath it. We have been present at Château Suduiraut on an occasion when the vintagers passed through the vineyard for the tenth time, each time collecting single berries, and it was believed that they would have to pass once or twice more. In general, however, the grapes are collected in three successive harvests. The grapes are crushed and pressed, and the sweet thick must which flows off is put into barriques. When the first must has run off the murk is stirred up and loosened, trodden by the feet of men, and again pressed, and this process is repeated once more; the barrels are then removed to the fermenting shed, or chais, and there allowed to ferment. The vintage of one day is always kept by itself, and not mixed with the vintage of another day. In October we observed in the chais of various great estates, including Château Yquem, twenty-one different sets of barriques, each in a different stage of fermentation, representing the results of the vintage protracted during twenty-one days. The first seven or eight days' collection, when many are made, or the first collection when only three are made, are kept apart—even after the wine is ripe—from those of the second and third seven days, or the second and third collections. The first series of collections give generally what is called the "head wines"—*vins de tête;* these are the sweetest and headiest. The second collection or series generally gives *vins de milieu*, or wines of middle quality, which are less heady or alcoholic, and contain less sugar; and the third class are wines of the tail, or *queues*, which are the result of the pressing of all the grapes that remain after the other selections have been made. These latter yield the driest wines; therefore in tasting the white wines of this district one has to taste first the three qualities of head, middle, and tail each by itself, and then a mixture of equal parts of the three, *ensemble.* By means of this particular treatment of the grape a must is obtained which is exquisitely sweet; this sweetness remains, to a great extent, throughout the whole life of the wine. Indeed, the Sauternes wines, and all white wines of the Gironde which are similarly made, and from similar vines, are now of such a nature that they are not

Fig. 25.—Vine supported by a Walnut Tree at Celles, Canton of Mont-agries, Arrondissement of Riberac. Department of the Dordogne.

preferred in England, France or Germany to fully fermented wines. The excessive sweetness is given to them on account of the great demand which exists for sweet Sauternes in Russia. The dry fine wines of Sauternes were once amongst the great favourites of the œnophilists' cellars, but they have now almost entirely disappeared. Indeed Sauternes are now, or will be soon, what Muscat-Lunel and

Rivesaltes have been hitherto, but there will be this difference, that the Sauternes never receive any addition of alcohol, whereas the Lunel and Rivesaltes are like the Spanish *dulces*, mere sweet grape-juice not fermented, but preserved from fermentation by the addition of brandy.

The fermentation of the Sauternes is allowed to proceed in the barrels, and the yeast is not allowed to be cleared out at the bung-hole, but is compelled to sink in the fluid. Thus a maximum of alcohol is obtained to preserve the great quantity of fermented sugar from subsequent secondary fermentation. During four or five years the head wines have a disagreeable flavour, but much alcohol and sweetness, commonly called body. The flavour improves as they become drier. The more liquorous the wine is the longer it must be kept before its strong and peculiar flavour is adjusted to the right medium.

The principal growths of the district are the Barsacs, Sauternes, and Bommes. From the heights of Sauternes and from the castle of Yquem a splendid view of the valley of the Loire is obtained, one of the finest landscapes in Europe.

§ 75. Description of the Wines.

The wines of Barsac have much body, alcohol and a fine bouquet. They are more heady—*capiteux* as it is termed in French—and have a more lively taste and a more amber-tinted colour. The first growth of the district of Barsac is that of the Château Contet. The wines of Sauternes proper are more marrowy, and fine, more transparent and agreeable. The Château Yquem produces the finest of all the Sauternes wines; its prices range from 12,000 to 15,000 francs per tonneau of four barriques. In 1869 we tasted the several vintages, amongst them 1844 and 1865; the latter was very attractive, the *tête* excessively sweet, and when it was mixed with the tail, it sank in it like syrup of high specific gravity. The 1866 was too hot, *i.e.*, too alcoholic. At Château la Tour blanche, we found the 1865 very similar in flavour to Rhenish cabinet wines, which also remain excessively sweet; the middles and tails suited our British palates better.

At Château Suduiraut, distinguished by rich sources of flowing spring water, we observed an amusing little incident illustrative of the view which one may take of the hypocrisy of *tasting* wines for purposes of business. In tasting, the wine is supposed to be spat out after being rolled about the mouth for a few moments, and the tasters maintain that they are not in the habit of swallowing any, and that they are not obliged to swallow any for the purpose of getting a perfect taste. While we were tasting the 1857 wines the proprietor's little son came near, and his father asked him whether he would have a drink. The boy replied in the affirmative, and then putting the glass to his mouth drank its contents; but as the company was not supposed to drink but only to taste, the father jocularly admonished the son to "spit a little"—*crachez un peu.* In reality, of course, no taster could exist if he had to swallow even a quarter of what he puts in his mouth for tasting.

The viticultual statistics of the Sauternes district producing white as well as red wines are fully given in Thudichum and Dupré, "Treatise," pp. 357-365.

§ 76. Wines of the Hill-sides or Côtes of the Gironde.

A chain of hills extending along the right bank of the Garonne from Ambarez to Sainte-Croix-du-Mont yield great quantities of vines termed "of the hill-sides," *Vins de Côtes.* The northern part of the district produces mainly dark-coloured wines, which are at first hard and rough, but ameliorate with age. These are exported under the name of "wines of the good hill-side." In the southern part only little red wine is made but much white wine of a dry quality, called "wine of the little hill-sides." Under this latter category the traders of Bordeaux include the wines of the right bank of the Dordogne, from Bourg, which is about twenty kilometres north of Bordeaux to Fronsac, which is about twenty-four kilometres north-east of

Bordeaux.   Among all these wines the most celebrated are those which are grown in the community of St. Emilion, and named after that district; the vineyards occupy 1,041 hectares.   The best qualities are obtained on the plateau of the Madeleine and St. Martin, and on the inclines towards the south and west of the St. Emilion hills.   The soil on the hill-sides is chalky clay lying upon rock; in the lower parts the territory becomes sandy, and rests frequently upon ferruginous subsoil.

St. Emilion was a stronghold of the Knights Templars,

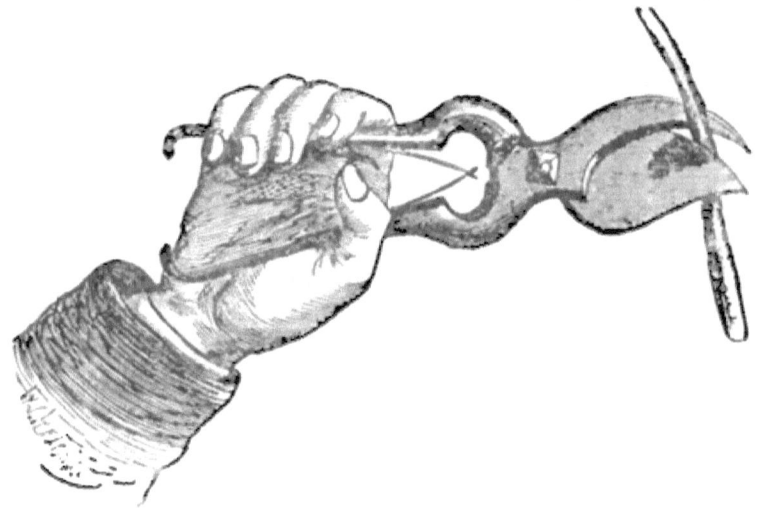

Fig. 26.—The Secateur as used for pruning Vines in the Gironde

and of their churches and order-houses innumerable ruins exist, interspersed with inhabited houses.

The varieties of vines met with in this district are the *Noir de Fressac*, the *Merlot* and the *Bouchet* or *Cabernet*. The Merlot is one of the vines of the marshes or Palus, and the Cabernet one of the best vines of the Médoc, where however it is designated by the synonym of Carmenet. These vines are represented at St. Emilion in the proportion of one-third of the whole set.   To the Cabernet the St. Emilion wine, in our opinion, owes its finesse; to the Merlot its body and lasting quality; and to the Noir de Pressac its particularly fiery and fresh quality. The mode of cultivation is very similar to the so-called basket cultivation of the Rheingau. The Noir de Pressac is pruned so that only short spurs are left. The Bouchet and the Merlot, however, are cut with long canes. The soil is worked by hoe and plough. The vines are tied to stakes,

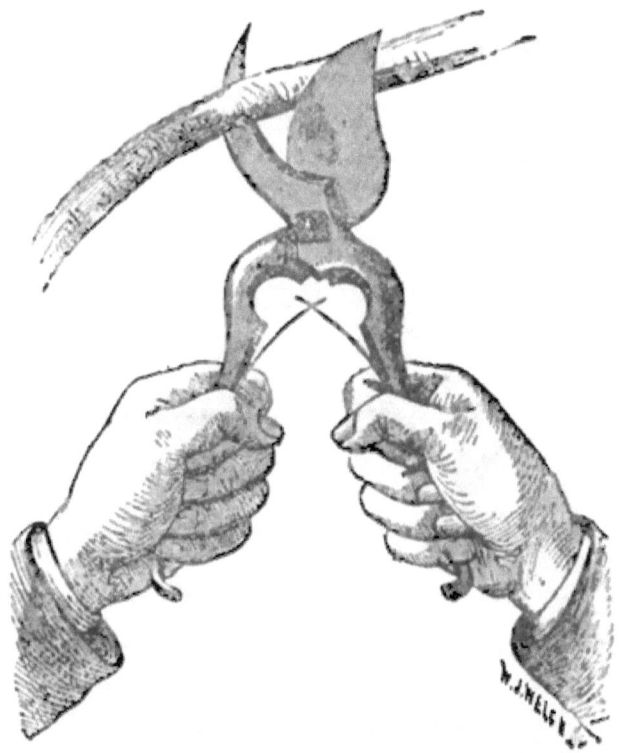

Fig. 27.—The Secateur as used with both hands to cut a thicker branch.

which here bear the peculiar name of *carasonnes*. A hectare of the best vineyards yields about six barriques or thirteen and a half hectolitres; the common vineyards yield double that quantity. The vintage takes place at the end of September and beginning of October. Most proprietors crush the grapes and put them by preference into middle-

sized vats. The rest of the treatment is the same as that
which we have described as prevalent in the Médoc.

St. Emilion of good quality can be put into bottle towards
the fourth year, and must, under all circumstances, be
bottled by the sixth year. If this period be overstepped and
the wine left in barrel beyond it, it loses its fruitiness,
freshness, flavour, and colour, and becomes incapable of
producing in bottle that fragrance which it would have
obtained had it been bottled at the proper time. It follows
that St. Emilion wine will be less injured by premature
bottling than by undue delay of this operation. It is singular
that the St. Emilion wine is not liked in England, although
like the best Montpellier it recalls many of the finest

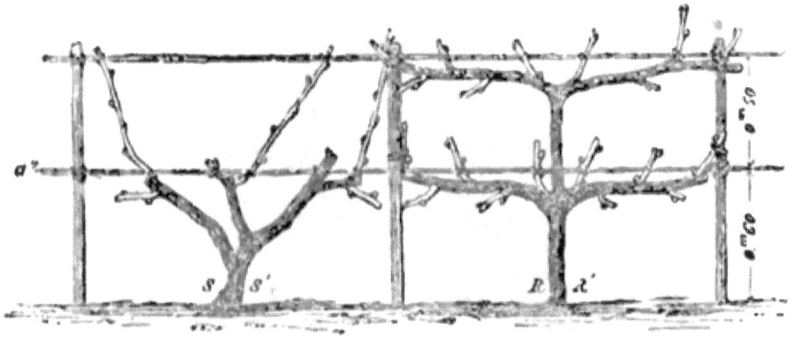

Fig. 28.—Vines of the Palus (Villenave d'Ornon) pruned for
spring growth.

qualities of fine port wines, leaving brandy out of the
question. Fine wines will sell at 300 to 350 francs the
hogshead, and will come to about £16 the hogshead in
London. Some qualities sell at 75 francs the hogshead.
Most of the good St. Emilion at present goes to Belgium,
Holland, Denmark and Sweden, the second class St.
Emilion is largely imported into Paris.

St. Emilion is the centre of a district called the *Libournais*, of which Libourne is the principal town. Towards the
north-west the Libournais is marked off by the river Isle. On
the other side of the river is the district called *Fronsadais*,
of which the principal town is Fronsac, upon the banks of

the Dordogne.   To the north-east of the Fronsadais is the *Blayais*, which has the town of Blaye, a fortress lying on the banks of the Gironde, for its centre.   The Blayais, therefore, lies opposite the Médoc, on the banks of the Gironde. In these districts considerable quantities of red and white wines are produced.   None of these are classified, but many are very useful.   Large quantities, particularly of white côtes, coloured up with Teinturier of Toulouse, are exported to America.

For statistics of these districts see Thudichum and Dupré, "Treatise," pp. 370-380.

CHAPTER XIII.

WINES OF ROUSSILLON AND LANGUEDOC.

§ 77. WINES OF ROUSSILLON.

THE ancient province of France formerly called Roussillon is now merged in the department of the Oriental Pyrenees.   Its name has been preserved, at least with foreign nations, by its wines; and certainly its wines were, and in part are yet, its only or principal wealth.   It contains more than 50,000 hectares of vineyards.   Three kinds of wine are produced: liqueur wines, or musts preserved with spirit without fermentation; dry wines by ordinary fermentation, and half-fermented wines, which are in such a condition that they can be used for the manufacture of anything—factitious port in particular.   It is to the fortified wines, particularly red wines, that Roussillon owes its main success.   The most celebrated vineyards of the district are at Banyuls-sur-Mer, Collioure, Port-Vendres, Rivesaltes, and Perpignan.   Banyuls-sur-Mer is very near the Spanish frontier, in the warmest part of the eastern Pyrenees, and its vineyards have an area of about 4,500 hectares; they are mostly on slopes of schistose rock, in the plain on alluvial soil.

The vineyards are planted almost exclusively with the *Grenache noir* and the *Carignane.* In the whole of the Roussillon district the Grenache is mainly planted on the heights, while the lower parts of the vineyards are populated by the Carignane. The bunch of grapes of the Grenache is large, loose, pyramidal, with uneven berries, and otherwise deformed by accident during blossom time. The bluish-black colour of its thin skin is overlaid by a strong waxy bloom ; in it fine taste, sweetness and perfume prevail, and it ripens early. The Carignane is less fertile and less delicate than the Grenache, and gives dry wine ; its bunch of grapes is long, round, and uneven, blackish-blue, with a strong bloom. It has a thick husk, ripens late, and tastes less sweet than the Grenache. The ordinary Banyuls wines are generally made of two-thirds of Grenache and one-third of Carignane grapes. Two other vines furnish some addition of grapes, one, the *Mataro,* bearing a blackish, sweet, and early ripe grape ; another, the *Picpoule,* which seems useful for bearing quantity ; for this it is grown in the lower Rhône valley, the Herault, and the Gard. These two adventitious vines, as far as Roussillon is concerned, according to Lenoir, yield only mediocre wine.

In the accompanying engraving Fig. 29, a view of the vineyards of Banyuls, Port-Vendres, and Collioure is given, which shows the remarkable steepness of the slopes on which the vines are planted. In consequence the labour here is manual, while in the plain the soil is worked with the plough. A hectare on the slopes yields about 15 hectolitres of wine, while in the plain it gives 25 hectolitres. Plastering of the must is not rarely practised, and helps to make Roussillon wine flat and mawkish, and to deprive it of that refreshing acidity which alone makes sugary wines palatable.

The so-called Grenache wine is not really a wine at all, but grape-juice preserved from fermenting by the addition of spirit., sulphurous acid, and frequent racking from any deposits, including any yeast which may grow. The richer

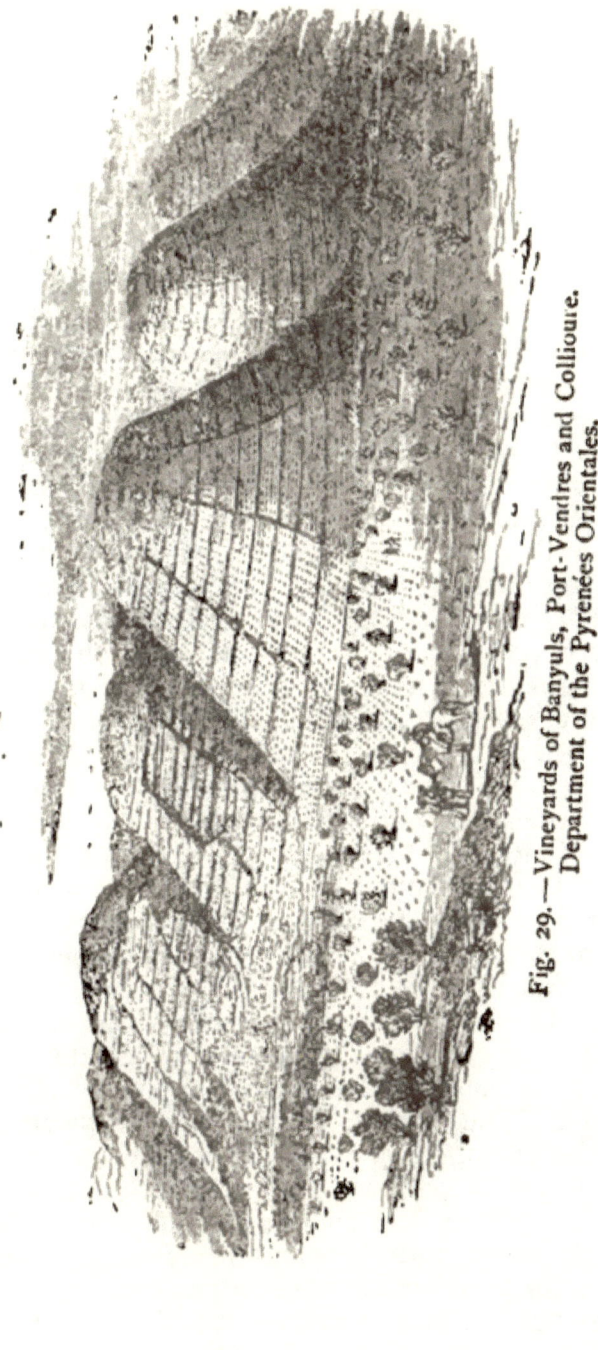

Fig. 29.—Vineyards of Banyuls, Port-Vendres and Collioure.
Department of the Pyrenées Orientales.

in sugar the must is, the less spirit does it require, but the amount of spirit added is never very great ; the main agents in suppressing fermentation are, besides concentration and alcohol, the vapour of burnt sulphur and frequent racking. It is said that the liqueur must remain in cask for fifteen years before it is fit for being drunk.   This is, therefore, a preparation resembling in every way to the Spanish *dulce*, except in this, that it receives less spirit than the *dulce*, and consequently requires more time for its perfection.

The vineyards of Collioure cover 800 hectares, those of Port-Vendres 600 hectares ; they resemble in every respect those of Banyuls, and the treatment of plants and product is the same.   The Collioure wines have much colour, body, and what the French call generosity, yet being drier than that of Banyuls.   They lose colour after ten years in barrel, and then are thought to be most fit for bottling, but such delay between growth and consumption is nowadays not very practicable.   When sold after the first spring racking the wines fetch very low prices, from 15 francs a hectolitre, being a penny-halfpenny for a litre, up to 150 francs, being a franc and a half for a litre.   Most of these wines go to the United States, to be there transformed into liqueur wines, and to the Brazils, to be there drunk as dry wines.   Cette and Marseilles take considerable quantities to work them up into whatever may be demanded.   The vineyards of Rivesaltes cover 10,500 hectares ; they yield a fine wine which is qualified to be transformed into effervescent wine after the manner of Champagne.

In the Collioure vineyards a peculiar vine is grown, the *Clairette*, also sometimes improperly called the *Blanquette*, but only intermixed with the main or prevailing sets above described.   The bunches of this vine are pyramidal, with wings, and among the grapes are many oval, half-transparent, golden yellow bloomy ones, having a thick skin and a sugary taste.   They ripen late and give a fine wine, which, when young, is sweet, and afterwards becomes dry, and is also qualified for transformation into Mousseux.

Rivesaltes produces what are called specialities, which have a limited reputation, such are the *Muscat*, the *Maccabeo*, the *Malvoisie*, the *Grenache*, and the *Rancio*. All these names are those of vines from which the beverages, mostly liqueurs, are produced; the *Rancio* alone is named after its age and dryness, and bears a Spanish name, which once indicated old wine, but by modern traders is held to be a term implying condemnation.

§ 78. MODE OF PRODUCTION OF MUSCAT SWEET WINE.

The grapes are shrunk on the plant, or on trays in the sun, until they are raisin-like shrivelled, but not dry. They are then crushed by any of the several methods, and on pressing yield a must of great density, which is put into barrels and allowed to ferment. The barrels are not entirely filled up, and when fermentation is completed the wine is racked. Owing to its great amount of sugar, this wine, like Tokay or Rota Tent, forms very little alcohol; in the first year therefore it resembles more to a syrup than a wine, and approaches the thick Sauternes in quality, though these are not artificially condensed, and form more spirit. In the second year the wine becomes clean, acquires finesse and fire, and that Muscat bouquet to which it owes its reputation. It should not be kept very long, for its bouquet is transient, but should be drunk while it is fresh. The Rivesaltes is sold young at about 100 francs the hectolitre.

§ 79. MODE OF PRODUCTION OF MALVOISIE AND MACCABEO WINES.

The grapes used for these wines are not dried or concentrated by the sun, but their expressed juice is somewhat concentrated in a pan over the fire. When the scum has risen and been removed, the liquid is allowed to cool, and put into barrels, together with a certain amount of proof spirit. It is racked once a month for six months, and thereby fermentation is completely prevented. In the making of the Malvoisie the grapes are carried to the press with the utmost care, for if they are at all injured they lose much of their flavour. The must, although mixed with

K

some proof spirit, is allowed to ferment as long as it will. When fermentation has ceased the wine is racked, and a little more spirit is added. Dry Malvoisie is also made with the aid of full fermentation. On the whole, the production of these sweet wines is very limited as regards quantity, and their prices are very low, on account of the long time during which they must be kept before they are approved of by the consumers.

§ 80. VINEYARD OF PERPIGNAN

Of the 5,000 hectares of this vineyard two-thirds are in the plain and of inferior quality to those on the hills, and even these slopes rise but little above the level of the sea. The soil is clay, here and there chalk, and everywhere there are rolled pebbles as in the Médoc. The wine is left in the cuves from twenty-five to thirty-six days; the lower class wines are always treated with gypsum or plaster of Paris; the white wines, if sweet, are put in bottle in March. The red wines remain in barrel much longer, but are apt to lose much of their colour. As they preserve it when bottled, they are put in glass early, and decanted from any deposit, and transferred to new bottles seven times in fifteen years. It is doubtful whether the resulting wines are worth the trouble bestowed upon them, and they would not bear the expense if they were not so extraordinarily cheap when newly made. Much of the wine grown here goes to North and South America, to Genoa, Cette and Marseilles, and to a few inland places of France, Lyons among them. In the Canton of Perpignan there is produced a wine called Torremila, which comes very near to average Madeira; at Torremila also a kind of Mousseux is made, which has a certain reputation.

§ 81. SUMMARY OF THE WINES OF ROUSSILLON.

The most esteemed liqueur wines, whether partly fermented or not, and treated as dulces, are the Muscat of Rivesaltes, the Maccabeo, the Grenache, and the Malvoisie.

Amongst the dry wines are esteemed those of Banyuls-sur-Mer, of Torremila, of Rivesaltes, and of Terrats; the Malvoisie and Picpoule are here also made of dry quality.

Among the red or commercial liqueur wines those which take the first places are of Banyuls-sur-Mer, Collioures, and Port-Vendres, Corneilla-de-la-Rivière, Pezilla-de-la-Rivière, Tautavel, Montner, and Banyuls-des-Aspres.

Among the dry ordinaries are to be mentioned the wines of Espira-de-la-Gly, Rivesaltes, Baixas, Salces, Millas, Saint André, and the two Cantons of Perpignan.

The barrels in which Roussillon wine is made and sold are of the size of barriques of Bordeaux. The wine is laden into ships directly from the producing district; but, as the ships cannot come near to the shore in that part, the barrel is rolled out to the beach, and then down the beach into the water, which may be a distance of a mile or two miles. When the barrel begins to float, the man who has rolled it pushes it on towards the ship, at last by swimming. When the cask arrives at the ship, it is lifted on board by a crane, and the man returns to the shore.

§ 82. WINES OF LANGUEDOC, OR THE MIDI OF FRANCE. TOPOGRAPHY AND SOIL.

Languedoc is the name of an ancient province of France, and comprises the greater part of what are now the departments of the Aude, of the Hérault, and of a portion of the Gard. The wines are mostly red, and the inspectors of the English Board of Customs, who were sent there on an official inquiry, found none which contained above 23·9 per cent. of proof spirit, while many contained less. In a great part of Languedoc viticulture was in a flourishing condition already at the time of the Romans; and now these wines are the objects of a vast commerce, which is daily increasing owing to the united advantages of climate, soil, and situation, by means of which great quantities of cheap and saleable wines are produced. The surface occupied by vineyards in the three departments mentioned amounts to 258,192 hectares, of which the department of the Aude owns 70,982, that of the Hérault 179,962, and that of the Gard 75,248 hectares.

The soil is chalky on the slopes, chalky and clayey in the plains, and silico-calcareous, with many rolled pebbles, on the high plains or plateaux. The same vines are raised throughout the whole of the departments, and the wines which are obtained from them are classified in the same manner throughout the entire province of Languedoc. They go generally under the name of *Vins du Midi*, which in the eyes of uninformed persons is equivalent to cheap, bad stuff. If they knew the quantities of such wines exported to all parts of France, and mixed with the Burgundies, the Bordeaux, and other varieties of French wine drunk in the country or exported, they would moderate their dislike ; and if they had the enterprise to study the wines of these countries themselves, they would find their quality and cheapness a sufficient recommendation to all consumers of the middle classes. The wines are divided into two categories : wines for the distillery, and wines for commerce. These latter are sub-divided, first, into ordinary red and white wines of commerce ; secondly, into the fine red wines ; and thirdly, into the white dry wines, and the white liqueur and Muscat wines. The sales are effected through the agency of brokers, termed *courtiers*, who formerly were of more importance than nowadays, when their only office is to obtain samples and bring them to the merchants.

§ 83. Vines Cultivated in Languedoc.

The vines prevalent in this province are the Carignane, the Terret noir, the Grenache, the Mourastel, the Aspiran, the Oeillade and its variety the Sinsaon, the black Picpoule, the white Picpoule, and the Clairette. These yield the wines of commerce. For the distillery wines only two vines are cultivated, namely, the Aramon and the Terret bourret. These two latter cover the whole of the plains of Hérault and of St. Guilhem upon the sea, the plain of Lunel, of Orbe, and of the Aude. The grapes of these vines are their most characteristic parts. The Terret noir has loosely hanging grapes of equal size, oval in shape, of a blackish-red colour, transparent and browned by the sun, with a thick skin of acidulous taste; the bunch is pyramidal and winged. The grapes of the Terret bourret are of similar shape, but of a light rosy or violet colour; they have a flat taste, and yield only the lowest wines used in the distilleries. The Aramon has a long exuberant bunch, with round, equal, violet-black bloomy grapes, of a flat taste, and provided with a thick skin. The Oeillade bears a magnificent pyramidal winged bunch, with voluminous grapes, hanging on

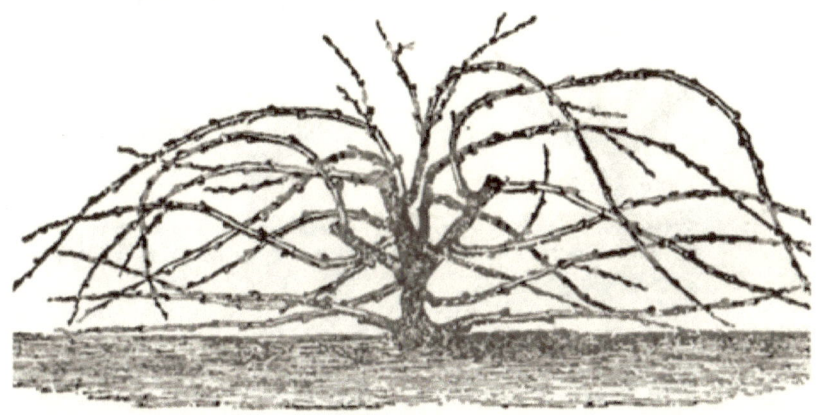

Fig. 30.—Vine of the Hérault, with all its wood as seen in winter.

very long green stalks, of blackish blue colour, with brown sun spots, ripening early; their taste is fresh, sugary, and agreeable. The Piran or Aspiran bears a middle-sized bunch with black-bloomed grapes of fine and sugary taste. The *white wines* are mostly made of Picpoule and Clairette. The vines which are planted on alluvial soil are called *vines of the plain;* those on ferruginous soil mixed with pebbles, the result of chalk denudation, are termed *vines of the terrain de grès.* They give esteemed commercial wines. The slopes, *garrigues,* yield wines which are fit for exportation, and are distilled only in years of plentiful harvests. In abundant years the distillery keeps up the prices of wines for consumption; in years of dearth even the wines of the plain, which ordinarily go to the distillery, are mixed with wines of good years and sold to the world.

The vines are not very carefully cultivated, the manuring in particular is very negligently performed. The vintage takes place in the middle of September and extends into October. In the rich alluvial plains a hectare may some-times yield 200 hectolitres of distillery wine; but on the slopes and gravels only from 25 to 30 hectolitres. Good ordinary soils planted with Aramon and Terret bourret yield up to 50 hectolitres.

The grapes are crushed as usual, powdered over with

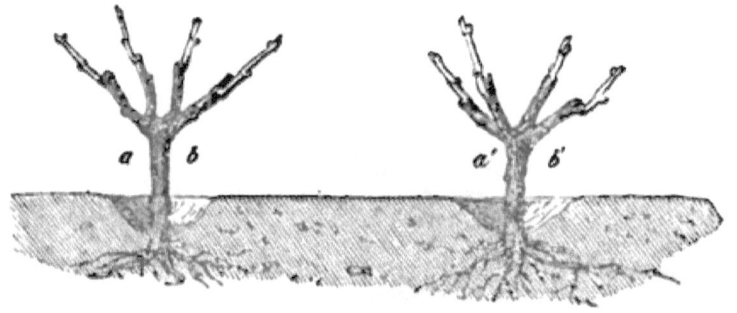

Fig. 31.—Vines of the Hérault pruned and their "feet" uncovered. *a. b.—a'. b'*. Stocks with four branches each.

plaster of Paris, and put into the vats; the wine is placed in *foudres* or large barrels of a capacity varying between 7 and 700 hectolitres.

§ 84. DISTINGUISHED GROWTHS OF THE DEPARTMENTS OF THE AUDE AND GARD.

The vineyard of Limoux yields a white wine passing as *Blanquette de Limoux*; of this about 3,000 hectolitres are made, which fetch double the price of the red wine; of the latter 10,000 hectolitres are produced. These wines are termed, after the localities, Lédenon, Langlade, and St. Gilles, all three in the arrondissement of Nismes. The

Langlade wine is left only three days in the vat, is light, of rich colour, and less alcoholic than other wines; as it is so well known, thousands of barrels of other districts pass under its name. The vineyard of St. Gilles, 5,000 hectares in extent, produces wines of brilliant purple colour, soft taste, yet of the quality which the French express by *nerve* and *mordant*, for which we might say *strength* and *grip*. They are called *vins fermes*, because they can be used to give colour and strength to wines which do not possess those properties, and hence they are also called *vins de remède*. The St. Gilles' wines have, however, and always bring into other wines with which they are mixed, a particular taste—so-called taste of territory. Considered in their character as dyeing materials for other wines, the products of this district are divided into six classes, and called accordingly the wines of one, three, five, or six colours, according to whether they can, on being mixed with one, three, five, or six times their volume of white wine, produce a well-coloured ordinary table wine. At St. Gilles wine is sold by the *barrel*, measuring a little more than 50 litres, and corresponding almost to the Austrian *Eimer*. The hectolitre may fetch up to fifty-three francs, and in good years sink to three francs. The average price is ten francs the hectolitre. Most of this wine goes to Paris and Holland.

In the vinification the care taken to extract all the colouring matter from the husks is very great. Before the vintage is mashed it is put into closed spaces, whereby a slight fermentation begins in the unbroken berries, through which the skin is predisposed to part with its pigment. The rest is not peculiar, except that little care is taken to avoid the effects of a tainted or acetous top or *chapeau*.

A peculiar process adopted to strengthen wines consists in concentrating entire grapes in cauldrons heated by steam; they shrivel, as if they were in the sun, and become cooked as well; the hard skin becomes macerated and the pigment loosened. Grapes thus concentrated are put into spirit or into new wine. Mild wines of dark rose colour, from the third day of fermentation, are sent off to Burgundy to serve in what is called the "arrangement" of Burgundy wines;

excess of colour and of acidity is thereby corrected and the Burgundy becomes earlier fit for sale.

At St. Gilles sweet wine is also made with the aid of sulphuring and racking, which delay fermentation and allow the wine to become clear ; when fermentation ultimately sets in it is much slower and less energetic than it would have been in the must not sulphured and racked, and leaves a great deal more sugar in the fluid than would otherwise have been left.

At St. Gilles is also made a speciality, by a proprietor, Dr. Beaumes, namely, a wine from the true Furmint or Tokay vine, after the manner of the Hungarian Tokay ; it is called Tokay Princesse, and sold in the place at the price of six francs the bottle.

§ 85. REMARKABLE GROWTHS OF THE HÉRAULT.

Amongst the red wines of the province those of St. Georges D'Orques, St. Chrystol, and St. Drézéry are best known. The Picardans are white wines, and the Lunels are Muscat wines. The wines of the arrondissement of Montpellier are amongst the finest of the department. The Picardan wines are sweet or dry, and mostly obtained from the Clairette. The grape of this vine must hang into October. The wines obtained from it are similar to Madeira, and are frequently mixed with alcohol, so as to contain from 13 to 15·5 per cent. of absolute alcohol. The wines are also heated in the sun, or in hot chambers as in Madeira. They are mostly cheap, selling at from 12 to 16 francs the hectolitre.

§ 86. REMARKABLE MUSCAT WINES.

The mode of their production has been above described. They are mostly made from white, more rarely from black Muscat grapes. At Frontignan from 230 hectares there are annually produced of white Muscat 800 to 900 barrels, containing from 220 to 225 litres each, while of red

Muscat only 20 hectolitres are made. The price per barrel varies between 120 and 200 francs. Lunel is rapidly diminishing its production, while Maraussan and Espagnac are not increasing theirs.

§ 87. MANUFACTURE OF SPIRIT DISTILLED FROM WINE, CALLED "TROIS-SIX" AND "EAU-DE-VIE," AT MONT-PELLIER.

In the department of the Hérault two qualities of brandy, called *trois-six*, are made from grapes, one of wine and the other of murk. The former ones are called "of good taste" (*de bon goût*) when the wine from which they have been made was neither spoiled nor sour. The spirit from murk, always called trois-six of murk, is less valuable than that of wine by from 25 to 50 per cent. The trois-six of good taste is obtained by stills, called after their inventor De Rosne, and other more modern ones, which will in twenty-four hours produce up to 30 hectolitres of brandy of 86 per cent. strength. The wines of the plain contain from 7 to 11 volumes per cent. of trois-six of 84°, in good years up to 12 volumes per cent : a large still can consume daily from 200 to 300 hectolitres of wine. The residues have a very repulsive odour, and when discharged into water-courses infect the air more than sewage. No use for them has as yet been discovered. The strength of the distilled spirit is mostly ascertained by the aid of the alcoholometer of Bories. This is a very ancient instrument, and the manufacturers and producers of Languedoc are as reluctant to give it up as the Germans are with regard to that of Tralles, or the English with regard to that of Sikes.

§ 88. MARKETS FOR THE SALE OF SPIRITS.

There are in the department of the Hérault four markets of *eau-de-vie* and alcohol, in the order of their importance : Béziers (principal sale day Friday) ; Pézenas (Saturday) ; Cette (Wednesday) ; and Lunel (Monday). If there are no stipulations made to the contrary, the manufacturers of **trois-six** are bound to deliver all produce to one or other of these markets, and let it be accompanied with a warranty of its quality. The inspector of the market verifies the analysis, and, if correct, admits; if incorrect, returns the piece. The inspector states the limpidity, which must be perfect; he observes that it is free from any colour; the taste must be pure and free. If a piece is declared of *mauvais goût*, it will be paid for only as trois-six of murk. All trois-six is paid for in cash.

§ 89. Designations of Spirits of various Degrees of Strength.

The several designations of spirits of various strengths used in Languedoc and other parts of France are derived as follows :—Common *eau-de-vie* is accepted as the standard, and supposed to show 19° Cartier at 12·5° temperature. It then contains a little less than 50 volumes per. cent. of absolute alcohol. *Trois-six* is a spirit of which three volumes added to three volumes of water were supposed to give six volumes of *eau-de-vie* at 19° Cartier. It is the common alcohol of commerce, marks 33° on the scale of Cartier, and contains consequently 84·4 volumes per cent. of absolute alcohol. *Trois-cinq* is a spirit of which three volumes added to two volumes of water were supposed to give five volumes of *eau-de-vie* at 19° Cartier, while *trois-sept* is an alcohol of which three volumes added to four volumes of water were supposed to give seven volumes of *eau-de-vie*. It is evident that by the more accurate methods of ascertaining the strengths of spirits these names have lost much of their meaning, the very standard of *eau-de-vie*, with 50 volumes per cent. alcohol, excluding the possibility of the existence of an alcohol called *trois-sept*. But whenever these names are used without the definition of the exact strength in volume per cent., or degrees Cartier, we may assume that by 3/7 is meant a spirit of 94 per cent. by volume; by 3/6 a spirit of about 84 per cent. volume; by 3/5 a spirit of 78 per cent. volume; by proof of Holland a spirit of 58 volumes per cent. [Rendu, "Vins du Languedoc," i. p. 71, gives proof of Holland as 52 volumes per cent.; Payen, "Chimie Industrielle," third edition, p. 712, gives proof of Holland at 58·7, and proof of London at 58 volumes per cent.; British (or Sikes's) proof spirit at 15·5° contains 57·06 volumes per cent., or 49·24 weight per cent. of absolute alcohol.]

Commerce and manufactures demand and produce now only the strongest kind of spirit which can be conveniently produced by mere distillation. While at Montpellier there are now produced annually only 2,000 pieces of *eau-de-vie*, equal to 6,000 hectolitres of 52°, the manufacture of 3/6 rises to 60,000 pieces, equal to 360,000 hectolitres of *eau-de-vie ;* 60,000 hectares of vineyards of the Hérault produce nothing but wine to be used for distilling. The average production of 3/6 in the four departments—the eastern Pyrenees, the Hérault, the Gard, and the Aude—has been 500,000, half-a-million hectolitres, or fifty millions of litres. The spirit distilled immediately after the fermentation is the best ; older wine gives inferior brandy. The alcohol from murk is expelled by steam. On an average 13,000 kilogrammes of murk yield 600 litres of spirit. The warm murk after expulsion of the alcohol can be used for feeding sheep. The alcohols of the Hérault are mostly sold in France to be drunk as *eau-de-vie*, or to be used for fortifying wine—*viner les vins.*

CHAPTER XIV.

WINES OF THE EAST OF FRANCE.

§ 90. WINES OF THE EAST OF FRANCE.

THE greater and most reputed part of the wines of the east of France is grown on the right bank of the Rhône in the communes of Laudun, Chuselan, Tavel, Roquemaure, all in the department of the Gard ; in the district which contains St. Péray, department of Ardèche, and at Condrieu and Côte-rôtie, department of the Rhône. On the left bank of the Rhône much less wine is grown than on the right, but it is celebrated by the name of Château-neuf-du-Pape, department Vaucluse, and of l'Ermitage, department of the Drome. The vineyards of Croyes, Larnage, and Mercurol, in the same department, produce wine which in quality follows immediately after Ermitage. The wines of the Gard have the character of the *Vins du Midi*. The white St. Péray has a character of its own, particularly in the effervescent or Mousseux state. The wines of the upper part of the Rhône, Côte-rôtie, resemble those of the Beaujolais and the Côte d'Or. The wines of l'Ermitage are distinguished by peculiar qualities, and a pleasing bouquet, coupled with great finesse ; and those of Château-neuf-du-Pape by spirituosity and colour, for which qualities they are taken to Burgundy to serve as improvers of lesser qualities.

The greater part of the vineyards of the Rhône is on calcareous soil, on the left bank mixed with clay and pebbles ; the upper parts of the borders of the Rhône are formed of granite, the more horizontal land of diluvium of alpine origin.

§ 91. CÔTE DU RHÔNE.

The name of Côte du Rhône as applied to vineyards is equivalent to vineyards of the Gard ; they are about thirty miles long by six miles in width. The black grapes grown here are the Terret, Picpoule, Piran (Aspiran), Camanèze, and Grenache or Alicante. The latter imparts the good qualities to the wine of this region. In some localities the Uni and the Bourboulenque are grown on a small scale with the others. Of the white grapes the Clairette and Calitor form about a fifth part, the others are Uni blanc, Picardan, and several other varieties. The wines produced on the Côte are classified as follows :

*Red Wines—First class ; not vatted. Tavel.—*Very dry, light-coloured wines, improve much by age. Annual produce,

3,000 pieces of 280 litres measure, and about 50 francs value each.

Lirac.—Very dry, firmer than Tavel, of a lively rose-colour. Annual produce, 1,000 pieces of 50 francs value each.

Chusclan.—Very agreeable liqueur wine. Produce, 2,000 pieces per annum ; value 50 francs each.

Second class ; not vatted. Orsan.—A tender wine of deep colour. Annual produce, 1,500 pieces, value 45 francs each.

St. Geniès-de-Comolas.—Of this wine, which has analogies with Chusclan, 3,000 pieces are annually produced, of 45 francs average value.

Third class. Saint Laurent-des-Arbres.—Wine of half a colour so-called, 3,000 pieces annually, average price 45 francs.

Roquemaure.—The better productions are "of good quality," and valued as dinner wines ; 5,000 pieces, at 45 francs each.

Of *white wine* there is only one staple variety, named *Laudun,* it is agreeable. The total production is 1,000 pieces per annum, of which 700 pieces remain dry, while 200 pieces are converted into sweet wine.

§ 92. Château-neuf-du-Pape.

The 600 hectares of this vineyard are situated on the left bank of the Rhône, a few kilometres from Orange ; the plantations have mostly a southward inclination ; some, however, are in the plain, and have contributed much to decrease the reputation of this vineyard. The black grapes cultivated here are the Grenache, Picpoule, Tinto, and Terret noir ; of white varieties, the Clairette, Uni and Muscat. The cultivators say that the Grenache gives alcohol and finesse, the Picpoule generosity, Tinto colours, and the Terret quantity. The best vines, the Grenaches, are the latest to bear and the earliest to decay ; a well-kept *Grenachière,* as a vineyard planted with Grenaches only is called, produces up to 30 hectolitres of wine per hectare : the average of other varieties is only 20 hectolitres. A piece of wine of 270 litres is sold at the price of from 25 to 50 francs. The red wine sheds its colour after three years in barrel, and preserves it then only when bottled. The most remarkable vineyards in this district are the following :—The vineyard of *La Nerthe* gained its reputation through the practice of the owner, the Marquis of Villefranche, of frequently treating his guests at Paris to old fine Nerthe wine. The product is not now husbanded to the same advantage. The *Cru de Condorcet* is situated below the Nerthe and measures 20 hectares; its wines fetch only a fifth of the price of Nerthe. The vineyard of *Fortia* occupied a place similar to that of Nerthe under its former proprietor, the Marquis de Fortia d'Urban; that of *Vaudieu* produces light-coloured and less alcoholic wines, several parts of it are planted exclusively with white vines, from the fruit of which a dry wine is made, as well as a sweet one by the addition of spirit to the must. In the commune of Château-neuf-du-Pape the land is extremely subdivided, and every owner is a wine-grower. The wines are mostly bought after the harvest by the commission agents of Roquemaure, who after having averaged, *i.e.*, mixed them, send the greater quantity into Burgundy to be used there as "doctors" to feeble, acid and pale wines of bad years. Bordeaux also receives a quantity of these wines for the same purpose. In consequence the wines of Château-neuf-du-Pape do not occur in trade in their original condition at all; when bought for mixing they are already in a mixed state. The principle of vinification is to produce black alcoholic wine, in great volume, and in consequence the ancient reputation of these vineyards is gradually diminishing.

§ 93. Vineyard of St. Péray, Ardèche.

The vineyard of St. Péray is situated on the right bank of the Rhône in the department of Ardèche; it is 172 hectares in extent and produces only white wine. The dominant vine is the *Grosse Roussette* (Roussanne of the Ermitage); it is mixed with a small proportion of the *petite Roussette*, but with no other vine. The dry wine is made in the ordinary manner, and is put into bottles in the third or fourth year. The Mousseux is produced in the same manner as Champagne: Grand Mousseux of the best years is sold at two francs a bottle retail; it is very heady and neither so fine nor so mild as Champagne. The wine in barrel is sold for 50 to 75 francs the hectolitre.

§ 94. Vineyards of the Ermitage.

The vineyards of the Ermitage are situated on the left border of the Rhône in the commune of Tain, twenty-eight kilometres from Valence, department of Drôme; have a surface of 190 hectares and are distributed over two slopes; one of these is on granitic soil, the other on alluvial. They are exposed to the south-west in such a manner that the sun strikes them from his rising to his setting. The name is derived from a place of retirement which one Gaspard de Sterimberg, a courtier of Queen Blanche of Castile, built thereabouts for his old age in the year 1225. The vineyards on granitic soil constitute the so-called " Mas de Bessas ;" those on the alluvial the " Mas du Méal ;" those on alluvial clay the " Mas de Greffieux." The high quality of the Ermitage wines depends upon the combination of these three vineyards, the produce of which is always sold *mixed ;* and a proprietor in order to have his produce classified as " premier cru " must hold property in the three vineyards. In short, what is called Ermitage, and has any quality, is always a mixture of the grapes of the three " Mas." The vines grown here are the " grosse Sirrah " and " petite Sirrah " for red wine; and the " Roussanne " and " Marsanne " for white ; the " grosse Sirrah " is remarkable for its fertility, but produces a common wine ; it is therefore gradually being driven out of the good vineyards and is grown in the plain. Nineteen out of twenty parts of the hill-district cultivate the " petite Sirrah," the rest is planted with white vines. The " petite Sirrah " has a fine elongated winged bunch, bearing slightly oval grapes, which are unequal, closely packed together, of a blackish-violet colour, much browned on the surface, juicy, very sweet and with a thin husk ; they ripen early. The grapes of the Roussanne are white, small, round, unequal, and very much browned under a thick bloom ; the bunch of the Marsanne is not so large as that of the Roussanne ; its berries are unequal and very closely set.   As the vines are kept very near to the ground, many of the bunches lie partially on the ground when nearly ripe, and become covered with earth.   This entails a special operation in August called "unearthing the grapes."   The vintage ordinarily takes place towards the end of September, but in early years it is made before the equinox, as heavy rains are not rarely experienced at that time.   A hectare brings about 24 hectolitres of wine ; a vineyard of this surface may be bought, if it produce first growth, for 60,000 francs, second for 48,000 francs, third for 36,000 francs.   The cultivation costs about 900 francs per annum. To make a barrique of so-called straw wine, *i.e.*, sweet liqueur wine, 760 kilogrammes of grapes are required, which without drying would have yielded three barriques of wine. The black grapes remain long, sometimes as long as forty days in the vats and are stirred frequently.   This seems required by the large amount of sugar contained in the must, of which the last portions are only slowly transformed into the strongly alcoholic liquid.   The wine can be bottled after having been in the barrel during four or five years. The best red Ermitage is sold at about 400 francs the barrique of 210 litres.   Red Ermitage of the best quality goes to Bordeaux, to be mixed with the colder growths of the Gironde ; anything sold in trade as Ermitage is always second class, if it be Ermitage at all.   When genuine it is distinguished by great richness, a lively purple colour, and a special bouquet, and becomes by these united qualities the best wine of the south of France.

There are a number of smaller vineyards resembling by their products Ermitage ; these are called of Crozes, Lamage, Mercurol (La Rochegude), La Rolière, Die, Condrieu and Côte-rôtie.   The wines are mainly red, and ripe for bottle in five or six years.   The piece of Ampuis, measuring 240 litres, is sold at about 200 francs.   The wines are fiery and heady, but have great finesse and much bouquet.

When the wine is made from the Vionnier grape mainly, it is lighter and more delicate, and does not lose its colour by age, but when made principally from the Terine, the wine is more harsh, and of darker colour; in bottle it forms a strong crust, loses its purple colour, and becomes of the light red colour of onion peel.   In ancient times much of the produce of the Rhône valley was exported to Rome, now it is dispersed over the world, mainly in admixture to less alcoholic wines.

§ 95. Vineyards of the Beaujolais, Mâconnais, and the Chalon Côte.

The districts which contain these vineyards are situated in the upper part of the valleys of thé French contributories of the Rhône, particularly the Saône.   The vineyards are agglomerated, partly on slopes running towards the Saône, partly on rich flat land.   The traveller by rail or road enters suddenly upon a viticultural district, continues in it, perceiving right and left nothing but vines, and after having travelled some miles he suddenly leaves it, when all viticulture ends and nothing but ordinary agriculture is perceptible.

§ 96. The Beaujolais.

The Beaujolais is an arrondissement with Villefranche as principal town, and extends from the confines of the Mâconnais to the district of Lyons.   It is divided by a chain of hills into the *high* and *low* Beaujolais.   The high Beaujolais consists of the cantons of Beaujeu and Belleville, where the best vineyards are met with.   The low Beaujolais produces a greater quantity of wine, but of a less distinguished quality.   There are now in this district 20,000 hectares of vineyards, stretching over a length of 35 kilometres and a breadth of 6 kilometres.   In the soil red quartzy porphyry predominates; in other parts a schistose formation comes out, and there are many mixtures of Plutonic and Neptunic formations.   In the lower part chalk, with alluvial soil, crops

L

up. Most of the vineyards, like those of Burgundy, slope towards the east.

§ 97. Vines, Vintage, and Classification of the Wines of the Beaujolais.

Two vines prevail in the Beaujolais, the *Petit Gamay* and *Gamay Nicolas*. Their bunches are elongated, conical and winged, and bear loose-hanging, unequal grapes of middle size, ovoid shape, black colour, bloomy surface, with thin skin, liquid juice and particularly sweet taste. Many vineyards are cultivated by tenant farmers, who occupy from 4 to 5 hectares, reside on the land, and pay as rent half the produce of wine. The hectare in the Haut-Beaujolais yields on an average 20 pieces of wine of 210 litres each; in the Bas-Beaujolais much larger quantities. The vintage takes place in the end of September, and vinification is performed in the manner usual in Burgundy.

The better wines of the Beaujolais may be arranged under three categories :—First, the fine, early maturing and little coloured wines of Chénas, Fleury, Lancié, St. Etienne-la-Varennes ; secondly, the fine, strong, deep-coloured and long-lasting wines of which Julliénas is the representative ; and, thirdly, the semi-fine wines which are esteemed but do not reach the quality of the former. The wines in this district are more delicate than the wines of the south of France. They taste juicy, and frequently are very sour. It is for this reason that they are esteemed in France, where it is usual to mix water with the ordinary wine drunk at table. The wines are not treated with plaster of Paris. The common wines fetch from 80 to 140 francs, the better ones from 130 to 400 francs the piece of 210 litres. The special examination of the *crus* can be seen in Thudichum and Dupré's "Treatise," *l. c.*, p. 418.

§ 98. The Mâconnais. General Division of District and Soil.

The district is situated round the town of Mâcon, also in the valley of the Saône, and may be divided into five belts.

of which four yield exclusively red wines, while the fifth gives exclusively white wines. The first belt includes the Thorins and the Romanèche, which yield the finest class of Mâconnais wine; the second belt is represented by the vineyard of St. Amour; the third by that of Davayé; the fourth belt includes the whole district north of Mâcon and the canton of Lugny. The wines of the latter are inferior to those of other districts, and remain common, but are abundant. While young they are rough, and become drinkable only after years of keeping. To the north of this district is the vineyard of Tournus, which produces much flat and dark-coloured wine; but this district no longer belongs to the Mâconnais. The fifth zone is represented by the vineyard of Pouilly, which gives the typical white wines of the Mâconnais. The good vineyards are mostly situated upon slopes, the soil is granitic and schistose, frequently chalky. White wines are mostly grown on chalky soil. The vines on the rich alluvial soil in the valley of the Saône produce only rough common wines, which go to supply the town of Lyons.

§ 99. PREDOMINATING VINES.

Formerly the black Burgundy grape called Pineau predominated, under the name of Bourguignon, but this has almost disappeared and given way to the Gamay, which is here termed *bon plant* and *plant de la dombe*. There are three varieties of this Gamay, the Gamay Picard, Gamais Nicolas, and the Petit Gamais. These vines have nothing in common with that particular vine called the Gros Gamay, the planting and cultivating of which was forbidden by a law passed by Philip le Hardi and the parliaments of Metz and Dijon. The *bon plants* of the Mâconnais bear much fruit, and this produces good wines, but they are never equal to the Pineau. In the vineyards for white wines the Chardenet, or white Pineau, the prevalent white grape of the Bourgogne and Champagne, predominates.

§ 100. MODE OF CULTIVATION, VINTAGE AND TREATMENT OF RED WINES.

The vines are kept near the ground, with low stems and short spurs for growing wood. The vintage begins at the end of September and is completed by the middle of October. The grapes are vatted, and allowed to ferment during thirty-six hours ; in the lower parts during five days. The wines, when in barrel, are treated like those of the Bourgogne and Gironde. They are fined with white of egg, and bottled in the fourth or fifth year. They are ripe for drinking six months after bottling, and are mostly sold in Paris, Lyons, and Geneva, provided they are cheap. The better Mâcon wines are sometimes carried into Burgundy to be sold as wines of that country. They are very alcoholic, and very acid at the same time, and if not mixed with water are not an agreeable drink, but excite the heart. It is possible that owing to the great acidity the alcohol remains unperceived in the drinking, and incommodes the consumer afterwards.

§ 101. WHITE GRAPE-VINES, AND CHARACTER OF THEIR WINE.

The typical processes of viticulture and vinification, so far as white wine is concerned, can be studied at Pouilly and Fuissé. The white vines are trained with long bearing canes, having ten eyes each. At the vintage, towards the end of September, the grapes are all deposited in *baignoires* and after slight mashing are pressed ; the must is run into barrels, and fermentation proceeds. All the white wines of the Mâconnais district go to the town of Mâcon, and are thence transported to Paris. The Pouilly wine is dry, but too heady ; it is not so transparent as the Chablis, but has a more golden colour, preferred by many consumers. At the end of four years, of which two are spent in bottle, the vinosity and bouquet of the wine are fully developed. The Fuissé is inferior to Pouilly in *finesse* and generosity ; it is therefore mostly "put under," *i.e.*, mixed with Pouilly.

Chaintré is a pleasing sort of small wine, and of good taste, but inferior to Pouilly. A hectare of the best Pouilly vineyard yields about 18 hectolitres of wine, each of which, at the vat, is worth 50 francs. The wines of Fuissé and Solutré are rarely worth more than 40 francs.

§ 102. CÔTE OF CHALON-SUR-SAÔNE.

The vineyards of the arrondissement of Chalon-sur-Saône are situated along the Côte of Chalon, and produce mainly ordinary wines, more rarely wines analogous to the half-fine wines and great ordinaries of the Côte d'Or, which are sold under the name of the latter. The vineyards are divided into three zones. The lowest is the plain; the next is the half côte; and the third, or upper côte, called côteau. The plain yields only common wines; the half côte wines of ordinary second quality; while the best wines are obtained on the incline which commences north of Chalon, runs through Sivry, and then subsides in the Mâconnais. The soil is chalk mixed with clay, silica and ferric oxide; much of it is alluvial. The best growths of the côte are protected by hills from the north wind, and the sun shines on them from its rising to its setting. The vines which here predominate are the Pineau, the Beurot or grey Pineau, in Germany called Ruländer; the Gamay, and the Giboudot, which is also called Malain, or "plant of Abraham." In this district also the desire of viticulturists for the production of quantity is increasing daily, and, in consequence, the black Burgundy grape is being diminished in number, while the more plenteous bearer the Gamay, is being substituted for it. The grapes of the latter ripen rather late, and as those of the Beurot ripen early, the mixture is harvested before the Gamay is quite ripe. The "plant of Abraham" has only one virtue, its enormous fertility. It has large bunches with loose-hanging berries; these have thick skins, so that with the ordinary mode of vatting they remain sometimes entire. The wine obtained from them is violet red, harsh and sour, and can be drunk only after it has been several years in barrel. The white Gamay yields a flat white wine

The wines of the Chalonnais are sold in pieces of 228 litres, and mostly go to Paris. The wine of Mercurey has for many years had a great reputation. The merchants of Beaune bought this wine in order to mix it with Volnay, to which it was very similar, and of which it increased the small quantity produced, but with the gradual diminution of its quality Mercurey wine lost even this value. A share in this decay is due to the general want of intelligence and care on the part of the vignerons. It is stated that the renting of vineyards at the rent of half the produce does not answer well in the Chalonnais.

Chapter XV.

WINES OF BURGUNDY.

§ 103. General Observation on the Wines of Burgundy.

Burgundy is probably the oldest viticultural country in central Europe, and the art of wine-making migrated thence to many parts of France and Germany. In the Middle Ages Burgundy was the standard wine on the table of great people. When the reputation of Burgundy wine had been established, many proprietors without that district desired to obtain the vine from which this beautiful beverage was produced; and the value of the plant may be estimated from the fact recorded in history, that reigning princes of Burgundy made presents of such vines to other princes whom they befriended. Then the Burgundy vine migrated across the Rhine, up the Maine, into Saxony, Bohemia, and Moravia, and with it the mode of cultivation which we see in Burgundy. The place which Burgundy wine formerly occupied in society is now taken by Champagne, and in those parts, for example, of Germany where formerly much Burgundy was drunk, now hardly any is met with. But the Netherlands and Belgium preserve much of this ancient predilection for Burgundy, and in these countries the best wine of this kind is to be met with.

§ 104. VITICULTURAL DISTRICTS OF BURGUNDY.

That part of Burgundy which produces the best wines of its kind has been called the Côte d'Or, or "golden hillside." This is formed by a series of hills, about thirty-six miles in length, which stretch from Chalon on the Saône to Dijon, their cultivated inclination and exposure being towards the east. They are from 200 to 300 feet high, and consist of a loose chalk mixed with little clay. Towards the east of these hills there expands an enormous fertile plain right to the Jura mountains, which in fine weather can be seen, with the Mont Blanc behind them. Along these thirty miles of declivity an uninterrupted series of vineyards have been planted. They begin on the upper third of the hills, never ascending to the brow, and then stretch down the inclination into the plain, and frequently extend for a mile or two in the plain itself. The good vineyards are all situated about the lower third of the inclines. The property in the good situations is very much divided, so that a vineyard of five hectares is very rarely met with. An exception to this is the *Clos de Vougeot*, which has about fifty hectares of vineyard and is surrounded by a wall. The vineyard of the Clos appears to the eye to be almost level. The *Clos Romanée Conti* has only about two and a half hectares, the *Chambertin* four to five hectares.

As these celebrated vineyards, and all others approaching them in quality of product, are very flat, it may be said that a vineyard which has an inclination of above ten degrees in the Bourgogne does not belong to the first class. Along the higher regions of the hills many deserted vineyards with old terraces may be discovered. They demonstrate that the vine does not succeed above a certain height along the incline. In the Champagne also the black Burgundy grape does not rise up to the crest of the hill, but at the upper third is replaced by the white Burgundy. Thus nature limited the production of Burgundy on two sides ; on the side of the mountain by spring frosts, and on the side of the plain by want of quality of the produce.

§ 105. Varieties of Vines planted in Burgundy.

The vineyards of Burgundy are populated by a mixture of vines termed by the vignerons *Passe-tous-grains*. The black-graped vine peculiar to, perhaps indigenous of Burgundy, the Pineau or Noirien, is the dominating variety along the Côte ; but in the ordinary situations, and in small vineyards, white and red grapes are found among the black. The Pineau is also the dominating grape in the Champagne. But by the side of it there is another variety, the Gamay, the dominant grape of the Mâconnais and Beaujolais. This latter grape gives a wine of much inferior quality, but the vine bears much more abundantly, for which reason it is preferred by those vignerons who get paid for quantity only. The must of the Noirien is much sweeter than that of the Gamay, showing one-eighth more sugar than the latter. The vines themselves are not easily distinguished from each other by external appearance, but more easily by their fruit, that of the Gamay being larger in the berries and frequently showing some unripe ones ; while the Noirien is always of equal ripeness in all its berries. The Gamay is the same vine with that planted at Bolle in Switzerland, and there called *La Dole ;* a great amount of effervescent wine is manufactured from it at Vévais on the Lake of Geneva. Another variety of vine which frequently occurs in Burgundy is one bearing light red, almost grey grapes, called Beurot, known in Germany as Ruländer. Of white grape-vines there is the Chardenay or White Burgundy, which is grown in the Champagne in the higher-lying vineyards, but also mixed with the other vines, and prevails in the northern part of Burgundy, yielding among others the celebrated wine of Chablis.

§ 106. MODE OF CULTIVATION.

New plantations follow the ordinary general rules ; young plants do not bear before the fifth or sixth year ; they are dressed upon two spurs, kept low on the ground, and supported by stakes. Single vines are replaced by sinkers. Rejuvenescence by sinking all the vines, as is frequently practised in the Champagne, a process which gives to many

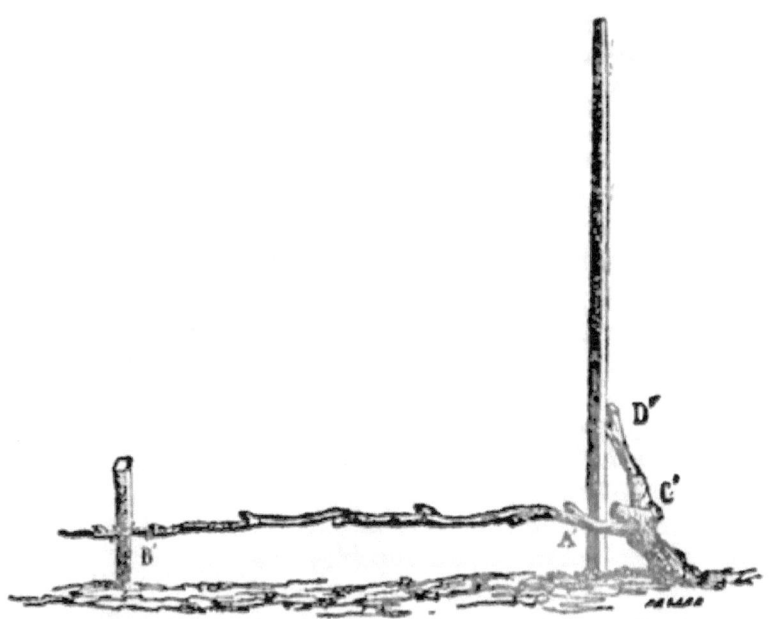

Fig. 32.—Burgundy Vine as it ought to be dressed, according to Guyot. *A′ B′* the bearing or fruit cane. *C′ D′* the space for growing next year's fruit cane.

vineyards of this district the aspect of great youthfulness, is not effected with regularity or extensively. Along the côtes of Beaune we have observed many vineyards with vines at least twenty years old, and having their bearing systems a foot and a half above the ground, a condition preventing excellence in the product ; moreover, the yearly branches are then so high that the stakes cannot carry them any more. Such vines would therefore be advantageously treated by the sinking process usual in the Champagne. Each plant shoots three new canes, which are allowed to grow until the middle of summer.   They are then tied together at the top, and when the grapes begin to colour the tops are cut off, excepting those of all canes which it is intended to sink, these are allowed to grow to their full length.

As the reproduction of the vine is practised very irregularly, the vineyards of Burgundy do not present that remarkably cultivated, orderly, and youthful appearance of the vineyards of the Champagne.   On the contrary, the peculiar sight is one of great inequality, very young vines being mixed with very old ones, and very low ones with very high ones.   The soil, moreover, is stony, and is not so well attended to as elsewhere ; many stones are brought to the surface by the sinking of ditches for the laying of canes ; these sinkers affect about one-fifteenth of all the vines every year, so that a vineyard is rejuvenesced gradually once every fifteen years.

The vineyards are manured as well as possible ; all the labour is done by hand, and there is no ploughing.   The vineyards are divided into *ouvrées*, or areas, which give a day's work to a man ; such an *ouvrée* has 3,645 square feet. The sinking, up to twenty vines per *ouvrée*, is included in the contract ; a higher number of sinkers has to be paid for beyond the wages.   In many parts of Burgundy the old arrangement prevails by which the labourer does all the work in the vineyard, and receives half the harvest as his payment.   Such a vigneron generally has from three to four hectares under his charge ; he is aided by his family.   He carries all the earth and manure, finds the poles or stakes, performs the vintage, presses the wine, and, in short, does every operation until the wine is in barrel.   In parts where the wines are very good and high in price the viticulturist has yet to bear the half of the State taxes and of the communal imposts.   The proprietor, however, allows him some collateral advantages, in the shape of plots of land for the keeping of animals, and free lodging.   This peculiar practice of dividing estates into *vintageries* or *vigneronnages*, has been carried into Saxony, particularly into the neighbourhood of Dresden, where the whole wine-producing district is cultivated upon the pattern of Burgundy.

Grafting.—In Burgundy also much grafting is practised, the slip, sinker, or sunken cane being grafted with its end into a groove made in the stem which has to be renewed or lowered. The labour of this process is no doubt great, but as grapes can be obtained from grafts sometimes in the first, mostly in the second year, the expense of the labour is sometimes at least partly repaid.

§ 107. VINTAGE.

The period of the vintage in Burgundy fluctuates between the latter end of September and first half of October. Early vintages are supposed to prognosticate a better wine, for of course they result from a favourable summer season. In some communes there is yet the *vintage ban*, a regulation intended to protect the grape-harvest by keeping everybody out of the vineyard from the time the grapes begin to ripen until the time of the vintage. Even the proprietors are not allowed to enter their own vineyards except perhaps once a week, during an interval which is announced by the village bells. When the grapes are ripe a commission is appointed, consisting generally of the mayor, a proprietor, a practical vigneron, and one merchant. This commission, while visiting the vineyard, forms an opinion whether or not the grapes ought to be collected. When they have fixed the time they announce it to the mayor, or the prefect, and it is published by the town-crier or by other means. This peculiar law does, of course, not affect enclosed properties. The Gironde abolished it effectually during the revolution. Burgundy did the same, but the law was re-enacted under the restoration. In the Rhenish provinces of Germany this law was also abolished, at least remained only in a harmless modified form, as a faculty never practised; but in Wurtemberg and some of the wine-producing districts east of the Rhine it has been retained, and exercises an impeding influence on the progress of viticulture; for the vineyard owner whose grapes, owing to situation or variety of vine, ripen early, has to let them hang until the late ripening grapes in the district have attained a tolerable maturity ; and when he comes to his vineyard he finds his crop either eaten by flies and other vermin, or rotten, or overripe, and in any case it yields him a lesser quantity or quality of wine. He who has late ripening grapes, cannot let them hang to ripen, because, from the moment that the vintage is over, he loses the protection of the public custody of the fields.

When the grapes are collected, they are put into a large vat, called *ballonge*, fixed on a waggon ; in this they are trodden down by a man as fast and firmly as possible. When the vat is full the carter dismounts, rubs his feet on the nearest bundle of grass, puts on his boots, drives the cart home, and sees the grapes put into the large vats. The carter then returns with his *ballonge*, until the whole of the harvest is at home. In this manner the great bulk of the Burgundy grapes are carried home ; but we have also seen instances of better treatment, in which the grapes were cut, cleaned, their stalks were removed, and the murk was fermented by itself. Here, as in the Champagne, many of the grapes are sold while hanging on the vines, and the proprietors collect them according to the prescription of the purchasers. Many wine-merchants buy the whole harvest of a vineyard and collect the grapes themselves. Frequently the grapes are bought by others after they have been collected by the proprietors, and during the vintage an active trade in grapes is carried on along all the roadsides in viticultural Burgundy ; there are the baskets full of grapes, and anyone who likes can come and buy. The grapes are measured by *feuillettes*, being barrels of 114 litres capacity, being *half a piece*, or a *quarter queue ;* the half queue or entire piece in Burgundy therefore contains 228 litres. The feuillettes used for measuring the grapes are provided with two iron handles. The grapes are filled in without pressure, and when the vessel is brimful the grapes are heaped on the top as high as possible. Ten feuillettes full of grapes generally give one queue, or two pieces of must ; or 1,140 litres of grapes give 456 litres of must ; or $2\frac{1}{2}$ bulks of grapes give one bulk of must ; until the wine be made this proportion is again changed, and nearly three volumes of grapes are requisite to furnish one volume of finished wine, having passed the spring racking.

§ 108. VATTING AND FERMENTATION.

The grapes are transferred from the ballonges to the vats or *cuves* by a coarse process in which a kind of hook, called a *grappe*, is employed. The ripest berries are broken, but many of the harder ones remain entire and have to be broken by the press. The vats are generally higher than they are broad, and narrower at the top than at the base. This shape has practical advantages on account of the facility with which the hoops can be kept tight. Their height is between five and six feet; they are not provided with any opening at the bottom or side for letting off the wine, but throughout Burgundy the wine is drawn from the vats by syphons. The cuves are therefore raised only one foot from the ground, instead of three or four feet as in the Gironde. Every proprietor endeavours to fill a cuve in one day. Some vignerons moisten the inside of the vat with brandy, to take away what they call the taste of the wood; but as they do not afterwards remove the brandy with the woody taste from the cuve, the process results in an addition of spirit to the wine. The cuve is filled to within a foot from the top. A narrow basket of the height of the cuve is fixed to the inner side, and serves as a well, or space free from the murk of the grapes, from which the wine is drawn by the syphon after fermentation. In many parts of Burgundy the addition of sugar to the must is very common. We have witnessed this addition, which in some cases amounted to twenty pounds to the piece. This increase of the eventual alcoholicity preserves the Burgundy better from secondary fermentations, to which it is so liable. A quick fermentation, completed in about six days, is desirable for Burgundy to effect a complete extraction of the colour and perfect decomposition of the sugar.

While the fermentation proceeds the murk rises to the top and forms the hat or *chapeau*. This being penetrated with or supported by gas, rises above the level of the liquor.

As long as the chapeau continues to rise or remain stationary, the fermentation must be allowed to proceed. In case the weather becomes cold, and impedes fermentation, it is necessary to warm the fermenting room, by means of stoves, up to 80 or 90° F. When the chapeau begins to sink it is necessary to draw the wine in order to prevent the upper or somewhat spoiled and acetified part from coming into contact with the wine and imparting to it a disagreeable taste. Another criterion of the proper moment for drawing the wine is the specific gravity of the liquor. This is ascertained by an areometer so constructed that its zero indicates the point at which the sugar has completely disappeared. The colour of the wine is also ascertained by means of a small vessel called a *tasse*, embossed with hollows, bumps and ridges, and highly polished, so that the light can be reflected through the wine in all directions. The wine is not often drawn before it is of a sufficiently deep colour. The extraction of the colour is completed by a process of distributing the chapeau in the wine repeatedly. This is done by men who in a state of nudity penetrate the chapeau, sink into the wine, and then mix the chapeau with the wine for half-an-hour or longer. The spoiled parts of the chapeau have been previously taken off. After the lapse of several hours the husks have again risen to the top, and, if not well decolorised, are mixed a second time with the wine by the men. The work is very severe upon the men, for, owing to the large quantities of carbonic acid evolved, they are mostly deadly pale or blue, and pant and hang their heads over the edges of the cuves, gasping for fresh air. We cannot approve this method of effecting the *foulage*, otherwise so necessary, any more than the dirty proceeding of treading the grapes observable in the Gironde or in Spain. Many more cautious proprietors avoid the spoiling of any portion of the chapeau, either by keeping it submerged by wicker-work loaded with weights, or by closing the vat with a wooden cover, luted by means of loam or clay ; the more rustic and poorer vignerons cover the vat with a layer of clay or loam, to which cow dung has been added to give it cohesion. No wonder, then, that much of the wine that is made in Burgundy has a strange, disagreeable taste, and does not keep ; that along the Côte there is made not only the best wine in the world, but also the worst ; that in not a single hotel or inn along the Côte a single bottle of Burgundian wine fit to be drunk by any traveller accustomed to fair wine is to be obtained, as we testify from personal experience ; what is set before the traveller is cheap *Vin du Midi*, and the growth of the vineyard within sight is as good as unknown. We cannot be astonished that Burgundy wine is subject to those many alterations called "diseases," such as bitterness, loss of colour, acetification, etc.

After the *foulage* the wine is drawn by means of a syphon fixed in the wicker-well already mentioned, and put into barrels or pieces of 228 litres each. The after-fermentation is completed in the cellar, and the wine is racked in February and ready for sale in March. Common wine may be drunk at the end of the first year. The good wines require four years in barrel and several years in bottle before they develop their full qualities ; but during that time they give to the proprietors and the wine-merchants a great amount of trouble, and require very attentive treatment.

When the wine is drawn the murk is put upon the press, and the wine thus obtained is added to the wine drawn by the syphon. The pressed murk is then sometimes used to make a second wine, or *piquette*, which is very much relished by the working vignerons. The presses commonly in use in Burgundy are the long-beam presses, which formerly prevailed everywhere, and are only gradually disappearing. The beams are of oak, from fifteen to thirty feet in length, and exercise their pressure upon a space of twelve feet square as maximum. The beam is weighted at its end by a box of stones, or a millstone, or even several millstones. The weights are made to exercise this influence by being raised by an enormous screw passing through the free end of the beam. In some parts presses like those in the Champagne are used. Of course, with the progress of time, the round or square screw presses take the place of these old constructions, which are difficult to manage and consume much time in their application.

The wines are mostly drawn into small casks, but on large properties, *e.g.*, the Clos Vougeot, the wine is laid in barrels containing from ten to thirty pieces, and is drawn into single pieces only after it has been sold. While the young wine is in the chais, the barrels are carefully kept full (*ouillé*). The fining of wines is effected by means of white of egg.

The wines of Burgundy are sold by the *piece* of 228 litres, the *feuillette* of 114 litres, the *quartant* of 57 litres, and the *bouteille* of 75 centilitres or three-quarters of a litre. In the case of great wines the price of the cask is always included in that of the wine. Quotations are mostly loco Beaune, the centre of the trade of the Côte d'Or.

An hectare of vineyard planted with Pineaus produces on an average annually fifteen hectolitres of wine, while the common varieties of vines produce from fifty to sixty hectolitres per hectare.

For further details concerning the statistics of viticulture in Burgundy, we refer the reader to the table of the " Comité d'Agriculture de l'Arrondissement de Beaune." This publication also contains a good map of the Côte.

Chapter XVI.

WINES OF THE CHAMPAGNE.

§ 109. Wines of the Champagne.

The Champagne is an ancient province of France, spread out under three degrees of latitude, the 47th to the 49th. At the division of France into departments it was cut up into four parts, which, united with other communes, were formed into the departments of the Ardennes, the Marne, the Upper Marne, and the Aube. The celebrated wine called Champagne is obtained only in the department of the Marne, which includes the prefectures of Châlons-sur-Marne, Epernay, Rheims, Saint-Ménéhould, and Vitry-sur-Marne. These prefectures contain 19,589 hectares of vineyards, which are situated on the territories of 453 communities, and belong to 27,018 proprietors. An average vintage produces about 700,000 hectolitres, of which more than a quarter is drunk by the inhabitants themselves. Good wine is produced only in the prefectures of Rheims and Epernay. The vineyards of the former are situated around the slopes of a wooded mountain, which is called the *Bois et montagne de Rheims*. No vines grow in the plain, and none grow above a certain height on the slopes of the mountain. About one-half of the vineyards lie on the north-eastern slope, and the other half on the southern slope of this little mountain. In the former are situated the celebrated growths of Bouzy, of Verzy, and of Verzenay, and if the tourist who visits the Champagne starts from Bouzy, and walks along the road northward and north-westward, he will gradually pass all these celebrated places one by one, and terminate his tour at Villers, a few miles south of Rheims. The growths situated on the southern slope include Ay, Haut Villers, and a number of others. These latter vineyards extend from the slope of the mountain to very near the border of the Marne, but the plain in which the Marne itself flows is destitute of vines. The *second district* lies south of the Marne, and its centre is Epernay. It is bordered on the west by the forest of Anguien, the smaller one of Brugny, and in the south by that of Vertus. It is one continuous, splendid vineyard, and besides the growths of Epernay, yields those of Cramant and Avize.

The soil of the Champagne is composed of chalk, sand, and clay in varying proportions. The vegetation does not show any particular signs of luxuriance ; the northern district, which slopes toward the north-east, would, on theoretical grounds, be supposed to be very unfavourable to the growth of the vine for wine, for throughout the world we find that the declivities of mountains sloping towards the meridian and exposed to the sun are those which produce the best wine, and that eastern and western exposures are less favourable, and northern declivities almost unproductive. The explanation is supposed to be this. · To the north and east of the Bouzy and Verzenay districts extends a great

M

plain, over which the sun exercises a free influence so as to warm the soil during the daytime to a very high temperature. Much of this land is barren and bears only a few wretched pines. It is termed the "lousy Champagne" (*Champagne pouilleuse*). Another part is cultivated, but no part of it is so covered by vegetation as to prevent the sun from striking the soil. During the whole of the summer months, from June to September, the prevailing current of the air over this plain is in the direction of the mountain of Rheims; the air thus passing abstracts heat from the soil, and thus, on reaching the vines, not only adds to the direct effect of the sun upon them, but is an auxiliary to their progress during the evening and throughout the entire night. This phenomenon seems fully sufficient to explain the magnificent development which the vines and grapes attain round the whole of that Côte.

§ 110. WINE-PRODUCING PART OF THE CHAMPAGNE.

The wine-producing part of the Champagne from its extreme north, namely Rheims, to the southernmost point, Vertus, has a diameter of about forty-five English miles. The centre of the whole district is Epernay, on the borders of the Marne. The slopes of Verzenay, Verzy, Saint Basle, Villers, Marcmary, and Bouzy are formed on a series of rounded promontories running out from the main mountain, the gentle valleys between which, down to the beginning of the plain, are all covered with vines. But the slopes of Mareuil, Ay, Dizy, and Haut Villers are more rapid. From the heights of Ay, one can see the extent of the whole Côte of the Marne in an easterly as well as westerly direction, and also perceive a great part of the vineyards south of Epernay.

The vineyards south of Epernay extend over an undulating plain southward to Vertus. From Pierry to Vertus the territory consists of an irregular accumulation of small chalk hills which slope towards the east. Epernay has 6,000 inhabitants, its only trade being in wine. Rheims has 40,000 inhabitants, and, besides a remarkable trade in wine, has a very important industry in spinning, weaving, and dyeing, particularly of woollen goods. To the east of the Champagne wine district, and almost out of it, lies Châlons-sur-Marne, which has 13,000 inhabitants, and an important trade in wine. This localization of the manufacture of Champagne at Châlons is due almost exclusively to the circumstance that the chalk hills running along both sides of the valley are composed of so favourable a material, that large cellars, which do not require any masonry to support them, can be easily excavated. In consequence, these chalk hills are pierced by cellars like honeycombs, and millions of bottles of Champagne are constantly stored in them and sent out of them to all parts of the world.

In coming from Rheims towards Sillery we observed a little plot of vineyards, said to be the celebrated Bruyères de Mailly, which used to form the pretext for the so-called Sillery wine. The Château of Sillery formerly belonged to the widow of Marshal d'Estrées, and as she possessed some of the finest vineyards in Verzy and Verzenay, and caused their products to be treated with particular attention in her cellars at Sillery, this name obtained a notoriety which its ten acres of vineyard actually situated there could never have obtained for it. The château afterwards went into the possession of Madame de Staël, and later into that of M. Ruinard de Brimont; some years ago it was owned by M. Jacqueson, of Châlons. Not very far from this little château is the estate of Romont, to which now a great part of the Bruyères and some of the vineyards at Verzenay belong, which yield the best so-called Sillery.

In one of our œnological peregrinations we started from Sillery and walked to Verzenay. The road crosses the great canal repeatedly, then goes along it, and, suddenly turning to the right, tends towards the mountain. From this road a most lovely view of Verzenay is enjoyed. It is a bright village, lying on the high part of the saddle formed by two promontories projecting from the main mountain. Behind it is the green forest of the mountain of Rheims. In front of it are open cultivated plains, and the tops of the two hills which mark its lateral limits are surmounted by two

enormous windmills, which impart to the beautiful view a
kind of animation. The soft verdure of the expanses of
vineyards is most pleasing to the eye. Passing through the
vineyards and the village we went across the heights towards
Verzy and Saint Basle, the character of the country remaining much the same ; but, as the promontories ran more towards the east, one of these declivities formed a good southern
exposure. The best among them were at Contures and
Minets. We everywhere perceived that the lower part of the
côtes bore the black Burgundy grape, while in the higher parts,
toward the forest, the white Burgundy grapes were mostly
grown, but in many parts of the vineyards which we visited
we saw a few white Burgundy among the black. Having
passed Verzy, we found an interruption in the continuity of
the vineyards of several miles in length ; continuing our
journey southward we came to Bouzy. This is celebrated
for its red wine, the so-called still red Champagne ; but
many of the grapes grown there are also used for making
white Champagne. The soil is chalky, ferruginous, and
contains many pebbles. A few miles south of Bouzy ends
the viticultural district of the côte of Rheims, and the
traveller passes ordinary fields towards the Marne to enter
upon the southern côte at Mareuil. In wandering through
the splendid situations of Mareuil, Ay, Dizy, and Haut Villers,
we saw an uninterrupted, undulating, splendidly green vineyard, wound like a mantle round the slopes of the Rheims
mountain. Below Haut Villers, which, as its name indicates,
is situated rather high, and nearly opposite Epernay, the
mountain projects more towards the Marne, corresponding
to a similar projection northwards of the mountain which
runs behind Epernay towards Pierry. By this arrangement
a wide kettle-like valley is formed in which Epernay appears
as the inhabited centre. Among the hills which form the
best situations from Mareuil to Haut Villers, the mountain
of Ay is distinguished by its form, inclination and exposure.
It has a height of about 200 feet and an inclination of about
20°, being exposed towards the south-south-west. Upon its
side lies the village of Ay, which in its environs has many
beautiful gardens and villas, giving signs of opulence and

well-being. Indeed Ay is the most lovely place in the whole Champagne. The côte runs uninterruptedly by Dizy towards Haut Villers, a length of six English miles. Here mostly black Burgundy grapes are grown. Most of the vineyards of Haut Villers lie below the village, so that, seen from a distance, this village seems to crown a mount of vines; its best situations are called *les quartières* and Hataut. From Haut Villers viticulture is continued along the right bank of the Marne to Chatillon.

Passing to the south of the Marne, and starting from Epernay to Pierry, we observed that the exposure of the vineyards became south-easterly. In the neighbourhood of Pierry the vegetation is much richer than in other parts of the Champagne. The grapes are larger and blacker, so that one is almost tempted to think they are another kind. In this part the variety called *Meunier*, or miller vine, is often blended with others. It is recognized by the white felt which covers the dark-green leaves, and particularly the tops of young shoots, and gives them an appearance of having been dusted with flour. The soil is very stony, a fact apparently incorporated in the name of the village. On passing over a considerable chalk hill, the traveller finds near Cramont, and more southerly, near Avize, a côte or series of hills having an easterly exposure, and being covered with vines. This côte runs from Cramont, Avize, Ojer, and Le Menil up to Vertus, where the vine cultivation terminates. In this part mostly white grapes are grown, and it is stated that the black grapes do not succeed so well. Avize has from 700 to 800 acres of vineyard, amongst them one with a southern exposure, called *Goutte d'Or*. This name is very common in France and indicates everywhere a place where a good wine is grown.

As the basis of the geological formation of the Champagne is chalk with pebbles, the fructiferous covering of cultivated ground could only have been formed by the superaddition of alluvial masses, and these we find, singularly enough, upon the high points of the mountains. Much clay has been washed down from them by the agency of rain, and enormous quantities of it are annually carried on the backs

of donkeys or mules, or in waggons and baskets, into the
vineyards.   One particular kind of clay is termed *cendrière*
(ash soil). We observed this black material in the neighbourhood of Verzy and Verzenay, where a trade was apparently
being carried on in it, there being depositories at frequent
intervals along the road, and establishments where it was
mixed with manure and other matters, and formed into a
kind of compost. We ascertained that it contained gypsum,
iron oxide, clay and sand.

§ 111. Cultivation of the Vine in Champagne.

The management of the Champagne vineyard differs in
some important particulars from that which prevails in other
districts.   The established wines are every three years sunk
into the ground, and one year's wood alone is allowed to
project from the ground and to form the new vines.   Every
vineyard, almost, thus becomes a continuous nursery for the
formation of young vines.   It is to this circumstance, that
no vine which appears above ground has older wood than
three years, that the whole of the vineyards of the Champagne
owe their juvenile aspect.   In the Médoc one sees vines
perhaps 150 years old, in the districts of St. Emilion and
Sauternes one sees vines which are seventy or eighty years
old, but in the Champagne district all that appears above
ground is only one, two, or three years old.   The method of
the Champagne viticulture might therefore be called viticulture by constant rejuvenescence.   The vines are pruned
so as to leave to each plant two or three branches, with
from two to four eyes each.   The soil is worked by manual
labour with the hoe, never ploughed, and manured as much
as possible.   The cultivation of an acre of vineyard costs
from 160 to 240 francs per annum.

§ 112. Value of the Vineyards.

Throughout the Champagne the prices of vineyards are
very high, because of the great subdivision of the soil, which
allows as many as 27,000 proprietors to participate in the

benefit of its cultivation by manual labour. At Verzy an acre of vineyard sells at from 4,000 to 10,000 francs; at Ay for 6,000 francs; at Epernay, Pierry and Haut Villers the acre frequently sells at from 12,000 to 16,000 francs; at Avize the average price is 4,000 francs, that of the better situations rises up to 8,000 francs.

§ 113. Varieties of Vines grown in the Champagne.

The prevailing vine in the Champagne is the one called *Plant doré*, black-graped, identical with the black-graped vine of Burgundy, there called Noirien or Pineau. The Pineau is sometimes distinguished from the Noirien and called *Gros Plant doré*. The bunches of the Pineau are less cramped or closely set, while those of the Noirien are more dense and rounded off; but the difference in other properties is so small as to appear irrelevant. The true *Plant doré* ripens its grapes equally, while the Noirien, here at least, always shows a few green berries among the black ones. The Pineau is the most fructiferous and gives on large bunches strong grapes. We have not been able to ascertain whether these popularly admitted varieties are true varieties or not. We have seen the *Plant doré* at Pierry with such thick, glistening and black berries that it seemed almost a different vine from the one at Verzy, and yet it was the same. Indeed the black Burgundy grape changes its non-essential properties according to situation, soil or climate, and its development into Pineau, or *Plant doré* is the effect of accidental circumstances.

Next to these black-graped vines, which yield the best white Champagne, there is grown in the neighbourhood of Epernay the *Meunier*, or miller. This gives a wine of inferior quality, but bears more than the Plant doré. The *white Champagne grape*, called *gros blanc* and *petit blanc*, and also the *white of good nature*, is identical with the white Burgundy grape, the *Chardenay* from which, among others, the wine of Chablis is made. About one-third of the whole of the vines in the Champagne are of this white kind. It dominates in the upper part of the Champagne, near Avize, Vertus, and Cramant; in the lower part of the Champagne, from Ay to Rheims, the heights are planted with this vine. The majority of the old vineyards are yet planted half with white and half with black grapes, a mixture which was formerly supposed to be the most suitable to produce great *mousse* in the wine. At the present time the Champagne makers prefer to keep the varieties separate, and to mix the young wine from white grapes with that from black grapes only in spring, after the nature of their separate fermentation is known. The white vines are more hardy, and less liable to suffer from spring frosts and other calamities. When we visited the Champagne in 1867 we found that the Pineaus had suffered greatly at various periods of the year, and yielded the most indifferent harvests, while the white Burgundy or Champagne vines, which stood mixed with the Pineaus which had suffered, were full of healthy, large and tolerably sweet grapes. Thus, to the cultivator of vineyards, the white Champagne grape is a kind of assurance in bad years; the Pineau failing, the Chardenay will at least give him his house-drink.

Here and there a little *Gamais*, the dominant vine of the Mâconnais, is met with, but it gives a sour wine unsuitable for the production of Champagne. Another white grape which occurs here and there is the *Marmot vert*, identical with the *Elbling* of the Moselle and the *Goix d'Orleans*. A variety is moreover met with which the Germans call Ruländer, and which is in effect a black Burgundy which has become half white, and hence is called "smoked." Of the German varieties, the Riessling, Traminer, Sylvaner, and Austrians, not a single plant can be discovered throughout the Champagne.

On the whole, then, the character of the effervescent Champagne vines is derived mainly from the black Burgundy grape—the small and large varieties—with which in good years is mixed a certain quantity of white Chardenay; the still Champagnes are made, the red varieties from the black Pineau only; the white varieties (for example, the excellent white Verzenay) from the white Chardenay only.

§ 114. Vintage in the Champagne.

Of the 700,000 hectolitres of wine produced annually in the department of the Marne, a quantity which would amount to eighty millions of bottles, only about 180,000 hectolitres, or twenty-two millions of bottles, are transformed into effervescent wine. That is, a little more than one-fourth of the whole quantity produced. The rest is

Fig. 33.—Gathering of the grapes in Champagne.

transformed to a small extent into white, but for the most part into red wine. The production of red wine is much like that usual in Burgundy, and therefore does not require here a description, but the production of white wine offers peculiarities which we must follow.

There is no vintage-ban in the Champagne. The proprietors either take off the grapes themselves, press them, and sell the wine in December or January, or they sell the grapes as they are on the vines, which is called "selling the

harvest." This is done either according to an estimate of
the quantity per acre, or the grapes are measured after
having been cut, and the agreed sum is paid for the grapes
delivered. In bad years from six to seven hectolitres of
grapes may be necessary to produce a hectolitre of wine,
while ordinarily five or four and a half would be sufficient
to produce that quantity. The vintage attracts great numbers of labourers of both sexes, and proprietors of mules,
donkeys, horses, carts, etc., to the district. It is preferred
to cut the grapes early in the morning, even though they
should be yet a little wet from dew, because it is necessary
to press them while they are cool, to prevent the incipient
fermentation from extracting any colouring matter from the
husk, for, although made from black grapes, Champagne is
nowadays the more valuable the more colourless it is. The
cut grapes are carefully cleaned, and carried in baskets or
panniers to the press-house. The animation of a harvest
day in the Champagne can hardly be imagined. Throughout all the green undulating vineyards hundreds and thousands of people are dispersed ; all the roads are lined with the
cleaners, and the heaps of grapes on trays and in panniers.
Everywhere donkeys stand to wait for new loads, or go in
long strings along the narrow paths of the driving roads.
So peculiar is this scene to the Champagne, that in our
many œnological peregrinations we have never observed
anything like it in any other of the wine-growing countries
which we have visited. The donkey is a symbol of the
vintage in the Champagne, as the great oxen are the symbol
of its culture in the Médoc. Nowhere else have we seen
grapes intended for wine carried home in baskets. The
grapes of the Médoc, for example, would lose half their
juice if they were so carried, as they become crushed by
their own pressure, or fall off the stalks by slight shaking.
On the occasions of our visits to the Champagne in harvest-
time we were much struck with the good-nature and hospi-
tality of the population. Many persons carrying home their
produce would speak to us, or answer our greeting, and
invite us to taste their grapes—an offer which had not always
the object of effecting a sale. The value of a hectolitre of

grapes in bad years is 5 francs, in middling years 10 francs, and in very good years it rises to from 12 to 15 francs.

§ 115. Pressing, Fermentation, Cellaring, and Fining of the Wine.

The presses in the Champagne are complicated and powerful machines. The nuts of the iron screws, of which

Fig. 34.—The wine press of the small proprietor.

there are two to each press, of the size of a strong man's leg, are worked by means of a toothed wheel, which is itself turned by a large upright wheel to which four or five men can apply their strength. This great power of the pressing apparatus is necessary because the grapes do not go through any process of crushing before being placed into the press;

the entire grapes as they are emptied from the panniers are thrown on the press, and the press is the only agent that extracts the wine. The first must which runs from the press is the best, and goes by the name of "the first drop." In middling years this must is kept separate for the production of the best quality of wine. The cake of murk is repeatedly trimmed, the sides are cut off and thrown upon the middle, and pressure is re-applied. The fourth drawing is generally a harsh must, with much stalk-juice, and can only in good years, when the stalks are very dry and yield no juice, be mixed with the first three drawings. Forty basketfuls of grapes are generally put upon the press at one and the same time, and yield ten pieces of wine. The entire process of pressing one quantity has to be finished in two hours; if that time be exceeded the must becomes coloured. The must obtained by the first three pressings (called *serres*) is put into a large vat standing by the side of the press; each such vat takes on an average not less than ten pieces. In these vats, called *cuves*, the must is allowed to stand at rest for from six to eighteen hours, to throw up a froth to the top, and deposit a mucous matter at the bottom. From both these impurities the must is separated and drawn into small barrels of two hectolitres capacity and left to ferment. This clearing of the must is also frequently effected by filtration, particularly in hot weather. If the season be warm this clearing must be favoured by sulphuring the must to delay fermentation. The purified must is then allowed to ferment in the *chais*, or cellar, and to lie quiet until the weather has become cold, about the middle of December. The wine, then mostly clear, is now drawn from the lees. As the wine has now, to a certain extent, declared its quality, purchases can be made with more safety than at harvest-time, but of a less speculative kind, and at higher prices; thus commerce becomes enlivened at that period. It is now that the Champagne-making houses carry to their own establishments the wine bespoke in autumn, or newly bought by their agents, particularly that which they stand in need of for mixing with the qualities which they may have themselves produced. This mixing is one of the most important operations in the production of Champagne. Every manufacturer is, of course, obliged to produce the varieties which the public demand, and the object of all the Champagne houses is to produce, by the art of mixing, wines which shall satisfy the particular demands, or represent particular qualities under particular names of localities. When these necessary ingredients have been brought together they are mixed by vatting, and drawn off into barrels for further treatment.

The wine is next fined by the introduction of isinglass. This is pounded small, soaked and swelled up in wine, kneaded with the hands, and driven through a sieve to disintegrate all solid particles, and then mixed with sufficient wine to produce a semi-fluid paste. It is then allowed to stand for twenty-four hours, when it has again formed a set jelly. The adding of wine and the kneading with hands is then continued daily, until the isinglass does not swell any more, or as it is technically expressed, "ceases to grow." The fining material is now ready; it is passed through a tammy once more, and the necessary quantity of it is then put into each barrel and mixed with the wine by strong agitation. The wine generally becomes clear in from twelve to fourteen hours. One hundred pieces, or little barrels, require a pound of isinglass, provided the wine was pretty clear when it was put into the barrels; but in case the wine was thick, each barrel requires a quarter of an ounce of isinglass, which is about double the quantity previously mentioned. Throughout the Champagne these operations of fining are effected in the small barrels. The reason for this is the facility with which the wine is kept cold in them, so as to prevent every chance of even the slightest degree of fermentation being set up. All these operations are carried on in a shed above ground, which is called a cellar or *cellier*, and corresponds to the *chais* of the Médoc. After the application of the finings, and their thorough incorporation, the wine is left at rest for a week or a fortnight, and if clear, is racked; if not clear it is left for another fortnight, and if not clear then, is racked from the lees, and fined a second time. During these finings and rackings much sulphur vapour is used for

the purpose of keeping the wine quiet, and making it as
pale as possible.

§ 116. Drawing into Bottles, or Tirage.

The bottles intended to receive the wine for manufacture
are tested by experienced persons, who strike two bottles
together with their sides; all badly annealed bottles break
at once; the bottles which are too thin, or which show
blisters or galls, are rejected.   The bottles which are not of
good shape are sold to the country people at a reduced
price, and it is partly owing to this fact that all the wines
which one gets throughout the Champagne in the small
public-houses, or sees among vignerons, is contained in such
faulty Champagne bottles.   The bottles are washed with
water, rinsed with spirit, and closed with a cork, and are
ready for use.   On each bottle the State levies a tax of
threepence.   The 100 bottles cost, at the manufacturers,
twenty-eight francs; of these ten per cent. break or are
rejected at the testing.

The wine is now so arranged by mixing with sweeter wines,
or with sugar, that it shall contain two per cent. of fermentable sugar.   In this state it is drawn into bottles; these
are now corked.   The corks are compressed by a special
powerful machine, and forced into the neck of the bottle
with a wooden mallet; they are then tied down with string
and wire.

The full bottles are carried into the fermenting vaults,
or *caves*, as true cellars are called, and put up in piles of four
or five feet in height and any convenient length and breadth;
the latter mostly four bottles deep.   They are held together
with thin wooden laths; single bottles can be removed at
any time.   The wine in the bottles begins gradually
to ferment; it becomes turbid, increases in bulk, and
shows the presence of gas when shaken.   Now some bottles
break, from the internal pressure, or leak.   When the breakage does not exceed eight per cent. it is cheaper to take no
measures to arrest; when it is higher the wine has to be
uncorked, or to be moved to a colder place; during this

operation the workmen wear masks and gloves, to prevent injury from bursting bottles. As winter cools the caves the wine becomes quiescent, and the breakage ceases.

§ 117. Clearing of the Bottles of Yeast, or Disgorging.

When the fermentation is complete the stacks of bottles are rummaged; all broken bottles are removed, all those which leak are put aside, and only those which have kept in good condition are re-stacked. They are then allowed to lie at rest until the whole of the yeast has settled on the lower side of the bottle. In that state the wine remains until it has to be prepared for sale. The preparations for clearing the wine consist in putting the bottles with their necks downwards on benches which are pierced with holes. A workman now gives the bottles a skilful turn, thereby effects the loosening of the deposit of yeast from the side of the bottle, and causes it to sink upon the cork. This has to be repeated until the whole of the deposit has been worked down and the wine is quite clear. The bottles are now what is called disgorged, that is to say, opened by a skilful extraction of the cork, and the yeast is removed; a little wine is lost as the cork is discharged with a loud report, and the froth, which immediately rises, carries with it all the impurities collected in the neck; the latter is moreover touched with the finger while the froth is rising, to detach the last traces of yeast. The bottle thus prepared passes into the hands of another operator.

§ 118. Liqueuring, Corking, and Finishing.

Champagne prepared in the manner above described is quite dry, that is to say contains no sugar whatever perceptible to the taste. But the operation of liqueuring is intended to impart to its taste some amelioration, whereby it may become more attractive, either by imparting to it some amount of sugar corresponding to the taste of the consumer, or to give to wine which has not had time to mature a certain finish and flavour, by mixing it with a small quantity of good old well-matured and fine-flavoured wine. For this purpose the Champagne makers provide themselves with the best wines they can get for the purpose of making these liqueurs, and in all these cases the liqueur consists of a mixture of cane-sugar and wine only. But the cheap kinds of Champagne, not admitting of the introduction of expensive wines, or requiring the addition of alcohol on account of the natural want of that ingredient, are only treated with a liqueur consisting of spirit of wine and sugar. Many of the so-called dry wines receive no sugar at all, but only brandy. The liqueurs have to be made stronger or weaker according to the nature of the wine, and to be added in larger or smaller quantities according to the taste of the consumer. For England strong-bodied wines are taken, and little liqueur is added, because in this country the dry and semi-dry qualities of Champagne are preferred. But there is also mild, sweet Champagne imported, such as also goes to Russia. In Austria and Germany Champagne is preferred with some sweetness in it. In France a nice medium of liqueur is commended. When the bottle has received its measured addition of the selected liqueur it is filled up with wine already liqueured, and handed to the corker. The cork is forced in, and is tied down with string and wire, and the operation of disgorging is complete. The bottles are washed externally, inspected one by one as to their clearness, and, if passed, covered with the usual tin- or bronze-foil. The desired label is attached, and the bottles are placed in boxes, or baskets, and exported.

Most Champagne makers keep their wine in an unfinished condition as long as possible, as wine which has been so lying is not apt to form a second deposit after disgorging. It sometimes happens, however, that the wine which has been disgorged and liqueured undergoes a second slight fermentation, and thereby becomes turbid again. It has then of course to be disgorged a second time, after the yeast has been collected on the cork as before. If the wine has become turbid without any fermentation, as it may from the development of microscopic fungi, the second disgorging involves the loss of much *mousse*, the wine ceases to be *Grand Mousseux*, and becomes simply *Mousseux*, or even only *Crêmant*.

§ 119. QUALITIES OF CHAMPAGNE AND QUANTITIES PRODUCED.

The wines produced in the Champagne are of four qualities. Of these the *first* is *Champagne non-mousseux* (*Still Champagne*). This is wine which has been fully fermented, fined, drawn into bottles, stoppered in the usual manner of the *Mousseux* wines, tied, and allowed to rest a long time. This is the original method of making bottled wine in the Champagne, and out of it arose the discovery of the *Mousseux*. Of such *non-mousseux*, many, if properly matured, have striking peculiarities of taste and flavour. The *second variety* is that moderately sparkling wine called *Crêmant*, which derives its name from its faculty of forming a slight cream of effervescent bubbles upon its surface when it is poured into a glass. The *third variety* is *Mousseux*. This wine, on the bottle being opened, projects the cork with an audible report, and begins to rise gently over the margin of the bottle. The *fourth variety* is *Grand Mousseux*, which projects the cork with a loud report, and immediately overflows from the bottle. When only a small quantity is poured out, the foam which it produces also rises over the edge of the glass. Champagne which contains less than four atmospheres of carbonic acid gas is not any longer saleable as *Mousseux* or *Grand Mousseux*. *Mousseux* must have from four to four and a half atmospheres; four and a half to five atmospheres constitute *Grand Mousseux*. Above five atmospheres of gas cause the wine to be lost by frothing, and six to eight atmospheres burst most of the bottles. There are distinctions made between ordinary wines, fine wines, and cabinet wines; between pale wines, reddish wines, the so-called *œuil de perdrix*, and those rather uncommon varieties which are sometimes made as articles of curiosity.

The prices of Champagne begin at 16s. the dozen bottles at the place of manufacture; some varieties are sold in

London in bond at 17s. a dozen.   Much is bought at 22s. and can be sold in London at 28s. per dozen.   The price of a good class of wine rises to 40s.; best sorts to 65s. and 70s.   Anything beyond is fancy price, for which special grounds must exist.

Champagne must be kept a few months after having been disgorged and liqueured, in order that the wine and liqueur may be perfectly amalgamated, and the new flavour become a little developed; after a year it has reached its perfection, and does not improve, but deteriorates after two or three years.   It becomes a little etheric, but it loses *mousse*, and becomes *crêmant*, and the danger of the stoppers leaking increases with the time during which the pressure has been exercised upon them.

Latterly, sound, rather dry effervescent wines from various parts of France have made competition to Champagne; they are like the prototype, useful dietetic drinks for persons of means or patients suffering from impaired digestion. The glasses from which to drink Champagne should be conical, seven inches high, and provided with a heavy base or foot, so that they cannot be easily upset.   In these glasses the sparkling is best observed, in which much of the attractiveness of Champagne rests.

§ 120. Historical Note on the Discovery of Champagne.

The Champagne has produced red and white wine ever since the time of the Roman Emperor Probus, A.D. 280, to whom, it is said, the Gate of Mars, still extant at Rheims, was dedicated by his troops.   It appears from the historical notes contained in the work of M. Perrier, that there was at the Abbey of Haut Villers a monk of the name of Dom Pérignon, who managed the cellars of the Abbey from the year 1670 to that of 1715.   One of his successors in the administration, Grossard, states that Pérignon was the inventor of effervescent wine.   Grossard had in his possession the documents of the Abbey up to the time of the French Revolution, and he asserts that before Pérignon, the art of stoppering bottles with corks was not known; the only stoppers which were used being bundles of hemp dipped in oil, as seen nowadays in some parts of Italy. It appears from a little book of the year 1718, which has been examined by M. Perrier, that white effervescent wine was in course of being made twenty years previously, which would put the first record of the making of such wine to the year 1698; it was then called *pétillant*, "stopper-jumper," or "cork-jumper," and "devil's wine." The new wine became popular, but the art of making it was kept secret, and all sorts of fables were current about it. The writer maintains that he possessed the true secret of the manufacture, and that it had been given to him by the dying Dom Pérignon. It was, therefore, probably first made at Haut Villers. The introduction of corks for stoppering bottles of young wine would lead to the formation and discovery of effervescent wine, and the rest would be done by art and study.

The production of Champagne has much increased during the century; in 1835 about 5,000,000 bottles were exported from France; of these America took 500,000; England 700,000; Russia 500,000; Germany 500,000; Sweden and Denmark 200,000; Italy 100,000; and 600,000 were used in France itself. In 1866, the export had risen to 22,000,000 bottles, and at present exceeds 30,000,000.

§ 121. PRODUCTION AND VARIATION OF THE MOUSSE.

One hundred volumes of wine containing 10 volumes per cent. of alcohol, and 90 per cent. of water at 12° C., at the ordinary pressure will absorb 132·969 volumes of carbonic acid gas. The excess of carbonic acid gas, which makes the wine *mousseux* can therefore exist in it only under pressure.

The fined Champagne wine, ready for bottling, called *Claret* hardly ever contains more than a half per cent. of sugar. This would be insufficient for producing a good *mousse*, and therefore sugar has to be added; its temperature also must be raised to let the fermentation begin. The Champagne maker carefully adjusts the amount of acidity in his claret; if it be intended for sweet wine it may reach seven per mille, while ordinary dry wine bears only four to five per mille. He then examines the amount of sugar contained in his claret, and adds as much to the quantity found as will raise the whole to three per cent. of the weight of the wine ; this percentage after complete fermentation would yield a *mousse* of five and a half atmospheres, which after disgorging, would fall to five. If the wine has been too much fined, and air has not been sufficiently in contact with it, it is liable to lose its power of passing into fermentation. To obviate this mishap some makers carefully ventilate the wine, and add a minute quantity of wine-yeast, not exceeding a teaspoonful to the hogshead, to the sugared claret, in order to make sure that a few spores may be present in every bottle.

The report on opening a bottle of Champagne is produced by the gas which is compressed in the air space. If this space be large the report will be full and deep ; if the space be small the report is high pitched, dry and short. A good report is only produced by a cork which fits equally all round, and does not allow gas to escape on one side before it is ejected entire. If the cork be unilaterally weak, or stand obliquely, it allows the gas to escape with a hissing noise on opening and no report is produced. This is so objectionable that manufacturers spare no expense to obtain the best corks. Champagne, after having been opened, and relieved of its pressure, is somewhat viscid, and disengages the carbonic acid slowly in the form called *sparkling*, in French *pétillement*. During the whole of this time the wine is over-saturated with gas, as is shown by many phenomena. Thus the gas bubbles rise mainly from projections and uneven portions of the surface of the glass. Almost invisible particles of dust give cause to the prolonged rise of strings of little pearls of gas. Any porous body, such as bread, or sponge cake, produces immediately a lively effervescence. When the glass is held tightly in one hand, and the palm of the other is struck gently on the top of it, bubbles are evolved on the entire inner surface of the glass. The glass being depressed suddenly, while the fluid is unable to follow as suddenly, a slight attenuation is produced in the fluid next to the glass, whereby the gas is liberated.

The disgorged Champagne has lost all traces of ferment, and possesses little tendency to ferment again ; the addition of brandy and sugar diminish the liability to ferment still further. Most Champagne, therefore, after proper treatment remains clear and at rest ; the bottles should be kept lying on their sides, so that the cork remains moist and swelled and does not allow any gas to escape.

The cane-sugar, sugar-candy, which is added in the liqueur to the sweet varieties of Champagne after disgorgement, is after a short time found to be entirely transformed into invert sugar.

Champagne after being poured into a glass contains carbonic acid to the extent only of its own volume, no matter what may have been the amount of gas in the bottle. It is therefore probably an error to endeavour to give to this wine a conventional *mousse* of six atmospheres. With such a pressure the cork certainly rises high up in the air with a loud report, the wine rises from the bottle and from the glasses into which it is poured, and is in part lost by overflowing ; but when it is drank, the wine does not contain more carbonic acid than it would if the wine in the bottle had contained only two and a half to three atmospheres. The more the wine is agitated by rapid development of overcharged gas the quicker it becomes flat. The artificial aerated waters show a similar bearing ; they become flat much sooner than the natural ones, which, though less charged, are less agitated.

CHAPTER XVII.

WINES OF THE VALLEYS OF THE LOIRE AND CHARENTE.

§ 122. WINES AND VINES OF THE VALLEY OF THE LOIRE.
IN the neighbourhood of Orleans there are considerable plantations of vines which extend through an extensive

plain towards Blois, and then towards Angoulême and Poitiers, and further towards the Charente into the district of Cognac.

The most common vine is the "miller," or *Meunier*, recognized by its white dusted leaves; it bears bluish-black grapes on middle-sized bunches, and is very fertile. Some vineyards are exclusively planted with the "dyer vine," the *Teinturier*. The grapes of this vine yield a dark red juice on pressing, and this juice becomes still darker by fermentation with the husks; they contain therefore two different kinds of colouring matter, one *soluble* in the acid, half-sweet liquid juice; and another *insoluble* in the juice, but extracted from the husk by the alcohol developed during fermentation with the aid of the acid contained in the juice. The wine made from the dyer grape is of itself very sour, but is very well suited for colouring white wines, one part being sufficient to impart a red colour to seven or eight parts of wine. Owing to the large quantity of astringent matter present in the *Teinturier* juice, the white wines treated with it obtain the character of original red wines, and are sold as such at Paris mainly, being unsuitable for transport to greater distance, or across the sea. The dyer grape, on account of its thick black colour is also called *Gros Noir*, in some places *Auvernat tint*, and at Cahors, in the department des Lot, it is called *Auxerrois*. Next to the "miller" and "dyer," the most commonly grown grape on the Loire is one called *Auvernat noir*, which on examination turns out to be the black Burgundy grape.

§ 123. MODE OF CULTIVATION.

The cultivation of the vines on the Loire is carried on by a number of methods; the most rational is that according to which the bearing canes form arches tied to a stake; the vines are sometimes planted in groups of four, and the new canes are united in the middle. From Blois towards Tours a low ridge of mountains stretches for about forty-five miles along the former wide bed of the Loire. The whole incline of this ridge towards the Loire is covered with vines; but all are lying on the ground, with not a single stake to support them, covering the earth in such a manner that neither a path nor a separation of property can be distinguished. From a distance the whole looks like a light green meadow; there is no interruption of its remarkable continuity. The canes are always rejuvenesced by sinking, as in the Champagne. The Germans call such a plantation a *hedge-vineyard*.

In some parts of the valley of the Loire men live in excavations in the rocks; in others there are luxurious villas, and splendid gardens with cypress, pomegranate, fig, orange and citron trees.

§ 124. WINES AND BRANDIES OF THE CHARENTE.

This viticultural district comprises a nearly circular expanse of country on both sides of the river Charente; its eastern border is marked by the town of Angoulême, its western by that of Saintes; it comprises portions of two departments, the department of the Charente proper, and the department of the lower Charente; its very centre is marked by the town of Cognac. In many parts of this land, the entire hill-country, as far as the eye can reach, is seen to be covered with vines; from Angoulême to Cognac, a distance of about fifteen miles, stretches an almost continuous vineyard. This area produces a wine which is not valuable as such, but only as the material for distilling from it the spirit or brandy named Cognac.

§ 125. VARIETIES OF VINES PRODUCING THE EAU-DE-VIE OF COGNAC.

Cognac brandy is produced from vines bearing white grapes, namely the *Folle-blanche*, the *Boillot*, and the *Blanc doux*, *Colombar*, *Sauvignon*, and *St. Pierre*. None of the latter varieties, however, gives so sweet and well-flavoured a spirit as the *Folle-blanche*. Its wine, nevertheless, although full of alcohol, is not agreeable. The spirit of red grape wine, which is sometimes made, does not possess

the soft and agreeable properties which are peculiar to that
obtained from the white. Here vines were formerly
allowed to attain the height of dwarf trees, to admit of
some herbaceous growth underneath them, but the practice
is very rare now.

§ 126. MODE OF PRODUCING THE EAU-DE-VIE OF COGNAC.

As the best brandy is obtained from the youngest wine,
distillation begins almost immediately after the fermentation is completed, and is carried on during the whole winter-
time. Almost every other proprietor of vineyards possesses
a still. Those vignerons who do not possess a still, sell their
wine to the large distillers, or have it distilled by any of the
migrating distillers, who go about from village to village,
and extract the spirit from any one's wine. In spring the
distillation is mostly effected and over. The spirit obtained
is for the most part, at first, colourless, and of the strength
called "four degrees of Tessa," equal to from 59 to 60
volumes per cent. of absolute alcohol. As regards this time-
honoured instrument, the alcoholometer of Tessa, it is
known and used mainly, some say exclusively, in the Cognac
district. Each of its degrees above four is said to be equal
to 3 volumes per cent. of alcohol, so that "five of Tessa"
would be about 63 per cent. by volume, and so forth.
Calculating the value of the lower degrees at that rate, the
zero of Tessa would be about 47 to 48 per cent. by volume
of absolute alcohol. We may surmise it to coincide with
the strength of *eau-de-vie* as formerly generally sold in
commerce, namely 49·1 per cent. by volume. The freshly
distilled Cognac brandy has a disagreeable, burning, rough
taste, without any flavour, and is, in fact, undrinkable. It
is kept in barriques of 200 litres for periods differing
between a year and four years. During that time it amelio-
rates, becomes sweet and tasty, and extracts from the wood
the light amber colour which it retains thereafter.

The quantity of brandy produced on the banks of the
Charente every year amounts to 180,000 hectolitres, being
the produce of the distillation of 1,400,000 hectolitres of

wine, which, together with 300,000 hectolitres of wine drunk in the country and sold as wine, make the 1,700,000 hectolitres of wine which grow on the 112,648 hectares of vineyards in this department. In good years six to seven bottles of wine yield one bottle of standard Cognac *eau-de-vie ;* in bad years eight to ten bottles are required to yield the same result. The value of wine, as such, in this part of France is perhaps the smallest that occurs anywhere, no more than from 8 to 10 francs per 200 litres being paid for white, and 18 to 20 francs for red wine. Yet wine continues to be produced, probably because climate and soil do not admit of the cultivation of other crops. The cultivable land rests everywhere upon a limestone, which covers the soil with fragments in the same manner as in Burgundy ; cultivation is by the hoe. The vines are pruned once in spring, and beyond that no operation is effected either upon the soil or upon the vine ; the rest is left to nature and the sun. Rakes are neither required, nor used. The vines sometimes have such strong stems and tree-like branches that children can mount them.

A part of the district bears the name of the *Champagne,* and hence the *eau-de-vie* produced here is called *Champagne brandy,* a term which has given rise to the erroneous conception that the brandy was made from the *mousseux* wine of the Champagne proper. All *eau-de-vie* of the Cognac district is ranged in five classes ; the best is called *fine Champagne brandy,* the second is termed *little Champagne brandy.* These terms are all supposed to be derived from the fact that vines were planted on clearings of forest, and the space cleared was called *a champagne,* or cultivated field. When at the beginning of the present century further clearings were made, new names had to be made for them, and they were called *bois,* or *borderies* (the latter is also the ancient name for common wines grown in the district) ; they were classified as *très bon bois, bon bois ordinaires,* and *troisième bon bois.* Thus Cognac brandy is classified in *five great categories,* derived from the assumed places of their growth. Some writers limit the classes of Cognac to four.

The Charente seems to have overcome the depression

caused by the ravages of the phylloxera, for it is reported that about a hundred new firms trading in brandy have been established at Cognac since 1875.

Those readers who would desire to read or consult a general classification of the wines of France are referred to Thudichum and Dupré, "Treatise," etc., *l.c.*, pp. 495-524, where will be found at least the name and situation of every wine-producing community. On pp. 493, 494 is a list of the names of the vines cultivated in the different parts of France, arranged according to climatic districts.

CHAPTER XVIII.

WINES OF THE UPPER RHINE AND MAINE VALLEY.

Wines of Alsatia; of the Palatinate or Rhenish Bavaria; of Rhenish Hesse; of Franconia, or the Upper Maine; of Baden, Würtemberg, and Hesse North of the Maine.

§ 127. WINES OF ALSATIA.

THESE wines bear the Rhenish character, and are quite distinct from the French wines; they are mostly white, and made from Riessling, Traminer, Burger, or Elbling and Grosser Räuschling. There is also Sylvaner and Ruländer or Grey Pineau. Peculiar to the district is the *Knipperle, Petit Mielleux,* which fills the vineyards of Thann, Rick-weiher and Ribweiler. The cultivation is peculiar: the vines are trained to form elements; each element at the pruning receives a long fruit cane, which is bent in an arch downwards and fixed to the stake. By this arrangement most of the grapes are situated too high above the ground, and ripen with difficulty. But the vineyards in the best situations are cultivated like those of the Rheingau. The vineyards of Zahnacker and Trotacker at Rickweiher are celebrated by the researches which Boussingault carried on in them, and from which we have taken many data contained in our general part. Some parts of Alsatia are said to be free from spring frosts, but all are exposed to the early autumnal rains, which destroy a great part of the harvest, particularly in Sylvaner. The wines produced are

Fig. 35.—Cultivation of the Vine. Rhenish Basket.

consumed in the district and in the adjoining parts of Switzerland. They were formerly added to Rhenish products of the lower districts, but now the reverse obtains. The Strassburg hotel-keepers and wine-dealers were very French as regards the labels on their bottles, but the contents of the bottles were all genuine Alsatian products; this we know from personal study and experience. Now this is somewhat altered, and the German market has raised their wines in the estimation of the Alsatians themselves. Most of the Alsatian wines are white and dry, those of good quality ranking in the second class; good old bouquetted wine can be obtained now and then in country inns; most popular wines belong to the third class, and yet are by no means cheap. The so-called liqueur or straw wines are more curiosities than articles of commerce, and scarcely leave the hands of their makers.

The wines of lower Alsatia, particularly those of the historical environs of Weissenburg and Wörth, have to be considered with those of the Palatinate, as the vines and viticulture are nearly identical.

§ 128. WINES OF THE PALATINATE, OR RHENISH BAVARIA.

The viticultural districts of the Palatinate are situated at the foot of the Haardt mountain, which is the continuation towards the north of the Vosges, and forms the western limit of the Rhine valley in Rhenish Bavaria. The mountain, which consists mainly of sandstone, rises rather rapidly to a height of from 600 to 800 feet, and is intersected by many valleys, which are mostly directed rectangularly upon the Rhine. The land at the foot of this mountain is, in general, from 50 to 100 feet higher than the level of the Rhine valley, and forms, therefore, a kind of plateau, inter-mediate between the Rhine valley and the Haardt moun-tain. The slope is distributed over a distance of about four or five English miles, and is therefore little perceptible in any one locality. Near Landau and Deidesheim the district is more hilly. The valleys which run from west to east produce many exposures, but on the whole the aspect of the vineyards is towards the east. The land upon which the vineyards are situated is chiefly of alluvial origin, drift from earlier ages of the Rhine, lacustrine shores, and washings from the mountain by water and ice-carried drift. Here and there basaltic formations are seen; the red sandstone of the higher mountain reposes upon clay schist and granite. At some places the grey old chalk becomes visible, as at Deidesheim and Neustadt, and influences viticulture favourably. Marl and sand are found over the whole district, giving to the soil the peculiar faculty of producing large crops. The whole of this alluvial formation, from the mountain to the plain, is covered with vines, and only rarely are a few small meadows to be seen in the troughs of the smaller valleys. From many eminences, *e.g.*, a mount near Burrweiler, the wine-fields can be seen extending over an area more than thirty miles long and seven miles wide. They produce one-seventh part of all the wine of South Germany, namely 70,000 fuder. The wine of the Palatinate is reputed for its medium good quality, the purity and freshness of its taste, and the extreme relative lowness of its price. The quality of the wine is partly the effect of the regular air-currents, which during the day pass from west to east, and during the night from east to west; this air has been warmed in the plain of the Rhine, and helps to bring the grapes to better maturity.

§ 129. Mode of Cultivating the Vine.

The mode of cultivating the vine is here altogether peculiar; it is called *double-chamber cultivation (Zwei-Kammerbau)*, and extends from Landau to Maikammer. At Hambach and Dittesfeldt the so-called *closed low-frame training* is usual. In all the villages east and south of the village of Haardt the *open low-frame training* is usual; this latter also prevails in the celebrated vineyards of Ruppertsberg and Deidesheim. The closed chamber-training or *Kammerbau*, is essentially the result of a particular *frame*, which is better understood by a drawing than a description. From twelve to fifteen vines are adapted to such a frame, and, when the leaves and branches are fully developed, form a low chamber, which is covered on all sides like an arbour or bower. This framing entails great expense for wood, and involves great agility on the part of the workers. It is partly owing to this cause that nothing is done to the vines throughout the growing season. They are allowed to spread and cover the whole of the chambers as best they may. In September only the viticulturists go out to cut

the superfluous branches, mainly for the purpose of producing fodder for their cows, which then begins to get
scarce in the meadows and in the fields. The branches
which cannot be consumed green are dried for the winter.
In the district of Weissenburg, and in Rhenish Bavaria, the
vine is, indeed, utilized as much to produce fodder as to
produce wine, and in some parts there prevails a practice of
planting mangold wurtzel underneath the chambers, whereby
the thicket is greatly increased, and the chances of the
ripening of the grapes are very much diminished.

The method of closed chambers is most developed in the
neighbourhood of Edenkoben, where the vineyards are
divided by many foot-paths and roads.

§ 130. PREVAILING VINES.

The vines which are most commonly planted in this
district are the Chasselas, called *Gutedel*, the Traminer,
the Austrian or Sylvaner, and the Riessling.   For some
decenniums the *Traminer* has gained a great preponderance,
and much good wine is now sold as being specifically made
from it.   Whatever may be the origin of the name of the
vine, it is certain that it cannot be traced to the little town
of Tramin in Tyrol, as the vine does not occur there.   It
occurs however in many localities under different names.
Count Odart and Guyot, the vitologist of the French
empire, term it *Gentil duret*, which we therefore accept as
the French name. The vine is medium-sized, its bunch
is small, generally dense, branched, pyramidal, multiple
and short.   The grapes are of nearly equal size, small, and
somewhat elongated, but the more ripe and juicy the more
round they become.   They are transparent, show veins of a
light red colour, whence the adjective (*Gentil*) *rose* used in
Alsatia, and a greyish-blue bloom.   The skin of the grapes
is thick and hard, and resists the autumn rains better
than do the thinner husks of the grapes of other vines.
The juice is of semi-viscid, mucous nature, very sweet and
agreeable, and with a peculiar taste, which is not musky, but
aromatic.   From this property the vine is also termed the

aromatic Traminer (*Gewürtz Traminer.*) It cannot bear spring frosts, as it does not shoot secondary eyes when the first shoots have been lost. It is trained with fruit canes, bent downwards; the leaves are shed early, and the harvest is sometimes taken off vines already entirely bared of leaves. The wine made from the grapes has great body, makes an impression of corporeality upon the taste, and is locally called *fat;* it is smooth, generally, with little acidity. In Tyrol, where it occurs, it is called *Francon*, and may have come from Franconia on the Maine.

The mixed sets of vines in the vineyards of the Palatinate offer several advantages to the viticulturist over single sets, and unitary plantations. The Chasselas ripens early, and almost every year, and although it does not give wine of lasting qualities, it yields tolerable substance without acidity. The Traminer gives wine of much body and smoothness, as already stated, but its lasting qualities during the first years are doubtful. The Sylvaner yields a very fine liquid tasting wine, without much particular flavour. The Riessling, in bad years gives much acidity, but in good years it imparts to the mixture of the other qualities a beautiful bouquet. This mixture of vines produces the best average of which the changes and vicissitudes of the seasons will admit. In the direction of Worms plantations of pure Traminer and pure Riessling are becoming more common.

There are in the Palatinate 33,048 morgen of vineyards; of these 12,576 belong to the first, 9,816 to the second, and 10,656 to the third class. It is estimated that a full harvest yields between 70,000 and 80,000 fuder of wine. As a fuder is about 1,000 litres, the maximum would be 800,000 hectolitres.

§ 131. WINES OF RHENISH HESSE.

The vines and wines of this province, the ancient archbishopric of Mayence, are very similar to those of the Palatinate on the one, and those of Rheingau on the other hand. The average annual production amounts to about one "Stück" (piece) of 1,200 litres per morgen; and as there are 27,842 morgen of vineyards, the total production of wine amounts to 334,104 hectolitres, being less than half the quantity produced in the Palatinate.   The vineyards of Worms include the one south of the Liebfrauenkirche, which produces the "Liebfraumilch," a Riessling wine of fine bouquet. The district of Oberingelheim produces much red wine of the character of Burgundies of the second and third class, from Burgundy grapes, and furnishes considerable quantities of these latter for the production of effervescent hock.   The district of Bingen is distinguished by the growths of Scharlachberg and Feuerberg.   The wines of Laubenheim, Bodenheim, Guntersblum, Nierstein and Selzen possess individual reputation, and are often substituted for wines of the Rheingau. Many wines of the other villages, particularly of the Kreis Oppenheim are sold under the title of Niersteiner, especially in England, where the name of this village enjoys marked favour.

The statistics of the area and production of the vineyards of Rhenish Hesse, according to districts and communities, can be seen in Thudichum and Dupré's "Treatise," *l.c.*, pp. 537-539.

§ 132. Wines of Franconia, or the Upper Maine.

The country anciently called Franconia, which is now comprehended under the name of the lower circle of the Maine of Bavaria, contains about 70,000 Bavarian tagmerke of vineyards, which is about the same surface as that cultivated in the whole of the kingdom of Würtemberg. Most of the wine grown there is consumed in the country, only a small quantity, grown in the proximity of Würtzburg, is exported. The slopes and heights surrounding Würtzburg are planted with vines in every direction, there being altogether 6,000 morgen of them visible from the town as centre. The best vineyard is the so-called Leiste, situated on the left side of the Maine, in a small side valley, between two hills, south of the former fortress.   Next in quality to this is the Stein, which is situated on the right bank of the Maine, close to the river.   To the north from the Stein is the so-called Middle Stein, and behind that the Harp and Schalks-berg; the vineyards continue eastward for some distance. The wines of these situations in good years have a particular strength.

The Leiste vineyard, 85 Würtzburg morgen, or nearly 17 hectares in extent, was protected from the north wind by the wall of the former fort; the grapes ripened a month or two months earlier than elsewhere. The vines, cultivated after the manner of Hochheim, are mostly Riessling and Traminer, also the so-called Franconia vine, or white Traminer, perhaps indigenous to this district. Odart, who had consulted and corresponded with Stoltz, the author of an ampelography of the Rhine, does not mention their supposed origin. Besides these a good deal of Elbling is grown. A peculiar grape is also grown here, the so-called Ermitage, of a yellowish-brown colour like the white Traminer, of fine flavour, the taste being between that of a ripe Riessling and a Muscatel, having neither the fine flavour of the Riessling nor the gross flavour of the Muscatel. A wine made from such grapes only might be something excellent. The greater part of the Leiste is a royal domain, and the wine made there goes into the cellars underneath the royal castle of Würtzburg.

The cellars of the castle are vaulted, and of splendid construction; on both sides of each vault there are casks holding from five to ten fuder, or 50 to 100 hectolitres. Many of these tuns date from the time when Würtzburg was the seat of a powerful bishop, who was also the ruler of Franconia under the Emperor. Many of the old casks are ornamented with apostles and other saints. The largest of them is so high that, in order to ascend to the top of it, it is necessary to make use of a ladder of twenty-four steps; this contains 660 eimer, and was built in 1784. Not far from this is another, called the "tun of the Swedes," because, it is said, the Swedes, when sacking Würtzburg in 1630, during the Thirty Years' War, left this tun unharmed. The number of tuns in all the cellars of the castle is 289; of these about ten per cent. are now supplied with wine. The Leiste wine of good quality is mostly carried to Munich and drunk at court: only a small quantity is sold to the trade.

The Stein, an abbreviation of Steinberg, or chalk-hill, slopes towards the Maine, and the vineyards reach the river-side. The best part of the Stein vineyard is the property of the town hospital, and yields the wine called "of the Holy Ghost." This can be bought only from the steward of the Bürger Hospital, and is sold by him in peculiarly shaped flasks called "Bocksbeutel," bottles with a wide belly compressed from the sides, and a short neck, containing thirty-two ounces of liquid. The vines prevailing in the vineyards are Riessling, Traminer, and Ruländer. The wine of many vineyards in the neighbourhood of the Stein is sold as genuine Stein, though of very inferior quality as compared to it. Much of the wine which is sold under the name of Stein wine in London is Palatinate wine, which at Mayence and other places is filled into bottles of the shape of the Bocksbeutel, and then sold as Stein.

The mode in which the vine was trained in Franconia is called "the head-knob system," an antiquated form, con-demned by experience. The best Rhenish methods are now almost generally introduced.

§ 133. Wines of Baden, Würtemberg, and Hesse, North of the Maine.

Würtemberg and Baden produce considerable quantities of wine, but as its quality is rarely above the fourth class none is exported. The area of the vineyards of Baden is 51,532 Baden morgen; the quantity of wine produced annually exceeds 500,000 ohm; its value is estimated to vary between seven and eleven millions of florins, or nearly a million sterling. Growths of reputation are the white Markgräfler, which is the product of thirteen village districts, and the Affenthaler, a light, agreeable red wine.

The government of the Grand Duchy of Baden have done more for viticulture and the science and art of wine making than any other authority on the continent. Only by the government of Napoleon III. was an attempt made, with the aid of the viticultural author, Guyot, to effect for France what had been initiated by Baden. The scientific referee and reporter to the Baden government was J. P. Bronner, an accomplished apothecary and vineyard proprietor at Wiesloch, near Heidelberg. He was commissioned to undertake scientific journeys into many viticultural districts, and report the results of his inquiries and inspections. Thus he reported on the Champagne, and the art of producing its effervescent wines ; on the Bourgogne, and the art of producing red wines; on the Gironde, its treasures and methods ; he travelled to French Switzerland, to Italy, the Tyrol, Austria, Styria, Hungary, and in detail examined the Rhenish vineyards, and studied the wild vines of the Rhine Valley in an exquisitely scientific, and, withal, almost poetical manner. He embodied his reports in small treatises, which were published at intervals during the years from 1830 to 1845. His works on the red wines, including a history of the black Burgundy grape, which is interesting as a chapter of the history of culture in general, were published in 1855 and 1856. Altogether his works are contained in some fifteen different publications, which are now very scarce and difficult to obtain. It was Bronner who mainly stimulated the adoption of improvement in viticulture, and to his description of the art of making effervescent wine is due the great development of this manufacture on the banks of the Rhine. He had enthusiastic support on the part of Dr. Batt, of Weinheim, and of the Director of the Botanical Garden at Heidelberg, Metzger, who himself published a work on viticulture, and formed a collection of vines in the garden under his direction. There was also the Baron von Babo, who, stimulated by Dr. Batt, the tutor of his sons, went in for viticulture, and wrote several encyclopædic treatises. A son of this Baron became teacher of viticulture at the Austrian Agricultural College at Kloster Neuburg.

The area of the vineyards of Würtemberg is 54,600 morgen, of which more than half are situated in the valley of the Neckar. The average money value of the annual product is only three and a half millions of florins. Much of the wine has a pale red colour, and hence is termed " Schiller."

Hesse north of the Maine, produces wine in the valley of the Kintzig, from Hanau to Gelnhausen, the ancient castle of the Emperor Rothbart, named after his daughter Gela. To the north of this is Büdingen, which has a favourably situated vineyard called the Pfaffenwald. Here, in a beautiful garden and vineyard, the author early acquired that love for viticulture and its resultant or adjuvant sciences which has remained with him throughout his life.

CHAPTER XIX.

WINES OF THE RHEINGAU, OF THE LOWER MAINE, AND OF THE MOSELLE.

§ 134. WINES OF THE RHEINGAU. HISTORICAL NOTE.

THE vine was cultivated in the Rheingau as early as the sixth and seventh century, therefore long before the time at which Charlemagne is related to have caused vines to be planted at Rüdesheim. Great extension was given to viticulture by mediæval monasteries, Johannisberg (1106), Eberbach, Steinberg (1131), and Gräfenberg. The corporations were swept away by the Reformation, and the wars consequent upon the French Revolution of 1789, and the properties, having been for some time in the hands of bishops, passed into those of Prince Metternich and the Duke of Nassau. During last century a great extension of viticulture ensued by the fact that many persons of property invested in vineyards and planted new ones.

§ 135. TOPOGRAPHICAL AND GEOLOGICAL NOTE.

The *Rheingau* is enclosed between the Taunus mountain on the north, and the river Rhine on the south; it forms a bay in the mountain, twice as long as broad, and filled with undulating hillocks. It is protected from sweeping northerly winds, and from south-west winds; the climate is most favourable to the production of the peculiar viticultural products.   The basis of the soil is the Rhenish slate, or clay-schist, the renowned *grauwacke*, which has been re-named Devonian slate, as it occurs massively in Devonshire; in some parts it contains much free quartz; at Rothenberg, near Geisenheim, much iron oxide.   The hills in the wider part of the Gau are alluvial, with loam, marl, clay, and gravel, the whole of the Rhine valley from Bâle to Bingen having been a great lake before the river excavated its present bed through the slate mountains from Bingen to Coblentz.

§ 136. Varieties of Vines cultivated in the Rheingau.

The characteristic and most frequently cultivated vine of the Rheingau is the *Riessling*.   It is durable, yields wood every year, ripens in time before the winter frosts, is little liable to be affected by the winter frosts, and is not easily nipped by the May frosts, as it grows tardily in the spring. It is a short-wooded vine.   It is also common in Rhenish Hesse and in the Palatinate, but in the latter the Traminer and Ruländer have much supplanted it.   It is, however, spreading in various parts of the world, even in Australia; only in France and Italy it seems quite unknown.

The Riessling is not only peculiar to the Rhine valley, but probably indigenous to it.   Being a small vine, its fruit is developed near the soil, and receives its radiation of heat at night; its bunch is not large, its grapes are also of a small size, with little juice and much acid, with hardy skins capable of withstanding much inclemency of the seasons, and with great ability to ripen late in the year while hanging on the vine, almost to the beginning of winter frosts.   When the grapes are very ripe they assume a rose-red hue. During the last ripening the stalks become dry and shrivel, ripe berries and some bunches drop off the vine, like other ripe fruit.   Of other vines, a small number of the Albe, or Elbling, are cultivated.   At Assmannshausen the black Burgundy vine, or Pineau, is grown massively, and gives the red wine for which the place is known.   In many vineyards white grapes are mixed with the black ones. Of these the *Klein-berger* is a variety of the Elbling, with small berries among larger grapes, whence its name *Kleinbeeriger*, contracted in speaking as just spelled. The small-berried large-bunched Velteliner in also grown here and there amongst mixed sets.

The Rheingau is densely populated, but lacks an agricultural substratum of fodder production, and this engenders a one-sided reliance upon viticulture, which in bad years produces great want. Good years, on the other hand, make up for the losses of many years. On the whole, however, the statistics of the Rheingau show that no proprietor can on an average make more than three per cent. per annum on his capital, and for the realization of this interest even he must be in a position to bide his time for selling.

The most important vineyards of the Rheingau are the following: *Ellfeld* or *Eltville*, the largest village in the Gau, is situated on alluvial loam, gravel, and clay ; the vines are disposed in groups of four, an antiquated arrangement called *stöck*, now on the decline. The vineyard faces the river. In *Rauenthal*, vineyards are situated on the side of a long hill, which appears to be placed across the opening of a large mountain valley ; it was a forest up till 1626, when it was transformed into a vineyard. Each rood of land was then charged by the lord of the manor with an annual impost of one pint of wine, which tax has remained the same during the centuries up to the present, and some years ago amounted for the whole Berg to eight pieces and four ohms of wine. On the west of the Rauenthaler Berg is an ultimate eminence of white quartzy sandstone, where there was formerly a chapel. From this point a view of the Rhine valley and the Gau can be obtained, which rivals in magnificence that from the Niederwald, or from Rüdesheim. The vineyards of Kiedrich include the Gräfenberg, formerly the property of the monastery of Eberbach, now held by private parties.

§ 137. THE STEINBERG.

The *Steinberg*, the most famous vineyard of Germany, also belonged formerly to Kloster Eberbach ; it became a

Nassovian domain, and since 1866 is public property of Prussia. The Steinberg is a hill about three miles distant from the Rhine; its vineyard is a long oval of about eighty morgen surface, entirely enclosed with a thick wall, twelve feet high, and protected from the weather by a roof of timber and slate. On the eastern side toward the convent the wall is pierced by a number of doors, through which the produce is carried to the Kloster. The vineyard is provided with carriage ways, so that all parts of the plantation can be reached by horse and cart; it is drained by drains of masonry, sunk below the sphere of the roots of the vines. The whole is ornamented by two pavilions. At the foot of the vineyard is a farm, which is kept for the sole object of producing the manure necessary for the vineyard; to this farm are attached 200 morgen of meadow land, and 400 morgen of arable land; the tithe contributories delivered, moreover, 12,000 trusses of straw, which, since the commutation, have to be bought. One hundred and sixteen head of cattle are kept, besides the draught animals, and the entire amount of manure thus produced, namely, a thousand so-called double-carts full, each being equal to a load for two horses, or twenty-four cubic feet, is annually carried into the vineyard. Each morgen of vineyard receives every three years forty such double-carts full, each double-cart being distributed to sixty-four vines. The farm carts enter the vineyard by gates leading into the enclosure of the farm.

It will thus be seen that the Steinberg wine is virtually the product of 680 morgen of land, and not of the 80 morgen of vineyard only. The vineyard itself is divided into parts, which produce different qualities of wine; the best grows in the part called "the golden beaker"; the second quality in "the garden of roses"; the third, newest part, bears the name of "plänzer." The work of dressing the vines is performed by specially appointed vine-dressers, called "Weinbergs Hofleute," who work by contract, according to a special code of instructions, which is an accurate and intelligible short guide to viticulture adapted to the Rheingau. The vintage is always very late, mostly in October, when the grapes are over-ripe. They are

trodden by men wearing special boots, standing in a pail
with a perforated bottom.   Stalks are never separated from
berries ; they produce a slight depreciation of the wine, but
it is less than the expense of removing the stalks.   The
presshouse is an old chapel, which the monks, having
built a new one, devoted to Bacchus.   Where before stood
the altar they placed ten magnificent wooden wine-presses ;
the rest of the chapel was filled with pails, baskets, vats,
and other apparatus to be used at vintage time.

Opposite this chapel is a smaller hall, where the cabinet
wines are pressed.   Close to this hall is the so-called *Cabinet*,
a vault above ground protected by double walls, and by
trees and shrubs from the external heat of the atmosphere
and the rays of the sun.   In this place the best wines are
kept, and hence called Cabinet Wines.   All other wines
are put in the large beautiful underground cellars, and
there prepared for sale.   All the produce of Steinberg is
sold by public auction at Erbach.   The day of this sale
resembles a festivity.   Each stranger arriving, presumably
a buyer, receives a dinner and a liberal allowance of good
wine, cabinet wines being given with the dessert.   The sale
afterwards proceeds amidst general merriment.

The wine at auction is sold in pieces of 1,200 litres each,
being 7½ ohms ; the cabinet wine is also sold in smaller
quantities by private arrangement, if the auction price be
below the reserved price ; it is also disposed of in bottle at
high prices.   The wines of other domainial vineyards, *e.g.*
Hattenheim, are sold at the same time ; so that with the
average of 84 pieces from Steinberg, 120 to 150 pieces may
be sold at one auction.   The price of the wine varies
between £65 per piece and £600 to £700, the latter
being the highest realized for exceptionally fine qualities.

§ 138. Marcobrunn and Johannisberg.

The *vineyards of Marcobrunn* are partly Nassau (Prussian)
domains, partly property of Count Schönborn.   In the
middle of the front of the vineyard is the gushing spring
from which the situation bears its name.   Other names are

Hattenheim, Oestrich, Winkel, Geisenheim with its Rother Berg. The *Johannisberg* is the only rival of the Steinberg; it is a conical hill, projected from the Taunus mountain to within about a mile of the river Rhine. The estate was originally a Benedictine abbey, founded in 1106 by Ruthard, Archbishop of Mayence. In the course of seven centuries the Johannisberg changed proprietors frequently: in 1717 it was bought by the Abbot of Fulda, Adalbert von Walderdorf, who built the present castle. At the time of the French Revolution the Johannisberg came into the hands of the then Prince of Orange, but Napoleon, after the battle of Jena, took it from him and gave it to Marshal Kellermann. In 1815 the Emperor of Austria took possession of it, and on August 1st, 1816, gave it to Prince Metternich, with whose descendant it now remains. The proprietor pays annual wine-tithes to the House of Hapsburg.

The vineyard has a surface of 62 morgen, and is manured by the entire produce of a farm of 450 morgen of arable land, and 70 morgen of meadow land. The vine is cultivated after the manner usual in the Rheingau. The grapes are selected with great care, and the vineyard is passed through by the reapers several times, when the best produce is selected berry by berry. Such *Auslese,* as it is termed, easily loses the character of Rhine wine, and becomes a sweet liquorous product, resembling Muscat or Sauterne. Much of the wine is bottled at the castle and sold to the public. Each cork shows the brand of the Metternich arms; after it has been inserted in the bottle, it is sealed over, and the wax is again impressed with the same coat of arms. A label, stating the name, year, and price of the wine, is now fixed upon each bottle, and the wine is then sent away in cases and baskets to its destination.

The cellars of the Johannisberg generally contain upwards of a hundred pieces of wine. The quantity of wine produced varies greatly with the years—between forty-eight and sixty pieces. The wines of inferior years are sold by auction after the spring racking, only the higher qualities are kept in the cellar, and are bottled at the age of four or five years, the time of their maturity in cask. After being bottled, the wines improve greatly in bouquet, and keep twenty-five years. The auction wines fetch from £50 to £200 per piece, and the cabinet wines from £500 to £1,000 per piece. The Johannisberg wines, like all white Rhine wines, are kept very pale, and any influence which would increase their colour is carefully kept away.

§ 139. VINEYARDS OF RÜDESHEIM.

The *vineyards of Rüdesheim* have perhaps the most ideal situation of any on the Rhine, but suffer easily from drought. They are now daily traversed by many tourists, who ascend to the Niederwald to inspect the national monument commemorating the results of the war of 1870-71. The *Rüdes-heimer Berg*, as the best part of the vineyard is termed, has an area of upwards of 400 morgen. The price of vineyards is very high, as the mere planting, terracing, earthing, and removal of stones from underground, etc., involves an original expense of from £600 to £700 per morgen.

§ 140. WINES OF THE LOWER MAINE, OR HOCHHEIM.

Hochheim is a village situated on the northern side of the Maine, about three-quarters of a mile from the banks of that river, 100 feet above its level, and about three miles above its confluence with the Rhine. The vineyards extend for two miles along the northern bank of the river; their area is 1,779 morgen of 160 ruthen each; their inclination to the south is slight, and they have no particular protection from the north wind; but the two most celebrated vineyards, the *Domdechanei*, and the *Stein*, are protected on their northern ends by a high church and the houses of the village. The so-called "church-plot" (or piece) of the Dechanei yields wines for which, in good years, as much as £600 per piece Rhenish are obtained. The soil is calcareous clay, mixed higher up with gravel. The vines and mode of their treatment are the same as in the Rheingau, as by its methods and results Hochheim is really a part, and a very typical one, of the Rheingau. The Riessling grape here attains its highest development; it is, when perfect, light brown and transparent, not green; the kernels are brown, and not white or light-coloured; the taste is *burning*, sweet, and accompanied with the peculiar strong flavour of the Riessling; the stalk of the perfectly ripe bunch must be dry and shrivelled, like that of raisins, and not green or succulent. Vinification offers no peculiarities. The wine is ripe for bottling after five years.

Hochheimer seems to have been the earliest and best-known Rhenish wine in this country, and has furnished the monosyllabic English term by which all Rhine wines are confused, the curious symbol of "*Hock.*"

The whole of the vineyards in bearing in the Prussian province of Nassau, including Hochheim, have an area of 10,974 morgen; the morgen contains 160 ruthen of 100 square feet each. The produce may be estimated as amounting to a piece of wine per morgen. Of all the vines in the province 51 per cent. are Riessling, 16·3 per cent. Kleinberger, 8·9 per cent Sylvaner, or Oestreicher, 16·9 per cent. are nondescript mixtures; the black Burgundies amount to 4 per cent, the Traminer to 2·2 per cent., and the almost extinct Orleans vine to only 0.8 per cent. The Nassau ohm measures 160 litres; the piece (German *Stück*) measures 7½ ohms, or 1,200 litres; the same measures obtain in Hesse Darmsdadt and Baden. The Frankfort ohm, by which wine is commonly sold to England, has a capacity of only 143·41 litres, or 31·56 imperial gallons. Of Frankfort ohms, eight are equal to one Frankfort stück of 1,152 litres, equal to 640 Frankfort maas. The Palatinate *fuder* is 1,000 litres.

§ 141. WINES OF THE MOSELLE.

The Moselle issues from the western slopes of the Vosges, and receives its principal contributory, the Saar, near Treves; it then runs nearly northwards, with many windings, and flows into the Rhine near Coblentz. The valley is deeply cut through the Rhenish slate formation, or Devonian schist, which on the right bank bears the orological name of Hunsrück, or Hundsrück, on the left that of the Eifel. Its undulating banks in Lorraine are mostly covered with black

Burgundy vines; but from Treves to Cochem white vines are planted.

§ 142. Cultivated Vines and mode of Training.

Of the cultivated vines of the Moselle, one, the *Albuelis* of Columella, or *Elbling*, or *Kleinberger*, seems to be indigenous to the Moselle valley. It occurs in all vineyards, and frequently prevails over the Riessling, but the latter is everywhere mixed with it. In five or six districts from Piesport to Trarbach are vineyards planted with Riessling exclusively. At Piesport and Kersten more red wine is already made, and in the neighbourhood of Cobern, Cochem, Carden, and a few places of the Lower Moselle, much red wine is grown, and the Burgundy vine prevails.

The small viticulturists grow their vines according to the *hedge principle*, as it is termed (*Hecken-Wingert*), that is to say, the vines get one pruning, no supports, and then grow as best they can: in August and September superfluous branches and foliage are removed for fodder, and in October any grapes are cut. The wealthier viticulturists all go in for quantity, and frequently injure their vines by leaving too much wood for bearing. The cultivation on the Upper Moselle is essentially French, specially Burgundian.

§ 143. Peculiarities of Moselle Wines.

The general character of white Moselle wine is that of thin Rhine wine, but it never attains as much flavour. It matures quickly, and does not possess the keeping qualities of Hock. Owing to the natural absence of flavour or bouquet, the producers of Moselle, and the merchants in their track, have devised an artificial flavour, namely, the tincture of the elder flower: it is used particularly in sparkling Moselle, and when properly applied affords a very agreeable bouquet. The tincture is made as follows. The little elder-flowers are cut from the bunches and infused with pure strong spirit of wine. After twenty-four hours standing the spirit is filtered. It may now be again infused upon new elder-flowers, and this process repeated several times, according to the strength which it is intended to give to the essence. Much care has to be bestowed upon the clarification of the essence. Of this tincture a small quantity added to common Rhine wine or Moselle gives it the peculiar flavour which is termed " muscatel flavour." But there is no grape grown upon the Moselle fit for wine-making which has this flavour, or any muscatel flavour, and not a single barrel of wine is made which has that flavour naturally, all which has that flavour derives it from elder-flower ; much of the " Moselle with muscatel flavour " sold in England is Rhine wine flavoured with the elder. There can be no objection to the use of this tincture, and there ought to be no concealment about it. Elder-flower is an agreeable flavour, in no way prejudicial to health, and has from time immemorial been used to make a high-flavoured infusion for the treatment of slight indisposition, particularly of the gastric organs.

The area of the vineyards on the Moselle is 20,606 morgen, which, with 15,080 morgen situated on the Rhine, make up 48,631 morgen of vineyards in Rhenish Prussia. The greater part of this area has been called into viticultural productivity by the protective duties which Prussia imposed on the exports of the small states before they joined the customs union, now merged in the empire.

CHAPTER XX.

WINES OF AUSTRIA.

§ 144. WINES OF AUSTRIA.

IN German Austria the young wine is put into new barrels of large size, provided with man-hole doors which are not pierced ; for as the wine is not drawn from the lees in spring, but is allowed to remain over them until sold and broken in smaller parcels, the purchasers do not like to buy casks which have the man-hole door pierced for the insertion of a tap, owing to a belief that such a condition of the cask would indicate that the wine had been disturbed, mixed, or tampered with.   The producers, on their side, know how to disarm such suspicion by providing every old cask which they use for receiving new wine, or any wine in their cellars, with a new man-hole door which has not been pierced.

In some convents and monasteries in Austria there are cellars filled with casks containing up to ten fuder of wine ; one fuder being equal to thirty-two eimer, or about 1,728 litres, the largest cask would contain upward of 172 hecto-litres.   Many of these casks contain wine ten and more years old still floating over the first lees.   In 1840 Bronner tasted wine at Neuburg which had been eighteen years over its first lees, and not been racked at all.   This practice makes wine expensive, and explains many of the short-comings which Austrian wines formerly exhibited.   No private producers could accumulate their crops in this manner ; on the contrary, they are compelled or induced to sell their wines somewhat too early, and it is for such reasons that Austrian wines have not taken that place in European trade which their otherwise good qualities might entitle them to.

§ 145. Red Wine of Vöslau, near Vienna.

About fifteen English miles south of Vienna, in the neighbourhood of Baden, are two viticulture districts, named from the villages of Vöslau and of Gumpolds-kirchen, which have, during the last forty years, obtained some notoriety.   The red wine produced in them comes from a particular black-graped vine, termed the Early Blue Portuguese.   The grape is early ripening, sweet, of some-what larger size than the Burgundy Pineau.   It is said to have been imported from Portugal, and to be identical with the Alvarilhao of the Douro district,[1] but we have not been able to substantiate these assertions by positive proof.   The wines made from this grape are fit for use in a very short

---

[1] Odart, _l.c._, p. 369.

time after they are made, and do not require a long sojourn in the cellar, while wines made from other grapes in Austria require to be kept in barrel sometime before they become drinkable.

The produce of Vöslau is mostly bought by the inn-keepers and speculators of Vienna and Baden, in the shape of what is called *gemesch*, that is to say, of grapes in a vat crushed by wooden stampers. The more advanced proprietors make their wines according to the best methods of France and Germany.

The vines are kept near the ground, but are so pruned as to produce many small grapes on many branches of wood. The soil of the Vöslau vineyards is chalky.

§ 146. WINES AND GRAPES OF THE TYROL.

. The wine-producing part of the Tyrol is situated along the valley of the Adige, beginning near Verona and running by Botzen up to Meran. The valley of the Adige is protected on the north by high mountains, and represents a kind of basin, over which eastern and western storms have no power, and the slopes of which are most favourable to viticulture, particularly where they are composed of a mixture of decayed chalk, gneiss, and porphyry. At Botzen and Meran sun and moisture vie in producing the greatest development of vegetation compatible with the temperature of the moderate zone. In ascending the Adige we find that with the Italian language ends the Italian mode of viticulture. With the German language commencing at Tramin and Neumarkt, the system called "bowers" commences, while that of the Italian "garlands" ceases. For some miles both systems are mixed, imitating the mixture of nationalities. At Roveredo appear the crossed stakes which prevail near Trieste. The garlands are trained nearer to the ground, and the plants are close together. At last there are no more twisted ropes of vine-canes, but only single canes stretching from stake to stake. These then also disappear, and the vines are kept near the ground, as at Seyssel, in Switzerland, in the form called "head-knob," or "willow-tree top."

By the bower treatment a great quantity of wine of the lowest quality is produced, which is only used by the country people, and quite unfit for any staple trade or export. But the German inhabitants now cultivate the vine after the Rhenish pattern.

The varieties of grapes cultivated in the Tyrol are in the Italian part entirely Italian ; in the German part there have hitherto been grown only large-berried white and blue varieties, among them the Vernatsch. This is a black muscatel, known as such in France and Germany under the name of Aleatico ; in upper Italy, under that of Vernaculo e Toscana. The grape is only fit for the production of so-called liqueur wines, that is to say, grape juice preserved from fermentation by the addition of distilled spirit. Such is the Tuscan Aleatico wine, and the French Lunels, Frontignans, the Cape Constantia, Cyprus, and many others. For the production of fermented dry wines the Vernatsch is quite unsuitable.

§ 147. THE TYROLINGER, OR "BLACK HAMBRO" VINE OF THE TYROL.

The *vine most characteristic of the Tyrol*, known in Germany as the Tyrolinger, or Trollinger, is that celebrated, and to all growers of vines in conservatories and hothouses, and particularly therefore to English viticulturists, most important vine, which they know under the name of Knevet's *Black Hambro*. The French, who received it from the Palatinate, called it Frankenthal. It is the usual table-grape in the belt of land which once constituted the Austrasian empire, stretching from Holland and Belgiuml through South Germany, down the Danube almost to Pesth· Odart (*l.c.*, p. 367) in consequence called it "the nationa, grape of the Germans"; and curiously enough speaks of it as a useless low vine, which he had torn out. However, it is certain that the Tyrolese or Black Hambro grape is of all eating grapes the most perfect, on account of its having thin husks, small pips, tolerably solid yet juicy flesh, and an agreeable acidity never in excess, mixed with a sufficient amount of sugar and mild flavour. The bunches are never very large, and not so close that the grapes have not sufficient space to develop themselves. The vine is always fertile, and even in bad years its fruit may be used, though not completely ripe, or may be used in good years somewhat under-ripe, on account of the modest amount of acidity. When the grape gets ripe and is allowed to hang a little beyond its actual period of ripeness, it yields a splendid wine; but this state of ripeness is hardly ever reached in the places where it is cultivated for the production of wine. There are two celebrated vines of this variety, one in a greenhouse in Hampton Court garden, and one in the conservatory at Windsor Castle; they are very old stocks, and annually surprisingly fertile.

The Tyrolese wines offer no points for observation, except that in late years they have been much improved, and several enterprising viticulturists have planted vineyards with the best vines of the Rheingau. A first harvest was obtained in 1869. But the treatment in the cellar was not yet developed, and difficulties have to be overcome to this day, consisting in the obstinate occurrence of so-called diseases produced by parasitic fungi. We also doubt whether the transfer of the Rhenish Riessling will be so successful as is hoped, mainly because we observe how vines are, so to say, related to districts, and perhaps autochthonous, and only succeed under other latitudes by special care or favour of local conditions.

§ 148. THE GRAPE-CURE AT MERAN.

The expression "grape-cure" is intended to signify the systematic eating of grapes on the part of patients afflicted with sundry chronic ailments which resist the ordinary modes of medical treatment, for the purpose of ameliorating their ailments. There are at Meran lodging-houses and hotels, where, in the proper season, people from many parts of Europe arrive and put themselves under the care of those medical practitioners who make a speciality of this kind of treatment. The patients are made to eat grapes in considerable quantities frequently during the day, the largest quantity

P

in the morning, and at the same time to take exercise. To the greater number of these patients the eating of grapes is more a pleasure than a privation, particularly when their digestive organs are not the seat of their ailment. The earliest effect of the eating of a certain quantity of grapes is purgative, but as the grape-juice nourishes at the same time, it is superior to the mere purging mineral waters. The selection of grapes at Meran is not easy, as there are only Trollinger and Vernatsche to be had—the Trollinger in a state in which it is still watery and acidulous, and the Vernatsche (*i.e.* Veronaccia, or vine of Verona, at Verona called Pavana) being also, at the early season, when the cure must be commenced, not sufficiently advanced in sweetness and concentration. The doctors of Meran have recognized the disadvantage that their only choice of material was between these two varieties, and have observed that at some periods their patients rather lost than gained weight, while with better grapes the patients mostly increase in weight during the treatment.

§ 149. WINES OF STYRIA.

The cultivation of the vine in Styria extends from Stein-brück, along the Save, and from Cille to Marburg, the vine-yards in the Bacher mountains being particularly extensive. Styrian viticulture has been described by many authors in that country itself, but it became known to wider circles only through the writings of the late G. P. H. Bronner, of Wiesloch in Baden. The wines of the western part of the Gallus mountain are generally known under the name of the place where they are usually sold, namely, at Saurish Winer, a name which lends itself to the suggestion of invidious reflections. Styria debouches not towards the Mediterranean, or the northern part of the valley of the Danube, but its long-drawn valleys are all directed towards the east, and communicate with the lower part of Hungary; as hitherto the sales could only take place in the direction of the river, and as just in that direction there was no want, the only market which the Styrian producer had for his wine was his

own country and the mountainous district of the neighbouring Alps. Nevertheless, wine is grown on 54,000 joch or
morgen, each joch bearing 4,000 vines. Near Pettau are
ranges of hills, so-called *Colles*, nearly thirty miles in length,
on which viticulture is carried on in the crater of the extinct
volcano, of which each hill is the remnant. The funnel-
shaped inside of the crater mostly measures ten morgen, but
there are some the area of which rises to twenty morgen. The
vines are grown on the slopes exposed to the sun; the slopes
turned to the north are mostly covered with forest. In the
mostly even bottom of the crater ordinary agriculture is
carried on. In the centre of each crater is mostly a central
volcanic cone, on which the residence of the cultivator is
built. The traveller who on a misty morning stands on a
high point, and looks over these craters, sees the houses
appear above the horizon, as if they were suspended to the
sky and had no footing on the earth, and thus enjoys an
apparently magical spectacle.

§ 150. VITICULTURISTS OF STYRIA.

Styria is divided into two nearly equal parts by the river
Drave, which comes from Carinthia and flows into the
Danube in Hungary. The part of Styria north of this river
is entirely German, the part south of it Wendish. All the
Wends are viticulturists, while the Germans engage here but
little in that occupation. The wine-producing Wends are
termed "Weinzettel"; they live on small properties, either
as renting farmers or as freeholders. Where the wine-
grower is only a tenant farmer, he frequently pays the most
curious rent or receives remuneration. The master gives him
two cows, and finds fodder and straw; the tenant takes
the grass from the vineyard and feeds the cows with it.
The calf of the cow belongs to the master, the milk to the
cultivator, but the master exacts not rarely eighteen pounds
of butter in a clarified state. On the other hand the master
pays to the cultivator thirty shillings per acre in cash, and
takes half the produce, so that there is a perplexing amount
of cross-calculation. In some parts the dung produced by

the cattle on the farm belongs for half the year to the master, and for the other half year to the cultivator. This complicated condition denotes a very elementary state of society, there being neither capital on the part of the proprietors nor resources of any kind on the part of the cultivators, and the effect of these circumstances unfavourably influences the wine produce.

§ 151. VARIETIES OF VINES CULTIVATED.

Some of the vines cultivated are probably indigenous to Styria, which has many wild vines, *e.g.* on the banks of the little river Svan. In the Gratz district dominates the Bellina, by the Germans termed "Heunisch," *i.e.* Hungarian, and by the Hungarians "German." In the mountains of Luttenberg and in the vineyards of the Drave the Mosler vine predominates, also called Schipon, identical with the Hungarian Furmint, or vine of Tokay. The Mosler always bears, ripens its wood, produces middle-sized grapes, which do not drop easily, and, when the sun is high, shrivel into raisins, from which, if need be, sweet wine can be made. The Rhenish Riessling also has been transplanted, but yields a fiery wine without much bouquet. In the less favoured part of Styria the dominant vine is the Tantowina, which bears copiously, but gives a mediocre wine; its German name is Mehlweiss. In the mountains of Gams white or yellow muscatels are grown, the juice of which is mostly consumed during fermentation. The Gonovitz red wine is made from the small round black grapes of the Kauka; the red wine of the Sausal mountains is made from grapes of the blue Wildbacher, an abundant bearer, which gives tolerable grapes even when grown as a climber on trees. One such vine, on a pear-tree, yielded to the late G. P. H. Bronner, of Wiesloch, in 1866, sixty litres of very good red wine. The wines of the Wildbacher resemble most the vigorous Bordeaux varieties, the Palus. This vine is no doubt indigenous to Styria; in the forests trees are here and there found covered by it; it produces long canes, some exceeding twenty feet in length: it bears every variety of training—low, like Burgundy vines, or along houses, or in frames, and everywhere brings great harvests. The berries are round, small, black, and covered with bloom. The skin is so thick and protected by bloom-wax, that it does not rot easily, resembling the Verdot of the Bordelais, and may therefore hang long on the tree without detriment to its colour.

The pruned canes, after cutting time, are thrown into the roads, to make them passable. Every proprietor abutting upon the road takes in autumn one half of the bruised and comminuted fragments of these vine canes, and puts them into his vineyard as manure. To avoid disputes, the two abutting proprietors sometimes agree to take the material alternately every other year.

§ 152. VINIFICATION, PRESSING, AND QUALITY OF WINE.

The production of red wine in Styria has, through the exertion of the œnophilist Trummer, been much improved, so that closed fermentation vats are used, when formerly only open, wide, flat wooden pans were employed. The bruised grapes are packed in the shape of a pyramid and bandaged with a long flat bandage made of the roots of the common juniper, and having a length of from 100 to 130 feet. The pressure is now applied, and the spiral lines of the bandage are pressed the one into the other, until the whole of the juice is squeezed out. This method is also common in Andalusia and in Dalmatia. The Wends use concentric hoops to contain the grapes under the press. The presses are mostly beam-presses, there being few screw-presses to be seen; the beams are up to thirty feet in length, the pressing beds are from ten to twelve feet square; stones are hung to the ends of the beams.

As each joch produces about twenty-five eimer of wine, the 54,720 jochs of vineyards in Styria give a total harvest of 1,367,500 eimer. The late Archduke John, quondam Reichsverweser of Germany, and Dr. Hlubeck improved viticulture in Styria greatly during the years from 1830 to 1850. In the Austrian exhibition of 1857 ninety-nine Styrian wines of good quality were exhibited; some Styrian produce is made into effervescent wine by the firm of Kleinoschegg. The Styrian wines are naturally so good, that with proper treatment they might become objects of a considerable commerce.

§ 153. WINES OF CROATIA.

The climatic condition of Croatia favours viticulture, but in consequence of the want of labour the producers cultivate the vine for quantity, neglecting all attempts at quality. The best vine is the Moslavina, known in Hungary as Furmint, but the dominating vines are the Grünhainer and the Heunisch, which cannot possibly give good wine. The vine arrives at its full bearing power only in the eighth year after being planted; it is sunk once or twice, to give it a large footing. It is pruned in spring, when also the soil is worked; then the vineyard is allowed to grow as best it can until the time of the vintage approaches. At that time the vineyard is a mere jungle. The vine-dressers, therefore, on entering the vineyard, cut their way through the tangled vines, and tie up what branches remain uncut, and in general make the vines accessible to the reapers. Behind the vine-dressers there go relays of women, who with sickles cut off the thick layer of weeds and grass on the ground. A Croatian vineyard, like some we know of at the Antipodes, is therefore a very picturesque scene at vintage time, and exhibits the power of nature and the luxuriance of the vine very well; but its produce is necessarily of low quality. The grapes are vintaged at the period of their greatest volume. The presses are mostly beampresses; there are are no proper receptacles for the murk, but this is mixed with old vine cuttings, as brick earth is with straw, and pressed. The must gets hot, and when it has completed fermentation has mostly an acetic taste. It is kept in a hole dug in the earth, covered by a reedy thatch, and this arrangement goes by the name of cellar. Even better cellars below houses are too warm in summer. The really great viticultural capabilities of Croatia are thus wasted entirely.

At the exhibition of Wagram in 1864 above a thousand specimens of Croatian wine were exhibited; they were all contained in well filled, beautifully corked and labelled bottles. But not one specimen out of ten was free from serious faults; nine out of ten exhibited the acetous flavour and the mouse-taste. This latter an Austrian juror of Neuburg facetiously termed the peculiar Croatian bouquet, while some Croatians themselves believed it to be derived from the soil.

§ 154. WINES OF DALMATIA.

A traveller intending to visit Dalmatia may leave Trieste on board a steamer, and pass the Istrian coast and the bay of Quarnaro. While the steamer passes between the island and the mainland towards the south, the tourist will perceive bare rocky mountains without any vegetation; only here and there will he perceive some shrubs rising from crevices in the rocks; if he were to draw a conclusion as regards the condition of Dalmatia from the appearance of the sea-coast, he would believe it to be a stony desert. On penetrating into the interior, however, he perceives that many valleys intersect the rocks, the bottoms of which are cultivated in various ways, while the slopes leading to them from the rocks are planted with vines. These vineyards exist altogether only by the assiduity of man. The earth is carried from the valleys up the steep inclines, and fixed by means of terraces; and as the strong winds from the sea would speedily blow the earth away, every small piece of vineyard is surrounded by a wall not less than six feet high. The stones from which these walls are built are mainly the produce of blasting operations, undertaken to diminish the inclination of the territory. The vineyards are thus real traps to catch the sun's rays and boil the vine. By these means Dalmatia was able, when the oidium had reduced Italian wine production to one-tenth of its average, to immediately supply the deficiency. Since then, Dalmatian viticulture has been steadily on the increase.

§ 155. VARIETIES OF VINES AND THEIR CULTIVATION.

Amongst a great variety of vines cultivated in Dalmatia, the Italian vines predominate, owing, no doubt, to the easy communication by sea with Italy. Amongst the blue varieties are the Hungarian Kadarka, the Crelenjack, the large and small Plavec, and the Modrulj. On the islands of Brazza, Glavusa, and Nicousa, the vines called the Vugava and Uva pasche predominate. The Dalmatians are particularly pleased with the Crelenjack and the small Plavec. The latter gives a slight wine, but bears largely. Among the white varieties is noteworthy a grape called the Maraschino (or Maraschina), small, long, and very sweet; it is cultivated particularly in the island of Brazza, and used in the production of the sweet liqueur wines called Maraschino. This must not be confounded with the liqueur which is drunk in Europe under the name of Maraschino, and which is distilled from the fermented mash of a small cherry called the Marasche. The Maraschino liqueur made at Zara is an excellent cherry brandy, and exceeds in *finesse* even the cherry brandies (Kirschenwasser) of Alsatia.

The Dalmatians term naturally fermented wine "sour," and liqueur wines with added spirit "sweet." The grapes, cut at the time of their largest volume, are put into bags made of the skins of he-goats, with the hair turned inside, and carried home. In this way all Dalmatian wines acquire the taste or flavour of the he-goat. Only in Zara and Sebenico are grapes carried home in panniers and other baskets. A third ordeal awaits the grapes during fermentation, which is conducted in open shallow vats. The presses are very elementary; the murk is kept together by a circular bandage, sometimes a rope made of straw. The new wine is put into new pine-wood barrels, and thus the ordinary Dalmatian wine presents a mixture of flavours, which disqualifies it for use by persons with an educated palate. A bottle of wine is sold for two pence, and we have been assured, that if all the faults were removed from this wine, its value in the locality would not rise to two pence halfpenny. The red wines are very dark, and so astringent, that we could not drink them without diluting them with their bulk of water. The wines going to Italy fetch only 1½*d*. the litre. Much wine goes into Thessaly and Epirus. The Austrian Government have done much to encourage the improvement and extension of wine production in Dalmatia.

§ 156. WINES OF ISTRIA.

There are viticultural districts between Trieste and Pisano, and near Rovigno and Pola. The islands of Vaglia, Cherso, and Lussin, also produce wine, but spoil it, like the Dalmatians. Viticulture at Trieste is practised as in Italy, and is faulty throughout; and the wine produced is sour and indifferent. Of vines, the blue Refosco and the white Malvoisie are the most esteemed and extensively planted (Odart says they prevail along the shore of the whole Adriatic sea). The wines made near Trieste have all the faults of the wines of Croatia and Dalmatia. To obtain a glass of good wine at Trieste one must ask for Austrian Vöslauer, Gumpolds-Kirchener, or Grinzinger. If the Istrians produced good wine they could export it to all the world, because much shipping leaves Trieste in ballast.

§ 157. WINES OF GÖRTZ.

The fruit of Görtz is highly esteemed in the markets of South Germany, and particularly of Vienna, but the wine produced here is mediocre, because all vines are overshadowed by fruit-trees. The tenant-farmers pay rent in wine, and some corn. The vines are Italian, Refosco being preferred. Some enterprising men at Görtz now produce a good red wine; others an effervescent wine, from a particular grape called Ribola. The latter was, some years ago, yet imperfect, as the art of disgorging had not yet penetrated to Görtz, and the connoisseur drank the sparkling wine in a turbid state. A sweet liqueur wine is also made and exported to Turkey and Russia.

§ 158. Wines of Bohemia.

Bohemia produces annually about 50,895 eimer of wine, of which 19,300 are red, and 31,595 are white. The best wine is that of Melnik, a town situated about twelve miles to the north of Prague, and is made from the black Burgundy grape. The production of wine in Bohemia is decidedly on the decrease, as the climatic conditions are not sufficiently favourable to make it a remunerative object of agriculture.

CHAPTER XXI.

WINES OF HUNGARY.

§ 159. General Observations.

THE wines of Hungary were the object of much discussion and controversy at the time when the principles of free trade received a generalized application in this country. The late Mr. Cobden used, *inter alia*, Hungarian wines as objects on which to illustrate his teaching, and relied for his information upon an extensive report of our then Consul in Hungary, Mr. Dunlop. The Consul, on his part, had to rely upon local information, which was in many respects delusive, and the consequence was that many erroneous statements on Hungarian wines became current, which found their final contradiction and extinction only during the last few years. Hungary no doubt produces much wine, and many varieties of it. On the occasion of the International Agricultural Exhibition at Hamburg, in 1863, a Hungarian reporter, Stefan Morocz, estimated the total annual production of wine in Hungary to be 25 millions of eimer; or, taking the eimer at 54 litres (it being actually 54·1527 litres), 13½ millions of hectolitres. Of this quantity a little less than one-eighth, namely three millions of eimer, equal to 1·62 millions of hectolitres, was supposed to be capable of being so prepared as to become fit for European trade. But of this latter amount a very small proportion is as yet actually so prepared; and in the year 1859 the exportation from Pesth, the principal market for Hungarian wines, did not yet amount to 100,000 eimer.

§ 160. VITICULTURAL DISTRICTS OF HUNGARY.

The principal viticultural districts of the kingdom are five in number, and may be defined as follows.

The northern district, on the left side of the Danube, is the continuation in an easterly direction of the viticultural regions of Lower Austria and Moravia. It includes the valley of the Waag, in which vines are cultivated from Trentschin to Szered; further, the valley of the Gran; but is mainly characterized by the Hegyalja mountain, containing the celebrated vineyards of *Tokay* and *Erlau*, and the less distinguished but fertile vineyards of the Bodrog, a river which comes from the Carpathian mountains, and the Samos, which issues from Transylvania.

The eastern district is confined between the Stein on the west, and the river Samos and Transylvania on the east; its southern frontier is the Banat. Its wines are represented by the products of Erdöd, Bakator, and Menes.

The central district is situated between the Danube on the west, and the Theiss on the east; its northern limit is at Pesth, and in the south it ends at the Woiwodina.

The western district is divisible into two parts; one to the west of the Raab river, which is a continuation of the viticultural district of Lower Austria, and is represented by the vineyards of *Rust;* the other parts to the east of the Raab, and further enclosed by the Danube and Drave, including in its centre the regions of the Plattensee. This part is characterized by the wines of *Ofen, Somlau*, and *Weissenburg*.

The southern district includes the *Banat* and *Woiwodina;* in the former the *Werschitz* mountain has vineyards on many slopes.

§ 161. Varieties of Soil on which Vines grow in Hungary.

Vines are grown mainly on slopes of hills, but also on plains, and even on marshy lands. The great wines are produced either on plutonic or volcanic land, or chalky soil. Thus the Hegyalja, a promontory of the Carpathians extending and sloping towards the south, consists mainly of porphyry and basalt. The best wines of Fünfkirchen grow on chalky hills, called the Deindol. The Ofner wine, termed Adlersberger, grows on volcanic soil, which constitutes a part of the series of hills running along the Danube from Pács-Megyer to Alt-Tétény. The wine of the mountain of Somlyo, or Somlau, in Veszprim county, near the Plattensee, grows on basaltic soil. The wines which grow on the shores of the lake of Neusiedl, and those which grow round the Plattensee, generically termed "lake-wines," are grown on basaltic soil, which slopes from the Badacsonyer mountains southwards towards this lake. All the lake-wine of Gyorköer grows on soil which is made up of one-third of chalk and two-thirds of clay. The wine of Packsdorf, in the county of Eisenburg, is obtained on strongly ferruginous soil, while the wine of Musai, in Beregh county, comes from a soil which is partly the product of the decay of alum-stone (schist).

§ 162. Varieties of Vines and Mode of Cultivation.

There are two dominant vines peculiar to Hungary—the *Furmint*, or Tokay, with white grapes, and the *Kadarka* (*Kadarkas*) with black grapes. In the county of Baranye there are some extensive plantations of *Burgundy Pineau*, and round Villary there is much of the Rhenish Riessling, the early Portugese, and the Oporto vine. At Ofen a black-graped vine, *Sar feher*, occurs intermixed with the Kadarka. There are also other varieties imported from Croatia and Lower Austria, including some degenerate Muscatels, which have lost the muscat flavour.

The Furmint (in Hungarian *Io Formint*)—syn. White

Tokay, Lake-vine, Moseler, Moslavina—is a strong vine, with woolly canes and shoots; the leathery leaves show a thick felt on the underside. The bunch of grapes is large, loose, pendulous, cylindrical, sometimes divided in several lobes. The fruit-stalk is short and thin, and its node does not carry a collateral bunch. The berry-stalks are all long, and the basal enlargement has a brown margin, and fine light green warts. The berries are medium sized, and, when uncompressed, round, with strong white bloom; their juice is sweet, and has a peculiar strong flavour. The grapes ripen early; the earliest burst and discharge a portion of their juice, which dries up, and forms, with the rest of the berry, a shapeless lump, full of sugar; these products are called "dry berries," and must not be confounded with the raisins of southern climates. The dry berries are mostly interspersed with fully ripe and plump, not at all passulated, berries. At the vintage these dry berries are separated from the plump ones immediately after the bunch is cut off, and collected in separate vessels, and further treated as will be described lower down.

Nearly all the red wines of Hungary are made from the *Blue Kadarka*. Its berries are oval and of medium size, black, covered with bloom; the bunches are of medium size. The dark green leaf, which is shiny above, and somewhat hirsute on the underside, shows the peculiarity that its two extreme lobes are generally turned or twisted a little upwards. By this twist the Kadarka can be distinguished from other varieties of vines, even at a distance. To get fully ripe, the Kadarka requires the great heat of the Hungarian summer; it is the only black-graped vine which yields dry berries like the Furmint, and thus enables the viticulturist to produce the sweet wine called by the Germans in Hungary "Ausbruch."

The *Mode of Cultivation* of the vines is that known as *small head*, or *knob*; this keeps the fruit near the ground, and avoids the necessity of stakes for support. Nevertheless, it does not yield the best quality of wine.

§ 163. Vintage and Vinification.

At Ofen (Buda) the white grapes are vintaged first, and the black ones afterwards. Both red and white wines are mostly fermented with the husks and stalks, and pressed after the fermentation. 150 eimer of mashed grapes (a quantity called a "gatzen") yields 120 eimer of clear wine and 30 eimer of murk. The first drawn wine is called "sweet wine," and amounts to 110 eimer out of the above 120; the remaining 10 eimer are obtained by pressing the murk, and are somewhat harsh. The presses are primæval beam-presses; the murk is kept together by hoops or boxes. The wine is preserved in large barrels, but for sale is put in barrels of from 162 to 270 litres each.

As regards Hungarian wines, we must distinguish between such as are really thoroughly fermented grape juice, and such as are more or less sweetened and alcoholized, so as to be, or to approximate to, liqueurs. What is called "*Maszlacz*," German "*Ausbruch*," whether made at Tokay, Rust, or Menes, or other places, consists of must from plump ripe grapes, more or less fortified, thickened and sweetened by means of "dry berries." In consequence, a portion of the harvest is deprived entirely of its dry berries, and this now yields only "*ordinary wine.*" When the dry berries are not removed, and are made into wine together with the entire harvest, and without any addition of dry berries from other vintages, the so-called "*natural wine*," or "*Szamorodni*," is obtained. *Maszlacz* is made of four qualities, called, one-, two-, three-, or four-"*buttig*," according to the quantity of dry berries added to each cask of must. A cask of wine contains ten "*butten*," and the addition of dry berries to produce the several qualities of Maszlacz, therefore, amounts to one butt, equal to 10 per cent. of the total volume of the murk; or to two butts, equal to 20 per cent.; three butts, equal to 30 per cent.; and four butts, equal to 40 per cent. of the total murk. Such wine is always highly alcoholic, and more or less sweet. When five volumes or more of dry berries are added to the must, so that the mixture consists of equal volumes of must and dry berries, or so that the volume of the dry berries preponderates, "*Ausbruch*" is formed.   The finest quality of Ausbruch is that which runs spontaneously from the must-infused dry berries after they have been allowed to macerate a short time, and is called "*Essence*."

§ 164. CLASSIFICATION OF HUNGARIAN WINES.

When Hungarian wines are compared with each other, they can be arranged in a certain series, which indicates their relative value.   But it is not intended by this list to attempt a comparison of Hungarian wines with other products, either as regards quality, value, or price.

A. Wines of the First Class.

First Order.—*Tokay:* (1) *Essence:* very sweet, containing slight amount of alcohol, not exceeding 7 per cent. (should not exceed 4 per cent.), and produced by extremely slow fermentation ; must be very old.   When fifty years old in bottle will fetch from forty to sixty-six shillings each small Tokay bottle. (2) *Ausbruch:* sweet, strong in alcohol (added); must be old : not rarely deposits, like the essence, sugar in crystals. (3) *Maszlacz:* of four different qualities : the quality with 40 per cent. dry berries costs at Tokay from 120 to 160 thalers per eimer, or six shillings the ordinary wine-bottle full. (4) *Szamorodny*, or dry natural Tokay : is fiery and acid, and requires age to develop its qualities, which then are remarkable.   (5) *Ordinari.*—The total production of all qualities in twenty-one communes of the Tokay district is about 268,000 eimer per annum, or about 14,500,000 of litres.   The *Mezes-Male*, or Imperial Tokay, grows at Tarczal, a market town, and is never sold in trade.   Next in quality are the products of Talya, Mad, Liszka, Kirsfaludy, Zsadany. Third in quality of so-called medium Tokays are the wines of Tokay town, Kerestur, Erdöhenye, Toloswa, Nagysaropatak (all four market towns), and of the villages Ond, Zzanto-Olassi, Ujheli, Sara, Golop, Zzegilong, Zombor, Erdö-Herwathi, Ratka, Kis-Zoronyia.   Around these vineyards of the third rank there is a large circle of twenty-five places producing annually 130,000 eimer, which form the fourth and last quality, and include all that can have the most remote title to be called *Tokay-Hegyalja*.

Second Order.—Menes Magyarat, county of Arad. Red and white Ausbruch and natural wines are produced annually in fourteen localities, and amount to 241,000 eimer annually. Vinification as in Tokay district.

Third Order.—Wines of Rust, Oedenburg county. 69,000 eimer produced annually in nineteen localities; white, strong, and sweet Ausbruch and natural wines. The vintage is here mostly very late, some grapes being allowed to hang until December.

B. Wines of the Second Class.

(1) *White Wines.*—Some grow at Somlau, Veszprim county, and are made into table and dessert wines.—Badacsony, on the Plattensee, county of Zala : table, dessert, and Ausbruch wines.—Neszeliny, county Gran.—Ermelleker, county Bihar : strong table and dessert wines.—Szeredny, county Unghu.—Neograd : table wines.—Krasso : dinner and dessert wines.

(2) *Red Wines.*—Erlau Visonta, termed Schiller, or Rubinette, Hevesh county.—Szegzard, county Zolna : wine of fiery taste and honey-like odour.—Villany, county Barany : red wine resembling Burgundy.—Ofner Adelsberger : a good strong wine.—-Krasso.

C. Wines of the Third Class.

Baranya : good red dinner wines.—Pesth, Steinbruch : white dinner wine.—Hont : good white dinner wine.—Presburg : red and white.—Vagh-Ujhelyer : good red dinner wine.—Weissenburg : good white dinner.—Somogy : red and white.—Bakator, Ermelleker, called Bratenwein : white.—Eisenberg : good white dinner.—Raab : good white dinner.—Balaton-Füred : white.—Erdöd : red and pale red (Schiller).—Fünfkirchen : white strong dinner.—Miszla, county Zolna : white, acid.—Oedenburg : white sweetish table wine.—Paulitsch : strong good red.—Neusiedl lake-wine : acidulous dinner wine.—Simonthurn, county Zolud : strong sweetish red.

The rest of the wine-producing places belong to *the fourth class*, which it is unnecessary to give a list of. Their products are mostly very inferior, and consumed by the population. What we have in the foregoing termed dinner or table wines, can be bought in Hungary in large quantities, varying between eighteen and thirty-six shillings per eimer. Clean ordinary wines can be bought at ten to eighteen shillings per eimer.

§ 165. WINES OF THE BANAT, WOIWODINA, AND SYRMIA.

The wines of the Banat and the Woiwodina resemble the small wines of Hungary, and are rarely above the third class. The mode of procedure in vineyard and cellar are still more faulty than in Hungary. The Werschetz mountain in the Banat yields annually about 400,000 eimer, the rest of the Temeser Banat 939,500 eimer, and Syrmia nearly 1,500,000 eimer. The free town of Werschetz is the centre of the most extensive viticultural district of Austria-Hungary, and produces from 200,000 to 300,000 eimer annually. Of select qualities, 150,000 eimer are constantly in store at Werschetz; of these, 15,000 are red, sweet, and alcholic; 15,000 are second class, also strong and red, but not sweet; 15,000 eimer are sweet, pale reddish wine of the first class; about 100,000 eimer generally are dry, spirituous, harsh, schiller-wine of the second class. Of white wine of good quality there are only about 8,000 eimer annually produced; the rest is a very low-class product. Karlowitz in Syrmia produces red and white Ausbruch wine, and a mediocre dry wine resembling low Burgundy; it is made mainly from the Magyocka (Magyarika, or early blue Magyar vine). There are other peculiar wines of Karlowitz. At this place are also produced the *Vermouth liqueur*, and the *Slibowitz*, or *plum brandy*, and exported to many parts of the Orient.

CHAPTER XXII.

WINES OF SPAIN.

§ 166. VINEYARDS OF JEREZ DE LA FRONTERA.[1]

Territory and Varieties of Soil of the Vineyards.—The territory of Jerez is entirely of the so-called tertiary period. It consists of undulating hills, with gently-inclined sides

---

[1] The topographical descriptions occurring in this chapter are best appreciated with the aid of the excellent map of the Jerez district, published in 1867 by Don Jorge G. Suter, the English Consul at Jerez, and sold by E. Stanford, Charing Cross.

The land measure, termed the *aranzada*, is equal to 44·72 French ares, and is therefore about one-tenth larger than the English acre, which is equal to 40·47 ares.

The measure of length, *vara*, is equal to 0·843 metres, or 2·782 feet English, and is therefore a little shorter than the English yard, which is equal to 0·914 metres.

The *bota* (*butt*) of wine or must (*mosto*) measures thirty *arrobas*, equal to 106·5 imperial gallons ; one arroba is equal to 16·133 litres.

The *real* is equal in value to 2½d. English ; four reals, value 10d., are equal to a *peseta*, the Spanish franc ; its value is five per cent. higher than that of the French franc.

The *peso* is an imaginary unit of value by which wines are bought and sold. It is equal to 15 reals.

For the purpose of its *topographical consideration and description* the district may be divided into nine parts, radial sections of a circle, of which the town forms the natural centre, and the roads which lead to and from it form the natural radii. Many years ago I made each of them the object of a special scientific reconnaissance. They are the following :—

1. Balbaina section and group of vineyards, N.W. of Jerez, S.W. of new road to San Lucar, between it and the road to Rota.
2. Corchuelo section, N.N.W. of Jerez, between old and new carriage-road to San Lucar.
3. Macharnudo section, N. of Jerez, between the old road to San Lucar and the road to Trebujena.
4. Carrascal section, N.N.E. of Jerez, between Trebujena and Lebrija road.
5. Section of the plain, or north-eastern section between Lebrija

accessible to cultivation over their entire surface, and slightly-excavated valleys between them. The hills consist of a sand and clay pervaded chalk-rock, which crops out at their tops, or is easily reached by digging a few feet—sometimes only one foot—into the disintegrated surface. It is mostly white, here and there coloured by some iron oxide, and contains chalk or carbonate of lime, clay, or silicate of alumina, magnesia, iron, quartz, and gypsum. The lower parts of the inclines of the hills and the flat valleys between them are covered by alluvial formations of different periods. These contain much clay, iron oxide, and sand, and in many parts pass into mere sand, more or less coloured red by iron-ochre, or white by clay and chalk. These chalk-rocks, clays, and sands give rise to the several descriptions of surface-soil distinguished by the Jerezanos under the denominations of *albariza, barros, barro-arenas,* or *arenas,* and *bugeo.*

The Albariza, also termed *Tierra de Anafes, Tierra blanca ó Tosca,* is the white soil of the hills, the disintegrated tertiary chalk rock According to the analysis of Louis Proust (the French chemist, who lived at Madrid from the time of the first revolution to the Napoleonic invasion of Spain) the soil contains from 60 to 70 per cent. of carbonate of lime, a considerable quantity of clay, a little silica, and some magnesia. When the clay and other ingredients disappear or diminish greatly, so that the soil is little more than chalk, it is no longer termed "tosca" by the natives. The coarse mixture of chalk, sand, and clay is more suitable to viticulture than the finer chalk. Its colour is a dead white; its texture fine-grained and rough, with harder nodules, which appear when the mass is left to dis-

road and Arcos road. This section I divided in two parts, one N. of the Seville road, the other between Seville road and Arcos road.

6. Eastern section, between Arcos road and Hijuela de Pedro Diaz.

7. Monte Alegre section, S. of Jerez, between the Hijuela of Pedro Diaz and the Carretera to Puerto, traversed by the road to the Cartuja.

8. Torrox section, S.S.W. of Jerez, between the carriage-road to Puerto and the bridle-road to the same place.

9. Carrahola section, W. of Jerez, between the bridle-road to Puerto and carriage-road to Rota.

integrate under the influence of sun and water. In that case it breaks up a great deal. When introduced into water it gives out bubbles of air, and falls gradually into a loose pasty mass. When dried again it falls into powder-like particles, and does not cohere in lumps or separate by deep fissures. On the hills it occurs in layers, which have a thickness of several yards, and become thin in other parts, so as almost to disappear. It contains no flints. It is an impure chalk, and reposes upon a sandy formation. The greater part of the vineyards of Jerez, San Lucar, and Trebujena, are upon albariza soil. The vineyards of Paxarete contain it in the immediate subsoil. It is here termed "albero." A thousand vines planted on albariza at San Lucar produce about eighty arrobas of mosto; exceptionally in favoured portions of special territory from 110 to 120.

Barros is the name given to quartz sand agglutinated by chalk and clay, and coloured red or yellowish by iron ochre. It forms horizontal layers of great extent along the coast, from the mouth of the Guadalquivir to Conil. These banks are traversed in all directions by fissures, filled with almost pure sand. The barros is never so hard that it cannot be disintegrated with the fingers. It is easily washed away by the tide and by rain, and becomes very slippery when wet ; but continued rain washes out the chalk and clay, and leaves the stones and sand on the surface. Clemente, the author of a celebrated work on the vines of Andalusia, believes the barros of Jerez to be a small portion of the immense formation of sandy chalk and clay which runs in one uninterrupted course from the shore at San Lucar to Gibraltar. The vines planted upon barros give double the harvests produced by the same number on albariza. Near Jerez, the barros contains many large stones of hard grey chalk, which occur in layers, and are repeated at intervals down to a depth of eighteen feet. It also contains fossil shells, such as ostrea, cardium, pecten, and others, which becomes so numerous in some parts, *e.g.*, near the Badalejo, as almost to constitute the bulk of the soil. Barros and sand mixed form the soil of the plain to the north and north-east of Jerez (*Tierra barro arenosa*).

Arenas (better, *barro-arenas*) form the third variety of soil. The pure, nearly white, shifting sand, such as occurs principally near the sea-shore, is only rarely found in the Jerez district, being limited to some localities in the East, towards Cuartillo, and along the road to the Cartuja.. This sand admits of being transformed into fruitful gardens and vineyards, as can be seen at San Lucar and Rota. At the latter place particularly I was surprised to see the work and care bestowed upon this mere sand, which has actually to be protected against the wind by frequent small enclosures, ridges, and deep furrows. These gardens are called *nabazos*. On such sand the vine produces as much mosto as on the barros, but its quality is as much inferior to that of the barros vineyards as the latter is inferior to that coming from the albarizas. The commonest arena mosto in these days is sold at about half the price of the albariza mosto.

Bugeo is the greyish black earth which at Jerez and San Lucar occupies the dales between, and lowest slopes of, the hills of albariza. It consists of clay mixed with carbonate of lime and fine sand, and a certain quantity of vegetable mould. During the heat of the summer this soil forms enormous fissures, and this is said to be the cause of its inaptitude for viticulture. But at Jerez, as well at St. Lucar, there are vineyards on bugeo. They are very fertile, bringing up to six botas per acre, but the wine is coarse.

The albariza vineyards give the finest, cleanest, and strongest mostos, but produce the smallest quantity. The barro-arenoso lands produce twice as much as the albarizas, and are also much easier to work, but their mostos are less fine and thinner. The bugeo vineyards produce as much as the barro arenasas, and give mostos of as much or even more body than the albariza mostos, but they are neither fine or clean; and the bugeo soil requires much labours because it becomes quickly covered with weeds, and cracks in a manner dangerous to the roots of the vines.

In the trade of Jerez wines are sometimes distingushed as wines of the pagos de arena, wines of the pagos de barro, and wines of the pagos de afuera. The latter term is not a geognostic distinction at all, as the pagos de afuera have soils of all descriptions, and is not comparative to the other two terms. It simply means pagos which are out of the circle of the city boundaries, and at such a distance that the labourers from Jerez receive an addition to their wages for distance.

There are few vineyards, and hardly any pagos, in which all the vines stand upon uniform soil; and if a pago is termed of a particular soil, this is to be understood to mean that that soil is the prevailing, not the exclusive soil. There are, further, a few special names for particular mixtures of soil. *Lustrillo* is a mixture of white marl and albariza and red barro-arenosa soil, interspersed here and there with strata of chalk, or gypsum. Another kind of earth, produced by the accumulation of old building rubbish, is termed *Tierra de villares*, or *Almaduras*. The names of *Balejuela*, and *Lentejuela*, are applied to greatly broken up albariza mixed with a certain material of agricultural improvement or bugeo. *Tajon*, the earthy vein in the limestone, and *toxa*, the rough earth, are forms of albariza which occur in special strata. There are also stony territories which surprise the proprietors by a curious phenomenon, namely, that the stones have a tendency to come to the surface, of course by the action of the rain. But the proprietors prefer the mysterious to the evident, and believe that these stones are constantly being formed, or being worked upwards by some mysterious power in the earth.

The different soils are planted with varying sets of vines, according to empirical traditions which do not admit of precise exposition. In the albarizas the palomino prevails, and is generally mixed with a certain proportion of perruno, cañocazo, albillo, Pedro Jimenez, and mantuo, which are said to impart to the palomino wine superior qualities. In the barro-arenosa territory the mantuo castellano prevails, mixed with much mollar, beba, and other vines in small numbers; on the sand there is a little tintilla, and much beba. The moscatels and Pedro Jimenez grow best in the black earth or bugeo.

§ 167. Climate of Jerez.

The climate of Jerez is determined by its geographical position between the 36th and 37th degree of north latitude, and under the 6th degree of longitude west of Greenwich.

The summer season is characterized by great heat and long-continued drought, during which most of the vegetation, except vines, olive trees, and pines, comes to a standstill, and most annuals die off. The arable land, the grassy plains, and the dry swamps then look like arid deserts, and are avoided alike by animals and man.

The autumn and winter consist in a rainy season, and frost is never observed. Snow has fallen at Jerez only twice in this century. The first fall occurred in 1819, and no particulars regarding it have come to my knowledge. The second and last fall happened on the 9th of December, 1867. The snow lay on the ground for two days, and destroyed many delicate plants. The autumnal rains are copious, not rarely very much so. Thunderstorms of extraordinary severity appear now and then. The north wind in summer is dry and hot; the west wind refreshing and agreeable. The east wind (Levante) easily becomes a storm, which may continue for days without intermission, and do much damage to all kinds of crops. It is said that the vines are kept low on the ground on account of the danger to which they would be subjected on the part of the Levante if they were raised higher and fastened to poles.

§ 168. Extent and Position of the Vineyards.

The vineyards are estimated to have a surface of 14,000 aranzadas, or 6,287 hectares. They are grouped round the town of Jerez in a manner which is best appreciated by inspection of the map. The districts to the N. and N.E. of Jerez are perfect plains, whereas those to the N.W., W., S., and S.E. consist of a series of more or less round hills and hillocks, separated by glens and dales. The hills are mostly covered with vines all over, whereas the glens are mostly not stocked with vines, but with fodder plants, or used for growing the strong reeds (cañas) which are employed for making the stakes for young vines, and the fork-like supports for fruit-laden branches, and give their names to the dales themselves (cañadas). Like land everywhere else in Europe, the whole of the cultivated land round Jerez is divided into sections bearing distinctive names, so-called *pagos*. These pagos, again, consist of several fields or properties; only rarely one entire pago, still more rarely several pagos, also form a single property. The pagos are very unequal in size; many are entirely covered with vineyards.

For a list of the Jerez pagos reference may be made to a brochure on the viticulture and trade of Jerez, by D. Diego Parada y Barreto, which appeared in Jerez in 1868.

§ 169. THE BALBAINA DISTRICTS.

The district of Balbaina is perhaps the oldest viticultural pago in the neighbourhood of Jerez. It lies in a north-west direction from Jerez, on both sides of the new road to San Lucar, mainly between that road and the road to Rota. It consists of five great divisions, of which three only belong to the community of Jerez, while two owe municipal allegiance to Puerto de Sta. Maria. The Jerez Balbaina, properly so called, lies on the north-west, or right side of the San Lucar road, past San Julian, and includes Cande-lero and the Llano de las Tablas. South-west of it lies the largest part of the district, termed Balbaina alta, to dis-tinguish it from the contiguous Balbaina baja, of the Puerto vineyards. Farther to the north-west, also on the left of the road to San Lucar, is the pago of los Cuadrados, with the contiguous Balbaina of Puerto, properly so called.

Balbaina, with Balbaina alta, and including the Puerto Balbainas, comprises more than twelve hundred aranzadas of vineyards. Its soil is albariza and bugeo; its vines are palomino, perruno, cañocazo, albillo, Pedro Jimenez, and mantuo, and its mostos are held in great esteem. The most reputed vineyards are the Cañas, la Campanilla, del Arcon, and del Sargento mayor. Jerez monasteries once held a great part of this district, and a particular plantation they termed the vineyard of God. Candelero, which is contiguous to Balbaina towards San Julian, is a pago of about eighty aranzadas, in the valley which bears its name. The soil is for the greater part bugeo, and its vines are palominos. A special vineyard in the pago also bears its name. North-west of Balbaina, and bordering upon the Cañas, is the Llano de las Tablas, a pago of forty aranzadas, bordering in the north upon Marihernandez.

Just across the San Lucar road is Balbaina alta, a vast expanse of green hills and dales. The first sub-pago nearest to Jerez is Sida, a pago of forty aranzadas, with albariza soil, planted with palomino and Pedro Jimenez. Noted vineyard, la Miranda. Sida derives its name from that of an old Jerez family. Farther on is the Cañada de Huerta, a pago with bugeo soil, and palomino vines. It borders upon the Gallega group of pagos, and upon the Rincones, a pago with albariza, bugeo, and lustrillo soil, and palomino stock. At the southern end of Balbaina alta, and close to and at the right of the road to Rota, is the pago Cruz de Husillo.

At the north-west end of Balbaina alta, and opposite los Cuadrados, we find the pago of Plantalina, forty aranzadas of bugeo and lustrillo soil, with palomino prevailing. Far to the north-west is the pago of los Cuadrados, two hundred aranzadas, with albariza and bugeo soil. The palomino reigns. A noted vineyard is la Soledad. Close by is the pago of las Peonias, with a good vineyard of the same name.

In this neighbourhood I observed a beautiful plantation of albillos. These vines are not ordinarily kept on separate plots of ground, like the palominos, or Pedro Jimenezes, but grown interspersed in uncertain numbers with the prevailing varieties. The Albillo castellano ought to be particularly good for wine making, as will appear from the following description. It is a slender vine, with many canes, lying on the ground, of a silver-grey reddish colour, small palmate leaves, with heart-shaped sinuses, green, but a little reddish when first developed, falling late; the bunches are pyramidal, of middle size; no side bunch; stalk very short; does not shed unripe berries. The ripe berries are very sweet and juicy, and are easily emptied of their contents. The juiciness of the grapes is their most striking characteristic. Clemente says that each bunch may be considered as a bagful of mosto. The ants are great friends of these grapes. Mosto weighed 11 and 12 B. on September 15th and 19th. It readily passes into wine of the quality called fino, but is less good for olorosos, and rarely produces amontillados.

There are two other varieties of albillo, which are less frequently planted in the Jerez vineyards than the former, they are :—

Albillo pardo, also termed *Uva pardilla*, has leaves which are more rough than those of the other varieties of albillo, its grapes are of a yellowish-green, light colour, less mild, and taste more sour, than that of the other albillos, but capable of yielding finos.

Albillo negro. Not frequently planted. Differs from the white albillo by the black colour of its grapes, its thinner husks, and larger bunches. Its canes are also lighter, and the leaves less incised and almost entire.

I also observed some Jaenes, vines which may be supposed to bear their names from a more northern province of Spain.

Jaen negro. Stock of middling size, with many short, greyish-red canes, small leaves of lively yellowish-green colour. They bear many dense bunches of medium size, round, blackish-red grapes, with hard skins, though fleshy. Mosto weighs eleven to twelve B. *Jaen blanco*, also termed *Garilla*, is analogous to the former, but its grapes are white.

§ 170. NEW PLANTATIONS, YOUNG VINEYARDS, MAJUELOS

Modes of working established Vineyards.—The soil is mostly prepared by deep digging, trenches being drawn, and the top earth filled in while the deep soil is brought up. These turnings are more than a vara in depth. They are generally effected in July or August, and if the soil turned up be lumpy, it is left to the atmosphere for a year without any plantation. The young vines are produced mostly from canes, rarely from rooted vines prepared in a nursery. Their distance from each other is from a vara and a half to two varas in every sense, so that each vine has a surface of four square varas allotted to it. This large extent of surface is necessitated by the peculiar mode of turning and working the earth, to be described hereafter. The canes to be planted are a vara in length, and are sunk into the ground in three different methods. Either a hole a vara in depth is dug for each, and after insertion of the cane, filled up (*plantacion por hoyes*); or the vineyard is traversed by ditches, which, after the canes have been laid in, are filled up (*plantacion por cajones*). The last form is that which employs iron bars for making narrow holes in the ground, in which the canes are inserted (*plantacion por barras*). During the early years the young vines are kept surrounded by hollows so as to catch all available water. In the second and third year they receive a support in the shape of a caña or strong reed, and begin to show fruit. They are then cut in a manner to establish the permanent four-armed stocks, and in the eighth year they begin to bear rich harvests. But it is not until the fifteenth or twentieth year of their growth that they produce the best wines. Up to that time these plantations are termed majuelos, only with the eighteenth to twentieth year they reach their majority, and then are termed viñas.

The growth of young vines is very vigorous indeed, particularly in rainy seasons. The first shoots are very long and thick. In dry seasons they come to an early standstill, and many die. Such partial losses in young, and also in old vineyards, are mostly replaced by layers, slips so-called *mugrones*.

A single layer or slip is made in the ordinary manner, described in the seventeenth section of this Treatise, if the object is to produce a single new vine from an old one. The burying is very deep, and the point of the cane projects in the bottom of a deep excavation, intended to collect as much water as possible, and to allow the new cane to be gradually covered up by earth, so that it may have a deep footing.

But when several layers or slips are required from one vine, the latter is buried in a pyramidal hill of earth, termed *voga*. Its four arms are allowed to project, and to grow from the four inclined sides of this hill, and all fruit is suppressed. The canes now grow much more vigorously, because they are fed by the stock itself, as well as by the numerous new roots which they develop in the voga. They may therefore be laid down in the winter following their growth, and in that case are only detached from the mother-stock in the winter following their growth ; or they, or some of them, may be detached entirely in the first winter and used as

Fig. 36.—The " Voga," pyramidal hill of earth, for multiplying a vine fourfold.

rooted plants. After the largest have been detached, the vine is disinterred, and again puts out new branches.

§ 171. ANNUAL LABOURS IN VINEYARDS.

The labours are all performed by men, and on no single occasion have I observed women or children to be employed, even in vintage time and for light work. The working day, which during vintage time lasts from sun-rise to sun-set, is interrupted by two periods allotted for meals and repose. For breakfast, one hour is given ; and for dinner and siesta, two hours. The labourers are paid for the day, practically of nine hours, and I have not learned that there are any who work by piece and contract. They receive the wages mentioned below, and five cigarettes a-day. During the time of active labour, particularly poda, chata, cava bien, and vintage, the men stay in the vineyards; they mess together, and their food, consisting mainly of arranque, is prepared for them by the common cook or housekeeper (*casero*). In cold weather they sit, during the time of meals and repose, around a great bonfire of vine and reed canes, which is lighted in a pit of masonry specially arranged for that purpose in one of the sheds of the vineyard. The smoke escapes through a long slit in the highest part of the roof. The labours which are performed upon the vines and vineyards in the course of the year, are the following:—

Poda.—The pruning, or cutting back of the vine, to maintain its shape and fertility, is performed during October, November, and December. Some viticulturists work the earth before, some after, the poda.

Alumbra, or *Chata,* consists in digging and dressing the land in such a manner that there is a large square basin round each vine, which may catch the rain-water. As the vines are from 1·5 to 1·8 metres apart, in every sense these basins are more than a square metre in width, and one-third of a metre deep. This work begins in October. When the digging is not so much a formation of basins, in case the rains were early and copious, as a stirring, it is termed *chata.*

Hechar Mugrones is the work of making layers or slips.

Resposicion de Marras is the replacement of dead vines.

Deserpia is the removal of suckers projected by the roots.

Desbragar (*desbarbar*) is the taking off of the highest roots, day or dew roots, which, particularly in young plants, become exposed by the chata.

Cava bien is the great digging and refilling of the holes (*cierra*) made by the chata. This is performed in February, after the rains are over, and before the new growth starts.

Castra is the operation of taking off all superfluous shoots and buds previous to and immediately after blossom-time.

Golpe lleno is a digging of the ground after the grape is formed, and before the branches of the vines have become entangled with each other, sometimes even as early as the end of April or beginning of May.

Levantar varas is the operation of supporting branches after the grapes have begun to get heavy, by little forks made of canes or wood. These supports are not higher than the stocks of the vine, and, consequently, the branches are kept in a horizontal position.

Vina is a light digging of the surface of the land, performed in the latter part of June, to destroy the weeds.

Recastra is the second removal of superfluous shoots.

Revina is another hoeing at the end of July, to remove weeds (also termed *aschalado*).

In August the vineyards become covered with the *correguela*, or running weed, a kind of convolvulus, whose roots grow very deep in the ground, and run quickly through great distances, reproducing the plant at the surface with great rapidity. Another common weed is the *castanuela*, a kind of cyperus. The removal of these weeds in August is termed *agostar*.

The vineyard from this time is merely protected by watchmen until the vintage.

Vendimia, the vintage, begins on the 7th or 8th of September, mostly with great regularity, in the best situations. It lasts until the 18th or 20th when regular, when interrupted by rain it may last till the end of the month. Generally it is a most rapid operation.

The vintagers (*vendimiadores*) receive three pesetas a day in money, and have a sleeping room, and mats of rushes (*enea*) provided for them. The pressers (*pisadores*) receive also three pesetas per day, and, in addition, for each bota of mosto pressed one peseta and half a bottle of wine; once during the entire vendimia each pisador gets a basketful of grapes (*un capache de uvas*) or five reals instead.

The removal of the mosto, or wine, from the vineyard to the bodega in Jerez costs for each bota about thirty reals for all distances below and up to one league. Above one league the cost is forty reals per bota. When the removal is by mules the vehicles used are *carros*, when by oxen, *carretas*. I have also seen mules laden with a bota full of mosto each, and believe the practice to be cruel and dangerous, and happily rare.

The day's work of a man is called *peonada*. The price paid for the peonada of each kind varies according to years, weather, and the labour market. In bad years and during bad weather, the day's labour is less valuable, and therefore paid less highly than in good years and fine weather. I witnessed a strike for higher wages in a vineyard at an approaching rain. The capataz defied the men, and the rain passed off. In 1865 labour was so dear that the chata, which ordinarily costs 14 reals per day per man, actually had to be paid as high as 38 reals.

A proprietor of a large well-kept albariza vineyard calculated the cost of his labour per annum, including vintage, to be from £15 to £16 per aranzada, or on the whole one-twelfth of the amount of capital sunk in the vineyard. A generally accepted estimate brings the cost of labour to one real per vine per year.

Manuring is never employed, partly because it is not frequently necessary, partly because the proprietors believe it to be injurious to the grapes. It is difficult to understand this, but the fact remains, that in albariza vineyards, which have been uninterruptedly planted with vines for 300 years, as shown by documents of tenure, no manure is ever employed. In such vineyards there are, however, barren and bald places, which baffle all attempts to replant the vine. They may possibly be chemically exhausted, and here manure should be tried. It is probable that the system of catching the rain-water may act as chemical manuring, for it cannot be doubted that the heavy rains of winter bring much of the constituents of sea-water from the near Atlantic, and in this a portion at least of the salts required by the vine.

Nowhere in this district have I seen vineyards cultivated by the plough, but all labours were done by the arms of men. On the whole, the labours upon the ground are the most serious of any which I have witnessed anywhere. But they seemed out of proportion to the amount of care bestowed upon the vine, and the ripening grape in particular seemed to me mostly neglected in an unaccountable manner. The consideration occurred to me that the bounty of nature is here so great that man has no necessity for husbanding the produce, but if he loses a considerable part of it he can, with the remainder, still make up a profitable account.

§ 172. Productiveness of Vineyards.

Albariza legitima is believed to produce, on an average, from 1½ to 2 botas per arranzada. The dark and arenas soils produce much more, namely, four or five botas, but the must is coarse. This depends mainly upon the quality of the vines, which, for the lower lands, are chosen from the richest bearers. It was stated to me that the arenas grapes commanded a uniform low price, and that therefore an agriculturist would do better to grow quantity rather than to grow fine vines, unless indeed he did not sell his grapes but his wine. The best parts of a Balbaina vineyard give from ten to eleven botas per aranzada. Other pieces give only a half to one butt, and some parts give nothing.

Competent estimates bring the average production on all kinds of soil to three botas per aranzada, or ninety arrobas for every 2,000 vines. If we assume the entire area of the vineyards of Jerez as 14,000 aranzadas, and of these 12,000 to be in bearing, there would be an average annual production of 36,000 botas, or 1,080,000 arrobas of mosto. The average price of mosto may be assumed as 75 pesos, or 1,100 reals per bota, and the value of all the vintages is therefore about 40 millions of reals. Now, as the 14,000 aranzadas all require labour at the rate above detailed (though only 12,000 return at the time), and as the wages for this labour, paid to a population of more than 10,000 men, amount to between 20 and 30 millions of reals, the interest and profit annually reaped by the proprietors of the Jerez vineyards amount to from 10 to 20 millions of reals.

§ 173. Prices of Vineyards.

The usual price for average good vineyards is from 15,000 to 18,000 reals—say 150 to 180 guineas—per aranzada. If the albariza were less absolute, and the vineyard were to enclose places with dark earth, its price would be less. Old vineyards fetch higher prices than young plantations. Young vineyards do not reach first-class value before the twentieth year. The grapes of young vineyards are mostly worked up into vino de color, or into dulce. While some vineyards increase in price (an example which cost 7,000 reals per aranzada in 1833, in 1871 had a value of 37,000 reals) others remain stationary, some lose in value; thus a large vineyard of 80 aranzadas was a few years ago sold for about £16,000; it had been established only about twelve years, and is believed to have been sold at a loss, although by otherwise firm hands. Most vineyard property around Jerez about 1860 had risen to very high prices, but the later years have depressed all prices greatly. This is due to political circumstances, and also to the fact that proprietors have ceased to take personal interest in their vineyards. Consequently returns diminish, and the satisfaction of personal success disappears. While twenty or thirty years ago every proprietor (not always resident in his vineyard) would go to the vineyard during the entire vintage time; now-a-days none superintend their vintages, and the consequence is everywhere visible in dilapidation, deterioration, and neglect.

Second-class vineyards are sold at 8,000 reals per aranzada. The total value of the vineyards of Jerez is estimated at 210 millions of reals.

In 1819 the barro-arena vineyards were held in greater value than the albarizas. An aranzada of vineyard in the pagos of Carrascal or Macharnudo, which have the greatest fame now a-days, was then not much more than from 3,000 to 4,000 reals, while an aranzada of vineyard in Toleze, San Antonio, or Peliron, fetched 7,000 reals and more. A careful consideration of all the conditions of the Jerez districts will show that the barro-arenas soil is economically the most suitable for viticulture. The albariza is being exhausted beyond redemption, unless the proprietors resolve to bring, at least, mineral manure into their vineyards. In fact, the albarizas are dear because fashionable; but if the barro-arenas were planted with the same select stock, they would produce the same quality, and much more quantity, than the albarizas, and therefore obtain a ready market.

The pagos of the Corchuelo and Añina group are situated to the north-west of Jerez, beginning at a distance of about three kilometres, and extending for about five kilometres over the entire space between the old and new roads to San Lucar. They are conveniently reached by either of these roads, or by a field-road running between them direct from Jerez to Corchuelo (the Camino de las Viñas). Close to the town are the vineyard pagos of Picadueña and Miraflores, the latter remarkable for containing on its commanding height the splendid reservoir of the waterworks which supply Jerez with water from the distant mountains (*deposito de las Aguas de Tempul*). These pagos include about eighty aranzadas of barro-arena soil, and are planted with mollares, mantuos, and the uva calona, the fruit of which is mainly used in the shape of verdeo, that is to say, eaten fresh. Close to them is a third small pago, Serrana, on the right of the road del Calvario, which separates it from Miraflores; it belongs to the barro-arena class.

The pago las Salinillas is an albariza hill stocked with palomino, and surrounded by swampy territory impregnated with salt, furnishing the name to the pago, next to Maricuerda. The soil is partly albariza, partly bugeo; its vines mainly palomino. Its surface is from fifteen to twenty aranzadas. In the direction of Corchuelo is the pago of Rui Diaz, of one hundred aranzadas, with the noted vineyard la Lebrijana. To the south lies the pago of Cortadedo, bordering upon Obregon and Rui Diaz. Its extent is ninety aranzadas, with bugeo, albariza, and lustrillo soil, planted with palomino.

The pago, el Corchuelo, is circumscribed by the pagos of Rui Diaz, Cortadedo, Obregon, and Cantarranas, and the lane of Añina. It comprises three hundred aranzadas, and its soil is what is termed lustrillo, being rocky and lumpy albariza, bugeo, and barro-arena mixed, just the same as is found in the pagos of Cuartillo and Majada alta and some others. Prevailing vines are the palominos, with perunno,

Pedro Jimenez, mantuo, cañocazo, and albillo. Its products vary in quality. Noted vineyards are la Recobera, los Desaboridos, and others. The name of the pago is sometimes connected with *corcho* (cork), and *corchuelo* may have signified a plantation of cork trees (*alcornóques*). The word also signifies blockhead.

Close to Corchuelo is the pago of Cantarranas, which borders to the west upon San Julian, and comprises two hundred aranzadas. Its higher parts have albariza, its lower ones bugeo soil. The predominating vine is palomino.

§ 174. Principal Vines most commonly Cultivated and their Distribution in the Pagos.

The principal vines which are most commonly cultivated in the albariza and bugeo districts are the following :—

Pedro Ximenes.—This vine gives mostos of all kinds, but is mainly reputed for the sweet liqueurs, conventionally called wines, which are made by mixing the juice of its sundried grapes with spirit. This dulce is also used for sweetening the ordinary sherries. The stock is large ; the canes are the most erect amongst all varieties of vines in the district. When weighted with a full harvest they sink to the ground, but after the vintage become again upright. The leaves are quite smooth, and not woolly or hairy ; medium to small, lobed or irregularly incised, and possess reddish greenish yellow nerves. By the erect position of the canes, and the yellowish colour of the foliage, a stock or vineyard full of this vine can be easily recognized at a distance. The grapes are not very large, greenish white, and bloomy, the sweetest of all grapes ; the bunches not very large, but yet of southern dimensions. The mostos are from 12° to 15° B., without *assoleo*, but rise to 22° B. after about ten days' exposure to the sun.

The legend that this vine had been brought by one Pedro Ximenes from the Canary Islands and Madeira to the Rhine, and had thence been transplanted to Spain, was first published by the German author F. J. Sachs ("Ampelographia," Lipsiæ, 1661, 8vo). It has since made the round of literature, and is an established, but nevertheless completely erroneous tradition. Odart says characteristically, that this story might flatter a German, but could make a Frenchman only smile. For if Pedro Ximenes had taken away any of this vine from the Rhine, he must have taken all. The vine is not found on the Rhine. It is a large-graped vine, which would never ripen in any German vine-yard. The fallacy ought therefore to be discarded.

A less frequent variety of the foregoing vine is the *Pedro Ximenes Loco*—a name reminding us of the French *la folle blanche*. It is also termed *soplona*, the tale-bearer, informer; names for which the reasons are not assigned. Stock strong; canes horizontal; leaves not provided with reddish nerves; bunches and grapes large, and of slightly rough taste.

The most esteemed of all the vines of the Jerez district is the *Palomino*, also named *Palomino blanco*, *Listan commun*, *Tempranilla*, *Orgazuela*, *Alban*, and *Ojo de liebre*. The stock is strong, the canes are thin and long, and numerous, reddish grey, or whitish red; leaves medium-sized, equal, dark green on the upper, woolly on the lower face. The blossoms come early, and develop into large bunches. The grapes are of medium size, of a greenish waxy colour and bloomy appearance, becoming very much bronzed when struck by the sun, which spoils their quality; they give mostos of 14° and 15° B. The wine obtained from it develops mostly into fino, but not into oloroso. This vine is the most common on the albariza soil of the Jerez district.

A very delicate variety of the foregoing vine is the *Palomino negro*, also termed *Centella*. Similar to foregoing, but with black grapes; very fine taste; little grown; used for *vino de color*.

Perruno.—Strong stock, with many erect, straight reddish grey canes, irregular shining leaves, many large bunches, with small, round, translucent grapes, of bronze yellow colour. They are very late and hard, not too sweet, and have astringent husks. The mostos have 12° B., and are good for olorosos of high flavour.

Perruno negra differs from the former mainly by its black grapes; it is not utilized for the production of wine at Jerez.

The Añina road separates the pagos of Mariañez, Cerfate, Orbaneja, Añina, Cerro, del Marmol, and Montana on the northern, from Marihernandez, Montana, San Julian, and Zarzuelo on the southern side of the group.

Mariañez is a pago of twenty aranzadas, between Añina and Corchuelo, and bordering upon Cantarranas, Cerfate, and Marmol. Its heights are albariza, its lower parts bugeo. Cerfate is situated at the entrance of the pago of Añina, close to the Cerro de Orbaneja. It has fifty aranzadas, and its soil and plantations are like those of Añina. Close to the old San Lucar road, and separated from it by the opposite pago of Amarguillo, which I shall describe in connection with the Macharnudo group, is the Cerro de Orbaneja. The Cerro borders upon Añina, Cerfate, and Mariañez, is 150 aranzadas in extent, its soil is albariza and bugeo, and other earth in the lower parts, and its principal vine is palomino. On the right of my road lay Añina, stretching towards the San Lucar road, bordering upon Orbaneja, Cerfate, and Marihernandez in the west. Its territories are partly bugeo, partly albariza, and partly villares, that is to say, soil formed by the destruction of ancient habitations. Its area is one thousand aranzadas, on which the ubiquitous palomino predominates. Prominent vineyards are del Aljive, del Alamo, del Caribe. Close to Añina is the Cerro del Marmol, twenty to thirty aranzadas in extent, with a rocky subsoil, whence its name is derived.

The most north-western end of the Añina group is formed by the pago of Montana, two hundred and fifty aranzadas in extent, with soil varying between bugeo and albariza. In the south-west it borders upon the pago of Marihernandez, which in the east touches San Julian, and in the south abuts upon Balbaina. It has eighty aranzadas, and bugeo prevails on its surface, although the summits are albariza. I returned by the Hijuela de Candelero, keeping on my left the pagos of San Julian and Zarzuela. The latter lies between Candelero and Cantarranas, and has lustrillo, bugeo, and albariza soil. Its vines are palominos, mantuos, and albillos. San

Julian has 300 aranzadas, and stretches from Zarzuela to the new road to San Lucar. Its soil is good albariza, its wines are mainly palominos, with interspersed perrunos, albillos, cañocazos, mantuos, and Pedro Jimenez. It yields wines of the first quality.

Passing out of the Candelero road into the old San Lucar road, the topographist passes the last pago of this group, completing the list, namely, the Cerro de Obregon, eighty-five aranzadas in extent, a plantation of albariza and bugeo soil. Along San Julian and Balbaina this road exhibits to the eye some good long and deep sections of the albariza territory, the white hard rock, softer surface, and overlying white or coloured bugeo earth.

The Cerro de Santiago is a pago of more than 200 aranzadas, bordered to the west by the old San Lucar road, and in the north passing directly into Macharnudo bajo. Its soil is albariza, and it contains the noted vineyards del Capitan and de la Trinidad. In a north-west direction is the pago of Doña Juana, bordering upon the bye-road del Alferez Tuerto, the low arable lands between Macharnudo bajo and the pago of Amarguillo. The name of this latter is derived from a spring of bitter water in proximity to the pago. Its vineyards are divided into two patches, situated on the right or eastern side of the old road to San Lucar, which road separates them from the pagos of Añina and Orbaneja. In the north, Amarguillo passes into Valcargado, Pelado, and Tizon. Its soil is, for the greater part, bugeo, its vines are palominos and moscatels. From a height one sees the pago of Puerto escondido, isolated between Amarguillo and the Cerro del Pelado. Its extent is seventy aranzadas of lustrillo soil, its vines are palomino, perruno, Pedro Jimenez, moscatel, albillo, and mantuo. On the right of the San Lucar road, past Amarguillo and Puerto escondido, between Tocina, Tizon, and Valcargado, one sees the Cerro del Pelado, with albariza heights, bugeo in the lower parts, and palomino prevailing on its ninety aranzadas. Farther to the north-west, close to the Cerro del Pelado, is the pago of Tizon, with 200 aranzadas of albariza and bugeo soil, and planted with palominos. Between Tizon and Amarguillo, close to the latter, is the pago of the Tocina, 100 aranzadas in extent, with soil varying between lustrillo of albariza, bugeo and barro-arena. Its vines are palominos and mantuos, and of its vineyards the most noted is the one del Garrotal, also named del Canónigo. East of Tizon, north from our point of view, and stretching towards Macharnudo, we see the pago of Valcargado, with a surface of 100 aranzadas, bugeo and albariza soil, and palomino vines. East of Valcargado and bordering upon Macharnudo bajo is the pago of Tabajete, of sixty aranzadas, with albariza and bugeo soil planted with palomino. We take the road which borders this pago to the east and divides it from Macharnudo bajo, termed Hijuela de Tabajete, and then turning towards the east take the Hijuela alta, which separates Macharnudo bajo in its entire length from the isonymous high pago. Thus we are in the midst of what is termed comprehensively Macharnudo, perhaps the greatest pago of Jerez, having more than 1,500 aranzadas of vineyards. In the east it abuts for several kilometres upon the Trebujena road.

Its soil is mostly white plastic albariza, with interspersed low-lying bugeo districts. Its vines are palomino, perruno, Pedro Jimenez, albillo, moscatel, cañocazo, and mantuo ; palomino forms half the set. It yields excellent wines. Noted vineyards are those of la Compania, and Domecq's, originally planted by Haurie, 400 aranzadas in extent.

§ 175. Pruning of the Vines.

The cutting instrument used for pruning is termed *hoz de poda*. The long part, *boca*, bears the oblique cutting edge with which the canes are cut downwards. The *peto* is a kind of light hatchet, and used as such upon trunks and dry old wood. In cold weather this hoz not rarely breaks the branches, particularly of young vines, therefore upon such advanced viticulturists now perform the poda by means of the secateur. Each established vine is generally so trained that it carries four arms on a low trunk. Ideally these arms should be at right angles to each other, but

as the vines have no supports, and the branches are heavily
dragged down by the fruit, they are mostly wonderfully con-
torted.   Long fruit-branches may bear from ten to twelve
eyes. The three remaining arms are mere stumps of old wood,
which, if any, have but one or two eyes left to them. There
is here a curious mode of cutting through the node of the
cane without considering the eye close by. When the fruit-
branch has been borne by one arm during one year, it is in
the following established on the next arm to the left, and the
arm with the obsolete fruit-branch is cut down to a stump.
In this manner the fruit-branch travels round the vine
like a game of cards, from right to left, once in four years.
This cycle is observed in the whole land of Sherry.

Fig. 37.—The " Hoz de Poda," or pruning knife and hatchet.

After the pruning, the vines look so mutilated and
stumpy, compared to their former richness in branches,
that the uninitiated can scarcely comprehend the manner of
their recovering the autumnal appearance.   This was
strongly felt by an English visitor, who expressed his
fear of what might happen if the pruned vines should take
it into their heads not to grow again, and caused him to ex-
claim anxiously, " Y si no mete? "

The pruning is always effected with the intention of
causing the branches to grow towards the ground ; therefore,
stumps which are directed towards the earth are preferred to
those which are turned upwards.   When old wood is so
situated that its cutting off might endanger the fruit-branch,
it is left.   This is the result of the use of the coarse instru-

ment, the hoz, above described. I have not heard of the use of saws, which in the Gironde now everywhere accompany the use of the secateurs.

In old vineyards young vines are practically all produced by slips. In new plantations the vines are produced by canes, or by rooted plants trained in a *plantera*, or nursery. The new stocks are always planted in a deep hollow, which is gradually filled up. When the plant has obtained a good

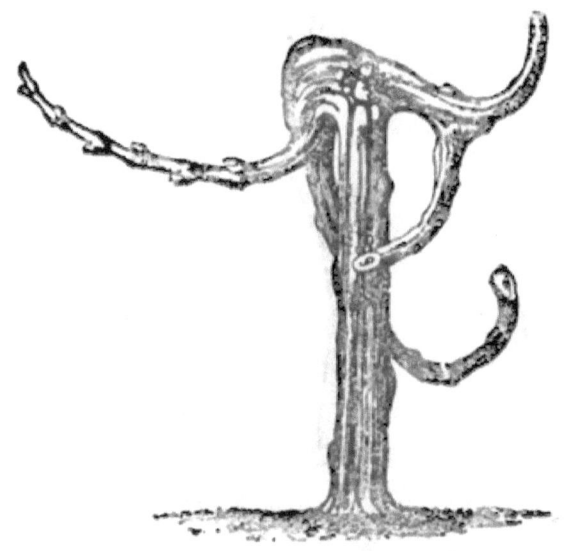

Fig. 38.—Vine pruned for spring growth.

size, and consists of a good strong cane, it is cut for establishing the foot, that is to say, whereas before it was cut close to the ground, now it is cut at a height of one foot from the ground. Two eyes only are left to it at the top, from which two canes grow. These two canes are in the next autumn cut so as to leave two spurs of two eyes each. Out of each eye a new cane is produced, and these four canes furnish the four permanent arms of the vine. At the top of the primary stem a little dead wood is left to indicate the spot at which the primary cane was cut from the establishment of the foot. This little stump is, curiously enough,

never removed by the vine-dresser. Here I also noticed
some striking cases of the diseases affecting the vine in
Xeres; the most remarkable of them is the *ageña*—the
insolation, or sun-stroke of the leaves, which causes them to
die in part or entirely. Many leaves in 1871 showed this effect
in the shape of black or brown patches of dead tissue. This
ageña also affected the grapes, and gave to many of them a
nice golden brown face, a feature considered a prime
quality in the chaselas of France, and termed *doré* (gilt).
But the grapes so affected at Jerez are always inferior, and

Fig. 39.—Vine in the second, third, and fourth year.

never attain either the sweetness or aroma of pale greenish
grapes which have ripened in complete shade of the leaves.
The ageña affects young vines more than old ones, and
causes great havoc in nurseries (*planteras*).

§ 176. RARER VARIETIES OF VINES.

The *Abejera* derives it name from the preference shown
to it by the bees (*abejas*). It has a thick foot, with many
canes, of silver-grey, yellowish colour, partly hanging, partly
standing erect. The canes have many laterals. The leaves
are entire, or nearly so, somewhat rugose, and of a pale
green colour on their surface, and woolly on the underside.
The branches are pyramidal, the grapes green, juicy, and

sweet, less cloying than those of the albillo castellano, which, in other respects, it much resembles. It occurs in Espera as the exclusive stock of vineyards or patches.

The *Agracera*, distinguished by the *agraz*, or acid taste of its grapes, which is said to make it useless for the production of wine. It is a late-ripening vine, forms flowers until the end of the spring, and ripens some of its fruit only in November. Its grapes are very large, black or violet; the bunches are mostly small, and poorly provided with grapes. Sometimes, however, when the vine is planted in good soil, they become large and close grained. It is almost exclusively grown in espaliers. The stock is slight, the canes are numerous, and have many branches; their colour is greenish-white, and sometimes reddish. The leaves are small, shining, dark green, and almost smooth. They remain long on the vine.

The *Agracera de soto* is a variation of the foregoing. Its grapes are less black and less acid, and ripen earlier than those of the ordinary agracera. It also resembles a little to the *melonera*. It is more suitable for wine (say the Jerezanos) than the other two varieties, because it is less acid.

The pago el Almocaden lies along the right side of the Trebujena road, opposite high Macharnudo. The road is here also termed the cross-road or thoroughfare of Almocaden, as if this pago were situated on both sides of the road. Its soil is albariza, with palomino mainly, mixed with some mantuos, moscatels, and others. The principal vineyard is that of Matamoros. The name of Almocaden is Moorish, and signifies captain or chief of troops guarding the fields. To the right is the pago of Cuadros, fifteen to twenty aranzadas of vineyards upon the rivulet of the same name, abutting on the road to Trebujena, between it and that of Carrascal. The soil is bugeo, with some albariza, mainly planted with palomino. Carrascal is a pago of seven hundred aranzadas, enjoying great reputation. Carrascal means a forest or plantation of evergreen oaks; it may, therefore, be assumed that these preceded the vines in this pago. The soil on the heights is albariza, in the lower parts

bugeo.   Its predominant vine is palomino, with some
cañocazo, Pedro Jimenez, and albillo. It yields fine mostos
and superior dulces.   It forms the centre of the group of
pagos which lie between the road to Trebujena and that to
Lebrija.   It contains large vineyards, and amongst them
that of Amoroso and that of the Corregidor.

Amoroso lies on a lower hill, surrounded by a circle
of higher ones, and therefore well protected from inclement
winds, particularly the dreaded *levante*.   It produces the
amoroso sherry, which is well known and frequently
imitated.   Some time ago, I saw an advertisement of a
London wine merchant, stating that he had fine amoroso,
that he did not know why it should be called so, but it was
much liked, and therefore, etc.   He and his customers
will perhaps thank me for the information, that Amoroso
was the name of the original proprietor and planter of this
vineyard, who lived at the beginning of this century, and is
remembered as a contributor to the work of Clemente.   But
for this reason the name might be considered objectionable,
particularly as the Italians play much with the root of amor
in the names which they give to many of their vinous productions, such as amorino, amoroso, amoretto, and others,
all of which occur not unfrequently on labels.

The vineyard contains some palomino negro, which is
generally used for dulce, or vino de color. The vineyard of
Romano is to be noted, because it used to be ornamented
with a great growth of Marvels of Peru (Suspiros), with
white, red, yellow, and violet flowers.   Some yellow flowers
were piebald, one-eighth of their entire petal being red.

§ 177. Vintage—The Lagar—Pressing the Grapes— Pisa.

The gatherers, or vintagers, all men, select the best grapes
for dulce, to be dried on the platform.   Each has a box
(*tineta*), with a strap of esparto fixed on one side, by which
the box is hung over arm or shoulder.

The full tinetas are taken to the platform, and their contents emptied on mats.   The next operation is the removal

of the main stalks, which is effected by cutting the side-branches of the bunches away from the stalks by means of knives. This is done for dulce only, and not for other wine. The buildings are, by their size and convenience, well adapted

Fig. 40.—The " Lagar,' or platform for treading and pressing grapes.

for vino-poetic purposes. In a large hall are the sleeping mats of the labourers, the pit for their nightly bonfire, and the copper for boiling the must. In a large shed behind this are the lagares, in number adapted to the size of the estate, and a hydraulic press.

The lagar used in Andalusia is a large square wooden trough, in which the grapes are trodden and pressed, but never fermented. It differs, therefore, greatly from the Portuguese lagar, which is mostly of stone, and serves for treading and pressing as well as fermenting the mosto, at least during the initial most stormy period. The platform or even bottom of the Jerez lagar is a square of about three yards on each side. The sides of the trough are from eighteen inches to two feet high, and slope inwards towards the bottom. The top of the trough measures, therefore, about three and a half yards in each direction. In the centre of the platform a wooden or iron screw is fixed perpendicularly. This is about seven feet long ; it carries a heavy nut, to which strong levers are attached, this entire piece from end to end being about two yards in length, The necessity of getting this piece out of the way of the workmen, when they are treading and manipulating the grapes, causes the enormous length of the screw—for while only the lower half or third of the screw is actually used for pressing grapes, the upper half or two-thirds serves to screw up the nut and levers to a height above the heads of the workmen. The lagar is raised above the ground about a yard or more, and slightly inclined in the direction of the side, where there is a spout for the juice to flow off. Sometimes the lagar is raised sufficiently high to allow a bota to be placed under the spout and receive the juice directly. But more commonly the spout delivers the juice into a tub, even when the lagar is high enough to allow the bota to be placed directly under its spout. Of such lagares there are generally a number kept ready in the building attached to each vineyard. In some vineyards, of which I knew the dimensions, I counted that one lagar was kept for every eight or ten aranzadas of vineyard, so that on each lagar there would be made from thirty to forty botas of mosto during each vintage.

The grapes are spread on the lagar, and immediately dusted over with burned plaster of Paris (*Yeso*). Perhaps from twenty to thirty pounds of plaster are thus employed, enough in any case to precipitate all tartaric acid and leave a large excess of sulphate. Two men (*pisadores*), lightly clad in short breeches, wearing leather shoes, the entire soles of which are covered with heavy iron nails, now tread the grapes in the lagar. The treading proceeds first in one direction, and then at right angles to it, over the entire lagar. The juice does not run from the lagar while the trodden grapes are lying spread, but begins to flow when they are heaped up in one corner and patted with the shovel. New grapes are now spread over the lagar, and trodden, and

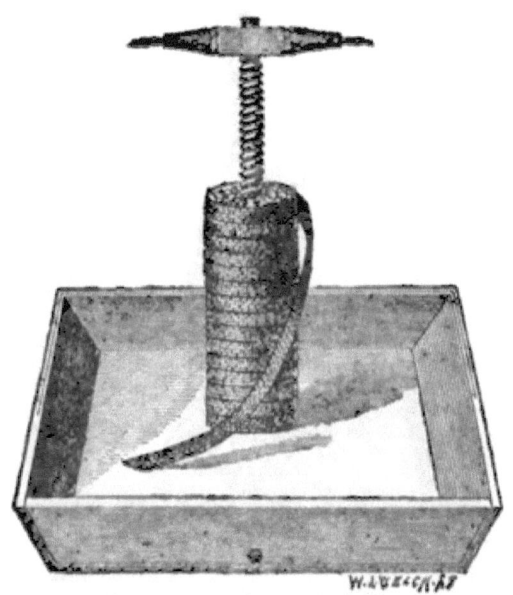

Fig. 41.—The murk bandaged with esparto band, previous to pressing.

shovelled aside; and this is repeated until a sufficient quantity has been treated to give a bota of mosto and a quantity of murk sufficient for a pressing, and for leaving a dry cake of sufficient size. The trodden murk is now heaped up around the screw, which stands in the centre of the lagar, and is with great labour and difficulty worked up into a high conical heap. The lagar is swept, and all is carefully collected. To see the pisadores building this *pie* with the shovel, and ever and anon patting it with the hands, cutting, bending, and adjusting it, and then see the murk bulge out here and yonder, and require a new effort on the part of the pisadores, reminded me greatly of the efforts of boys to construct a snow man in thawy weather. At last, however, the column stands, and is now ready for being bandaged. A long band, made of esparto grass, three to four inches broad, is wound round the cone of murk from below upwards in a spiral direction; both ends are fastened by being clenched between two rounds of the band itself. Frequently the

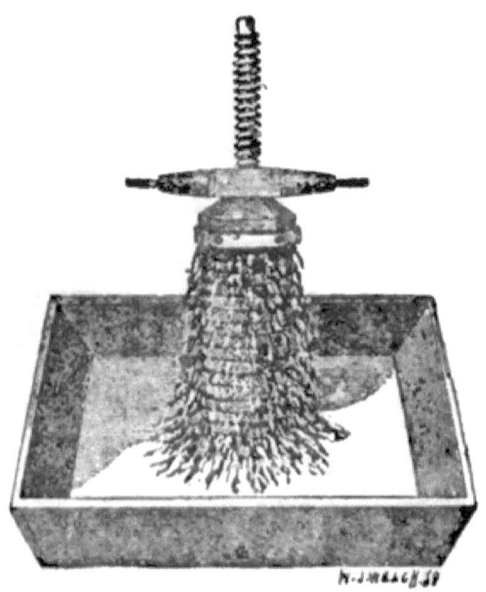

Fig. 42.—Pressing of the bandaged murk with the screw. Juice flowing.

windings are not uniform, so that no spiral result is obtained. When well built, the structure resembles much the representation of the tower of Babel in Merian's picture Bible. About fifteen rounds of the band are required to cover a cone about a yard in height. The top of the murk is covered with a plate, over this passes the nut of the screw to which the levers are fastened, and the murk is now compressed by turning the nut downwards. As this proceeds the murk gives out juice, and the spiral circles of the esparto bands are pressed, the upper ones behind or inwards of the lower ones.

At last the labour of turning the screw becomes severe. To overcome the friction of the plate, the men have to jerk their bodies violently, and as they might thereby lose the grasp of the levers and fall, they tie their hands to the levers. When the murk is compressed so that the two men jerking simultaneously at the levers can no longer move the screw, the pressing is complete. The cake is allowed to remain in this compressed state for a time and is then removed.

Some now subject the entire murk, distributed on mats, to a second compression in hydraulic presses ; others remove the stalks by working the murk on sieves, treat the murk with water and then compress between mats, others, again, simply pour water on the murk and press it between mats. The product is not put with the must or used for wine, but kept and fermented by itself and ultimately taken to the distillery.

The juice which runs from the most inclined part of the lagar through a spout passes through an iron-wire sieve, of the shape of an oval basin, hung over the end of the spout to retain pips and husks, and then flows into a tub (*tina*), whence it is ladled by flat spoons resembling bankers' money shovels, into jugs, and from them poured through a finer sieve, placed inside a wide funnel (*embudo*), into the butts.

This mode of pressing is highly laborious, and yet does not yield a dry cake of murk. Its only advantage is that it is not strong enough to press juice out of the stalks ; but, as no care is taken to exclude the last portions of juice from the husks, which are always harsh, from the mosto, this feebleness is only a partial protection against the coarse elements of the murk. We can judge of this process better by comparing it with the method of pressing used in the Champagne. Here the must is collected in four or five different stages and mixed consciously only, *i.e.* after trial of each portion by gustation, with the distinct object of obtaining the finest and purest juice and excluding acerbity. Compare also with the Jerez mode of pressing, that which is used in Styria and Dalmatia, and the description of good wine-presses as used in the Gironde.

§ 178. Further Description of Pagos, their Soils and Vines.

The pago nearest to Jerez reaching from the Lebrija road to the Sevilla chausée is the Cruz de las Caballeras. Thirty aranzadas of barro-arena are here planted with mantuos and mollares. United to this is the Pié de Rey, a pago of eight or ten aranzadas. Farther N.N.E. lies Bogar, (or Bogas), a baro-arena pago of ninety aranzadas, extending from the Ducha to the Sevilla road.

About one and a half kilometres from Bogar, in the direction toward Ducha, on both sides of the Ducha road, and looking towards Carascal on the west, and Val de Pajuela on the east, is the pago of Doña Rosa, barro-arena with some albariza, about thirty aranzadas in extent. Its vines are mantuos and mollares. The most extreme pago in this section on the Sevilla road, and stretching on its eastern side to the railway, bordered on the N.E. by the cañada ancha is Val de Pajuela, a barro-arena pago of one hundred aranzadas. On it mantuo predominates.

The second section of the north-east district lies between the Sevilla road and the Arcos road. The pagos nearest to Jerez are Jarreta, pago of barro-arena near cemetery, between the road de la Zanja and the carriage road to Arcos. Here also lies Membrillar, close to the rivulet of the same name; its extent is about forty aranzadas. Laguna del Jabonero is a pago which may have been a swamp in which soda-plants, yielding ash fit for soap-making, grew. A part is occupied by the cemetery. Close to it and the cemetery is the Peral del Cangrejo, a pago of barro-arena, and close to this, bordering upon Jarretta, is Peliron, barro-arena, forty aranzadas in extent. Close to the Peral del Cangrejo is the pago of Cuatro Novias, barro-arena, thirty aranzadas. It borders upon the suburbs of Jerez.

On the right side of the Sevilla road, between this and the road De la Zanja, below Valdepajuela, lies the la Zanja, and a side-road called of Largálo, lies the barro-pago of Santo Fé, barro-arena, twenty aranzadas in extent. Between the long narrow lane which runs almost parallel with the Sevilla road, called Callejon de arena pago of Largálo, with a surface of 200 aranzadas. Close to this, and in the direction of Las Abiertas, is Pelona, a barro-arena pago. Here also is Percebá, a barro-arena pago of twenty aranzadas, planted with mantuos and mollares.

The most eastern pago, situated close to the high-road to Arcos, between the olive-groves of Alcántara and land belonging to the Cortijo de la Peñuela, is the pago of Alcántara. It gave its name to the Marquisate of that name, which was bestowed in the seventeenth century upon the Jerezano D. Agustin Villavicencio. Its soil is albariza, its surface one hundred aranzadas—the palomino predominates upon it. Its most notable vineyard is that called of the Cartuja, formerly the property of the monastery of that name on the Guadalete. The last pagos of this group to be described are the Abiertas de Caulina vineyards, in the plain of Caulina, forming the extreme E.N.E. end of the group, and bordering upon the Llanos de Caulina. They extend from the Arcos road to the Callejon de la Zanja, and are traversed by the railway. On the north they are bounded by Santa Fé, on the south by El Pinar. Their soil is barro-arena, their vines are mantuos and mollares, and their surface is one hundred and forty aranzadas.

§ 179. FURTHER DESCRIPTION OF JEREZ VINES.

The vines most commonly grown in this and the following district are the mantuos, mollares, the ferral and beba. I subjoin a short description of them and of their subordinate varieties :—

Mantuo Castellano.—This vine occupies one-half of the Jerez vineyards. Its stock is strong ; its canes are numerous and large ; at the thick end they are greyish red, towards the point whitish red ; the leaves are yellowish green, and reddish when they are shed ; they are of medium size, entire, and woolly on the lower face. The numerous bunches are large ; the grapes large, equal, of good taste, and ripen a fortnight later than those of the palomino ; they rot easily in rainy weather. They are peculiarly consistent, without being hard, as if the juice was shut up in many small receptacles. Many dark stones make the grape disagreeable to eat. Its mosto is very heavy, ranging from 9·7° to 14° B, and developes into wines termed finos.

Mantuo de Pila.—The canes are somewhat irregular; the grapes hard; sweet, but late; this lateness necessitates that they should hang on the vines beyond the time of the general vintage, which causes them to be inconvenient grapes for wine-making, if not kept by themselves. Its name is derived from Pila, the town in the province of Seville.

Mantuo morado.—Similar to the other mantuos, but differing by the violet colour of its grapes.

Mantuo Cordovi.—Whitish strong canes; leaves yellowish green; grapes large, bronzed, and translucent.

Mantuo lacren, ladrenado, or layren.—Name derived from the Arabic, of problematical meaning. Similar to the former; its grapes are less translucent and later ripe; its bunches more pyramidal.

Canocazo.—Arabic name, signifying soft mild grape. Is also termed *mollar blanco.* The stock is strong, its canes are numerous and straggling, some being upright, others on the ground, hanging in all directions; they are thick, and of a greyish red colour, with some yellow admixed. The large leaves are almost entire, yellowish green; the branches are large, with many grapes, and giving a mosto of from 11° to 12° B, which produces high-flavoured olorosos. When well dried in the sun it may be advantageously combined with Pedro Jimenez for dulce.

Mollar negro, also termed *Sevillano.*—Stock middling; canes numerous, hanging, greyish red; with large and almost round leaves of yellowish green colour, which become red before the fall. The bunches are large and numerous, the grapes black. Very commonly grown in Jerez, and used for verdeo. Mosto weighs from 9° to 14° B.

Ferrar, also *ferral.*—Stock strong, with few short, thick, erect canes, of a greyish red colour. Leaves yellowish green; bunches large; grapes nearly black, large and very late. In unfavourable years and conditions the husks remain violet, even green, though the contents are quite sweet. It should be grown on espaliers in protected places, upon the so-called extension system, with many branches, like the so-called Hambro' vine of English conservatories, the Tyrol grape, to which it has much resemblance. It is supposed that from the richness in branches (when it is grown on espaliers) the Arabic name *ferrar* is derived. Its mosto is not very heavy, Clemente finding it $8 \cdot 5°$ B. I have observed it at $14°$ B, from very ripe ferrars. Clemente says that its must was not good for wine, as it was too acid. This has been so often repeated, that it is now generally believed; but it is an error. The nonsuitability for wine of the ferrar arises from its liability to form scud immediately after fermentation, and to shed its colour and lose quality. As regards acidity, it must not be forgotten that what in Andalusia is acidulous, would be very sweet indeed even in the Gironde.

The last of the favourite vines in this district is the Beba. Its stock is of middling size, with canes which are red, and have the silver-grey hue; they sink to the ground. The leaves are large, and appear whitish, owing to a downy covering; in shape irregular, palmate, lobed, and of uneven surface. The bunches are pyramidal, and dense, and the grapes are large and hard, and frequently bronzed. They are late, and therefore are suitable for being hung up for later use, or for being transformed into raisins. Large quantities are sold as verdeo. As I have repeatedly used, and shall have again to use this expression, I give some explanation of its meaning. Verdear is the selling of fruit for the purpose of its being eaten fresh, or transformed into other products. Thus it is said that the inhabitants of Velez transport to Malaga, in the month of July, "para verdear," or "para verdeo," 250 mule loads of sugarcane. The grapes which are sold as such at Jerez are termed "verdea," but it does not follow that they are all eaten. A portion, no doubt, is made into wine, although produced and sold, in the first instance, as verdeo. (See Clemente, p. 136, footnote 1.)

Calona.—This vine has a medium-sized stock, and few

straight and erect canes. The leaves are almost entire, unequally punctured, and of a yellowish green colour. The bunches are large, the grapes large and white, tasty, but sour; this is indeed indicated by its name, which is Arabic and indicates acid or vinegar. It is an early grape and used for eating. Its black brother, the *Calona negra*, also termed *Carchuna*, has yellower leaves than the former, and large thick black grapes. They are sweeter and earlier than the white ones, and liked for eating.

The *Uva de Loja* belongs to the class of datileras, has numerous straggling canes, and small and light yellowish leaves. The grapes are large and frequently two-winged; when single they are conical; the berries have thin husks, and are good for raisins and for eating. The name is derived from the town of Loja.

A kind of vine, not frequently grown here, and possibly identical with the Malvasia of Greece, is the *Malvasia*. Canes erect, short, whitish red. Leaves large, irregularly lobed or palmate; grapes transparent, white, very delicate to eat, sweet, and early, but with a thick skin. Comes from Cataluña. Another interesting vine is the *Vigiriega commun*. Middling-sized stock, many canes, and yellowish leaves, of middling size, almost entire and round. Bunches few; grapes almost round, greenish white, and very sweet, being good for mosto and for eating. A variety of it is the still more rare *Vigiriega negra*, black, and much less sweet than the former.

§ 180. CLASSIFICATION OF GRAPES, IN THE ORDER OF THEIR QUALITY FOR MAKING WINE.

Pedro Jimenez—the finest grape, little grown in Jerez, mostly used for dulce; sweetest grape.

Palomino—the dominating vine; produces finos and amontillados; made pure.

Perruno—produces high-flavoured olorosos.

Mantuo castellano—solid fleshy grape.

Mantuo de Pila—late grape.

The foregoing alone form sets in vineyards.

The following never form sets, and are not prized for wine :—

Beba—esteemed for eating.

Cañocazo—scarce ; produces high-flavoured olorosos.

Ferral, Mollard, and Palomino Negro—are used by proprietors for making vino de color, as if from white grapes, not red. The ferral and mollar are rejected by the purchasers of partidos.

Almuñecar and Albillo—the most juicy or fluid of grapes.

The proportion in which any of these vines are reared in vineyards may be seen under the description of each district. For common vineyards no proportion can be stated. I inspected some crops while they were being emptied on the lagares (September 15, 1871), and found them to consist of a mixture of the following grapes, enumerated in the order of their apparent frequency :—Beba, Mantuo Castellano, Palomino, Albillo, and Mollar.

§ 181. Eastern, Southern, and Western Group of Pagos.

The eastern group comprises the section between the Arcos road and the Hijuela de Pedro Diaz. The first pago out of Jerez by the Arcos road is that of San Antonio, situated close to the town, upon the drain or sewer de los Alunados, between the carriage-road to Arcos, or footpath del Badelejo on the one and the footpath of the Canaleja on the other side. Its extent is thirty to forty aranzadas ; its soil is barro-arena, its vines are mantuos and mollares. On the south-east of, and close to the former pago, is that of the Pozo de Ramos, twelve aranzadas in extent. It is close to Jerez, and approached by the long narrow lane La Manga del Toril. Its soil is barro-arena ; its vines are mantuos and mollares. East of San Antonio, and bordering upon the road of Badalejo, is the mantuo-bearing pago of Barbadillo. Between this, the Arcos road and the pago El Pina, is that of Cabrestera, forty aranzadas in extent. In this group also lies Garrido, a pago of about twenty aranzadas, and Piedra del Mirabel, of thirty aran-

zadas. Continuing by the Badalejo road, we meet on the
left the large pago of El Pinar, which bears its name from
a plantation of pines contained in it, and includes one
hundred aranzadas. On its north side this pago is bordered
in its whole length by the Arcos road, in the east it borders
upon the Caulina plain and Badalejo. South of El Pinar,
and on the right of the Badalejo road, is situated the long
pago of Canalejo, confined on its south side by the road of
the same name, with fifty aranzadas of vineyard, The name
is probably derived from criadero de cañas, cañaveral, or
more probably from canaléja, a drinking trough. The soil
of all the foregoing pagos, when not differently characterized,
may be assumed to be barro-arena, and to be planted with
mantuos and mollares.

East of the Canaleja is the small barro-arena pago of
Catalana, forming a compact mass of vineyards, with the
larger pago of Badalejo. This is situated where the Canaleja
and Badalejo roads join, and, branching off from the road
to Cuartillos, make a semicircular loop towards the Arcos
road, winding round the eastern end of El Pinar, already
described. The pago lies close to the rivulet of the same
name, which flows in a southern direction towards the
Guadalete, and joins its waters, profuse in the rainy season,
almost nil in dry summertime, with those of the Guadalete,
at a point between the Cartuja and the bridge close by.
The name of pago and river is spelt by Suter in his map
" Albaladejo," so that we have here an Arabic article pre-
fixed, and some letters transposed. The spelling which I
adopt seems justified by the probable derivation from the
Arabic guadalec or guadalejo, derived itself from guada,
river. The soil of this pago is barro-arena, with much
chalk, containing great numbers of fossil marine shells of the
tertiary period. The mantuos prevail, and their products
are esteemed. The total area of the vineyards amounts to
forty aranzadas. To the south-east of the pago and rivulet
of Badalejo is the isolated pago of Culebra, with twenty-five
aranzadas of barro-arena soil, planted with mantuos and
mollares.

Due east of Jerez, and about ten kilometres distant, is

Cuartillos, forming, with Majada, an isolated group of important vineyards. It comprises about four hundred aranzadas of lustrillo soil. Its vines are palominos, perrunos, albillos, mantuos, and bebas. The most noted vineyard is that de las Animas. Majada, also termed M. Alta, measures twenty aranzadas, and resembles Cuartillos in soil and plantation.

Returning to Jerez from a visit to the plain round Culebras, I passed the pago, which from a neigbhouring flowing spring is called Fuente de la Teja. It is situated at the eastern end of the group of vineyards which are enclosed between the road of the Canaleja and that of Pedro Diaz. It passes westward into the pago of Pedro Diaz, thirty aranzadas of barro-areno soil, and is also blessed with a living spring of the same name. From this pago all the way to Jerez the vineyards lying along the Hijuela de Pedro Diaz, belong to the pago of San José, barro-arena vineyards of forty aranzadas surface, with the mantuos and mollares usual in this district.

The plains all round this eastern district are, if not barren, at least mainly uncultivated. Their soil is clay and sand, and suffers from stagnation of water in winter and drought in the summer. They are covered by groups of palmitos, and were adorned, when I first saw them, with numberless squills in full bloom. Herds of cattle were roaming over them. I was informed that before the Revolution of 1833 these lands were the property of the commune of Jerez. In consequence of the revolution a plan was started in Jerez to cure the poverty of the labouring population by giving them lands. The public lands were divided, and somehow distributed amongst the citizens. The plots were large enough for separate settlements, or the establishment of small farms. But not a single one of the new proprietors was found to settle on, or even work, the newly acquired land. Some sold it on the evening of the day on which they had received the boon, for more or less of wine or money, an arrobe of wine being no uncommon price for an entire lot of several aranzadas. A few monied persons and landowners in the neigbourhood acquired the whole of what had been the common land, for a ridiculously inadequate price; and thus the community was not only cheated of its property, but the mass of its poor inhabitants were deprived of the greater part of the common land on which their animals had, during a great part of each year, found their subsistence.

The first pago close to the south side of Jerez, bordering upon the plain of San Telmo, is that of Mancebia, a small vineyard, of one aranzada, in bugeo soil. Where the road to Monte Allegre branches off that to the Cartuja there is situated the pago of Pozillos, fourteen aranzadas in extent, with barro-arena soil, and planted with mantuos and mollares. In the angle formed by the Monte Allegre and Cartuja road is situated the barro-arena pago of Barrial. Not far off is the farm of Vallesequillo, on barro-arena soil, with orchards and vineyards. In this part the soil is remarkably red when freshly worked, paler when long exposed; some parts are almost reddish brown, and the colour changes frequently with the situation. To the east of the pagos just mentioned, between the Hijuela de Monte Alegre and that of Pedro Diaz, lies the pago of Manjon, or Majon, twenty aranzadas in extent, with barro-arena soil, and the vines appropriate to it. Contiguous to this is the Llano del Moral, a barro-arena pago, of from fifteen to twenty aranzadas. To the south-east of these pagos, and occupying almost the entire space between the road to the Cartuja and that of Pedro Dias, is the important pago of Monte Allegre, of about four hundred aranzadas. It is divided in its middle by a road bearing its name. Its soil is in one part barro-arena, in another portion plastic albariza. The dominant vines are mantuos with interposed bebas, mollares, and palominos. The point of Monte Alegre close to the Cartuja is termed Cabeza de la Azeña, and contains twenty aranzadas of barro-arena soil.

To the south of the road to the Cartuja, between it and that to the Granja, lies the pago of Buena Vista, which derives its name from certain high hills in its midst, whence a fine view of the old monastery, and of the valley of the Guadelete is obtained. It comprises about sixty aranzadas;

its soil is barro-arena, with some chalky underground; the prevailing vines are mantuos. More towards Jerez, and to the west of Buena Vista, we see the ten aranzadas of the pago of Flamenco, traversed by the three roads of the Cartuja, la Granja and Solete. The Cartuja road separates it from the Moral, and the Granja road from the pago of Geraldino. This pago is, in its turn, circumscribed by the road to the Granja and that to the Solete. It contains twenty aranzadas of barro-arena, and is planted with mantuos. The name is said to have been selected in honour of a Jerez naval man, who fought with unsuccessful glory at the naval battle of Cape St. Vincent. At the southern extremity of Buena Vista, and close to the Guadalete, we find the pago of la Granja, with a farm of the same name, to which its main vineyard belongs. The road which leads to it bears the name of Camino de la Granja. It is thirty aranzadas in extent; its soil is barro-arena, and its vines are mantuos, mollares, and others.

West of la Granja, and between it and Solete, is the barro-arena pago of Lazo. It is a long strip of land, with twenty aranzadas of vineyards, abutting in the north upon the Granja-road, in the south upon that of del Rio viejo. The last of the large pagos of this district is that of Solete, due south of Jerez. It borders in the west upon the Carretera del Puerto, in the east upon the pagos of Lazo and Geraldino, and is traversed by a road which bears its name, and farther west by the railway to Cadiz, running parallel with the road. Its soil is barro-arena, and its vines are mantuos and mollares.

On the outskirts of the district above described are yet a few small pagos, which may be conveniently here enumerated. S.S.E. of Jerez, and at three leagues' distance from it, is the pago Torre de la Cera, of forty-two aranzadas, with albariza soil. In the same direction from Jerez, but at a distance of five leagues, near the ex-convent del Valle, is the pago of Parrilla, of forty aranzadas.

The road to the Cartuja is a quagmire of sand and dust, with here and there a fragment of macadamized road, a remnant of a better past.

The Torrox group of vineyards, sometimes also called group of las Anaferas, is situated S.S.W. of Jerez, in a pentagonal space, bordered to the N.N.W. by the Trocha de Jerez al Puerto, on the W.S.W. by the Cañada del Carillo, and the northern slopes of the Sierra de San Cristobal. On the N.E. it is skirted by the carretera del Puerto a Jerez, the railroad from Cadiz to Sevilla and the Rio Guadelete, three roads which run close together at the former port of Jerez, el Portal. The entire group is within five kilometres from Jerez, and is easily reached by the Puerto roads mentioned, or by either of two field-roads, the Hijuela of Torrox or that of las Anaferas.

The pago of Torrox is S.S.W. from Jerez, in the place where formerly was a laguna of that name, abutting upon Gibalcon, and giving its Moorish name to the entire group. Its extent is two hundred aranzadas, its soil albariza, with bugeo in the lower parts. The vines are palomino, mantuo, Pedro Jimenez. To the east of this, and due south of Jerez, lies Gibalcon, a pago with an Arabic name, and fronting towards the cerro del Fruto and San Telmo. Extent, ninety aranzadas; soil, albariza; vines, palomino and mantuo. Next to the former two pagos, and almost in the centre of the group, lies the pago of Cibullo, being albariza with some bugeo, fifty aranzadas in extent, and mainly planted with palomino.

The pago nearest the river and railway is that of Parpalana, one hundred and sixty aranzadas in extent. Its soil is white plastic earth, with bugeo in the lower parts. Vines: polomino and Pedro Jimenez intermixed with peruno, cañocazo, albillo, and mantuo. Noted vineyards: Nuestra Senra de la Merced, Perla de Parpalana, borders upon la Calderera and Bonaina. The former is an albariza pago, with sixty aranzadas of palomino, but Bonaina has more bugeo soil, fifty aranzadas in extent, and is also stocked with palomino. To this district also belongs the pago de Galera, a strip of land lying between the river Guadalete and the carriage road to Puerto, extending from the Portal to the olive-grove del Duque. Its soil, of which only half an aranzada is as yet planted with vines, is exclusively bugeo.

The pago o this group, which is third in importance and most distant from Jerez, is las Anaferas. It borders upon the Cañada (brook lined with reeds) del Carillo, and the pagos of Cibullo and Torrox. Its soil is white albariza, of so plastic a nature that it can be carved with a knife, like soap, and is in that state worked into portable little stoves for charcoal, over which the common people cook their dinners. From these stoves the pago derives its name. The palomino predominates on its ninety aranzadas.

Bordering upon las Anaferas is the pago termed after the brook Cañada del Carrillo, fifty aranzadas, with albariza in the high and bugeo in the low portions. On the outskirts of the group we have yet to notice the pago of Colores, situated on the right of the bridle-road from Jerez to Puerto. It measures twenty aranzadas, with bugeo soil and some albariza. Its stock consists of mantuos and palominos. Close to it, on the left or south side of the same road, is the pago of Matacardillo, about fifty aranzadas in extent.

South of las Anaferas and of the Cañada del Carillo is the pago of the Sierra de San Cristobal. The vineyard is situated on the northern slope of this mountain. Its soil is bugeo, some albariza, and arena, products of the disintegration of the sand and chalk-rock which forms the mass of the hill. The soil on the whole is therefore lustrillo. Extent, fifty aranzadas ; vines, mantuos and palominos.

§ 182. MOSCATELS.

Close to el Portal is the Vega del Moscatel. It forms about six aranzadas of vineyards in bugeo soil, on which choice varities of moscatels are cultivated, amongst them the following :—

Moscatel gordo blanco, also termed *romano* and *flamenco*. The stock is strong, the canes are yellowish, like those of reeds, the leaves small and entire, or almost so, and the grapes are large, and have the peculiar flavour.

Moscatel gordo morado, similar to foregoing in shape, but its grape is violet, and the canes somewhat greyish-red.

Moscatel menudo blanco, also termed *morisco* and *fino*, is a more delicate plant than the former ; its canes are intensely greyish-red.   The grapes are small and very sweet, and give the best moscatel wine, or rather, sweet liqueur.

Moscatels require dark territory ; even in this warm climate their flowers set very imperfectly, but the grapes which become developed at all attain a high degree of perfection.

Farther towards Jerez, to the east of Gibalcon, bordering upon the side-road of las Coles, and the carriage-road to Puerto, are yet two small pagos, the Cerro de Paez, a single vineyard of from six to seven aranzadas, with barro-arena soil, and pago de Palmosa, a small vineyard with bugeo soil.

§ 183. Density of Jerez Mostos.

Many a sherry-drinker has heard the oft-repeated tale, that in the south the grapes are so sweet, so highly charged with sugar, that the mosto made from them is unable to consume the whole of it, and remains sweet, to some extent, even after fermentation has produced the ordinary quantity of alcohol.   This tale is often made to justify or explain the sweet taste of sherry, and the large amount of distilled spirits which is added to it.

In the "Treatise on Wine," of Thudichum and Dupré, p. 638 *et seq.*, a special chapter is devoted to the comparison of the density of Jerez must with the specific gravity of must produced from different wines in various countries and years.   This comparison led us to the conclusion that sherry is not naturally stronger than the principal wines of France and Germany ; that it is able to consume the whole of its saccharine matter by natural fermentation, and become natural wine, and, if properly treated, does not require either plastering, or the addition of brandy, spirit, or boiled must.

I have been able to confirm this conclusion by many observations made at Jerez upon mostos as they came from the lagars, and subsequently fermented in the bodegas.

Out of 103 mostos, at the average temperature of 70°
Fahr. :—

1	showed specific gravity	10·75	Baumé.
3	,,	,,	11·00	,,
1	,,	,,	11·25	,,
1	,,	,,	11·33	,,
6	,,	,,	11·50	,,
1	,,	,,	11·70	,,
24	,,	,,	12·00	,,
3	,,	,,	12·10	,,
16	,,	,,	12·25	,,
12	,,	,,	12·50	,,
4	,,	,,	12·75	,,
14	,,	,,	13·00	,,
6	,,	,,	13·25	,,
4	,,	,,	13·50	,,
7	,,	,,	14·00	,,

All these mostos came from the mantuo castellano grapes
(grown in barro-arena soil) and transported to the bodegas
on mules' backs during the time from September 20th to
October 2nd, that is to say, very late in a very hot Jerez
season. The grapes had, indeed, been subjected to such a
heat that many were shrivelled, and others transformed into
dry raisins. These latter do not influence the specific
gravity of mostos made on the lagar, but are mostly lost to
the wine-makers. When the dry murk is subsequently cast
into the roads, or carried to the dung-heaps or fields, one
can see numbers of poor children rummaging it, and picking
out these raisins. I state this in order to show that the
mostos above described were really highly concentrated
liquids, which is indeed also shown by the specific gravities
themselves, to all those who know that Spanish musts
fluctuate between specific gravity 9 and 14 as extremes, and
are more frequently near the lower than the higher figure.

I next observed eight mostos which were made from
assoleated grapes, and showed specific gravity 13·3 ; 13·5 ;
four = 14° ; two = 14·25. Each bota received six arrobas of
brandy of 40° Cartier, whereby the specific gravity was de-

pressed by six or seven degrees. Of mostos made on October 2nd, from long-dried mantuo de pila, two showed 15°, one 16°, and one 17° Baumé. The heaviest mosto I observed at all at Jerez had 22° B, and came from Pedro Jimenez grapes exposed to the sun during ten days, from September 5th to 15th. All these heavy mostos were expressly prepared for dulce, and were not allowed to ferment at all, but had their fermentation prevented by the addition of one-fifth of their volume of alcohol.

I found the best palomino mosto from albariza soil, on many samples, weighed between September 11th and 30th, to have a specific gravity of 13° B. All these mostos, as well as the mostos of mantuo castellano from barro-arena soil, fermented readily and rapidly, and in the space of ten days or so, had completely lost all sugar, and were new, dry, thoroughly fermented wines. Thus it is shown, by overwhelming evidence, that the assertion so frequently made to screen the true nature of sugared and brandied wines is untrue. Sherry wine is never sweet, except when it is expressly and intentionally sweetened by makers and exporters. Sherry is so sweetened, and coloured, and brandied, in order to cover the natural defects of the taste ; and no sherry of any claim to quality is ever sugared or coloured, because the makers know very well that pale, dry wine, with the least possible amount of alcohol, is far more valuable than the cooked and drugged, coloured sweet and hot liquids.

§ 184. SULPHURING—AZUFRADO.

The wines in Jerez are all plastered. But the common wines are not only plastered, but sulphured in addition. For this purpose a complicated apparatus is employed, consisting of the following parts. A vat, closed on all sides, of the size of a bota, is raised upon a stand, so that its bottom is about breast-high ; to the side of this is attached a little furnace in which the sulphur matches are burned. The fumes of the sulphurous acid are conducted by a tube to the top of the vat, and then diffuse in its cavity. The mosto is kept in a reservoir under the vat, mostly buried in the ground, and is repeatedly raised to the top of the vat by means of a pump. It is spread out in the vat in the form of a fine shower by means of a rose, or sieve-like distributor, and in falling becomes impregnated with the sulphurous acid. The matches which are burned are made of broad cotton bands, and the products of the imperfect combustion of these bands are, of course, also admixed with the must. The quantity of sulphur thus burned to impregnate each bota amounts to one-third of a pound, or more than five ounces, and this will yield more than ten ounces of the sulphurous acid gas, and ultimately nearly a pound of sulphuric acid. As the plastering introduces several pounds of sulphuric acid into each bota, it is now explained why some descriptions of sherry contain from three to five pounds of sulphuric acid. The acid introduced with the plaster is in a combined state, but that introduced by sulphuring is ultimately contained in the free state.

The sulphuring process has the effect of somewhat retarding fermentation, in warm weather one, in cooler weather two days. The process also lasts a little longer than in must not sulphured. The freshly fermented wine has an awful smell and taste of brimstone and rotten eggs, and contains considerable quantities of sulphuretted hydrogen and other products of the reduction of sulphurous acid.

The object of sulphuring is said to be to prevent the wine from running into the acetous fermentation. We believe, however, that the main effect of sulphuring the mosto is the destruction, partial or entire suffocation, of the fungus of scud or viscosity, as it is called in wine, a fungus which, when it invades fresh sweet must, destroys the sugar, and prevents true alcoholic fermentation. Incidentally the free acid of the wine is increased in quantity, and thus approaches more to the condition of unplastered mosto. It seems also that sulphured wine becomes clear more quickly than unsulphured. In return for this advantage, the sulphured wine remains in the objectionable state of contamination with sulphuretted hydrogen for a very long time; and after oxydation of this remains turbid from

T

finely-divided sulphur, which is removed with difficulty
ouly. The sulphuring deteriorates the taste of the wine, even
after complete oxidation of the sulphur to sulphuric acid,
and for this reason producers and extractors never sulphur
the better classes of wine, but only the low common qualities.

§ 185. TEMPERATURES OF FERMENTING MUSTS.

On September 21st, when the temperature of the outer
air was 76·5° Fahr., I ascertained the temperature of fermenting palomino mostos to be 90° Fahr. When the casks
lay in a warmer place, their temperature rose to 92° and 93°;
when in a cooler, it fell to 85°. Thoroughly fermented
mostos about twelve days old showed 74·5°. When the
casks were laid up in rows three high, called *andanas*,
I found that the lower rows quickly assumed an even temperature of about 75°, while the temperatures of the middle
rows was about 80°. The third or top rows varied between
81° and 92°. The highest temperatures were found near
open windows. I have no doubt that, although these botas
completed their noisy fermentation on the even ground,
they carried a portion of the heat acquired by fermentation
up to the andana, and that the entire heat cannot be placed
to the account of position. But a certain portion of the
heat is, no doubt, communicated by the hotter air in the
upper strata, which in the day-time rose to 97°, and at night
fell to 74°. Now, here is the easy explanation of the observation, that so much wine at Jerez and in other parts of the
south passes immediately from the vinous fermentation into
the acetous. The temperatures of the casks of one of the
top rows observed were the following :—87°, 90°, 87·5°, 88°,
90°, 88°, 90°, 92°, 91·3°, 76°. All these casks had just completed their fermentation, and were turbid, but beginning to
deposit their yeast. They were lying in warm places, and
following in a certain measure the lead of external
changes of temperature, and kept near their actual temperature by the heat of the air in the day-time, which at this
period (the middle of September) was excessive, that is to

say, much higher than in ordinary years. All the casks were with vacua, that is to say, not filled by a least one-sixth of their capacity. Under these circumstances, it is, in my opinion, impossible that they should not directly suffer at least some acetous fermentation; indeed, the wonder is, not that they form vinegar, but rather that any escape from this contamination, and remain sound wine. This stage is, indeed, the most dangerous one for Jerez wines, namely, the time from cessation of the fermentation, at which the wine has a temperature of 90° to 96° Fahr., and is turbid, to that time at which the wine has reached 75° and less, and, not being disturbed by external fluctuation of temperature, has desposited its yeast and become clear. The danger is generally diminished by the addition of spirit. But it is well known that much spirit hinders the development of wines, and has, therefore, to be avoided. Now, as by the exclusion of air in hot seasons the acetification of wine can be prevented, a great part of the necessity for adding so much spirit to wine is done away with. Consequently, the wine is in a position to become more quickly developed, and, being developed, it may be either left in its natural state or brandied for the taste of consumers desiring to have it thus treated.

The fermented wine remains stacked in the andanas of the bodega until it is pretty clear of floating yeast, which is mostly in January or February. It is then racked (*desliado*), and some brandy is added to it. Finos receive half an arrobe per bota. Common wines receive from one to one and a-half arrobes, of 40° Cartier. On the whole it may be said that the better the wine, the less brandy is added to it. Those botas which have become bad are sent to the still, and those which are retained are marked, if they have developed any specific qualities, or left unmarked if they remain doubtful and on trial. If a wine goes wrong in any of several ways, the only remedy applied to it is brandy, never any change in its other chemical or in its physical conditions.

§ 186. STAGES OF WINE, AND QUALITIES.

Mosto is not only the freshly pressed juice of the grapes, but the name is retained for all fermented wine up to the time of the first spring racking. *Vino d'un anno* is wine which approaches or has passed the age of one year. Quantities of wine of this quality are generally termed *añadas*. A regular heavy Jerez wine from albariza soil remains, as a rule, in an unripe state for several years, and then gradually becomes fino. It remains so from the 5th to the 8th year, and then may pass into *amontillado;* when continued in open casks, and allowed to develope, it remains in this state from the 9th to the 14th year, and then passes into *oloroso;* this condition lasts from the 15th to the 20th year, whereupon the wine becomes *secco;* this is, properly speaking, a passed wine, all its qualities are exhausted and gone : it is more properly termed *passado.* In other parts of Spain very old secco is sometimes called *rancio,* but in Jerez this word is not used in the same sense, but signifies a rancid, bad, sour, and mousy wine. From stout fino all subsequent qualities may be obtained directly by accidental development. The wine, as it were, skips a stage or two, and becomes either oloroso or secco, without having been in the amontillado stage at all.

When distinguished according to quality simply, wines give rise to the following names :—

Palma.—The fine, dry, wines in the second and third year are thus called. They may yield amontillado in time. Some extractors say that the amontillado obtainable from palma is thin, and never becomes oloroso. Others mark the amontillado by the sign of the palma.

Double palma signifies the same general qualities as the former, but more general and ripe.

Treble palma is the highest intensity of this modification, essence of amontillado.

Palo cortado, the broken stick, or cut stick, the mysterious sign for oloroso.

Double palo cortado, a better wine than the former.

Treble palo, the highest perfection of oloroso, " Oloroso muy vièjo."

Some place the oloroso before the palma as to quality. Probably the palma speaks more to the taste, the palo cortado to the nose.

Out of a large number of butts of wine from the same vintage and vineyard, only a small number develope into any of the above qualities. The largest quantity remains

Raya, or *rayea*, the third quality of wine. This in its natural state is sound and dry, but without prominent qualities. Perhaps three-quarters of all albariza sherry is raya. It is the bulk of the sherries exported to and drunk in England. This quality (*raya primera*) resembles in colour and dryness, but does not equal in merit, old secco.

Dos rayas is a common wine, not clean, but affected with some fault or other.

Tres rayas signify wine which nobody will buy—refuse. Thus it will be seen that with raya the multiplication of the sign goes along with the increase of badness, while with palma and palo cortado the multiplication signifies increase of good qualities.

Vinagre, wine which is more or less affected by acetous fermentation.

The sign of a grating signifies wine destined for the distillery.

The foregoing distinctions yield nine different qualities of wine. Of all wine produced in Jerez only a small proportion reaches the highest quality, and it was the opinion of one of the first extractors that there were not 200 butts of treble palo in Jerez at the time of my visit. These signs and distinctions are mainly used by the extractors for their guidance in buying, and during maturing, and are not generally applied to wines as shipped.

§ 187. The Criadera. The Solera.

This name signifies a kind of nursery, in which wines are placed which have already arrived at a certain quality in the partido. The *partido* is the entire "parcel;" that is to say, the total number of casks of one vintage from one particular vineyard. When this partido has been dissolved into its separate qualities, either by the proprietor or purchaser, these qualities are now added to other quantities of similar quality, or are simply laid by their side to undergo their probation. We will assume a hundred botas of palma to have been selected from ten different partidos. The hundred casks may all develop equally, or all unequally, or only a number may take the normal development; the others may go back before having their character permanently determined. This result is attained and observed in *the criadera*. The name is derived from the idea that the wine while thus situated grows. The extractors say that they *grow* the wine, which has to be interpreted, that they stand by while the wine undergoes its changes for better or for worse, and observe and register these changes from time to time. If the wine shows signs of an unfavourable kind it is treated with some spirits, but no other application or regimen is applied to it. When wine in the criadera has attained certain desired qualities it is either arrested in its career and prevented from changing any further by receiving its full complement of spirits, or it is taken to the soleras.

A number of botas, which are kept together, and as far as possible supplied with wine of similar character, are termed *a solera*. This institution has for its object to enable the extractor to supply constantly good wine of the same general quality, or, at all events, wine which differs no more in the variation of years and seasons than can be disguised by careful mixing. If, therefore, a solera, say of amontillado, consists of sixty butts, and the sales of the extractor have diminished their contents to one-half, then he has to supply thirty butts to make up his solera. These he must obtain either from his own criadera or from that of others.

Now suppose that in the criadera of a hundred butts of palma assumed in the previous paragraph, thirty had turned into amontillado, then the extractor would probably distribute these thirty butts over his solera of sixty butts, and have it complete; but if he obtained only ten butts of amontillado in his criadera he would distribute these ten over his entire solera, and the butts of the solera would contain a void of one-third of their capacity. On the contrary, if the extractor were to sell thirty botas of his solera, consisting of sixty, he would not sell half the number of his casks; but he would draw from each of the casks half a bota, arrobe by arrobe, and distribute them equally over the botas about to be sold. The criadera, therefore, and, still more, the solera, in one sense, destroys all individuality of wine as to origin and year. When large soleras have to be made up from numerous small partidos, they represent, of course, a mixture of an infinite variety of wines; and old soleras represent a mixture of small residues from a great number of years, the latest addition being probably the largest in quantity. All the deposits which the wine forms while in the soleras are, in the practice of some extractors, left in the butts. I was informed by an extractor that he once bought the entire and only solera, consisting of 1,000 butts, of an old Cadiz house, who made only one quality of wine. Each cask contained about four gallons of black deposit, which was carefully moved with the wine when it was taken to Jerez. These deposits must not be of yeast, or they will be injurious. Later deposits are said to improve the wine, and the stirring up of old deposits in soleras, *e.g.*, during the addition of wine from the criadera, has a tendency to clear the wine. So say some extractors. Others have no belief in these deposits; they mostly consist of drowned mycoderma vini, and their significance as such must be nil, because they are dead, and unable to effect the change ascribed to the living ferment.

§ 188. COLOURS OF SHERRIES—ARROPE, COLOR OR VINO DE COLOR, DULCE.

All young sherry wines which are produced from sound grapes are very slightly coloured greenish-yellow. With advancing age they get a little more yellow, but the finos and amontillados are, on the whole, pale, and it is only the olorosos which become as dark as amber. The seccos are amber to brownish. I assume all such wines to be genuine dry, free from sugar and boiled mosto. Now, as colour in good wine is an undoubted sign of age (colour in young wine indicates that there were rotten grapes employed amongst others), and as many people believe that age is the highest quality to be desired in wine, the greater part of the occupation of the Jerez wine trade consists in imparting to young common wines a sham colour, by means of which it may pass as aged. But as, happily, the finos, amontillados, and olorosos are highly valued in the pure state, they are scarcely ever coloured by extractors who understand their business. The Englishman of position drinks raya, of ten or twelve years of age, and it is to the imitation of this that many efforts are directed. In this process the following agents are employed.

The plastered must, as it runs from the press, is boiled in a large copper, which is mostly fixed in a building in the vineyard. While boiling it is constantly skimmed, and the impurities and syrup adhering are thrown with the refuse, to be fermented and distilled. Seventy-six arrobas of mosto, fresh from the press, yield ultimately, by evaporation, seven and a half arrobas of skimmings, and fifteen arrobas of arrope. When five butts have been reduced to one, which takes from fourteen to eighteen hours, the mass is constantly kept stirred to prevent burning at the bottom of the copper, and promote evaporation. It is now a dark brown or reddish syrup, in thin layers. The colour is due to caramel, produced by the united action of heat and acid. Its taste is partially aromatic, partially bitter and nasty, owing to the concentrated mass of sulphate of potash which it contains, as the result of plastering. It is sometimes so acrid as to blister the tongue of delicate persons who taste it. The arrope is not used by itself without preparation, but is always transformed into a dilute menstruum.

To one bota of common wine about eleven gallons of arrope and a quantity of spirit are added and dissolved by agitation. By adding varying quantities of this colour to other wine the shades are produced. Brown sherry receives about 25 gallons of this *vino de color* to the bota. The pale brown (sometimes also termed pale) receives about

20 gallons. A butt of golden sherry requires 15 to 17 gallons of *vino de color;* and the least coloured, called pale (*i.e.,* golden), receives 7 gallons of colour. It is perhaps due to this large addition of colour and of boiled matter in the shape of *vino de color*, that this "golden" sherry can be shipped with about 34 per cent. of proof spirits, while "pale" sherry, with the smallest amount of colour, is said to require 40 per cent. to 42 per cent. proof spirit.

In exceptional cases *vino de color* is made by boiling mosto down to one-third, and adding spirit to the coloured liquid.

All *vino de color*, and wine made with its aid, fluoresces green. This is easily observed when the wine is exposed to the direct rays of the sun in an otherwise dark place. Natural wine never fluoresces in this manner, but requires a cone of concentrated sunlight for showing fluorescence; then it is pale green, nearly white, whereas that of color is green.

Natural good wine has a mild sweetish taste, without containing sugar. But common wines have no such taste, and are therefore mixed with sugar. The most genuine sweetening material is mosto preserved in spirit, termed *dulce.* To produce the best dulce, either Pedro Ximenes, the sweetest of grapes, or palomino, is selected. The grapes are exposed to the sun until they begin to shrivel, and then they are trodden and pressed. I examined a mosto made from palomino *assoleadas*, that is grapes which had been strongly passulated in the sun, and found its specific gravity to be 22° Baumé. The first and later runnings, when the grapes had been more crushed, had the same specific gravity, although the men working the press believed that the many raisins contained in the grapes would make the mostos heavier. The sugar of true raisins is never extracted by mosto in the short time during which this is in contact with them. Therefore, unless raisins are picked out from amongst the plump grapes, and treated separately, they are lost in the murk. Murk from which mosto for dulce has been pressed, is treated with water and pressed in an hydraulic press, and then yields a mosto of full 15° B. But this is not of good taste, and goes to the refuse vats to be distilled after fermentation. The sweet thick mosto to be made into dulce is mixed with one-fifth of its bulk of spirit of 40° Cartier strength, so that a bota of dulce consists of 24 arrobas of mosto and 6 arrobas of spirit. According to my observation it has then from 8·5° to 9° B. specific gravity. It is not subject to fermentation, but forms a deposit; and when decanted from this becomes clear, amalgamated, and a little darker by age. Old dulce (*dulce muy viejo*) is frequently drunk as a liqueur, and the working men take a glass of it the first thing in the morning, a practice which they call *tomar la mañana.*

By the addition of such dulce, the various kinds of mixed sherry receive their sweetness. No sherry of any kind contains a sufficient amount of sugar to have a sweet taste of itself. In fact, all wine in Jerez which has fermented is perfectly dry and free from sugary taste. Grapes not passulated by assolation yield always a mosto, which ferments perfectly, and never any sweet wine. Mostos of as much as 22° B. require twenty per cent. of strongest alcohol to be protected from fermentation. The ordinary sherries receive of such dulce as much as may be required by the taste of the customer. It is found by chemical analysis that the sugar thus imparted to wine amounts to from one to four per cent. of the total weight of the wine. In some bodegas the common dulces are kept in closed casks in the open air, in order to let them be heated by the sun. Much colouring and sweetening material is now made from cane-sugar, and is preferable to the arrope, as it is not saturated with sulphate of potash. The sugar, when mixed with wine, is quickly transformed into grape-sugar, and the caramel is identical with that of the arrope.

I here summarize once more what I have already partly discussed in connection with mosto, namely, the observation on the vacua in botas as affecting wines. The casks containing the wine are at no time filled up to their bunghole, but there is always an empty space left, to which the air has free access. This space is called *vacio.* The wine is allowed to ferment in seasoned botas, of from 37 to 38 arrobes, and in these a vacio of from 5 to 6 arrobes is customary, so that after two gallons of lees are abstracted and a little brandy added, a full bota of clear wine may be obtained after the first racking. In butts of 30 arrobes the vacio amounts to from 3 to $4\frac{1}{2}$ arrobes. This empty space causes the wine to offer a great surface to the action of the air ; the surface favours all kind of change, the best and the worst, according to the external temperature. In warm weather, the *mycoderma vini* is quickly developed, also the *mycoderma aceti*, and the wine changes with great rapidity from fino to vinegar, to mousetaste, to basto, or amontillado. All these varieties are observed side by side, or one above the other, in the same lot of originally identical qualities of wine. This vacio, together with the changeable temperature of the bodegas, is the great danger of Jerez wines. No doubt by its means these wines mature quicker in a low temperature, though even here it is dangerous, as we know, from the Arbois vaults. But in hot weather the wines go quickly to their ruin if not suffocated by and pickled in brandy. It would, therefore, probably be advisable that the practice of the vacio, at least in summer time, should be abolished, and only be adopted during the time from October to March.

§ 189. EVAPORATION OF WINE FROM CASKS. FLOR.

All wines kept in wooden casks diminish in quantity by evaporation, partly through the wood, partly through the corks and the bunghole. Young wines lose less than old ones. The former are estimated to diminish by $2\frac{1}{2}$ per cent., the latter by 3 per cent. per annum. Some extractors maintain that all wines become stronger in alcohol by keeping, but I am not aware that this has been proved by reliable experiment.

With the expression *Flor* the extractors signalize the whitish fungus which grows on the surface of wine; the Germans term it *Kahn;* botanists give it the name of *Mycoderma vini*. In November, 1871, all the wine of that year which

I examined (and I examined many hundreds of botas) was covered with this mould. On expressing my astonishment to the extractors that they allowed their wines to lie with a vacio and to be covered with this mould, they admitted that it was an unfavourable feature if the flor appeared on mosto or young wine yet on the first lees ; but they said they liked the flor on wine after the first racking, or on the añadas, or wine in criaderas and soleras. They said that wine, otherwise sound and growing flor, developed best. It is not easy to understand why, or how the fungus should be unfavourable at one and advantageous at another time. Flor is most commonly associated with the amontillado development, rarely with the oloroso stage. But I have also seen it together with mouse and other nasty tastes, and spoiled wine. But this might be defined as a case of mixed ferments ; the effect of the flor was spoiled or neutralized by collateral objectionable ferments. The German winemakers consider kahn their greatest enemy, and carefully prevent its formation. All countries producing red wines avoid its formation on these wines, as it completely spoils their purity and high taste. Only at Arbois, in the Jura, is wine allowed to be covered with mycoderma vini, as we know from Pasteur's description. This chemist also made it probable that the flor absorbed oxygen from the air, and gave it to the wine, but not so as to form vinegar. This latter function he attributes to the vinegar plant, or mycoderma aceti, which he found frequently mixed with the wine-plant, and observed also that it displaced and drowned the wine-fungus. At Arbois the wine is kept in cold, deep cellars, with vacios in the casks, which are never filled up. The moulds are never removed. Many casks of wine perish by becoming vinegar ; some, however, assume an admirable development. This quality is said to stand in a direct proportion to the development of flor. But here the proof of the flor causing the good development is also wanting. On the whole this subject requires a scientific investigation.

§ 190. SCUDDINESS, VISCOSITY, NUBE AND OTHER DISEASES OF WINE.

· A white pertinacious turbidity of wine is called *scuddiness*, and the matter causing the appearance, *scud*. It is not necessary that the matter should be in the shape of clouds (*nube*) when the liquid is moved in a glass; but this kind of scud is the most unfavourable. Most of these turbid conditions of sherry cannot be removed except after the addition of large quantities of brandy. Indeed, scud is the main cause of the brandying of wine. No other wines being subject to such pertinacious turbidity as sherry, I made a special study of this matter, and found that the extractors comprise under the one name scud a considerable variety of conditions of turbidity. I distinguished the following varieties:

The albuminous scud.—This is due to suspended albuminous matter in a fine state of division, and occurs after fining with white of egg. Removable by Spanish earth.

The bacteria and vibriones scud.—This arises in new wine of feeble alcoholicity, and is counteracted by sulphuring. This is the most dangerous scud, as it leaves indelible traces of its presence in the wine, and is itself difficult to remove.

The tartrate of calcium scud.—This is the whitest scud, and deposits gradually as a white deposit, but a cask of wine affected with it would perhaps not become entirely clear before some years.

The sulphide of potassium scud.—This is caused by the sulphate becoming reduced in the wine in the absence of oxygen, and the production of peculiar sulphur compounds.

The reduced sulphur scud.—This is caused by the reduction of sulphurous acid in sulphured wines. Sulphuretted hydrogen is first formed, and causes the wine to stink horribly; then this gas is gradually oxidized and deposits finely-divided sulphur, which is one of the most difficult turbidities to remove. This scud is regularly found in all Portuguese white (and not rarely red) wines during their first year, and sometimes does not disappear until the third year, or some time after all the sulphuretted hydrogen has been oxidized, and all sulphurous acid has been oxidized or otherwise decomposed.

While the albuminous and vibrionic scuddiness are removable by ordinary reasonable treatment and fining, the tartrate of calcium and sulphate of potassium scuds are the result of plastering, and most difficult to remove without brandy. The reduced sulphur scud, and the stinking qualities of wines, are the products of the sulphuring which some wine-makers adopt to protect their wine from acetification, or to give it more acidity, if that should be required.

§ 191. FININGS.

Animal Charcoal.—Much turbid and putrid evil smelling wine is treated at Jerez with animal charcoal. There are, indeed, extractors who use charcoal as the sovereign remedy for all evils. Putrid and evil smells can be removed from spoiled wines by charcoal, but the clearing such wines is only a temporary success. The wine dissolves phosphate of calcium out of the charcoal, and this is deposited from the wine subsequently in minute quantities and reproduces the turbidity.

Much wine is fined with blood, which is put warm into the bota. The albumen precipitated by the alcohol causes the turbidity to be enveloped, and drags it to the ground. Jullien's powder consists of dried blood. Blood mostly leaves a little hematin in the wine, and makes it darker. It also leaves some acid albumen and the salts in the wine, not rarely also the particular smell which is peculiar to the blood of all animals.

Meat is also used for fining wines; slices of steak are merely hung up in the wine, and their albumen is extracted, and causes a precipitate.

Most commonly albumen from eggs is used for fining the brandied wines. Fifteen to twenty whites, together with a quantity of *common salt*, are put into a bota and stirred. After that a quantity of *Spanish earth*, in the condition of a smooth thin paste, is added and stirred. The mixture is allowed to stand, and the wine becomes clear. In this case, also, the formation of a heavier and copious precipitate drags down the lighter slight impurity called scud. *Milk*, so frequently used in this country for clarifying sherry, is not used at Jerez.

In general, the difficulty of clarifying Jerez wines permanently is very great, and is said to be the principal reason for the addition of so much brandy to wine as we observe in it.

§ 192. TINAJAS. CASKS.

The wines of all southern provinces of Spain, particularly those of Montilla, used formerly to be made and kept in *tinajas*, buried in the ground of the bodega. The tinajas were either large earthenware vessels, containing about a hogshead each, or they were constructed of bricks and cement. I have seen both forms in the Jerez district, and believe them to have been here also the general receptacles. In a vineyard I saw a large tinaja used as a dog-kennel; and in a shed at San Lucar I saw several tinajas of brick and cement, holding six botas each, in a disused but hardly dilapidated state. The dangers of these vessels are well represented in the legend about Don ——'s Sheep. Don —— was a celebrated producer or extractor of wine at Montilla. His reputation grew, it is said, out of one particular tinaja, and the beginning of the rise was marked by the disappearance of a family sheep, a merino ram. After the lapse of years the celebrated tinaja which had made the fortune of the house, had at last to be cleared out, and in its muddy deposit were found the fleece and skeleton of the unlucky carnero. It is said that, in imitation of this remarkable event (a discovery without intention), the montillanos to this day are in the habit of putting the entrails of sheep into their wine. But whether this is true or not I cannot say from my own experience; I know, however, that sheep's blood, and that in a warm state, is often put into these wines.

We are now in a position to appreciate why botas and bodegas do not fit one another. In olden times wines were kept in tinajas, underground, which, in a covered space, is virtually in a cellar. When tinajas were discarded and botas adopted, burying was discontinued. The necessity of providing for export and transport antiquated tinajas; but the bota exposed wine more to the influence of heat and air. It is curious to speculate what anxiety this change must have given to the producers. But the enormous convenience of the wooden cask conquered the tinajas and their security. Now, the necessity for security must send the botas underground, and they will therefore have to go, not into the bare earth, where the tinajas were, but into vaults, to remain accessible and movable.

Jerez casks are mostly made of Memel oak staves, and of Canadian oak staves. One bota now costs 9 dols., equal to 36s.; but in productive years the price sometimes rises to 15 dols. and 16 dols.

½ cask	5 dols.	= 20s.
¼ ,, ...	3 ,,	= 12s.
⅛ ,, ...	2 ,,	= 8s.
barrille (4 arrobas)		8s.
2 arrobas		5s.
1 arroba		3s.

The practice as regards the treatment of new casks differs greatly. Some cause the casks to be burned inside when the staves are being bent, but do not steam the casks. Some extractors, possessed of steam-boilers and every necessary apparatus, have abandoned the practice of steaming casks, as either unnecessary or hurtful to the wood. Other extractors do not burn, but steam the casks. A third series of houses both burn and steam their casks. All these gentlemen, however, agree in soaking the inside of their casks with water for a very long time, and frequently renewing this water, until it remains both colourless and tasteless.

The new wine, of good quality, is here mostly fermented in old casks, which are retained in the bodega and never sold. But the rich proprietors lend new casks to less fortunate producers, to ferment their wine in; after the spring

racking and sale the seasoned casks go back to the proprietors.

§ 193. BODEGAS AND WANT OF CELLARS.

A cellar is an apartment underground, so constructed as
to withdraw its atmosphere from the fluctuations of temperature of the external air. The necessity for such apart-
ments is felt more by the inhabitants of rigorous climates,
with severe winter frosts, than by those of southern countries
with mild winters. Accordingly the knowledge and practice
of building cellars is more developed in the north than in
the south of Europe. Cellars have been most developed in
their application to beer and effervescent wines, so that the
best are met with in Bavaria and the Champagne. In Bavaria
they fulfil a twofold purpose. The beer is fermented as well
as preserved in them after fermentation. Owing to the low
temperature the fermentation is slow ; it need not be quick,
as exposure to the air does not injure the beer at that low
temperature. But the exposure to air has the advantage of
ripening the beer by oxidizing and precipitating the dissolved
albuminous matters. For these reasons the thin or light Bavarian beer keeps better than stronger beer prepared by ordinary
hot fermentation, when both are similarly exposed to air and
heat. The cellars of the Champagne country are not so
much used for fermenting the must as for fermenting the
wine a second time after it is drawn into bottles to give it the
mousse. This fermentation might take place in any apartment above ground, and for it the cellar is not absolutely
requisite. But the equable temperature of the cellar is required for the deposition of the yeast formed in the bottles ;
in other words for the perfect clearing of the effervescent
wine.

In Jerez, and generally in the south of Spain and Portugal,
there are no cellars such as I have defined above. The
wines are always made, fermented, and kept in buildings
above ground constructed for the purpose, and termed
bodegas—in Portuguese, *adegas*. These structures are frequently of very large size and rather lofty, but they have

many windows and doors, and their roofs are made of two
layers of tiles, resting upon wooden rafters.   The tiles next
to the wood are flat, like large bricks; the tiles facing the
sky, however, are corrugated, and so laid as to form parallel
ridges and furrows.   The two layers are fixed upon each
other with mortar.   Now, this roof conducts the heat of the
sun with great facility, and radiates it easily into the space
of the bodega.   The bodegas, therefore, are very hot indeed;
during the daytime their oppressive condition is only mitigated a little by draughts of air.   In the night they become
cool again.   The wines in the botas follow all these changes
within certain limits.   They become cool at night, warm in
the day—though they never reach the extremes of the air.
The botas which lie highest on the andana which may form
the third or fourth tier from the ground, are the most
affected: those in the second tier less, and so on to those on
the ground, which are the steadiest in their temperature.
Those botas also which lie near apertures and windows are
liable to great changes of temperature.   Accordingly, it is
often found that the upper tiers contain the greatest and the
lower tiers the smallest proportion of spoiled wine.   Botas
near windows are frequently spoiled, and all this is just
as it ought to be.   Scud, mousetaste, and vinegar threaten
constantly every bota.   With anxious mien the capataz tastes
the wines and marks the changes.   This basto of to-day was
new amontillado a week ago; these finos are all in danger
of becoming vinegar.   He shakes his head while observing
all, and cannot alter it; he does not know the reasons for
these ruinous changes; he consoles himself with the few
palmas which he can inscribe here and there, puts brandy
over the heads of the naughty children, and condemns the
worst of them to the still.   But he has no power over the
changes of his wines, either for good or evil, simply because
he cannot regulate their relation to air and temperature, and
such regulation he cannot possibly effect because he has no
cellar.   It is unquestionable that the great mass of Jerez
wines is greatly deteriorated, some even ruined, owing to the
absence of cellars.   I need hardly include in this category
of ruined wines, those which require and receive brandy for

being preserved from acetification and fermentation, in order to prove my proposition, but everybody admits that brandy deteriorates wines, more particularly those of good quality, and therefore the fact of wine having been brandied is suppressed and disguised by every possible means.

How different would be the case if the Jerezanos were possessed of proper underground cellars, where their products might be maintained at the average temperature of the earth in that region. I ascertained what that temperature is in the usual manner, by taking on October 3rd the temperature of three deep wells :—

Pozo in a cooperage . . . . . . 64°73 F.
Ditto en casa de Don N. '. . . . . 64°33 F.
Ditto en casa de Don M. . . . . . 64 33 F.

Consequently a good underground cellar in Jerez ought to have the average temperature of 64°5, with a very light increase in summer, owing to the heat radiated into it by windows and doors. But never would the temperature reach 70, or fluctuate between 70 and 85, as I have observed it to fluctuate in bodegas in September. The temperature in those buildings must be very high in summer, but had never been ascertained by the thermometer.

In such cellars the Jerez wine would undergo a perfectly normal developement. It would ferment thoroughly, would not be liable to the acetous or mousy change, and would become clean in a short time. It might be left to develop with the vacio, for at the low temperature the contact with air would be hardly dangerous, probably beneficial. It would probably be always beneficial, for as all botas would be under identical conditions, they could not fail of producing identical results. In any case, I am conviced that with cellars the Jerezanos would produce 90 per cent. of fine wine, where now they produce 10 per cent. To this some of the extractors have objected that if they were to change their style of growing the wine ("growing" is here used as an active verb by the extractors, who also speak of "rearing" and "educating," whereas their only action consists in standing by and seeing the wine behave and misbehave, "kick," and mark the result with chalk upon the barrel), they ran the risk of failing to produce any of those very fine qualities which constituted their reputation and main profit, and of depressing their wines to one common low level.   To this the answer was that the mass of their wines was at a very low level indeed, that half their wine had to be exported at £15 per bota, and that £30 per bota was a high average to assume for the total export, and that of fine wine at £100, about which so much boast was made, not two hundred botas were annually exported from Jerez.   That the loss of these very high wines, if it were a necessary consequence, which I by no means admitted, of a change of vinification, would be very small compared to the loss—the enormous loss—inflicted upon the average wines by the faulty condition of the bodegas ; for as an example it was notorious in the fortnight following the harvest of 1871 all wines suffered an immense depreciation owing to the great heat, which caused them, yet hot from an active fermentation, to pass at once into the acetous fermentation, (the loss in money value which the Jerezanos suffered during that fortnight was something like a quarter of a million of pounds sterling).   If these wines had fermented in cellars, or had been put into cellars after their fermentation, this deterioration could not have occured, and the cellars would in one fortnight have repaid the cost of their construction.

This is a matter entirely apart from the question of the vacio.   To prevent misunderstanding, I point out that I am quite convinced that wines ripen quicker with the aid of the vacio than without—that wines ripen quicker in warm air than in cooler air.   But warm air and vacio together force the wine to go wrong, and compel the addition of brandy. Warmth without the vacio does not easily spoil wine, and vacio without warmth is a safe condition for Jerez wine. Therefore, the Jerezanos, by transferring their wines to cellars, would only insure themselves from loss, although their wines, if left altogether in the cellars, would ripen a little more slowly than in the bodegas.   But what would compel them to leave their wines always in the cellars ? Having got them clear and cool, having timed them over the dangers of great autumnal and summer heat, what would prevent them from placing the wines in the bodegas for the temperate months of the year, October to April? Why should they not in this respect do as the Champagne makers do, transport their wines to that cave which is most suitable to their then condition? Surely, to introduce the conditions of certainty into these operations is a desirable thing, and not an innovation to be dreaded, and it can by no means alter the character of their wine except for the better, and, therefore, can affect their trade only in the sense of expansion.

§ 194. Notes on the History of Viticulture and of the Trade in Wine at Jerez.

It is probable that viticulture in Jerez is not of very great antiquity. In Roman times no wine seems to have been made there, while the provinces of Catalonia and Valencia produced plenty. The first reliable historic evidence of the existence of vineyards at Jerez dates from the year 1268, when Alonzo el Sabio, after having defeated the Moors, rewarded forty of his knights by giving to each of them vineyards in bearing, as the document of donation preserved in the archives of the municipality at Jerez has it—"sex aranzadas de viña" and land on which they might plant vines—"sex aranzadas de tierra para majuelo." It does not appear in which district these vineyards were situated, but an Arabic document, a diary of the field operations of the Moorish army, published by the Royal Academy of History, recites that in 1285, when General Jusuf laid siege to Jerez, he encamped the body of his army between the river Guadalete and the town, in vineyards and gardens. This is the place where up to this day we find the greater number of Jerez gardens, and a great number of vineyards. The army was ordered to cut down the vines in the vineyard during the fourth, fifth, and sixth days of May, in order to clear the fields for the encampment, from which we may conclude that the vineyards had considerable extension. The vineyards presented to the knights in 1268 amounted to 240 aranzadas, and if they had planted their fields, might have risen in 1285 to double that number. Probably there were other proprietors besides these knights. The vines which the Moorish general ordered to be destroyed were in the shape of *cepas*, the low stocks at present in use, and *parras*, or vines nailed up to walls and espaliers, with which the properties were surrounded. From those times dates a Castilian proverb, which is said to have originated as follows :—Diego Perez de Vargas was pruning his vines, when the King Alonzo el Sabio happened to come by, and entering the vineyard began to collect the cut-off branches. On Vargas expressing his astonishment, the King is said to have replied, "à tal podador, tal sarmentador," meaning that the labourer was by no means too good for the bricklayer, in this case. In the fourteenth century, the Jerez vineyards seem to have been neglected, mainly in consequence of epidemics of pestilence ; in 1402, Enrique III. expressly forbade their destruction by the proprietors. But after that the cultivation of the vine took a fresh start, and in 1431, when the inhabitants of Jerez and Puerto de Sa Maria agreed upon the boundaries of their relative communes, and recorded them in documents, they mentioned the enclosures of the vineyards of Barbaina and of La Gallega.

In the fifteenth century vineyards were also fully established at San Lucar, and in a manuscript from that period, preserved in Madrid, it is related that they were dug round in March.

The Jerez wine of the fifteenth century, which was the most esteemed, was red wine ; for on September 13th, 1410, the town council of Jerez, desirous of making an important present (*un presente grande*) to Alonzo Nunez de Villavicencio, the Alcade Mayor of Jerez, who was then assisting at the siege of Antiquera, sent him ten arrobas of the best red wine. In 1456, the town council, in expectation of the visit of Enrique IV. to their town, ordered that all persons who had wine to sell, should sell the best of red, as well as white, at the price of six maravedis the azumbre. Nowadays, says a modern writer, "the mode of making red wine is no longer known at Jerez ; and the wants of its population and its traders are supplied by the viticulturists of Valencia, Cataluña, and La Mancha. The maravedi of the fifteenth century is supposed to be equivalent to fifteen maravedis in the present day; consequently the arroba of wine was fixed in 1456, at a little more than 21 reals; the bota of 30 arrobas, therefore, at 42 pesos (a peso being the imaginary unit by which all wine in Jerez is bought and sold, equal to 15 reals). This price is almost the same as in the present day. In 1479 the harvest failed, owing to rains in May and continuous Levantes and great heat, and the azumbre of wine rose to 40 maravedis, which is equal to more than 141 reals the arroba, and 282 pesos the bota. Such prices were, in subsequent years, only realized once, namely in 1863, when all extractors believed the Millennium had begun.

§ 195. VINEYARDS OF SAN LUCAR DE BARRAMEDA.

The situation and extent of the vineyards of San Lucar is best appreciated by an inspection of the map of Consul Suter. They are mainly situated upon albariza hills, and are worked upon the same principles as the Jerez vineyards. But at San Lucar all vineyard labours throughout the year are performed a fortnight earlier than at Jerez. The vintage is in the beginning of September, when the grapes are in a much less ripe state than that in which a fortnight later they are harvested at Jerez. This is probably caused by the proximity of the sea, which in September brings rains and winds, both of which are destructive of ripe and over-ripe grapes. The wines are mostly "listanes," the same as those which at Jerez are termed palominos. Vinification is the same as at Jerez; plastering, vino de color, dulce, and brandy are used to make up the semblance of sherry. But there is a speciality produced at San Lucar, which may be termed the parallel to the Jerez amontillado, namely, the so-called *manzanilla de San Lucar*. This wine has a particularly nice, though thin flavour, while young; with age it becomes very dry, and somewhat bitter. It has the character of all wines made from somewhat under-ripe grapes, and becomes *passado* at less than one-third of the age of genuine sherries. It should always be termed "manzanilla de San Lucar" in full, to distinguish it from the wines of Manzanilla, an important viticultural district not far from Seville. The production and trade of San Lucar are in the hands of growers or *cosecheros*, holders, or *almacenistas*, and *extractores*, or shippers, as at Jerez. In the viticultural pagos of El Merino on the east, and La Malaya on the west of the new road from Jerez the vineyard labours begin immediately after the harvest. The vines are kept even lower on the ground than at Jerez. Close to San Lucar are orange-groves of great beauty. In San Lucar I visited several bodegas, among others that of an old gentleman who was supposed to possess the oldest wine in the place. I heard him relate that in 1804 he had in his bodega three botas of vino de color, which were, to his knowledge, at least twenty years old. These three botas had since then, by simple evaporation, become concentrated to one. It was sold in my presence for ninety pounds sterling. I looked upon this *so-called wine* as merely a pickle of sulphate of potash, caramel, and spirit, from which the soul of wine had fled ages ago. In the same old bodega in which this relic was kept I also observed some of the underground tinajas of 130 arrobas, or six botas capacity each, executed in brickwork, which in former ages used to receive the wine. They had evidently been disused for generations, and now served as the playground of a numerous colony of rats.

Fine Manzanilla de San Lucar, ten years old, will obtain a price *in loco* of 300 pesos, equal to £45 per bota. Good wine, three years old, will sell at 140 pesos, or £21, per butt. On the whole, the San Lucar wines on an average command less than half the average price of Jerez wines. The wines in the bodegas are not highly brandied, but they do not come to England in that state. They are always suffocated in spirit before shipment.

§ 196. THE ALGAIDA AND ITS INDIGENOUS VINES.

The Algaida is a forest of about 9,000 aranzadas in extent, on the south bank of the Guadalquivir, to the east of San Lucar. It is reached by a long journey, along the sandy and marshy banks of the river, through fields and forests, and over uncultivated plains of vast extent. It is surrounded by swamps (*marismas*) and during the rainy season is itself inundated to a great extent. The soil consists partly of clay, partly of sand, and in many parts it contains deserts of pure sand. It is planted mainly with the sea-pine (*Pinus maritima*), but contains also groups of the silvery elm, and large tracts are covered with shrubs of lentiscus. Almost its entire border, and many large and small open spaces in its interior, are lined with the wild vines, first described by Clemente, which were the principal object of my excursion to the spot.

I was accompanied by some friends, and we engaged two foresters to guide and guard us, all being well armed. There are no roads whatever, and paths, beaten by the herds of goats of the distant villages, exist only round the circumference and in the shrubby parts. In walking along I soon perceived some wild vines covering an oleander bush ; further on, wild fig-bushes and trees in numbers. Then more vines, much pulled about by men and beasts. When, after a long walk, I arrived in a part where white silver-elms form a large continuous group, I found vines covering the whole of large fir-trees ; there were at the same time brambles and sarsaparilla in blossom, creeping up shrubs and trees. From a formidable rampart of brambles, covered with vines, one of my companions fetched some vine branches upon which were (on October 13th) eight bunches of blossoms. By this means I was enabled immediately to diagnose and to demonstrate, that these *garañonas*, as the Spaniards term the wild vines, are really indigenous wild plants, and not stray children of vineyards; for all the flowers had the *stamina recurvata*, which we know to be the characteristic of the female type of the *dioecic* wild vine, and no erect stamina ; and the recurvation was so strong and typical that I observed several stamina which had grasped the little cap ordinarily pushed off the bud, and kept it closely pressed to the flower-stem. As often as I bent it back so as to cover the umbilicus, the stamen returned again with the cap, and showed its nature.

Such flowers are represented in figs. 1, 2, and 3, p. 6, of this treatise, and the account there given of the indigenous vines of European countries is confirmed in all essential particulars by the foregoing observation in the Algaida. Some vine leaves were red, indicating black grapes. The shepherds and goats had not left a single berry on this side of the forest. We were informed by the foresters that the shepherds not only eat these wild grapes, but make wine from them. After a long struggle through miles of forest, brushwood, and brambles, through sand and difficulties of every kind, I at last came to the place described by Clemente:— "In this place the vines form impenetrable thickets, magnificent banquetting halls, most graceful pavilions, grottoes, places, covered walks, winding footpaths, crossed walks, labyrinths, walls, arches, pillars, and a thousand other original and indescribable caprices." This description, which dates from the year 1803, is literally true in the present day. From a large tree I took a vine branch fifty feet in length. Many other canes of the same size were hanging down, and forming a perfect screen, in the shade of which I rested for some time to admire the phenomenon.

We then passed miles upon miles of vines; at last we struck across the sandy interior of the side of the forest on which flows the Guadalquivir. A march of two hours through loose sand brought me to a part where all the forms of wild vines were found, round a swamp, in their most intense concentration. A wild fig-tree was covered with a wild vine full of grapes. They were small and black, acidulous, but good to eat. The vine was much affected by the oidium. The swamp gave me a good idea of the circumstances under which the fossil vines described in the Treatise, pp. 14-15, were living. At Salzhausen, the fossil vine leaves are found together with the leaves of a fig-tree. The vines are growing in such masses in this forest, that the foresters

estimated the quantity of wine which could be made, if all
the grapes could be collected, at a hundred botas. It is
probable that these garañonas have, by cultivation, yielded
the black palomino, also called tempranillo of the south,
identical with the graciano of the Ebro valley. The doctrine
which I advocated some years ago, in a paper printed in
vol. xviii., p. 109 of the "Journal of the Society of Arts,"
namely, that the peculiar wines of the great viticultural districts of Europe were derived from wild vines indigenous to
these districts, and not imported into them by the agency of
man, has thus obtained an important confirmation.

§ 197. VINEYARDS OF ROTA.—TINTILLA DE ROTA.

The soil of the Rota district is almost pure sand. All
the celebrated Rota vegetables and fruit, as well as the
tintilla, are indeed grown upon sand thrown upon the shore
by the sea. The parcels of land are all surrounded by sand-
walls, and these latter are fixed by stockades of reeds, the
well-known cañas. The parcels are mostly small, or, if
large, are frequently subdivided by such reed-palings, to
break the force of the wind and keep the sand in its place.
The wines in the bodegas of Rota I found to be of three very
different qualities. The first quality, the principal product
of the vineyards of Rota, is the *tintilla*. This is not wine in
the ordinary significance of the term, but more of a syrup,
made from passulated grapes or raisins by a peculiar process.
The black grapes of the tintilla vine are dried in the sun,
taken off the stalks, and put into upright barrels open at the
upper end. Must, which has been evaporated to the consistence of a fluid syrup, arrope, is now put over the raisins,
and the mixture is allowed to stand and macerate, the tops
of the casks being covered with mats. The raisins now
become disintegrated, until the mass is like a jam. More
arrope is added from time to time; in January the mass is
trodden on the lagar and pressed. The resulting thick,
dark, reddish brown liquid is the tintilla. No spirit, as I
was informed, is added to it at any time, and therefore the
finished tintilla, which is said not to ferment, ought not to

contain any alcohol. But on tasting the product of 1870, in one of the bodegas, I found it to be in a slightly effervescent state, producing the well-known prickly sensation on the sides of the tongue. And on subjecting a quantity of old solera tintilla to distillation I obtained 5·89 per cent. by weight of alcohol, or 12·87 per cent. of proof spirit. Another specimen of tintilla from another bodega contained 5·6 per cent. by weight of alcohol, equal to 12 per cent. of proof spirit. It is therefore certain that the tintilla of Rota contains alcohol, and that this is probably the product of a very slow fermentation. But some vendors in this country add spirit to the tintilla and thus transform it into a brandied counterfeit. On subjecting a quantity to distillation with oxalic acid it yielded 0·228 per cent. of acetic acid, another specimen 0·2 per cent., which, considering the process by which the wine is obtained, is not excessive and not hurtful. Distilled with some caustic potash the tintilla yielded an alkaline distillate, containing ammonia and compound ammonias, easily recognized by the peculiar and disagreeable smell. The existence of these ammonias is accounted for by the long maceration which the albuminous matters of the raisins undergo in the casks while moistened with arrope. Although the tintilla is made from black grapes, it does not contain the red or blue colouring matter of their husks, for this would require much alcohol and acid for their extraction ; as the alcohol is not added and is not produced until after the juice is separated from the husks, the colouring matter remains behind. The great amount of sweetness and the flavour of dried grapes, together with the mass of extractives and the little alcohol in juxtaposition to the free acidity, make the tintilla an article of the class of agreeable, drinkable sweets. A bota full of the best quality costs at Rota about £40, but the current price of the great bulk of the produce is about £20 to £24 per bota.

The second product of importance of Rota is vino de color. The tinto grapes are plastered, pressed, and the white must is allowed to ferment. Another quantity of the same white must is evaporated to the consistence of a syrup, and is added to the fermenting natural must, and the mixture completes its fermentation. Then spirit is added in larger or smaller quantities. This vino de color has a horrible taste, and is, in fact, undrinkable. Its principal, perhaps only use, is for mixing with pale country wines, to give them the external falsified resemblance to the similarly prepared brown, pale, and golden sherries.

The third quality of Rota product, and the one which approaches nearest to wine, is the tinto, or tent of English authors. It is made by fermenting the juice with the husks, and thus becomes a truly red wine. I have tasted tinto thoroughly fermented, dry, free from sugar and adventitious spirit, which was really delicious, and showed what tinto might be if properly prepared and left alone. But such is not to be, for it is not to the taste of the wine merchants, who want Rota tent with burning spirit and lots of sweet. This treatment completely ruins the peculiar fine flavour of this wine. The tinto grape of Rota therefore fares like the same grape of Tarragona. It is misused for the production of imitations of port wine and sold to the British public as *Spanish Port*. The inmates of hospitals and other charitable institutions are its principal consumers. The prices of this wine at Rota varied formerly between £4 and £9 per butt. As Catalonia can undersell Rota in this particular article, the manufacture of Rota has had to endure great competition, and may, perhaps, cease entirely.

§ 198. Wines of the Val de Penas.

The wines produced in this district, mostly red, were, up to a late period of this century, preserved in hides as of old. But some enterprising wine-merchants brought casks and coopers to the Mancha, and now its wines go by rail to Cadiz, and thence come to this country. The white varieties have all been treated with gypsum, the red ones mostly, but some escape it. These wines are commendable for their generally good quality and low price.

§ 199. Wines of Catalonia.

Catalonia yields annually 20,000 butts of wine, which is mostly red, and shipped to England as a cheap drink for the general public. The plain of Ampurdan is covered with vines, and of many other parts of this province four-fifths of all cultivated land is occupied by viticulture. Catalan wine is shipped largely also to America.

§ 200. Wines of Valencia, Benicarlo, Alicante.

Valencia wines are perishable, and therefore have no great reputation. They are mostly grown in the plain, only small quantities on suitable hill-sides. The bulk of these wines, stated to amount to 100,000 butts annually, a figure which is probably in excess of reality, is distilled for brandy, of which 600,000 cantares, or 2,130,000 gallons, are annually produced. Owing to the perishable nature of the wine, stocks are not kept longer than a twelvemonth.

In the district of Benicarlo, a town situated about sixty miles to the north-east of Valencia, and Vinaroz, near the mouth of the Ebro, wine is made in the ordinary way, but is fortified, less for home use than for exportation. Here, also, little stock is kept, each year's produce being generally sold for exportation before the new wine is made, so that the emissary of the English Board of Trade, in 1861, could not obtain samples of natural wine from former vintages. The wine for export is brandied twice as strongly as that used in the country, namely up to thirty-two per cent. proof spirit.

At *Alicante*, a town about ninety English miles south of Valencia, much wine is produced, both on hill sides and in the plain, from a kind of vine which occurs in a black and a white variety, and passes under the name of Alicante in the outer world, but at Alicante is termed *Tintilla*. It has a large loose bunch, hanging by a long stalk, which forms the axis and does not form wings or strong branches. The berries are fleshy and juicy and provided with a thin skin, and resemble much those of the black Hambro', the Tyrol vine so well known in this country. The black Alicante is immensely fertile, steady in blossom, but ripens late, so that it yields good wine only in the best situations even in its home. The black Alicante, and its paler variety, the red, are the vines the juice of which forms the basis of most Spanish wines. It is largely cultivated in the south of France. In the Dordogne it is termed Benicarlo; in Provence, Mourvède; on the east side of the Pyrenees, Mataro; in some other places, Tintillo; at Malaga, Alicante; and at Jerez and Rota, Tintilla. The reader may find the argument for these synonyms in Odart's "Traité des Cépages," pp. 513 and 531. The white Alicante ripens earlier than the blue, but is much less cultivated. Alicante wines also are fortified to at least thirty-two per cent. before exportation.

The wines of *Valencia*, *Benicarlo*, and *Alicante*, being rich in colour, are made up to imitate port wine, and even the casks are made up to resemble port-pipes in size and appearance. A very large proportion of these wines finds its way to France, for the purpose of being blended with other wines which are themselves deficient in strength and colour.

§ 201. WINES OF GRANADA, MALAGA.

The wines of Granada are better known under the name of wines of *Malaga*, the centre of the renowned viticultural district called *Axarquia*. The hills bearing the vineyards consist of clay and schist, superposed on limestone. The more solid schist is termed "*herizza*," that which easily disintegrates "*lantejuéla*" or "*pizárra*;" the latter forms the most suitable soil for viticulture. The climate of the district is so favourable, that the vine almost becomes a perennial evergreen, and bears three crops of grapes every year. The first harvest takes place in June, and is transformed into raisins exclusively. The second harvest takes place in September, and yields a dry wine somewhat resembling sherry. The last vintage takes place in October and November, and gives the particular wines known as Malagas. Of Malaga wines the following varieties are distinguished. 1. *Pedro Ximenes*, in reality a dulce. 2. *Colour-wines*, *i.e.* solutions in wine of must boiled down to brown syrup : these are used to impart the amber-colour, the Pedro Ximenes to give sweetness to the Malaga wine of trade. 3. *Muscatel*, also a dulce, *i.e.*, must preserved in spirit ; of this two varieties are distinguished, Malaga-Muscat, and "*drip*" or "*tear*" Muscat. 4. *Dry wines* resembling sherries, which are made up into "Malaga" as just related. 5. *Malvoisie*, resembling Madeira. 6. *Tintos*, coloured, mostly very dark, sweet and alcoholic wines. 7. *Cherry wines*, being liqueurs made with the juice of acid cherries, so-called morellas. The dry wine is brandied up to 37'5 per cent of proof spirit ; the sweet wines do not much surmount 30 per cent.

The *amount of wine* annually produced in the Malaga district is 80,000 arrobas, or 2,666 butts. Of these the greater part is exported, mainly to America. Much, also, goes to England, and the wine for both countries is prepared in the same manner.

§ 202. WINES OF ARAGON AND OTHER PROVINCES OF SPAIN, MAJORCA, MINORCA.

Aragon produces dark-coloured, strong-bodied wines of good taste and flavour, from the celebrated vines, the Grenache of Sabayes and the Carineña and delivers them up to the trade of Saragossa. *Navarra* does not admit of much viticulture ; the vineyard of Roncesvalles alone supplies a local want. *Galicia* produces a little good wine for exportation at Ribadavia and Tuy. In *Biscaya* much wine is produced for the people, but is quite unfit for exportation. *New Castile*, with the *Mancha*, produces besides the lightest and least-coloured but most agreeable wines of Spain, already mentioned above under Val de Peñas and the muscat of Iuencaral, near Madrid. Near to these are the wines of the Spanish Tagus, from Arganda del Rey above Madrid to Talavera de la Reyna. *Murcia* produces thick rough wines, of which those of Cartagena sometimes come up to common sorts of Alicante.

The *island of Majorca* produces a Malvasia wine, which is exported by way of Palma : and *Minorca* produces a dark red wine round Alcyor, which is not exported, as on sea it spoils in bottles and casks; while the "alba flora," a light white wine with some bouquet, bears keeping and exportation.

The wines of Spain are, on the whole, of good quality, but are easily and quickly spoiled in part by unskilful and unscientific treatment. They are subject to many accidents, caused by fungi, so-called diseases, which destroy their value; and to counteract these or their results, the producers use plaster, sulphurous acid, boiled plastered must, brandy and sweet must preserved in alcohol, so-called dulce. These admixtures, however necessary some of them may be in default of better means of preservation, are deteriorating the naturally excellent qualities of the wine. As regards plastering, some Spanish œnologists have strongly protested against the practice, and termed it an adulteration and a fraud. However this may be, the wine is deteriorated thereby, while the practice is so universal that it must have some deep reason at present unknown. It is not unlikely that it was discovered by the practice of keeping wine in underground cisterns of masonry, of which the binding and lining material is plaster of Paris. Of course the plaster itself does not dissolve in the wine, but it removes the tartaric acid, and substitutes sulphuric for it; the sulphate of potash thus produced remains in the wine and gives it a bitter taste. When this can be once avoided by improved modes of vinification, the wines of Spain will be much better and much more valuable than they at present are.

CHAPTER XXIII.

WINES OF PORTUGAL.

§ 203. VINEYARDS OF THE ALTO DOURO.

THE vineyards of Jerez are so beautiful and productive that they might well be termed the vineyards of Venus. Undulating hills, easily accessible from all sides, are covered with a luxurious growth of vines, which every September finds heavily laden with an enormous mass of luscious fruit. A poetical enthusiast might call these hills the very breasts of nature. Very different is the aspect and condition of the vineyards of the Alto Douro. Here all is rock, gorge, almost inaccessible mountain, precipice, and torrent, while over, or along, all these rude features of nature are drawn countless lines of stone walls by which man makes or supports the soil in which the vines find their subsistence. When opposite Tua, I had counted 150 stone-built terraces, one above the other, covering the rock which rises almost out of the waters of the Douro, I thought that if Jerez was the vineyard of Venus, this Alto Douro vineyard must be termed the vineyard of Hercules.

The vineyards of the Alto Douro may be visited from Oporto. It is convenient to travel in a hired carriage, particularly when the traveller desires to make œnological studies by the road-side. In former times when the great exodus of British merchants to the vineyards took place, the hire of a carriage and pair was, as a rule, eight pounds sterling for the single journey. This journey was often described after the manner in which the Phœnicians related the dangers of their sea-voyages ; along it were supposed to be found defiles like those of Scylla and Charybdis. My surprise was therefore agreeable when I drove to the very foot of the vineyards on a beautifully constructed macadamized road, while the scenery during the whole journey surpassed in beauty many of the reputed great sights of Europe. Indeed, the rise from the side of Amaranthe up to the watershed of the Douro valley is not surpassed by anything I have seen in Switzerland, the Pyrenees, or the mountains in central and southern Spain. The ascent should be made on horseback, while the carriage is being drawn up by the steady bullocks, which take half the labour from the carriage-horses.

§ 204. VINES OF THE PROVINCE ENTRE DOURO E MINHO.

During the entire journey up to the water-shed the observer sees no vineyards, properly so-called, but he sees all round the houses and villages, along the roads, along the margins of woods, vines creeping up trees, and competing with their foliage for air and sunshine. I observed only black grapes on these vines, and all those which I tasted were very acid and astringent. From them is made the beverage called " green wine " (vinho verde), from its resemblance to wine made from unripe fruit. The fruit is, in fact, unripe, and, moreover, never becomes ripe in any year, owing to its being grown high up in the air. I have not been able to ascertain what kind of grapes and wine these vines would yield if they were cultivated in good situations and low on the ground. On the whole, what I saw gave me the impression that these nondescript vines, which I also observed in forests and in woody valleys, covering shrubs and brambles, were like the vines of the Algaida, described in a former chapter, true children of the soil, indigenous plants, which, with a minimum of help on the part of man in the shape of pruning, produce an enormous quantity of harsh fruit, having the same relation in taste to the wine-berry as a crab-apple has to a fine French pippin. The vinho verde is only produced in this province of Entre Douro e Minho, and no other wine, particularly none of the quality produced in the Alto Douro, termed " vinho maduro," ripe wine, is here grown.

§ 205. SOIL OF THE ALTO DOURO DISTRICT.

The river Douro, in Portugal, flows through a valley
with precipitous sides, mainly formed of a clay-schist formation.   This reposes upon or alternates with granite, and

Fig. 43.—Vines ascending a tree, such as produce the *vinho verde* in
Entre Douro e Minho.

the latter rock not rarely appears on the heights forming the water-sheds.   The clay-schist forms the viticultural
soil, for many reasons.   It is easily broken into parallel
slabs, with which terraces can be built, so-called dry walls,
requiring no mortar or other binding material; it is easily
disintegrated by the atmosphere, and forms a clay soil,

which retains the water with pertinacity, and allows it to sink deep into the fissures of the schist, where also the roots of the vines are able to follow to great depths. The granite, on the other hand, lacks most of these properties ; it does not easily break up, and becomes very dry in summer, and then is generally situated so high above the level of the sea that the vine becomes excluded from it by the coldness of the climate resulting from the elevation. A great part of the soil of the wine districts could not be planted with any other crops; the valleys bear a few strips of land used in maize cultivation ; here and there are some olives. Corn, and a few fodder plants are grown on the mountains above the wine region. It is the vine, and the vine alone, which has made the rocks of the Alto Douro a cultivated part of the earth's surface.

§ 206. TOPOGRAPHICAL NOTES.

The topography of the Alto Douro is best understood with the aid of the maps which have been elaborated by the late Baron Forrester. The largest and most beautiful of them has, I believe, never been published for sale, but only printed for private distribution by the baron. A useful copy, on a reduced scale, was published by Parliament in 1852, in the Report of the Committee on Import Duties on Wines. The limits of the cultivation of the vine are on this map marked by a red line, which includes what was formerly the district under the surveillance of the so-called Agricultural Company. The cultivation of the vine is most extended, and as regards the production of a particular class of wine, most successful, on both sides of the river Corgo, a tributary of the Douro, coming from the north. The district west of the Corgo, usually called the Lower Corgo, has the most ancient cultivation. This begins at a distance of about forty-two miles English above Oporto, and occupies the triangular space between the Douro and Corgo. The part east of the Corgo, ending near the river Taah, is termed the Upper Corgo. On the south of the Douro there is also a strip of mountainous territory planted

exclusively with vines, but it is much narrower than the
district on the north bank. On the whole it may be said ·
that the vineyards of the Alto Douro extend over a piece of
mountainous country thirty English miles in length from
east to west, and ten miles in width from north to south.
The part of the district above Tua, which contains several
excellent though relatively new vineyards, is now frequently
termed the Douro Superior, as distinguished from the Alto
Douro.

§ 207. Modes of Planting and Training the Vine.

In the Alto Douro one can see nearly all the varieties of
culture side by side, but the prevailing mode is a rational
low cultivation. Near and below Regoa there are yet
many espaliers, forming covered walks, about two yards
high, over which the vines are trained ; all these give bad
grapes and bad wine.   Above Regoa they disappear entirely,
and the vines are trained low on the ground, but the pruning
is not so methodical as at Jerez, and consequently with the
age of the vine its bearing part rises higher, sometimes a
yard above the ground. Grapes grown at that height
mostly remain sour, and, particularly in dry years, form acid
raisins, which spoil the wine from the lower fully ripe grapes.
The viticulturists renew such vines by forming layers or
slips, bending the highest branch towards the ground, drawing it through a trench, and allowing it to project at a
distance. The young vine is never separated from the old
stock, and the old stock is never allowed to grow branches ;
such old loop-shaped vine-trunks, projecting from the earth,
and destitute of leaves, are seen in great numbers, particularly in old vineyards. There are vines trained to stakes,
as in France and Germany, and vines trained without them ;
in some vineyards the vines were planted through holes in
the perpendicular walls ; but it appeared that many so
planted had died from drought and heat.

The operations on the soil are not so methodical as at
Jerez. There is an excavation made round every vine in
autumn to catch the rain-water ; at the same time the vine

is pruned. Each of the two or three, or more, main branches of the vine is allowed two or three eyes for the bearing branches, and a spur of one eye with the subsidiary small eye for the growing of wood. All the vineyards are kept carefully free from weeds, so that the sun has free play in heating the soil.

The Douro vines have this peculiarity in common, that their fruit is not large-sized like the grapes of Andulasia, nor small-sized like the grapes of Burgundy or the Rhine, but medium-sized like those of the paludal vines of the Gironde.

§ 208. VINTAGE AND MODES OF VINIFICATION.

The Vintage in the Alto Douro begins at the earliest on the 20th of September, and ends about the 10th of October. The vineyards in low situations, close upon the Douro, are the earliest to harvest, and even then the grapes are some-times over-ripe, so as to be partially passulated; the latest vintages are in the third or top region of the slopes. The vintage is executed by men and women, all from Gallicia, hence termed Gallegos. These also do all the other labours on the ground required throughout the year; the settled population of Portuguese is too small in numbers, and too sickly for heavy work; for the entire district is extremely unhealthy. The Gallegos receive on an average seven pence per day in money, and food, which, however, does not include bread. The daily food consists of a pound of salted dry cod, of which large quantities are imported into Portugal from Newfoundland, and of a quart of a kind of soup, consisting of cabbage leaves, beans and lard, boiled in water. The Gallegos of each vineyard not only mess together, but also sleep together in the same shed, and any attempt to separate the sexes is immediately followed by protests, and, if these are unheeded, by an exodus. The women assist in the collection of the grapes only, but the disintegration of the grapes, their pruning, &c., is all done by men.

§ 209. THE LAGAR, THE PRESS, TREADING THE GRAPES,
FERMENTATION.

The receptacle in which the grapes are collected while the vintage is proceeding, in which the grapes are mashed, extracted, and pressed, is termed a lagar. It is always built of stone, generally granite, more rarely slate or masonry. In size it varies, so that it may hold the grapes for only a few pipes of wine, or for many up to 10 and 16. In the large vineyards there are, therefore, lagars of several sizes, so that they are immediately adapted for large and small harvests. The shape of the lagar is mostly square or oblong, its depth about 2 feet, or a little more, and its sides vary in length between 3 yards and 8 or 10 yards.

Over and across each lagar is fixed one of the old-fashioned lever or beam presses, of which the sketch gives an idea. Such presses do yet occur in Würtemberg, but they are not any longer in use on the Rhine.

After the lagar has received its full complement of grapes, or as much as it can conveniently hold during the entire operations of vinification, a number of Gallegos, with their legs bared to the upper thighs, go on to the lagar and tread the grapes into pulp. This operation lasts from twenty-four to forty-eight hours without interruption, the men being changed from time to time for refreshment and rest. During or after this operation fermentation begins, and proceeds, according to temperature, quicker or slower, but it is hardly ever very tumultuous; more frequently it falls below the necessary energy, owing to the stone walls of the lagar abstracting too much heat. In that case, as many men as can stand in the lagar are put on to it, and they are kept slowly stirring the mass with their feet until they have communicated so much heat that the fermentation can again proceed alone. When the fermentation has so far progressed that the amount of alcohol formed counter-balances the specific gravity of the remaining sugar so far as to bring the glucometer to the zero point, the fermenting mass is again trodden by the Gallegos, this time in order to extract the colouring matter from the husks. When the wine is as dark as may be desired, and a sample runs over a white plate so as to leave streaks of thick, dark red dye behind, fermentation is considered complete. The wine is now drawn off by a pump, syphon, or tap, or through a hole in the bottom of the lagar, the exit being guarded by some sort of strainer, and run into a large wooden cask, which may hold from five to thirty pipes, and is termed a "tonnel." From four to eight volumes of brandy, of about 40° Cartier, are added to every hundred volumes of wine, and the mixture is left to clarify itself by gravity.

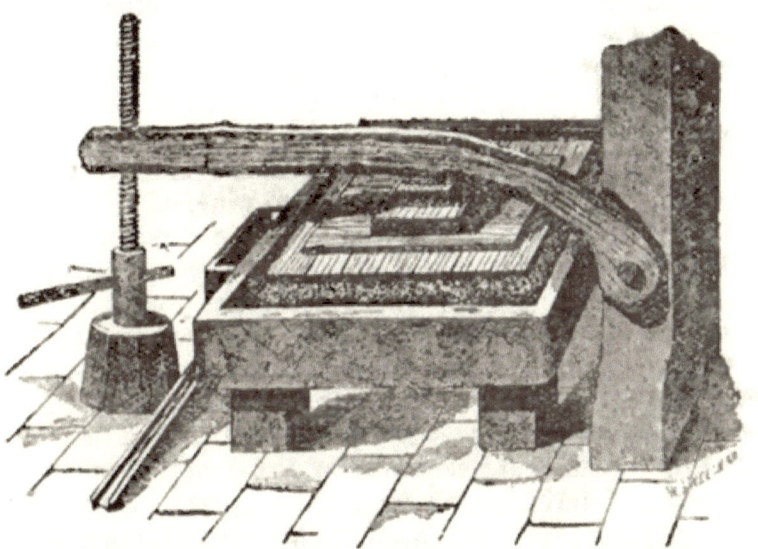

Fig. 44.—Beam or Lever Press, as used in the Alto Douro.

§ 210. REMARKS ON THIS MODE OF VINIFICATION.

The mode of making port wine is extremely unclean, and the proceedings are very crude and elementary; nevertheless, so good a product is obtained that its faults are, as it were, drowned in its good qualities. The great object of the wine makers must be to produce good and durable wine with only so much alcohol as shall not be injurious to the wine drinker. This cannot be said to be the case with the ordinary thick, heavy, so-called loaded ports of 40° to 42° of

proof spirit, and for this reason whole classes of society in
Britain have ceased to drink any port wine whatever. Yet
good port wine is one of the most wonderful productions of
the earth ; and I am sure, when vinification in all its
branches and variations shall be once fully understood on
the Alto Douro, it will produce such excellent red wines as
hitherto have not been exported from the Peninsula.

§ 211. ELDERBERRY AND LOGWOOD.

It is said that port wine is coloured with elderberries and
other dyes, and sweetened with jeropiga and treacle, besides
being dosed with brandy ; but I have been unable to find
any evidence of this, at least as regards Alto Douro wines.
Elder trees are very scarce in the Alto Douro, and I can in
this respect fully confirm the statement of Mr. Consul
Crawford. Moreover, the Alto Douro wine, of a good year
at least, is so deeply coloured, in fact, so excessively loaded
with colouring matter, that it cannot by any means require
any addition of colour; the elderberries exported from
Oporto are really used for colouring other wines than port
wine, particularly the Spanish ports, Mountain ports, Cape
ports, and Sicilian red wines which are carried to England,
and thence exported to countries where people buy wine
rather by the name it bears than by any quality it possesses.
It is also not rarely stated, upon the evidence of Mr. Cyrus
Field, in the report of the Parliamentary Committee of
1852, that port wine is now and then coloured red by means
of Brasilwood, commonly called logwood ; but this is a
great error, as it is quite impossible to dye wine of any kind
with logwood—for the colour of logwood is purple only in
alkaline solution, and not in acid, in which it is only tawny.
Moreover, it is very astringent, a quality which almost all
port wine possesses in excess. Logwood is never used in
trade for dyeing anything purple, and the large quantities of
logwood shipped to Europe are nearly entirely consumed in
the production, by means of iron mordants, of firm black
colours on many kinds of tissues ; and, although it may
occur that particular artists in mixing and counterfeiting,

dye some pipes of white wine with elderberries, and give them astringency with logwood, nevertheless I believe that such products would commercially not pay the cost and trouble of their production, and are, at all events, only an exceedingly small fraction of the wines which constitute the bulk of the exports from Oporto. I am, therefore, of opinion that the sooner we dismiss these prejudices and errors regarding elderberry and logwood in port wine, the better.

§ 212. White Varieties of Wines produced in the Alto Douro.

Many thousand pipes of white wine are annually made in the Alto Douro, and exported mainly to Russia and Ireland —very little goes to England. These wines are not distinguished either by the grapes from which they are made, or by the qualities which they obtain in the course of their development. The great qualities of Jerez wines are dependent upon a few dominant species of vines, sweet wines are derived from the Pedro Jimenez; high-flavoured amontillados and finos, from palomino; oloroso qualities from mantuo castellano; Rota wines owe their important characteristics to one vine, the tintilla. In a similar manner the wines of Burgundy come from one kind of grape, that of the pineau; and Rhine-wine is characterized by the Riessling. But the Alto Douro white wines are not thus characterized; they are not produced from any dominant vine, or vines, but are the product of the commixture of a great variety of fruit from frequently heterogeneous varieties of vines, amongst them the arinto, boal, verdelho, codega, malvasia fina, estreito, or rabo de ovelha, carnal, Donna Branca, gouveio estimado, moscatel. Of these the rich bearers, yielding coarse musts, termed castas grossas, are most favoured by the growers, and the result appears in the wines. The white grapes are not grown in the best situation, but only in second and third-rate vineyards. The Alto Douro wine districts, as a whole, may be considered as consisting of hills only, without any valley-bottoms between them; the declivities of the hills, all

supported by numerous terraces, as described, may be conveniently divided into three zones. The lowest zones,
nearest to the river and its tributaries, produce the first
class of red wines; the second zones, occupying the middle
of the slopes, produce the second-class; and the upper
zones, situated near the top of the hill, or covering the tops
of the lower hills, are mainly planted with white vines. These
latter are also planted on the lower zones of the higher lying
valleys away from the Douro. The white grapes are, like
the red ones, fermented with the husks and stalks, and in
this particular the vinification differs from that of most other
wine countries; for in these, white musts are generally
pressed out of husks and stalks before fermentation. In
consequence of this practice the Alto Douro white wines
acquire an astringency frequently amounting to harshness.
This may make them more firm and less liable to spoil, but
it greatly prolongs the time necessary for their maturation.
They are also arrested in their fermentation by the addition
of brandy, and, not being so sweet or so fully ripe as the red
musts, require more frequent admixture of artificial saccharine ingredients, such as arobe, jeropiga, or sugar. In consequence of this they acquire no very high vinous character,
even when kept long in bottle. On the contrary, they frequently develop in bottle a heavy disagreeable odour, termed
bottle-stink, which can only partially be removed before the
wine is placed on the table by decanting the wine and ven-
tilating it, so that the air may influence the wine, and dispel
or oxidize the bad smell. This is also a fault of many of
the red ports, which they acquire by being bottled at improper periods and while in an improper condition; the
cleaner the wines are when bottled the less they develop of
this bottle-stink, and perfect Alto Douro wines have not,
and ought not to have, any of it.

§ 213. TRANSPORT OF ALTO DOURO WINES.

Many of the vineyards are so situated that no animal can
be led to them, and their produce has therefore to be carried
to the lagares on the backs of men. Many of the lagares,

again, cannot be reached with vehicles, and the wines made on them have therefore to be transported downhill on the backs of animals; and as it would be impossible to use casks for that purpose, the wines are carried in bags made of the skins of animals. These wine skins are called "odres." An odre is made from a goat-skin, and is taken from the dead animal in such a manner as to injure it in the least possible degree. The hair is only shortened, not removed, and the hairy side is turned inwards. This is done in order to leave the epidermis or scarf-skin intact on the surface of the thick, strong, leathery skin; for this scarf-skin is very impenetrable to moisture, whereas mere leather would be very penetrable. The skin is made more impenetrable and imputrescible by being covered over the entire inside with semifluid pitch, or wood tar. I have seen thousands of these bags in use in the Alto Douro. Some merchants in this country seem to think that these odres are a matter which must be kept a secret from the lovers of port wine; and it happened to me, at a meeting of the Committee on Wines, of the International Exhibition, in Kensington, that, when speaking about these odres, I was flatly contradicted by a port wine merchant, and told that there was no such thing used in the Alto Douro. And yet I had, but a month before, seen strings of horses, mules, and donkeys, each carrying two of these odres full of wine, in the establishment of the partner of this very wine-merchant who so vehemently contradicted me, and had seen the wine from the odres poured into the tonels of the partner, whence no doubt it found its way to Oporto in due course. The odres are also used in Spain, as is popularly known from the romance of "Don Quixote," by Cervantes. A tourist who, during vintage time, travels in Italy, Spain, or Portugal, may frequently see a number of these skins, mostly distended with air, hanging up, either to be prepared for use, or to be washed after use. They frequently impart a pitchy taste to the wine, which is never got rid of; when made from the skin of he-goats, they also communicate the goat-flavour. In Spain odres are frequently made from pig-skins.

When the wine is collected in the tonels in the adegas

attached to the farms, it is ready for the travellers of the mercantile houses, who now taste, select, and buy. The wine is left in the adegas, until, in winter time, the water in the river Douro is high enough to admit of loaded barges travelling to Oporto. The wine-merchants from Oporto then send up their wine-casks, some filled with brandy (I have seen many casks of Berlin shape, with Berlin brands in the adegas of the Alto Douro, and therefore believe that much Berlin spirit is put into port-wine), the brandy and wine are mixed, put into the casks, returned to the river, and shipped to Oporto. The manner in which the wine-casks, all of the size called pipes, holding 116 gallons, are brought down the hills to the river, is very remarkable. They are brought on strong carts, each laden with one pipe only at a time, and drawn by two oxen. The carts are of the rudest but most solid construction, and the oxen are of the finest breed, large and very powerful. The labour which these oxen perform in bringing such a pipe of wine down the stony, rocky, horrible mountain roads, is really a most astonishing performance of muscular work. The wheels of the carts are fixed to the axle-tree on which the top of the cart rides by two forks. This arrangement causes much friction, by which a creaking noise is produced, which can be heard at great distances, particularly at night. The more noise an axle-tree makes the higher it is valued, and the peasants vie with each other for the possession of the cart which makes the greatest noise.

At last the wine in the pipes arrives at the river-side, and is shipped in boats to Oporto. The manner in which these boats are loaded and steered is well represented on the map of Forrester. Arrived in Oporto, the wine is carted to the sheds, called lodges, and stored. The treatment which it receives there mainly consists in the addition of brandy from time to time; the brandy is kept as low as possible, in order not to increase the expense more than is necessary. The last and principal dosing with brandy is only inflicted just before the wine is shipped. If the wine is not sweet enough, a quantity of jeropica is added; this, when legitimate, con-sists of sweet must preserved by the addition of one-fifth of

its volume of brandy of 40° Cartier, and therefore corresponds to the Jerez dulce. If in bad years, or from any other
cause, the colour of the wine is not so deep as may be wished,
some deep-coloured wine is added; and some elderberry
may be used now and then, but, as already stated, this is
not frequently used in making up Alto Douro wine. Those
wines which are not mixed with anything except brandy, not
even with other wines of similar quality, but of different
origin, are called vintage wines, and are kept by themselves.
Their date is preserved, and they are made much of by the
merchants. Those wines which are not kept by themselves,
but are mixed with other qualities, the product of different
zones and different years, are termed factory-ports, and constitute the great mass of the wines exported.

§ 214. Change in the Taste of the Public as regards Port.

Much has been written and said regarding the injurious
character of strongly-brandied port wine, and in consequence
the more polite classes of society have almost entirely turned
from port wine, and do not drink it any longer. I have
been present at dinners to which ten or twelve gentlemen
sat down, and not one took port when it was brought round.
An Oporto merchant in London gave a dinner party to
twenty gentlemen, and not one of these was found to drink
even a single glass of the merchant's own best vintage wine.
If this antipathy should continue, it might, perhaps, aid in
the reduction of the brandy in port wine to below *delirium
tremens* point. (This disease is common among spirit
drinkers, and those who consume much strong port; it
cannot be produced by drinking natural wines with less
than twenty-six degrees of proof spirit, even in large quantity.) I have no doubt that when the objection, namely,
excess of brandy, shall have vanished, many œnophilists
and persons of good taste will return to port, the natural,
full-flavoured, fine-coloured, invigorating, and wholesome
wine, which, as regards bouquet, body, vigour, and lasting
qualities, and as regards its wonderfully exhilarating effect

upon body and mind, is not surpassed by the red wines of any other land. But, it must be observed that, although some classes in England have ceased drinking port, others have taken to it, and in consequence the trade in port wine has not at all diminished, but has rather increased. The fact is, the port which was formerly generally bought by gentlemen, clergymen, noblemen, etc., and laid down in their cellars to mature for years, is now mainly bought by publicans, tapped, and sold in glasses at 4*d.* each. This is the case, not only in this country, but in America, and even in Newfoundland. The fishermen there, a great proportion of whose fish is consumed in Portugal, in return get a quantity of this port wine, and ease the difficulties of their climate and situation by enjoying this most delicious drink.

The price of port wine in the district varies between fourteen and fifteen milreis per pipe of 636 litres. In Oporto, £15 to £20 is an average price of good factory port. Fine wines and old wines rise to £80 per pipe.

§ 215. Wine Country of the Bairrada.

This is a very new wine country, but probably in the course of time it will develop into something of importance. The Bairrada lies between Oporto and Lisbon, rather to the south of Coimbra. The Portuguese Railway runs through the middle of it. The wine grown in the middle of the district, which includes both red and white varieties, is called *vinho de embarque*, or that which may be exported, whilst that grown in the outer belt, and its prolongation towards the north and the south, which is not fit for exportation, but is used in the country, or distilled for brandy, is called *consumo*. The soil there is chalky, of the so-called lias formation. The wines of that country are frequently taken to Oporto, and there made up into common class port wines by a small admixture of Alto Douro wine. They are brought to London mainly for the purpose of being re-exported to the colonies, and many butts of them go to Russia and to America. The wines are peculiar in this, that though dark coloured when young, they quickly lose their colour, and in four or five years, if not assisted by other means, they get so pale as to resemble old port. But they also lose their quality, and therefore they cannot be advantageously reared and kept by themselves. That arises again from the want of consideration for the principles of œnopoesis; and because there is in the Bairrada no dominant grape, but the peasants who grow these vines mix up every sort of grape they can lay hold of, and the consequence is a want of character and firmness in the product. The grape mainly grown there is the *baga*, which means berry. It is a small-berried, dark-coloured grape. There is also grown a little of the *souzao* and a little of the *bastardo*, which gives some flavour, but there are no coloured grapes like the mourisco or tinta, or tinta Francisca. There is also a white wine, made, as in the Alto Douro, from the *boal* and ten other vines; and the jeropiga, or sweet juice made by mixing spirit with sweet must, is largely produced, and further *abafado*, or must stopped in the middle of its fermentation by spirit, etc. Must is sometimes boiled down, and to the syrup is added brandy. Then there is also made *arobe*, which is the juice of the grape itself boiled down to a thick syrup, either alone or in company with a quantity of quinces, apples, and other fruit. I quote from the Government report of Portugal, where it is stated the arobe can be of two kinds, viz., simple and compound. The first is the concentrated must produced by the action of heat; the second, or compound arobe, is made with sugar and quinces, apples, and other fruits. I have been very careful to lay before my readers accurate information, to eliminate that which is erroneous, and to know and state only that which is true. Now these practices are not at all done with the purpose of imposing upon the customer. They are the results of dire necessities and difficulties in the vinification, such as it would really require the highest skill and science to obviate; for the poor peasant has no means and no scientific guidance, but simply the help of a copper and a little brandy.

Y

§ 216. The Vineyards Around and near Lisbon.—
Vineyards of Collares.

There is a quantity of wine grown round Lisbon. It is
called *termo*, from being grown within the bounds of Lisbon,
but there is not much of it, and it does not constitute an
article of commerce, and therefore need not further detain
our attention. Along the Tagus, south-west from Lisbon,
there is that beautiful village Carcavellos, which once had
a very flourishing production of from 1,300 to 1,500 pipes
a year, and still enjoys a reputation, though the production
is now entirely destroyed. It was one of the first fields
invaded. by the oidium, and some years ago the whole production did not amount to five pipes, for most of the vineyards had died out.

Going along the shore of the Tagus, and turning northwards round the mountain of Cintra, we come to the
celebrated vineyards of Collares. They can also be reached
by coming down the valley from Cintra, and perhaps that is
the most agreeable way of getting there. The vineyards of
Jerez are situated on undulating hills of chalk. Those of
the Alto Douro are rocky, but those of Collares are situated
on sand, thrown up by the billows of the Atlantic. Owing
to the shifting nature of this land, the peasant proprietor is
obliged to adopt some device to keep his vineyards and his
wine too. The vineyard is divided into a number of small
parcels, of the size of an ordinary sitting-room, each of which
is surrounded by a hedge of green reeds or cañas. The
doors which lead from one to the other are also formed of
these living reeds, so that when you pass from one department to another you bend the reeds asunder with the hands,
and walk through, and the curtain of reeds closes of itself
behind you. In spite of this precaution, when after a windy
night the owner of the vineyard comes to look at his vineyard,
he often finds his vines covered up with sand, and he is
obliged to dig them out. But this apparently barren and
unpropitious soil yields a very excellent product. The soil
is constantly moist, the heat of the sun strikes it all day long,
and the vines lie on the ground, in immediate proximity to

pure sand. The result is the excellent wine of Collares. Some of the red wine is made from a grape called the *ramisco*, and from that only. The qualities of this wine are based upon one dominant vine, and it is for that reason that it has such good substance. It quickly matures, is uniform, greatly improves in bottle, and will keep, although its alcoholicity is one of the lowest, being only between eight and ten per cent. It is a very firm wine also, as it requires no spirit to be added to it. It has a flavour of its own which cannot be compared with any other, derived entirely from the ramisco grape. It is a most agreeable and wholesome wine. About 1,500 pipes are made in the district, and the whole is consumed at Lisbon.

§ 217. Vineyard of Bucellas.

Passing from Collares to Cintra, and thence inland, we come to the vineyard of Bucellas. It is said that the Bucellas wine is made from the hock grape, alleged to have been transplanted there by the Marquis of Pombal. All over Portugal the Marquis of Pombal is remembered as a viticulturist, and a man who took great interest in the promotion of viticulture and wine making. I have gone through pretty well all the vineyards there, and have asked many experienced persons, but have not been able to find any hock grapes there whatever. The only grape grown there, from which the genuine Bucellas is made, is the Arinto. At first sight the Arinto has a little similarity to the hock grape called *Riessling*, as it is small-berried, but it is dissimilar in other respects, particularly by its possessing a large bunch. It reminds me of the grapes on the south slopes of the Alps, and has nowhere the small size of the grapes indigenous to the Rhenish countries. Its wine somewhat resembles hock in preserving a little sweetness in good years, and, on the other hand, in being excessively sour in bad years. The Lisbon wine-store keepers add sugar and brandy to the Bucellas, and transform it into the semblance of a low-class sherry. They add boiled must to it just before bottling it, and the consequence is that a thick brown crust deposits on one side of the bottle. This artificial product has no trace of the original high flavour, refreshing, acidulous, wholesome nature, of true Bucellas wine.

§ 218. WINES OF TORRES VEDRAS—LAVRADIO.

Torres Vedras is a celebrated name in the history of the British army. A good many thousand pipes of wine are grown there, but owing to the disregard of the principles I have mentioned, and owing to the fact of the wine being made from mixed grapes, it acquires no particular quality, and, though apparently good to drink in the first year or two, in the third year it falls off and loses its quality, although it does not spoil.

Wines of Lavradio.—Of the many names for which Portugal had a reputation in the vitilogical world, there remains yet to be mentioned Lavradio, which lies on the Tagus, nearly opposite Lisbon, and produces a mild, though somewhat sweetish, but to some people very agreeable wine. It requires very careful keeping for several years, but afterwards acquires all the fine properties of the natural and finer Alto Douro wines. If it were more scientifically treated, and if there were more of it, the Lavradio would soon acquire a high reputation.

§ 219. GENERAL FEATURES OF PORTUGUESE WINE MAKING.

In the Alto Douro, as well as in the Bairrada, and everywhere else in Portugal, all the wine is made in the lagars, peculiar troughs, made of stone mostly, but sometimes of wood, in which the wines ferment. They are very large, about six yards square, and, though in good years that entails no disadvantage, in years when the heat of the season is excessive, or when the harvest is interrupted by rains, the lagar entails every disadvantage which injuriously affects the wine. Sometimes the lagar is partly filled, a quantity of grapes being heaped in one corner; then rainy weather comes, and the grapes are allowed to lie in the corner for a week; then, perhaps, the vintage is continued, and new grapes—perhaps more rotten than the first—are thrown in, and the lagar is filled up. During that time, if the grapes were ripe, a partial fermentation would set in. If the mass were heated, a portion would ferment, and the air having access, it would produce a process of decomposition. Then when the wine is made it has to be sulphured, not only for the purpose of preventing the acetification, which has begun already under these unfavourable circumstances, but to destroy those fungi which in every Portuguese white wine declare themselves almost from the moment it is made, producing scud and viscosity. The wines when made are not put into cellars, but are all kept above ground, in large casks or tonels, and these are never full. In a good year they may be three parts full, whereas in a bad year they may be only one-third or a quarter full, and there is always a greater or a smaller surface of wine exposed to the air. Then if in these sheds the temperature rises very high, the surface being covered by mould, a quick acetification takes place. At Bucellas, I was in the shed of a poor woman, whose only property consisted of a vineyard, and of a shed and tonel of wine, worth, perhaps, £60. She had not tasted it for a long time, and when I tasted it, I told her it was vinegar. I shall never forget the face of the poor woman when she tasted her wine, and she said, " Yes, it is vinegar." So throughout the place, owing to the absence of underground cellars, where the wine can be kept away from the excessive heat in the summer, and owing to the omission of proper precautions in the making of the wine—owing, further, to the poverty of the people, who can only afford to buy one great vessel in which they keep their wine, being unable to buy new casks of a smaller size, which they could fill to the bung, and thereby prevent the air getting at the wine when hot and in a dangerous state—owing to these disadvantages, and to the peculiar climate, there are produced masses of fungi in all Portuguese wines, just as there are in the Jerez wines. These are called *nube*, and when these small microscopic fungi, visible only by the microscope magnifying 600 diameters, grow more numerous, the wine becomes at last thick and viscous, and is called *gordo*. Then the wine acquires this horrid mouse taste, which is the destroyer of many of the most beautiful Jerez wines. The finest Jerez wines are liable to have this horrible mouse taste, and the merchants will tell you that if wine gets a mouse taste, it will become a good wine; but that is rather a paradoxical assertion. Out of 100 butts of wine having mouse taste, perhaps about ten good ones are obtained, but a vast quantity never recover, and these the extractors send to the still. At Bucellas I saw in the sheds of a marquis twenty large tonels full of thick, horrid tasting, sulphury, abominable liquid, which nobody could ever guess would in the course of a year or two transform itself into potable wine. When the wine merchant gets this wine he treats it according to his science, for it need not be wholly lost, but can be purified by chemical means. It is simply a process for taking out the dirt, bad colour, and fungi; although it is very unpromising at first, by means of a little chemical operation a perfectly nice, clean-tasting fluid is produced, and all the mouse taste is gone.

The power of these fungi is so great that in some Portuguese vintages not only a portion of the must is concentrated to increase the sweetness, but the producer is actually obliged to put the whole of his must into the copper, and give it a boiling up, in order to kill the fungi. He does, in fact, on a large scale with his must that which M. Pasteur at Paris has proposed as a general principle for the purpose of preserving wines, namely, heat the wine so as to kill the spores, and thereby set up a healthy fermentation, whereas otherwise there would have been a diseased fermentation, and consequently a very bad product.

Wine Fungi.—Plants live on carbonic acid, water, and ammonia and salts, and fungi are no exception to that rule. It is frequently said that fungi do absorb compound materials —that they are not dependent upon the carbonic acid in the atmosphere, as other plants, but that they do, as it were, like animals, devour compound food. That may be the case with regard to some which live in the air, but those which

WINES OF PORTUGAL. 327

live in fluid do not do so, for when the carbonic acid is with-
drawn by other means than heat the fungi cease to live, sink
to the bottom, and are inert : that is to say, they are killed
or suffocated, and do not live much longer, and consequently
it is proved that the nube fungi require for their existence
the presence of carbonic acid. And it is for this reason
evidently that they are present in the largest quantities in the
youngest wine. The younger the wine the more nube, and
the older the wine the less carbonic acic it produces and the
quicker the nube goes down. Every Jerez merchant will
tell you that any wine which succeeds at all cures itself. It
requires no particular process for getting rid of the nube.
The flor also cures itself, provided the wine has at least twenty-
nine degrees of proof spirit. This flor is a fungus on the top
of the wine, which requires a large quantity of carbonic acid
in order to live. Remove the carbonic acid, and the fungus
dies. That has not been understood, but the practice has
been based strictly on that plan. If the wine containing
this nube be strongly shaken, the fungi condense, and sink
to the bottom. The evolution of the carbonic acid escapes
attention ; however, if the wine, after having been shaken,
be analyzed, it is found that a large quantity of carbonic acid
has been evolved. If the wine be put under the air-pump,
the carbonic acid be exhausted, and air excluded, the wine
will in a short time be clear and sound. The communications
of the highest importance offered by M. Pasteur will make
the producer of wine independent of all these accidents.

There is a peculiar affection now and then incident to the
wines of the Alto Douro, called the *agredoce*, or sweet-sour ;
the Viscount De Villa Maior, in his work on wines, mentions
the vinagre disease ; the amargo, or bitterness ; the *gordura*
(which, according to my opinion, is only a continuation of
the *nube* disease) ; and then he gives the *agredoce*, which, he
states, is a form of disease different from the first four, which
spoils port wine. The *agredoce* is not always a particular
disease, it is a transformation of a part of the alcohol into
vinegar in such port wine only as contains from two to
three per cent. of sugar which was not previously fermented ;
thus a wine is obtained which tastes on the one side of

vinegar and on the other side of sugar, in fact, a compound which, if it was a little sweeter, one might very well drink as people do raspberry vinegar. It is not at all like the bitterness of Burgundy wines, which arises from a totally different cause. This is one form of *agredoce ;* another arises from the production in sweet wine of *lactic acid ;* this latter is less detrimental to the taste of the wine, as lactic acid tastes purely acid or sour without any special flavour.

Portugal in itself, poor, yet climatically highly endowed, is capable of producing a variety of the most beautiful grapes, and a variety of wines, which, if properly made, would not be surpassed by those of any other country. The people are good-natured, industrious, and hard-working, and they have what is very agreeable to a person who comes from this country, a great regard for an Englishman. If these good people would continue to plant their vineyards with particular sorts of grapes, such as have been proved in the great Alto Douro districts, in Bucellas, or Collares, to be so excellent ; if they were to abandon that horrid practice of making sweet and cooked wines; if they were to study the conditions by means of which they might avoid the natural climatic difficulties which produce fungi and acidity ; if they introduced more cleanliness into their sheds, and if they were to have their cellars underground ; if they were to avoid large tonels and adopt small casks, I have no doubt Portugal, one of the most essential English vineyards, would produce other wines besides port, which would be of the greatest use hygienically and socially to this country. We have a great trade with Portugal in other respects, taking there our manufactures, and bringing away in return large quantities of produce,— cattle, grapes, figs, apples, and a variety of other articles too numerous to mention ; and an improved quality of wine would find in this country a very ready and grateful market.

CHAPTER XXIV.

WINES OF THE ATLANTIC ISLANDS, MADEIRA,
THE CANARIES, AND THE AZORES.

§ 220. WINES OF MADEIRA.

WHEN the Portuguese had discovered Madeira in 1418,
they forthwith set about to destroy the forest with which the
island was covered. The settlers were occupied seven years
in the destruction of the trees on the south side of the island
round the bay, now called "of Funchal." In their place
they planted, *inter alia*, vines imported from Cyprus and
Candia.

Soil.—Madeira is a relatively new production amongst
islands; it consists of a basis of tertiary chalk, whereby it
is demonstrated to have been part of a larger island or
continent now submerged; even this base would also have
been submerged and destroyed had it not been overlaid,
and, so to say, preserved, by vast masses and countless layers
of eruptive products of a now dead volcano, the ruins of
which, some 6,000 feet in height, pass under the name of
the Pic Ruivo. The basalts, trachytes, tufas, and different
later lavas form mounts and hills with steep slopes, many
and deep ravines; these rocks disintegrate under the influence of rain and sun, and become a soft stone (*pedra
molla*), which is now easily transformed into a gritty soil, in
which all kinds of plants grow readily. The territory slips
easily, and requires much support for access and cultivation.

§ 221. VARIETIES OF VINES AND THEIR CULTIVATION.

The Malvasia, said to have been brought from Candia
and Cyprus, is supposed to yield the best Madeira wine, so

called, but it is cultivated less frequently than the Vidogna, a vine resembling the Chasselas, and yielding dry wine. In smaller proportion are grown the Bagoual, the Sercial or Escanagao, the Muscatel, and the Alicante. These bear white grapes; but the following produce black grapes, which, with the exception of the Tinta, are all used for making white wine: the Batardo, the Negramal (perhaps the same as Tinta), and the Ferral. The latter is a grape quite unfit for wine making. The vines are mostly fastened to espaliers of wood and reeds, from three to six feet in height; sometimes trained in arbours, with grapes hanging overhead; in other parts the vines are trained on pollards; all these elevated trainings produce mediocre grapes.

Vinification is effected as in Portugal, lagars, presses, transport, etc., all being the same. The must, carried in barrels or bags of goat-skins, is carried to the cellar of the wine maker and there fermented in barrels. Must is called *vinho in mosto*, meaning wine as yet in the state of must, while after the first fermentation and settlement of the yeast it is called *vinho in limpo*, wine in a clear state. The must receives some addition of brandy at once, as it is rather watery, and would not keep by itself; after racking the wine receives more spirit; a month later it is again racked and receives a third addition of spirit. During the process of preparation the wine is placed in magazines, which can be heated, and are called stoves (*estufas*), and left there for some weeks or months. This process assists the formation of ether and softens the wine by oxidation, but it has the probably much more important effect of destroying any fungi which are capable of making the wine scuddy, or of otherwise changing it unfavourably by viscosity, bitterness, or acetification. The maturation also succeeds well, if the wine be sound, by the aid of heat and motion, as imparted to it by a sea voyage as merchandise to the West Indies, Hindostan, Java, or China. Wine which has thus been made to travel was termed, technically, East India Madeira.

Madeira Wine is a more or less amber-coloured liquid of a peculiar, agreeable, though weak flavour; in it lives the genius of the Malvasia and Vidogna grapes. The Sercial also contributes its particular qualities, namely, astringency, and with this some lasting powers; but the roughness imparted thereby retards its maturation. Most Madeira is dry, *i.e.* free from sugar, and is therefore suitable for being preserved with less brandy than sweet wines. The best qualities improve in barrel during ten years, and in bottle during another ten; but these periods are now shortened by art and the estufa. The red wines of Madeira are not distinguished by quality, and their production is small.

The best vineyards of the south side are the property of the royal family of Portugal, and their products do not occur in commerce. The district yielding the best salable wine is the Pago de Pereira. Vineyards of the second class are Calheta, Porto da Sol, Ribeira Brava, Cama de Lobos, Estreto, Santo Martinho, and Santo Antonio. The wines on the northern side of the island are used mainly for distilling brandy from them. The most notable vineyards in this part are those of Porto da Cruz, Santo Jorge, Ponta del Gada, Portomoniz, Santo Vincente, and Seycal da Norte. Before 1852 Madeira produced annually about 20,000 pipes of wine, and in good years 30,000; but then the vine-fungus, the oidium, destroyed the entire harvests, and subsequently the vineyards. No wine was made up to 1857, a calamity which involved an annual loss of a quarter of a million sterling. Since 1860 the vine has gradually been replanted, and the oidium repressed. The territorial law of Madeira is one of great complication, which makes the purchase and sale of land, if not impossible, at least very difficult. This is is alleged as another of the causes which have made Madeira sink to the present low economical condition.

§ 222. WINES OF THE CANARIES AND THE AZORES.

These volcanic islands, comprising Teneriffe, Canaria, Lanzerote, Fuerteventura, Gomero, and Ferro, produce wine from the Malvasia and Vidogna grapes. The wines from the latter are dry, and similar but inferior to Madeira. The Malvasia is a sweet liqueur wine, and, like Madeira, tastes of pineapple, a perfume probably derived from that fruit. Canary sack of former times was the sweet white wine of these islands, "vino secco" or "seccato," so called because it was made from grapes which had been dried and passulated to a certain extent before vinification. Before 1852 most Canary wine was sold as Madeira; at the present day it is transmuted into "sherry" by being vatted with small quantities of wine of the Palomino grape.

The Azores formerly produced much wine, the island of Pico alone 5,000 pipes annually; the sweet Malvasia was called *vino passado*, the Vidogna *secco*. Most of these wines were sold to North and Central America and to Brazil. The islands suffered the fate of Madeira, and now produce less wine, but many other exportable products of agriculture.

CHAPTER XXV.

WINES OF ITALY AND OF THE BALKAN PENINSULA.

§ 223. GENERAL OBSERVATIONS ON ITALIAN WINES.

ITALY is very active just now in promoting its agriculture; there are many viticultural societies throughout the peninsula, and they organize exhibitions and lotteries to sell the produce which is brought to them; but all these efforts will avail but little before viticulture, as a whole, is placed upon a more rational basis, and grapes are grown near to the soil, instead of, as now, high in the air. Italian wines, including those of Sicily, are singularly destitute of flavour, and in those which have any it is too often artificial, and in the white varieties produced by aromatic resins or gums. This artificial flavour I have, however, never found in the sweet and brandied wines of Sicily. The Marsalas, though brandied up to 36° proof-spirit, and sweetened with raisins or condensed must, are ordinarily not plastered, and apparently not provided with extraneous flavours. Lately, some new kinds of Sicilian wines have been introduced into England which deserve commendation.

§ 224. Wines of Piedmont and the Island of Sardinia.

Of these wines those of Asti and Chaumont have acquired a reputation. Only second to these are the wines of Alba and Montferrat. We found some Piedmontese wine, which we obtained directly from Turin, inferior and dear. The effervescent wine (*spumante*) mostly had fungi in the bottles; the red were all in a state of fermentation, frisky (Italian *fresco*) and turbid; some retained a peculiar biting taste after complete clearance. A number of red wines are made from the Grignoli grape, and named Grignolinos; the better qualities of these have great merit. The Grignoli vine is closely related to the Carmenet of the Gironde on the one, and to the Kadarka of Hungary on the other.

At many places of the island of Sardinia Malvasia wines are produced; at Sorso, Posa, Alghiere, and Naxo; those produced at Caunonas, Monai, and Garnaccia are exported. The wine of Giro resembles the Tinto of Alicante.

§ 225. Wines of Tuscany.

The best Italian wines are produced in Tuscany, not only because the climate favours viticulture, but because the former government, and many intelligent members of the nobility, paid attention to the improvement of the vineyards and of vinification.

At Monte Pulciano, between Sienna and Rome, the Aleatico, or red Muscat vine, is extensively grown, and furnishes the liqueur wine known under that name; similar wine is made at Monte Catini, in the Val de Rievole, and at Ponte a Moriano. The wine is purple in colour, sweet, and slightly astringent. A good red wine is made at

Chianti, near Sienna, from a peculiar grape   At Arcetri, near Florence, was prepared the best Verdea, or green wine, so-called from its colour: it is reported that Frederick the Great favoured it by his patronage.   The Trebbiano is a golden-coloured syrup, produced from grapes passulated on the vine by torsion of the stalk.   The vine is termed Trebbino.

The nobles of Florence, like those of Vienna, sell their wines by retail from the cellars in their palaces, in *fiascos*, or flasks, of the well-known Florentine pattern, containing about three quarts each.   The wine is not corked, but covered with a small quantity of olive-oil, which is either flung out, or soaked out with tow previous to the pouring out of the wine.

§ 226. Wines of Lombardy, Venetia, Central and Southern Italy.

In these provinces the vines are grown on trees, mutilated for the purpose, on the margins of cultivated pieces of land, or in rows intersecting them.   The grapes consequently grow high in the air, and although they look picturesque make very bad wine.   The wine which one can get to drink in the plain of Venetia is always very poor; it is not dark red, owing to the imperfect ripening of the grapes, it has a very astringent taste, contains very little extractive, little alcohol, much acid, and is destitute of any vinous flavour.   It is an exceedingly cheap drink to quench the thirst in summer and winter.   The indolence which has laid hold of the population of the peninsula, the result of centuries of oppression, misrule and superstition, favoured by the ease with which life can be carried on, affects viticulture here as throughout Italy, and proves the truth of the sorrowful but hardly hyperbolic words of Matteucci: "*Este in Italia ni studio ni lavore.*"

In the former papal state are produced the wines of Orvieto, and the Muscat of Albano and Montefiascone.   At Naples a wine called Lachrymæ Christi is produced at the foot of Vesuvius.   Although reported to be the strongest wine produced in the district, a sample obtained from a grower contained only 18·9 per cent. of proof spirit.

The wines of Gallipoli and Taranto are produced in the province of Puglia or Terra d'Otranto. These wines receive mostly an addition of spirit, but we have had perfectly natural Taranto; it was sold at first at a reasonable price, but this was raised and the wine went out of the market.

§ 227. WINES OF SICILY.

The light amber of brown Sicilian wine exported in large quantities passes under the name of the exporting town of *Marsala*. This place is situated near the western termination of the northern coast of Sicily. The vineyards extend along the coast towards the east and west in a band of upwards of twenty miles in length and twelve broad. The soil is a mixture of chalk and clay, coloured yellow or reddish-brown by oxide of iron. The varieties of vines are not scientifically defined, so that Odart does not mention any. To conclude from the nature of the wine they must be many, and are cultivated mainly for the production of quantity.

All the wine shipped from Marsala is strongly brandied, but it is generally not plastered. Much of it is sold as such, but large volumes are mixed with a little sherry and sold as "Amontillado."

Red wines are also grown in the island, and being of low price, are exported to other parts of Italy and to America. Faro, grown in the neighbourhood of Messina, contains from 18 to 23 per cent. proof spirit. Near Mount Etna is made the wine of Terre Forte, in vineyards formerly held by Benedictine monks; this is mostly brandied up to 30 per cent. proof spirit, and, according to Redding, has a taint of pitch.

The total quantity of wine produced in Sicily has been stated to be 200,000 pipes, which is probably greatly exaggerated. Probably the one-fifth of this quantity believed to be fit for exportation represents the quantity of marketable wine actually produced much nearer than the larger figure. The Marsala pipe contains 93 gallons. There are less than

300,000 gallons of Marsala consumed annually in England ; its consumption has increased by one-fifth beyond the quantity, which was imported before the reduction of the duties nearly thirty years ago.

§ 228. WINES OF THE BALKAN PENINSULA.

The productions of these countries are not suited for the use of western Europeans, as they are impregnated with tar, as a means of their preservation.   On Mount Athos (Hagion Oros) German monks have introduced some better mode of vinification.   Wines which pass into commerce are produced in *Macedonia* in the following places :—Chatista, Florina, Kuprio, Castoria ; in the district surrounding the lake of Ochrida ; in the plain of Serres ; at Piliori, Crotova, and in the valley of Resne.   In *Thessaly* : at Larissa, Cachia and Arta.   Much simmered wine for the use of Mahommedans is made in the village of Galistas, on the slope of Mount Bernos.   Albania produces much red and white wine, which keeps without the assistance of pitch.

§ 229. WINES OF GREECE.

A mountainous country composed of schistose, chalky and volcanic ranges, with slopes in countless valleys, with a climate tempered by the neighbourhood of the sea, and engendering the most beautiful seasons, would seem to be an ideal territory for the culture of the vine.   But these advantages were counterpoised by the liability to the occurrence of terrible earthquakes ; by meteoric influences which denuded the mountain-sides of cultivable earth ; by exhaustion of the soil in consequence of the ceaseless export of its produce to foreign lands ; by the absence of labour, live stock, and manure ; and the want of security from brigandage, which kept the population in terror and uncertainty.   In consequence of these deplorable conditions, which have been only partially remedied during the last thirty years, the production of wine in Greece, which was considerable at the time of the supremacy of the Venetians, has sunk to a relatively insignificant amount. But the production of currants is still a highly important branch of Greek agriculture.

§ 230. VINES CULTIVATED IN GREECE.

The currant-vine *Vitis Corinthiaca*, also called *Apyrena*, the *stoneless*, and from its product, in Italian, *uva passa*, is mostly grown as a shrub, on a strong stem, without support. The bunches of its grapes are long, loose and pendulous, and carry small unequal berries; the berry stalks themselves are long and thin. The berries are the smallest of all grapes, have a thin husk and contain no stones. The several varieties of the plant are recognized by the colour of the grapes. The commonest is *yellowish-green* with a strong grey bloom. Odart, however, believes the *black* variety to be more commonly cultivated for commerce; a third variety is violet. This vine is also much cultivated in Italy and Asia Minor. The raisins termed currants are produced by twisting the stalks of the ripe bunches, and letting the grapes dry in the sun.

Another Greek vine is the *Greco*, so termed by the Italians, the red variety of which is also grown in Corsica, where it is called *Barbirono* (Odart, *l.c.*, p. 553). A third is the *Cipro*, the vine peculiar to Cyprus. Its berries are large, and while unripe are round at the insertion of the stalk, and pointed towards the umbilicus; but when ripe they have the shape of acorns, and are dark blue with few points. The bunch is large, long, and has mostly short branches. The *white* and *black Moscada* of Greece are identical with the Muscatels of Frontignan. The *Malvasia* exists in several varieties, not yet well diagnosed from each other. The *Sultana* is cultivated for its stoneless raisins, but not on so large a scale as in Asia Minor. The most important vine for the small islands seems to be the *Assyrticon*, which prevails in Santorin. Besides these there are cultivated in Greece about sixty varieties of vines, of which names and descriptions are not yet accessible.

z

§ 231. VINIFICATION.

Vinification in Greece is very imperfect, so that the wines contain more volatile, *i.e.*, acetic acid, than any others. Many wines last only through the winter, and in summer turn to vinegar. To avoid this result the proprietors still adopt all the objectionable preservatives of antiquity : smoking with wood smoke, or vapour of resins, such as mastic, olibanum, cloves, Rhodus wood, Bucharis-Tagh, and labdanum ; the Commendaria (Cyprus) wine is said to get its flavour from those resins, gums, and spices, which are suspended in the wine, enclosed in a bag ; pitching the barrels ; adding turpentine and pine-cones; addition of gypsum, chalk, salt, and of tannin, particularly in the form of *hypericum perforatum*, a resino-tannous plant, which is said to conserve and to colour wine yellow. Most wine has also the taste and smell of the goats, in the hides of which it is kept or transported. In Cyprus and other parts, jars, pitched inside, are still in use, but in Santorin and other islands, barrels are becoming more frequent. The several parts of Greece produce, according to the "Journal des Travaux de la Société française de Statistique universelle," the following kinds and qualities of wines :—Akarnania produces wine at Arta, Limni and Komboti. Ancient Greece proper, Livadia, has its principal vineyards near Lepanto, Chæronea, Megara, and on the slopes of Mount Poligouna ; second-class vineyards are near Koskina, and in one of the valleys of Mount Helikon. Not far from Athens is Mount Hymettus, known by its bees and honey ; the wine bearing its name is grown in the plain surrounding the mount. Near Megara, twenty-seven miles west of Athens, upon the frontiers of Livadia and Morea is the port of Cendura, from which much wine, and large quantities of currants are exported. Upon the isthmus is situated what remains of Korinth, the ancient town known by games and currants, often destroyed by earthquakes.

The northern part of the peninsula of *Morea*, *Achaia*, has extensive vineyards near Patras, Blattero, Voltizza, and Kalavrito. Near the latter town is the monastery of Megaspileon, where the monks make and keep wine in large quantities, some of their tonnels holding from 7,000 to 15,000 litres. In the county of Elis, circle of Gartonin, much red and white wine is made; the best wine of the Morea is made near Pergos, and amounts to 100,000 barrels annually. Red and white astringent wines are produced near Barbacena and Budschaka, on the left bank of the Alpheus. Schiron, near Palacropolis, produces currants and wine of 280,000 piastres annual value. Argolis, east of Achaia, has vineyards near Argos, and in the valley of St. Giorgio, twelve miles from Argos; Nauplia, or Napoli di Malvasia, the place whence Malvasia wines derived their name, was nearly destroyed during the Greek wars of independence, and produces but little wine in the present day. Arcadia, in the centre of the Morea, produces annually 15,000 barils of wine, value 150,000 piastres. The largest vineyards are in the valley of Phokia, 18 miles north of Tripolizza. The district of the latter town, known as Tripolis, produces 15,000 barils of wine. A similar quantity is produced in the vineyards near Androuna and Nisi, together with 600 barils of brandy. The promontory of Modon, west of Koron, produces 2,000 barils, value 20,000 piastres. The south-east of the Morea, Lakonia, makes much Malvasia, particularly at Misitra. The wines are mostly only third class, and much below.

§ 232. ISLANDS OF THE GREEK ARCHIPELAGO, SANTORIN, IONIAN ISLANDS, CANDIA, RHODES, CYPRUS.

The Islands of the Greek Archipelago producing wines or raisins are in this order from north to south : Scopolo, Sciati, Skyro, Negroponte, Andros, Tine, Zia, Myconi, Thermina, Naxos, Amorgo, and Santorini. Near Skyro (Syra), a red wine, Como, is grown, and Scio (formerly Chios) produced more wine formerly; the "nectar" of Merta is bitter and astringent. Samos exports grapes, raisins and wines, amongst the latter a Muscat. Zea, or Zia, is ancient Cos. Of Tenedos the only production and trade is in wine, and it sends annually 100,000 barils to Constantinople, Smyrna, and the Euxine for Russia; all table wine in the East, wherever wine is drunk, is called Tenedos.

Santorin, ancient *Thera*, a series of islands, consisting of fragments of a volcanic ring, and its centre craters, produces much wine. There are sixty varieties of vines cultivated, but the dominant vine is the Assyrticon. Some of the vines are large-bunched. The quantity produced is said to amount to 9,000 pipes; it is principally exported to the Black Sea, and supplies the wants of the interior of Russia. The wines of these islands were for a time much spoken of in this country, probably as the result of the accounts of enthusiastic travellers, but their eastern course has not thereby been diverted.

Ionian Islands.—The red wines of Corfu, of which 33,000 barils are annually produced, are light; a liqueur from raisins produced here is called *Rosolio*. Cephalonia produces upwards of 40,000 barils of red wines of the fifth class. Zante produces dry and sweet wines, amongst the latter a liqueur, made from currant grapes, called Jenerodis. Thiaki (Ithaca) produces 6,000 barils of currants, and Sta. Maura 50,000 annually. All wines made in the Ionian Islands are plastered.

Candia ancient *Crete*, produced formerly a kind of Malvasia wine, stated by A. Baccius (" Naturalis Vinorum Historia," Romæ, 1696, fol., p. 331) to have amounted to 200,000 barils annually. But this production is now much reduced, and of the viticulture, *e.g.*, of the monastery of Arcadi, now in ruins, there remains only the monument of the fine vaulted cellars, now disused. The best vineyards are near Kanea, Kisamos, Spacchia and Kandia.

Rhodes produces sweet luscious wine from large grapes. Here, as in Malaga, three harvests can be annually obtained.

Cyprus.—The vineyards of Cyprus are on the slopes of hills, covered with flinty stones and blackish ochreous earth. The prevailing vine is the Cipro, already alluded to above. The *wines* produced are of three classes. The first class consists of the wines of the Commandery of the Knights Templars, and is made in the vineyards near Paphos, in the district of Orni. It is fermented and matured in about

40,000 earthenware vessels, of the ancient shape of amphoræ, of which each holds from ten to twelve litres. The wine is of a dull red colour, and becomes tawny by age, or of a golden yellow, a little sweet, with an astringent by-taste, fiery, of great and peculiar flavour and bouquet, supposed to be imparted to it by the introduction of resins and spices suspended in bags in the amphoræ. The second-class wines are sweet Muscats, made mainly at Arnodos. The third class are common red wines, which speedily shed their colour. Two centuries ago this island exported 365,000 cuses (or guzes) of wine; sixty years ago the export had fallen to 65,000 cuses. Cyprus wines are shipped mainly from Larnaka, the southern port of Cyprus, to Venice and Livorno. At Venice much Cyprus wine is still drunk. The Cyprus wine measures are the *cass*, equal to $1\frac{1}{4}$ English gallons, or 4·73 litres; and the *carica*, equal to 10·414 litres. The baril repeatedly mentioned in the foregoing, is the Venetian *barilla*, equal to 64 *boccalis* (beakers), or 64·3859 litres, or 14·17112 English imperial gallons.

CHAPTER XXVI.

WINES OF ASIA.

§ 233. WINES OF CAUCASIA.

THE production of wine in *Cachetia* amounts to 2,000,000 of *eimer* annually; the price of good red is one *abass* (sevenpence) for one *tunga* (five bottles); common wine is sold at from five to six kopecs, or twopence per tunga. The natives keep the wine in skins of buffaloes and goats, with the hair turned inside, and pitched with black naphtha or asphalt; better class proprietors keep the wine in earthenware vases, of the size of hogsheads, which are buried in the ground. The vines are being improved by new varieties introduced from the Russian plantations in the Crimea.

Georgia produces wines at Tiflis, Signack, Elizabethopol, Gandjea, Mokozange, Vachery and Tscheniedaly.   At Tiflis the vines peculiar to Shiraz are grown, and viticulture is mainly in the hands of vintners from Suabia or their descendants.

Mingrelia, Imeritia, Armenia, and Shirwan also produce wine; the best Mingrelian is that of *Odischi.*   In many parts German colonists are settled, who produce wine in casks, and realize good prices.   The produce is estimated to amount to 7,500,000 bottles.

The Caucasian wines are mostly colourless, like water; the red ones are only pale red, and lose their colour while assuming a bitterness, thus resembling some Burgundies and their diseases.   Much of the Caucasian wine is distilled for *brandy*, of which Cachetia alone produces 20,000 hogsheads annually.   A society " for the manufacture of Champagne from indigenous grapes," carries on a considerable trade in such wine throughout Russia up to St. Petersburg.

The marine, wine and general trade of Caucasia, which formerly was considerable, has been completely destroyed by the Russian blockade, which was kept up for more than a generation, for the purpose of aiding in the subjection of the Circassian people.   This conquest has now been effected, but the trade of the east of the Euxine has not been restored.

§ 234. Wines of Persia.   Shiraz and its Vines.

The ancient traveller Strabo relates that in the district of the coast of the gulf of Persia called Makine, the vine grew in swamps, and was cultivated in these morasses by people who placed baskets of earth into the water, in which the vines were planted.   The vines in these baskets were as detached from the land as flower-pots in a conservatory, and were now and then carried out of reach from the shore by floods or winds.   In such a case the cultivators replaced them again to their former positions by long poles.   Such paludal cultivation of the vine can also be seen in Egypt.

In Persian legends frequent references are made to King Dchemshid as having raised the accidental discovery of wine to a method of making and keeping it. As he was fond of eating grapes he caused great vessels full to be collected in order to enjoy them beyond the season. But they ran into juice, and boiled so suspiciously that it was believed a new poison had been discovered, and the liquid was put aside for appropriate use. Gulnare, the beautiful, one of Dchemshid's seven hundred wives, grew melancholy and resolved to take her own life. She selected the new poison as the means for self-destruction, and drank a long draught, which became a deep one when she found that the supposed poison, contrary to expectation, tasted very nice. The poison soon acted, however, and Gulnare sank on her couch and fell asleep. Awaking to despair, she doubled the draught, sought destruction in vain, but found happiness in frequent small sips of the suspected liquid. Shah Dchemshid discovered the effect of the condemned grape juice upon his mistress, tried a draught, approved, and henceforth was the patron of wine.

The wines of Persia most renowned in ancient times were those of Ariana (Iran), Bactriana (Turan), Hyrcania, (Mazanderan), and Margiana (Chorassan). Their reputation survived for some time the introduction of the Islam. All the fertile parts south of the Caspian still produce wines, but their reputation is now overshadowed by that of the wines of Shiraz, in Ferdistan.

The vineyards of this celebrated place are situated on the lower ranges of the Zagros mountain, which runs from the gulf of Persia to the Caspi Lake; the best of these are situated at the foot of the mountain to the north-west of the town. The vines are mostly trained low on the ground, and are rarely tied to stakes; some are trained over stone walls, up on the one side and down on the other, the latter being drawn down by stones tied to the ends of the canes. At Casvin the vine-growers irrigate the vineyards annually, twenty days after the feast of Nokooz, or about April 10th, and the clayey soil thus treated retains sufficient moisture to last throughout the period of vegetation, which is rainless. There are twelve principal varieties of vines.

The *Kishmish*, Sultanieh of the Turks, carries a beautiful

large bunch of white grapes ; the berries are oval, of medium size, have a tender, thin husk, no kernels, and are of an agreeable acidulous taste ; they serve for the table, and the production of raisins and of wine.

The *Damas* yields a black grape, from which the finest full-bodied and durable red wine is made. The *Samarkand* occurs in several varieties, some of which bear bunches up to twelve pounds in weight. The *Richbaba* (Rish baba), the principal or dominant vine, has large berries, without seeds ; according to Pallas, the name was derived from the cylindrical form of the bunch, and the compressed state of the berries. The *Askery* has small berries. The *Imperial of Tauris* is juicy and delicate. Besides these a great number of variously and strikingly coloured grapes are grown, of which the names are given by Odart (*l.c.* p. 584, *et seq.*), after a communication made by a Persian ambassador to a Duc Decaze. They have been described by many travellers, *e.g.*, Pallas, Chardin, Olivier, Ker Porter. Odart does not mention either the Damas or the Imperial of Tauris, and we apprehend that these names were introduced in the Russian vineyards in the Crimea, and are not Persian. The wine of Shiraz is fermented in large egg-shaped vases of earthenware, four feet high, and holding 250 to 300 litres, or more than a hogshead. The vases are glazed inside and out, covered with purified mutton tallow, and are kept buried in the earth in cool cellars. The made wine is bottled in glass flasks holding from four to five (old Paris) pints ; the bottles are stoppered with hard-pressed cotton, covered with wax, enclosed in matting, and packed in boxes holding ten. It is a little harsh on first gustation, but gains upon the palate by habitual use ; this refers to wine as drunk in Persia. The red Shiraz now and then brought to this country has always been fortified with spirit, and perfumed with peculiar resinous matters, which at first suit the European palate as little as does the rose-flavoured confectionery of Turkey. There are also white liqueur wines, with peculiar perfumes, made at Shiraz. The wines of Shiraz are sold in Persia by weight. A popular proverb considers them as essential to happiness : "Who will live merrily should take his wine from Shiraz, his bread from Yesdecast, and a rosy wife from Yest." Next to Shiraz as wine-producing places are Teheran, the capital of the Shah, Yezd, (Yest), Shamaki, Gilan, Casvin, Tabriz and Ispahan. All these places are situated on the slopes of mountains.

The wines of Persia are mostly consumed in the country, and only a portion is exported to Hindostan, China and Japan. Through the influences of Mahometanism, the consumption and production of wine in Persia has much decreased; nevertheless wine and spirit drinking are done in secret, and with the usual result of the Sunday drinking of intolerant populations. The Persian of to-day buys his wine from the Gueber, Jewish or Armenian grower, who is licensed upon payment of a tax. The wine is frequently mixed with raki and saffron, or the extract of hemp, which is added to make small quantities more intoxicating. In the East the idea prevails yet, that the use of wine legitimately terminates in intoxication, a fallacy which was yet prevalent with us a few generations ago. We may therefore hope to see it superseded by that amelioration of customs, which has changed the ethics of Western banquets.

CHAPTER XXVII.

WINES OF AFRICA.

§ 235. WINES OF THE CAPE OF GOOD HOPE. VINES; MODE OF CULTIVATION.

AT the southern cape of Africa, originally called by its discoverer "The Stormy Cape," but renamed by his King "of Good Hope," vines were first planted by Dutch settlers under the governorship of Jan van Riebeck in 1650. Their knowledge of viticulture being deficient, they omitted to select the most suitable situation, and this error has operated against the wines of the Cape for almost two centuries. Governor Riebeck is related to have imported vines from the Rhine, France, Spain, Greece, Madeira and Shiraz. In the best situations the muscat of Frontignac prevails, and is kept pure, its grapes serving for liqueur wines only. Most expanded are perhaps the German Riessling giving white, and the Burgundy grape giving red wine. Two not otherwise defined vines pass under Dutch names, the *Groene-druyf*, (green grape) and the *Steen-druyf* (stone-grape): probably the former is the Sylvaner, and the latter synonymous with Riessling; for Odart, (l.c. p. 593), says, that they both came from the Rhine. The *Haenapop* (has no pip) is easily recognised as the Persian Sultanieh, which yields the stoneless raisins. Odart gives a mistaken derivation of this name, from *hanap*, meaning a large pot or crock.

The modes of cultivation are those usual in the countries from which the vines are derived. During the dry season the vines must be irrigated, or they drop their fruit. The vineyards of Constantia are regularly irrigated. The vineyard proprietors have to combat many enemies, Kaffirs being the worst thieves; the grapes are devoured by wild dogs, Cape badgers, monkeys, and sometimes enormous flights of birds, which do not only devour, but damage and defile what they do not eat. The ordinary agricultural boer takes little care in vinification; but he is also in a difficult situation: he must import foreign casks, because Cape wood of any kind is unsuitable for wine-barrels; to carelessness he adds absurd practices, such as hanging up freshly killed meat in the fermented wine, or adding spirit in the shape of indigenous brandy called *Cape-smoke*, from its being contaminated with the flavour of the smoke from the fire by which it is distilled, like Scotch Whiskey. Only when the wine has passed into the hands of the exporter begins its transformation into Cape-brands.

§ 236. QUALITIES OF CAPE WINES AND IMPORTATION INTO ENGLAND.

The sweet pale-red Constantias are liqueur wines of the second class; they soon lose the muscat flavour, but gain ripeness instead. A simmered wine called *Kokwyn*, made from muscat grapes, resembles Malaga, and belongs to the third class. The red wines called dry Pontac and Burgundy, made from the relative grapes, sometimes become wines of the third class, but mostly remain below the fifth class. The Cape Hock of the village of Paarl in the valley of Drakenstein is a very characteristic wine, which belongs to the fourth, sometimes the third rank of white wines. The unnamed wines of South Africa are also red and white, the latter being dry. When properly prepared they have none of the so-called earthy or slaty taste so often complained of; it is probable that these and other faults are the result of their being made in too many instances by the unaided efforts of ignorant Kaffirs or other negroes.

In 1859 the importation of Cape wine into England had, owing to the favour shown to the Colonies by the mother country in the imposing a much lower import duty upon it than upon European wines, risen to 781,581 gallons. After the reduction of the wine-duties in 1860, the importation fell in 1862 to 182,282 gallons, or from 10·84 per cent. of the whole imports of wine in 1859 to 1·8 per cent. of the imports in 1862. This wine was not consumed as such, but worked up into the similitude of sherry and port and sold to whoever would buy it. There is no reason, however, why the Cape should not produce and bring to Europe good wines.

§ 237. PRINCIPAL VITICULTURAL DISTRICTS AND ESTATES IN THE CAPE COLONY.

Stellenbosh, a considerable wine district north of False Bay, received its name from a former governor, Van der Stell, who acquired large portions of territory in that locality, then covered by bush, and constructed a reservoir in the mountains to irrigate his farms and vineyards during the dry season, and to grind his corn in a mill by the side of the wine stores.

Drakenstein, a settlement north-east of Stellenbosh, was founded by a colony of French refugees after the revocation

of the Edict of Nantes in 1685. Land more suited for the
growing of corn was planted by them with vines. The
Dutch farmer imitated the example, but the produce acquired no reputation. On the western side of the valley of
Drakenstein stands the village of *Paarl*, surrounded by a
fertile tract of land, and especially distinguished by a curious
mass of granite surmounted by a number of large pebbly
stones like the pearls of a necklace, to which it owes its
name. Here the best white wines of the Cape Colony, so-
called *Cape Hocks*, are produced.

§ 238. THE CONSTANTIAS.

The Dutch governor Van der Stell, made three plantations of vines at the Cape, and named them after his wife
Constantia, with distinguishing adjectives High Constantia,
Great Constantia, and Little Constantia. The vineyards
are situated at the eastern base of Table Mountain, about
eight miles from Cape town, and midway between False
and Table Bays, all upon very gentle slopes, just sufficiently
inclined to admit of the distribution of water by irrigation
channels. The dominant vine is the red muscat of Frontignan, which gives to all Constantia wines their peculiar
character. There are also a few other varieties of vines
grown here, but with the exception of the Rhenish Riessling
they yield no characteristic products. The vineyards have
a surface of about 250 acres, or 101 hectares, and produce
annually from 700 to 800 hectolitres of wine. The product
is treated as at Frontignan, and owing to its good quality
and limited quantity, its price is well maintained. Another
notable estate near Constantia, is Witteboom, which also
produces red muscats. Seal Island in Table Bay also produces some good wines.

§ 239. WINES OF MADAGASCAR.

This island possesses an indigenous vine, which the
natives declare to bear a poisonous fruit; probably the
effect of this grape is similar to that of an American vine,

the husk of the berries of which inflames the lips; ripe Riessling also causes the lips to burn. Some Frenchmen made wine of that grape, and found it quite innocuous, so that the irritating matter, like that of the manioc, disappears in the preparation of the product. The inhabitants of Isle de France and Bourbon cultivated the vine only as an ornamental shrub in the garden, and did not multiply it in vineyards, as they found vinification to be impracticable.

§ 240. WINES OF MOROCCO.

In the north-west of Africa the vine is cultivated down to 33° lat. The grapes grow larger and sweeter, and are mainly reared on espaliers in the air, to produce shaded walks; what business viticulture there is resembles that of Andalusia, including the hedges of agave and of prickly pear cactus. There are seven varieties of vines, one with very large berries, called "hen's eggs," supposed to be identical with the Spanish *teta de vaca*. Wine is made by Jews only, is light and acidulous, kept in large earthenware jars and in skins, and does not keep beyond one year. The best and largest amount of wine is made at Uadnum, Tarodante, and Tangiers.

§ 241. WINES OF ALGERIA.

In 1860 there were only about 220 hectares of vineyards in Algiers, but in 1870 their area in Oran alone had risen to 3,200 hectares. The wines resemble the small wines of Languedoc. Viticulture has been somewhat extended since, particularly after the collection of vines made by Chaptal was transferred from the garden of the Luxembourg at Paris to Algiers.

§ 242. WINES OF THE NILE VALLEY.

In ancient times the valley of the Nile produced the wines of Arsinoë, Mendes, Koptos, and Mareotis; its Delta the liqueur wine of Sebenytus, of which latter large quantities were exported to Rome; since the spread of Islam only grapes and raisins are produced.

CHAPTER XXVIII.

WINES OF AMERICA.

§ 243. GENERAL OBSERVATIONS.

WITH regard to viticulture in America we have to record this remarkable fact, that vines from Europe do not succeed in that country, and that long continued and often repeated experience shows, that to produce grapes and wine in America of any quality, recourse must be had to indigenous vines. In California, European vines seem to grow, and bear fruit, but it lacks the essential quality of specificity; the wines made on the west coast have no flavour.

Viticulture has of late years not progressed much in America even on the Ohio, which was termed the Rhine of North America, and where there were some 1,550 acres of vineyards under cultivation. At St. Louis some very good effervescent wine was made and even brought to London. But the supply was soon exhausted, and none of it has been seen since the American Exhibition.

§ 244. INDIGENOUS VINES OF NORTH AMERICA.

In 1830 Prince counted more than eighty-eight varieties of American wild vines, but of these only a few were cultivated either for making wine or for eating as fruit. The vines were also described in a monograph by Durand, translated into French by M. des Moulins. In consequence of the ravages of the oidium and the phylloxera French viticulturists turned their attention to American vines, which were said not to be liable to the attacks of these vegetable animal parasites. But no good wine could be obtained from any of them, and the only way of utilizing the immunity of their roots from the phylloxera was to graft European vines upon American stems. This was, however, so costly and slow a process, that it could be only rarely adopted.

The American vines are either polygamic or dioic. In Thudichum and Dupré's "Treatise" a full description of ten varieties will be found : of which the following are the more important ones. (1.) *Vitis Labrusca* L. termed in America *fox-grape* or *northern fox-grape*. The berries are large, purple-black in colour, and have nearly the same taste and flavour or odour as black currants ; they ripen at the end of August or beginning of September. In the wilderness it is a very handsome climber, and rises to the tops of the highest trees. Under cultivation its berries become round and large, even of the size of damsons ; but the pulp always remains tenacious and does not easily melt in the mouth ; on pressure it slips as an entire lump out of the hard thin skin and has to be crushed expressly. It is assumed that from this V. labrusca a variety of hybrid vines have been produced, namely the Isabella, Catawba, Schuylkill, Alexander, Bland's grape and others. The Labrusca is not subject to the oidium, even when its branches intertwine with those of ordinary vines covered with the fungus. (2.) *Vitis æstivalis*, (Michaux) Summer grape, Chicken grape, Little grape. There are two varieties of which one goes by the adjective of the *genuine*, the other by that of the *sinuated*. The former has berries of a saturated sky-blue colour, smaller than that of the Labrusca. Although it is called summer-grape for reasons unknown, it ripens only in October. It is found in the Atlantic region, on the Mississippi and beyond. The sinuated variety has small sky-blue berries of an agreeable but austere taste. It is found in the South Atlantic region up to Louisiana, where it is called Pine-wood grape. It does not climb so well as the Labrusca. From it the Delaware grape is derived.

The Vitis Caribæa was named by Decandolle. It has large, purple-black, little juicy, sour berries, and is very common in the Antilles ; it also thrives in Florida, South Arkansas, and Mexico. (4.) *The Vitis Candicans* (Engelmann) is the Mustang grape of New Mexico, Texas and Arkansas. The grapes are purple-black, the husks contain a very red and extremely acid juice, the pulp however has a softer, not burning taste, and is eatable. The vine, as a

parasitic climber, is a great plague of the countries in which
it lives, as it destroys the greatest trees in forests and plantations. It is a great bearer; a plant of eight years yielded fifty-
four gallons of juice; the must is, however, so acid, that each
gallon requires the addition of three pounds of sugar, and
the made wine requires the addition of some spirit to make
it keep. The wine thus obtained is good, strong-bodied,
agreeable to drink, and nicely coloured. Of this vine,
several varieties are known, some of which have a red pulp,
others a white pulp, all having purple-black husks. The
wild plants are dioic, the males bear no fruit; they acquire
an enormous size, stems two feet in circumference, and extend
their branches over five or six trees, seventy to eighty feet
high. In Texas it reaches such a great size that stems of
eighteen to twenty inches in diameter have been cut down.
When the grapes are ripe, they seem to cover all the foliage
as a black mass; their taste is detestable, owing to an acrid
principle contained in the husks, which inflames the lips and
the mucous membrane of the mouth. When this husk is
peeled off, the pulp, which remains as a solid lump, may
be eaten without evil effects (5.) The *Vitis Californica*
has small black berries of agreeable taste; it is common in
California, Sonora, and the eastern part of New Mexico.
The five varieties of vines described in the foregoing have
leaves which on their underside are woolly, or felted, as if
with a spider's web. The following varieties have leaves
which are either quite smooth on both sides, or slightly
downy on the underside. (6.) *Vitis Cordifolia*, so called
from the heart shape of its leaves (Michaux), inhabits the
whole of the Atlantic region; it occurs in two varieties, the
genuine, and the one which lives on the banks of rivers.
The former is also termed fox-grape, winter and frost-grape;
it forms long bunches not very full of berries, which latter
are small, black and late, have thin husks, and are of an
acid taste like that of black currants. The vines overgrow
entire trees, and while they were plentiful, flights of wild
turkeys frequently settled upon them to eat their fruit. The
second variety, the *riparia*, by French immigrants into
Texas termed *Vigne des Battures*, is a sweet-scented grape,

more acid to the taste, with blood-red juice; it becomes softer in taste after having been frozen, as do sloes; each grape contains only one seed. It blossoms in May, and its flowers have the odour of mignonette; the male plant used to be termed *Vitis odoratissima* while it was believed to be an independent species. (7.) *Vitis rotundifolia* (Michaux) termed by Americans Bullace, Bullet grape, Scuppernong, southern fox-grape. Its small leaves have a shape somewhat between a kidney and a heart; its bunches are small, the berries have a great odour, a purple, sometimes amber colour, a hard skin, and an agreeable taste. It is cultivated for the table, and for wine-making in Virginia, Florida, Texas and North Mexico, passing everywhere under the name of Scuppernong. To the north of the Potomac it remains sterile, and is frequently destroyed by the frost.

A third section of American vines are characterized by erect or decumbent shoots, without the climbing faculty. (8.) *Vitis rupestris* (Scheele) commonly termed *mountain grape*, has heart-kidney shaped leaves, small purple-black berries, which ripen early and have an agreeable taste. Grows in chalky soil on the banks of rivers in Texas and Arkansas. (9.) The *Vitis monticola* (Buckley) has also short branches, compound strong bunches, with large, closely set, white or amber-coloured berries. It is said to have the most agreeable taste of all American grapes; it grows in Texas. (10.) The *Vitis Lincecumii* (Buckley) passes in Texas under the name of post-oak grape, or pinewood-grape: its berries are purple-black, sometimes amber coloured; they have an agreeable odour and ripen in August. It grows in Western Louisiana, Arkansas and Texas, and its name was given by Buckley in honour of the Texas doctor Lincecum.

§ 245. Vines Cultivated in North-America.

Viticulture in America is probably not yet typical, though adapted to local conditions; it has certainly hitherto not been very extensive. The vines cultivated are hybrids of native with foreign vines, and several are of excellent quality. We quote the *Catawba*, found wild along the Arkansas, cultivated since 1802, first by a major Adlum; nineteen-twentieths of all the vines of Ohio are Catawbas. The wine made from it is good, it can be produced effervescent. Such as we have obtained in England, directly from St. Louis, was strongly flavoured with, apparently, elder flower. Longfellow wrote an enthusiastic poem in praise of Catawba wine. (2). The *Cape grape*, also termed Alexander or Schuylkill Muscadel, is indigenous to the environs of Philadelphia, Pennsylvania; its must always requires an addition of sugar. (3). *The Isabella* is indigenous to South Carolina. In Ohio it is frequently injured by frost, while on the shores of lake Erie and in the neighbourhood of New York it bears amply and ripens well; it is cultivated for the table only, as it requires sugar to acquire a sufficient alcoholicity in its wine. The wine resembles light Madeira. (4). *Bland's Madeira* gives a good grape for eating, but the vine is too delicate for cultivation even in Ohio. (5). The *Ohio* or *Cigar-box* vine yields a handsome, black, soft, melting grape, with small berries; its wine is dark red, and has little perfume when young, but acquires some by age. (6). *Lenoir* yields a sweet and well-flavoured, melting, black grape. (7). *Missouri* the same, but is more suitable for wine-production than the former. (8). *Norton's seedling* has a small soft berry, but its wine is of inferior quality. (9). *Herbemont's Madeira* has small black berries, to which, as to No. 9, the name is by no means appropriate; the wine, though of a rosy colour, resembles Manzanilla in taste. (10). *Minor's seedling* is a muscat, useless for wine. (11). *White Catawba* is much inferior to the red; it has not been tried for wine. (12). The *Mammoth Catawba* is a large variety of No. 1. (13). The *Scuppernong* does not succeed north of the 35° lat.

§ 246. RISE OF VITICULTURE IN AMERICA.

The name of Longworth is associated with the history of the development of viticulture in America; he it was who made extensive experiments with European vines, and found them unsuitable, even the indigenous vines were found to degenerate quickly, and not to obtain any very high age. The vineyards were mostly cultivated by Germans from the Rhine-country; many were farmed by the viticulturists at the rent of half the vintage. At Cincinnati an acre of good land could be made to yield a profit of from 50 to 100 dollars.

It will thus be seen that viticulture in America has to contend with many difficulties. We studied the subject in detail some years ago, but have not to report any great progress since. The Chicago exhibition will have afforded a good opportunity for summarizing the present condition of viticultural affairs.

CHAPTER XXIX.

WINES OF AUSTRALASIA.

§ 247. GENERAL OBSERVATIONS.

THE founder of viticulture in Australia was an early colonist of New South Wales, of the name of Busby; he obtained 574 varieties of European vines, from France, and secured the grant of an experimental garden from the government at Sydney. Other enterprising men then took up the subject, *e.g.*, James Macarthur, and Patrick Auld. They were followed by many gentlemen of property, who were desirous rather of producing fine and creditable wines, than of obtaining large or immediate profits. Many cultivated the art as an interesting scientific experiment. Thus viticulture expanded in Australia and gradually assumed large dimensions.

The generally favourable climate of Australia is not invariably favourable to the vine, on account of the severe droughts and heavy rains to which it is alternately exposed, and which destroy other crops as well as vines. In December the growers desire some rain, which they term vintage rain; but when rain falls upon the nearly perfected grapes in February, that makes them swell and burst, lose their juice, causes them to rot, and destroys much of the harvest in a short time.

The condition of viticulture in Australia is most fully and correctly represented in the annual reports of the several Vineyard Associations. We would ask our readers to consult these rather than those reports which have no authentication at all. Products from a new country must be judged not only absolutely by reference to established standards, but also relatively with reference to their capability for improvement, if faulty or imperfect. We have said long ago, that by applying this principle to Australian wines, we had come to the result, that many good qualities had already been obtained ; that, if the process of vinification were better, these qualities would be greatly enhanced ; that many wines, evidently made from excellent grapes, are spoiled by faulty preparation, or by want of proper nursing during maturation. To prove these points, we gave vouchers from Australian literature, mercantile, journalistic, and private, from official reports on Australian exhibitions, etc. Time has fully borne out these notes, and their continued correctness can be proved any day by the comparison of mercantile articles with well-established models.

CHAPTER XXX.

GENERAL OBSERVATIONS ON WINES.

§ 248. RATING OF THE WINES OF THE WORLD.

THE most important practical distinctions of wines are marked by their relative prices. According to these, wines become beverages or luxuries for use on festive occasions. It has been proposed to call *table* wines all those which can be sold in this country at prices varying from twelve to thirty shillings per dozen bottles. Wines at prices varying between thirty and sixty shillings per dozen we will, in accordance with commercial custom, term *fine wines*, and those at prices above sixty shillings *cabinet wines*. The fine and cabinet wines are so limited in quantity, and so much sought after, that they can never have a wide area of usefulness. But amongst the table wines there are excellent qualities fulfilling all the hygienic and gustatory conditions demanded for comfortable and wholesome living. The great bulk of all the wines of Jerez, Oporto, Lisbon, Barcelona, Valencia, Alicante, Cette, Bordeaux, of the Rhine, of Austria and Hungary, etc., are, commercially speaking, cheap wines. We may read of high prices in the lists of sherry exporters, such as £1,000 per butt; but these partake of the nature of romance, as the objects, if there were any of such an ascertained value, never change hands. The great mass of sherry is exported at £15 per butt, and the average value of all sherry exported is £28 per butt. The same applies to Oporto. The mass of port wine is exported at a price somewhere between £22 and £25 per pipe, and the finer wines at £50 to £80 are few and far between. And so it is with all the places mentioned. The great bulk of their exports consists of cheap wines. There are exporters who pretend not to sell cheap wines, but they sell them in fact in large volumes, while omitting to place their names amongst the brands on the barrels in which they sell them. It was upon the importation into England of low-priced natural wines that the attention of the legislature was directed when the duty was reduced in 1860; to this object the attention of enterprising wine-merchants was directed, who have thereby opened a new era in the English wine trade, and broken the aristocratic pretensions with which the dealing in wines was formerly surrounded. Wines of all qualities can now be had from one shilling per bottle upwards, and the agitation carried on for so many years in the interest of temperance and free trade has resulted in great public benefit, the full extent of which has however to be obtained by further exertions.

A classification of wines is always a process of the utmost

difficulty because opinions are liable to be governed unduly
by the element of taste, and not by all the elements from
which a valuation has to be elaborated.   It might be said
that prices were a sufficient classification of wines, but this
is not really so, as prices are inflated by many fallacious
elements, including past reputations.   What can be more
disproportionate than the prices and the qualities of the so-
called dry champagnes, the prices enhanced by an abnormal
impost, which disarranged the settlement of 1860.   With
the import duty increased the nastiness of many of the
products of the Marne as well as the lower priced ones of
the Loire.   Another objection to any kind of classification,
on however broad a basis of recognized distinction, is the
fact that it is liable to cause much displeasure to the owners
or vendors of qualities not rated at cabinet value.   We have
observed this vivacity of sentiment particularly on the part
of foreign and colonial exhibitors, whose products we had
to report upon.   Further, a classification of wine would
have to specialize so many places and years in districts
which are liable to great variations in their products, that
the result would be unintelligible.   There are years in which
the products of vineyards ordinarily passing as first growths
are of the sixth and seventh class, and out of such accidents
no average can be constructed.

We would place sherry at the head of all wines, had we
not to admit that it is deteriorated by plaster, brandy,
colour and *dulce*.   Jerez wines and their congeners have
the greatest future, on account of their equability and in-
trinsic vinous quality.   They only wait for another reform
like that to which a Scotchman treated them when he substituted pale and dry for the brown and sweet concoctions ;
when he discovered and purified the amontillado flavour.
Let us hope that another reformer may succeed in turning
aside the plaster and brandy which now denaturalizes this
splendid product of viticulure.   We would claim only a
second place for wines of the Alto Douro or port wines so-
called, were they not much deteriorated by the quantities
of brandy with which they are mixed.   No doubt port has
properties which make it a peculiar product ; it is full

of extractive, apart from the fruit sugar, and therefore
requires treatment differing in some respects from that
which will mature the thinner wines with less extractive.
Nevertheless it is much denaturalized by the large quantities
of brandy which it receives, and which disqualify it for use
for so long a time as to cause its cost to exceed its value.
The wines of the Gironde are superior to the former two
classes, by the absence of brandy and other admixtures;
but they are inferior in body, that is to say, in extractives
apart from alcohol and vinosity, and are not rarely very
acid.   With these rank Champagnes of the better years,
white Burgundies and wines of the Rheingau; now follow
the red wines of Burgundy, Mâcon and Beaujolais; then
the white wines of the Palatinate. Now follow Greek,
Austrian, and Hungarian wines, Tokay excepted, of which
the sweet, thick varieties take a place by themselves, as not
being wines in the sense here defined; but the *szamorodnies*
are comparable, and take a place after those previously
mentioned.   Any rating of wines has to be based upon the
absolute qualities, total quantities of product, prices, average
success in years, absence of variability and of faults, in
short, upon the average result of a consideration of all the
factors which make a wine of the greatest use to the
greatest number at the least cost.

It is a general experience that the stronger wines are
preferred in winter, while the natural wines are sought after
in summer, when the others are avoided. This is caused
by the excessive stimulating qualities of the alcohol, popularly termed heating, which are not very useful at any time,
but bearable in cold weather. Similarly it is found that
delicate persons cannot bear brandied wines, but are able
to digest and to be benefitted by natural wines.   All
these conditions have been so ably put forth by many
members of the medical profession, that we need not dwell
upon them at length, but can leave to the public the care
for still more softening the rough drinking habits which
past generations left over to us.

All wine imported into the United Kingdom, pays a
customs' duty, which for natural unfortified wine, and for

wine fortified up to 30 per cent. of proof spirit, has been fixed by Parliament as 1s. per gallon. The law has most liberally defined as natural wine all wine which contains less than 26 per cent. of proof spirit, equal to 12 per cent. of absolute alcohol by weight, and 14·6 per cent. of absolute alcohol by volume. All wine which contains more than that proportion of spirit, or alcohol, is assumed to have received an addition of distilled spirit, or of wine containing distilled spirit, and was charged with a customs' duty of 2s. 6d. if it did not surmount in its alcoholic strength 42 per cent. of proof spirit. But this arrangement was altered some years ago to this extent, that the 26 per cent. limit was raised to 30 per cent., so that 4 per cent. of proof spirit in wine may come into the country duty free. But the advantage concerns only a small proportion of the wine imported. For no one would think of raising Bordeaux, Burgundy, Champagne, Hock, and other natural wines to anything like 30 per cent. proof spirit, and on the other hand, this strength is insufficient for any sherry, port, Madeira, or other southern wine of their kind. And this was the main reason for which the anomaly was acceded to. The relaxation is abused mainly in this way, that Spanish white wines are imported at a strength just below 30 per cent. of proof spirit, and afterwards mixed with wines imported at the highest alcohol strength, compatible with the 2s. 6d. duty, so that a wine of 36 per cent. proof spirit, supposing equal parts of the weak and strong to be mixed, will have paid only 1s. 9d. import tax instead of 2s. 6d., equal to a gain of more than £4 sterling per butt. All alcohol above 42 per cent. of proof spirit is charged the same duty per degree as distilled spirit, i.e. 10s. 6d. per gallon of proof spirit. Another anomaly was inflicted upon the system of wine taxation adopted in 1860, namely, the increase to 5s. a dozen of the import tax on sparkling wines; this raised the price of sparkling wines very much beyond the addition of the 5s. per dozen bottles; and acted as an almost forbidding increase of the price of the cheap effervescent wines from the Loire, which are imported at prices, in the River Thames, beginning at 17s. per dozen, and rising to 28s. Upon protest being raised on behalf of these wines, the impost upon them was limited to 3s. per dozen. Of course, the actual price also rose, and the quality deteriorated, and the policy of Mr. Goschen has produced only disadvantage to the community, and a very trifling increase to the takings of the customs.

§ 249. ACTIVE INGREDIENTS OF WINE.

The great uniform power in wine, as in all so-called intoxicating liquids, is of course *alcohol ;* and the main effect upon the body is produced by alcohol, and in direct proportion to its quantity. Equal amounts of alcohol, whether taken in strong or dilute admixture, will cause nearly equal effects, but dilute beverages will produce the effect quicker than strong; for these latter require more time for their absorption. Alcohol is, however, by no means the only active ingredient of wine ; were it so, mere alcohol would by this time have superseded wine altogether. Pure alcohol, indeed, in a state of drinkable dilution, is not a desirable beverage at all. It acquires its highest attractiveness by the presence of that union of flavours produced by the fermentation of grape juice, called *vinosity*, and represented mainly by the *œnanthic ether*, the wine-flower or bouquet ether, described in an earlier chapter. A number of other *ethers* no doubt contribute to the sum of the effects, but the œnanthic ether is the specific one, without which wine has no existence. This ether, and its helpmates, have a very remarkable effect upon the organs of taste and smell, which results in pleasure, and a desire to drink the liquid exhaling the odour; and again when drunk, the ethers produce an effect of a pleasureable kind besides, and independent of the effect of the mere alcohol. It is for these ethers, and their combination as bouquet, that the high prices are paid for fine wine. Brandied wines never can rise to the quality, in respect of bouquet, of the natural wines, for although they contain the œnanthic and other ethers, their olfactory effect is overcome by that of the newly added brandy. It is for this reason that few persons accustomed to sherry and port ever scrutinize their wines with the nose for the pleasure of the bouquet, as all connoisseurs unfailingly do with Burgundy and Hock, or Claret ; but rely upon broad gustation for the satisfaction of the taste and upon alcoholicity for effect.

Amongst the evil effects of wines, and spirituous drinks made with distilled spirit, several have been ascribed to the undue admixture with the beverages of alcohols of a more complicated composition than common or ethylic alcohol. Thus *amylic alcohol*, or the oil obtained by the distillation of dregs, called *fusel oil* by the Germans, is believed to cause great excitement and to aggravate to madness the evil effects of the habitual use of distilled spirit. Apart from the fact that fusel oil can be removed from any spirit by charcoal, as Döbereiner showed early in this century, and that the art of distillation is so far advanced as to admit of and mostly result in the production of almost chemically pure alcohol, which, owing to the absence of any kind of flavour, is termed *silent spirit*, it must be remembered that the production of fusel oil in wines occurs only under circumstances of the lowest uncleanliness, and, as regards natural wine in general, is not a question of practical importance. But as regards wine to which spirit is added, if the spirit be produced from potatoes, and not carefully purified, the introduction of some fusel oil might be possible. We believe, however, that the mere interest of the trader would prevent such an impurity from being introduced, for it would infallibly diminish the value of the wine by a greater sum than that which would be saved by the difference between a pure and an impure spirit.

There are effects of wines upon the nervous system which are as yet unexplained. Thus, to some men otherwise accustomed to the use of various wines, the higher kinds of white Burgundies do cause excitement of the heart ; the modern Champagnes also cause palpitation to many who formerly enjoyed the natural Champagnes, and used them to advantage; this arises from the fact that their alcoholicity is high out of proportion to the amount of their extractives. Champagne as now drunk in England is mostly *a brandied liquid.* Burgundies are liable to be a little brandied, even as regards the higher qualities, but the higher qualities of Hocks, or Bordeaux wines are never brandied; and this circumstance makes these wines particularly valuable for hygienic use as well as medicinal purposes.

Red wines contain an *astringent element*, which is a useful agent in hypercatharsis, and, on the contrary, is the cause of persons of slow peristaltic habit being obliged to avoid them. The astringency may act as a tonic upon some; it is the more likely to do so if it be combined with that peculiar *colouring matter* of red wine which contains *iron* as an element of its chemical constitution. But even of this only little is assimilated, and most of it is found in the detritus as dark sulphide of iron.

Red wines are liable to cause a feeling of *acidity in the stomach* to some persons; we have known such idiosyncrasy to appear and disappear at varying ages of the persons who manifested it; white wine suits such persons better. Again, we have known both white and red wine to become obnoxious to certain conditions of life, and in such cases diluted distilled spirits were the most suitable substitute for the discontinued wine. Beer disagrees with such persons still more, for reasons no doubt connected with the peculiar action of hops, and the fact that beer is a far more suitable medium for the propagation of many kinds of fermenting bacteria than wine, and wine more so than dilute spirit

Wine with *excess of natural acidity* surmounting five pro mille expressed as tartaric acid, is neither pleasing to the taste nor agreeable to the digestion. That such acidity can be removed by plaster of Paris, without making the wine absolutely flat, has no doubt contributed to the use of gypsum, as well as chalk. Wines treated with gypsum have a slightly cathartic action upon delicate persons, and therefore this effect must be noticed in given cases of intestinal disturbance. We have never known port wine to be plastered; sherry always is; and the wines of the Mediterranean countries, even the natural red and white ones, certain sorts of Marsala excepted, generally are plastered.

The *extractive matters* of wine, apart from sugar and glycerol no doubt have a distinct stimulating action upon the nervous system, analogous to the extractive agents contained in meat, milk, and vegetable juices. Their quantity is greatest in wines of the best years, and these are the most potent and wholesome. In old wines extractive matters have accumulated by concentration, and this circumstance is the main cause of the value of age in wine.

The *philosophy of the use of wine* as illustrated in history is a subject so large and important that it would occupy a separate treatise of the size of the present one. Its intimate connection with the life of most nations is demonstrated by the frequent symbolic use in religious observances. This can only be explained by the long-continued observation of its beneficial effects, as derived from its active ingredients; and for this reason antiquity sought after *good wine* as much as do modern nations.

§ 250. USE OF CHEMICAL ANALYSIS OF WINE.

The use of chemical analysis of wine for the purpose of sale and barter may be said not to exist. Wines have been made for ages, and developed to their present high state without any application of chemistry; they have been bought and sold by the test of mere gustation. Even now producers and sellers of wine do not use or employ chemical analysis for ascertaining any quality of the object of their trade, except with regard to alcoholicity, for this governs the amount of import duty they have to pay in several countries. Nevertheless chemistry could be of great value to wine producers if it were properly applied at the suitable conjuncture, particularly with reference to the remedial measures required by the accidents of faulty seasons and abnormal fermentations. We will take excess of *natural acidity of the must* as an example of a case in which chemistry might be useful. The amount of acid having been accurately ascertained, the amount of anti-acid required to be added to the must, in the shape of potash, would be given by a chemical equation. Or the chemical data would furnish the basis for the application of the process of Gall to must of excessive acidity. But while such an adjustment of the elementary properties of the raw material to be fermented has been developed to a high state of perfection in the brewing of beer—a process which is now literally in the hands and under the absolute direction of chemists—in the production of wine such interference is looked upon as akin to adulteration and denounced with sycophantic ardour. We hope that this erroneous conception of the *rôle* of chemistry in vinification may be discarded, particularly in view of the many empirical remedies which are applied to wine to correct faults which are the result of the neglect of chemical rules at the earlier stages of preparation.

One of the empirical processes most frequently employed in the making of wines in districts round the Mediterranean is the addition of *plaster of Paris* or gypsum to the must. We will now assume it not to be a mere adulteration intended to remove acidity from wine, and improve its colour to the standard cochineal red. We will also admit that it may be a question whether the removal of all tartaric acid, which is the main effect of plastering, may not be equivalent to the removal of a material from which certain fungi can produce compounds injurious to the quality of the wine ; or, putting it quite generally, whether the removal of the tartaric acid may not protect the wine from a possible deterioration greater than that which the abstraction of the acid inflicts on its part. Now it has been ascertained that when this danger is over, and the wine is made, its taste is greatly deteriorated, as compared to natural wine containing the tartar, by the presence of the free sulphate of potash, and it has a bitter and metallic taste. It has therefore been attempted to remove from such wine the sulphuric acid, and substitute instead the tartaric acid, which it naturally contained ; in other words, to restore to the wine its natural composition. The removal of the sulphuric acid is easily effected by baryta, but as that might be objected to on account of some remotely possible toxic effects, the sulphuric acid should be taken out by strontia, which is absolutely innocuous, and at the same time the potash should be re-combined with tartaric acid. A deposition of the excess of tartar then would clarify the wine, and after a short repose the product would be fit for use. In this process chemistry proves its usefulness, but it also proves the necessity for great caution. For it was found by experiment that some wines do contain not only sulphate of potash, as the result of the plastering, but, in addition, sulphate of soda, which was no doubt added as such, and these wines, when treated as just stated, do not only deposit tartar, but retain tartrate of sodium in solution, and are at least not improved by the process, for while bi-tartrate of potash is precipitated by alcohol, bi-tartrate of soda is not so precipitated.

Chemical analysis might inform the wine maker of the amount of *extractive* in his wine, upon which the ultimate development and durability to a large extent depend. It might inform him more precisely than mere taste of the presence of fermentable sugar and of its quantity, and thereby aid him to put his wine in a state of preservation from the risk arising therefrom in the shape of secondary fermentation after the bottling.

But at present chemistry is mainly applied to wine for the sorry purpose of what, owing to its exaggeration, we cannot help comparing to sycophancy. The discovery of the addition to must of any kind of sugar has attracted the highest ingenuity of food analysts so-called, who strain gnats out of their scientific solutions while allowing camels to pass through their filters. It would be preferable if so much ingenuity and work were applied to the enlargement of general scientific knowledge rather than to the tracing of petty remedies which a poor producer applies to his inferior products in order to give them a chance of being sold at any price. We have always been surprised that analysts who denounce a little salicylic acid as an adulteration never apply themselves to the plastered sherries ; that they do not even discover the wines the *acetic acid* of which has been neutralized by chalk, or the sweet wines the *lactic acid* of which has been neutralized in the same or some other way.

§ 251. USE OF WINE TO THE HEALTHY AND SICK IN YOUTH OR AGE.

There are some classical phrases to denote superfluous attempts, such as "carrying owls to Athens" or "coals to Newcastle." We would consider it equally redundant were we to say anything in praise of wine and its effects in general. A late professor of hygiene made a series of elaborate experiments upon a healthy guardsman, from which it seemed to follow that the use of wine was of no appreciable advantage to him. Some disciples of this professor went further, and endeavoured to prove that alcohol did not only not raise the temperature of the body but lowered it. Now warming a body does not include the raising of its natural temperature, and it is certain that wine does not produce fever heat. But wine can warm a body which feels, or is what is popularly termed cold, by stimulating the heart to action, and the mind to vivacity. It may not make him think better, but it will make him think quicker; it will exhilarate the healthy, as it will allay pain and spasms of the sick, and reinforce the wounded or exhausted.

The experiments in which alcohol was made to lower the temperature were performed on *corpora vilia* truly so-called, old, hardened drinkers, who were allowed to soak *ad libitum*, and then had their temperature measured. Of course it was depressed by the paralytic action of the toxic excess, but not very considerably. The effect was in fact known as necessary before the experiment, which proved only once more that when alcohol is made to act as a poison by excess, even upon persons habituated to excess, it still produces toxic effects. Such experiments also are "coals to Newcastle," for classic antiquity knew as much, and then the knowledge is of no use to anyone whatever. However interesting by its external precision, it is liable to serve as a basis for false inductions.

The foregoing experiment was not made with wine at all, not even with such as contains more than double the amount of spirit which wine can naturally attain, but with distilled alcohol, mere brandy. It therefore does, in reality, not illustrate the question which we are considering in any direct manner, though it does so indirectly. We believe that with natural wine, with an alcoholicity of less than 20 per cent. of proof spirit, the effect exhibited by these old topers would not be obtained at all. For there are certain peculiarities by which even the evil effects of wine are limited to its comparative advantage. Thus we have never known of an authentic case of *delirium tremens* produced by the drinking in whatever excess of natural wine. It was indeed this well-known immunity of wine drinkers, on the one hand, from, and liability of spirit drinkers, on the other hand, to the *tremor cum delirio potatorum*, which induced, in countries where wine is a daily popular beverage, the belief that the alcohol of distilled spirits was different from that of wine, or was mixed with a poison not present in wine, which many identified with the amylic alcohol, or fusel oil. Further, the habitual consumers of natural wine enjoy a remarkable immunity from gout, gravel and calculous diseases arising from the uric acid diathesis. Such immunity does not accompany the use or abuse of fortified wines, and goes the farther out of sight the greater is the amount of added alcohol. We therefore meet with men who present all the symptoms of chronic alcoholic intoxication, whose only beverage is sherry, and gravely maintain the mysterious nature of their complaint by assuring the physician that they never touched distilled spirits, not knowing or forgetting that the full half, or more than half, of the alcohol contained in their wine consists of distilled spirit.

The great physiological question of *the use of alcohol* in the body has in years gone by engaged my attention, and I endeavoured to answer it by serious experiment. A number of young men, engaged in athletic exercise in the open air, consumed a certain amount of wine of known strength, at reasonable intervals, with the precaution of avoiding all excess and any and every symptom of intoxication. It was ascertained by physiological analysis that 99 per cent. of alcohol were oxydized in the body, while about half a per cent. was exhaled by lungs and skin, another half per cent. re-appearing in the renal emunction. This proved therefore that the teaching of animal chemistry, according to which alcohol in the body was oxydized and produced power, was correct; the then teaching being faulty only in this respect, that it was supposed that the power produced was limited to heat; the theory caused the non-nitrogenous substances like fat, starch, sugar and alcohol to be called heat givers; but more extensive research showed that the power which they yielded was more general, and that while a portion might be heat, another undoubtedly was mechanical energy, and another, again, nervous. These experiments, which I was the first to institute, have been repeated since by others, always with the same result, and it is now generally admitted that alcohol is food in the true sense of the word.

Beer has an effect upon the body which is distinctly different from that of wine; it is no doubt an alcoholic liquid produced by fermentation, but it contains, at the same time, a principle of great sedative power nearly related to that of opium, namely *hops*. There is therefore between the alcohol on the one, and the lupulous principles on the other, a kind of antagonism, which, perhaps, neutralizes a portion of the effect of each in the first instance. As the composition of beer so is its effect upon the digestive organs more complicated than that of wine. It contains more extractive matter, in the shape of dextrine, sugar and salts, than wine, and by this means affords a material for the more copious development of bacteria in the intestinal canal, which wine, if at all, offers only in a much lower degree. The extract of hops is as powerful a sedative as that of poppy, particularly for the production of drowsiness and sleep, but it has not the anæsthetical effect of the latter. Its sedative effect shows itself in the lowering of all the higher nervous energies long before the arrival of alcoholic effects; wine has sedative effects by its alcoholic effects alone, and by these only at the later period of its action.

Distilled spirits have this danger in their use, that, in the case of insufficient dilution, they can be drunk in a more concentrated form than is good for the body. On the other hand, they develop the effects of alcohol in its purest form. *Rum* formerly possessed this advantage over other distilled spirit, that if unmixed with whiskey it was certainly free from amylic alcohol, so-called fusel oil. The progress in the art of distillation has imparted this quality to other spirits as well. Brandy from French cheap wines not rarely contains fusel oil to this day, and French chloroform made from such spirit is highly impure, from the admixture of chlorinated amylic products. But the finest French brandy, *Cognac*, made from the wine of the *folle blanche* is the most ideal, the finest perfumed, and most wholesome of distilled spirits.

CHAPTER XXXI.

DISEASES OF VINES AND OF WINES.

§ 252. DISEASES OF VINES AND THEIR TREATMENT.

MOST of the abnormal conditions, so-called *diseases of plants*,[1] particularly of vines, of which we have any precise knowledge, are of a *parasitical nature*, that is to say, caused by the settlement of living organisms of the nature of plants or animals upon the surface or in the tissues of the plant; drawing their nutriment out of the tissues of the vine, crippling or destroying them, and leading eventually to the death of the entire plant.

Thus a *fungus* of *the mushroom type*, an *agaricus*, the mycelium of which settles upon the roots of many forest and cultivated trees, and while its cycle of life was little understood, was called *rhizomorpha*, in some years infests many vines, and either makes them permanently sick and atrophic, or destroys them entirely. The French vignerons term it *Blanc des Racines;* it has been observed also in the Vaudois, on the lake of Constance, and on the Rhine.

---

[1] The reader who may desire concise information on the *Diseases of Plants* should consult the author's "Cantor Lectures" on that subject, delivered before the Society of Arts in January and February, 1887.

Chestnut and apple-trees not rarely fall victims to the *rhizoctonia*, or root-killer.

Of the *mildew fungi* or *blights*, the *Erysiphes* (Hedw.) a division of the *Pyrenomycetes*, comprising at least seven genera, and in these more than thirty species, the best known and most terrible is the *oïdium* of the vine, known after its discoverer, the Gravesend gardener Tucker, as *Oïdium Tuckeri*. It lives on the outside of the green parts of the vine, sends suckers, so-called haustoria, into their tissues, and

Fig. 45. Vine-leaf, covered and crippled by the oïdium.

thus gradually destroys them. The *leaves* shrivel, crumble up and die; the *young shoots* become atrophic and cease to grow; the *young grapes* cease to grow, or shrivel and die, the *larger grapes* burst, lose their contents, or rot and die. These changes are represented by the accompanying sketches after Du Breuil.

Most viticultural countries were visited by this plague during several decades of the present century. The wine production of Madeira, for example, was for years entirely destroyed; in that island 10,000 butts of wine were at one time produced annually; a few years after the invasion of the oïdium no wine at all was produced. In Portugal I have seen the vines of entire districts, such as Carcavellos, Bucellas, and others destroyed by that calamity. It has been found that the presence of sulphur in a finely divided state is fatal to the oïdium, and by the use of such sulphur only have the wine-producing lands been liberated from this plague. Du Breuil's work contains many illustrations of the manner in which the sulphur may be distributed over

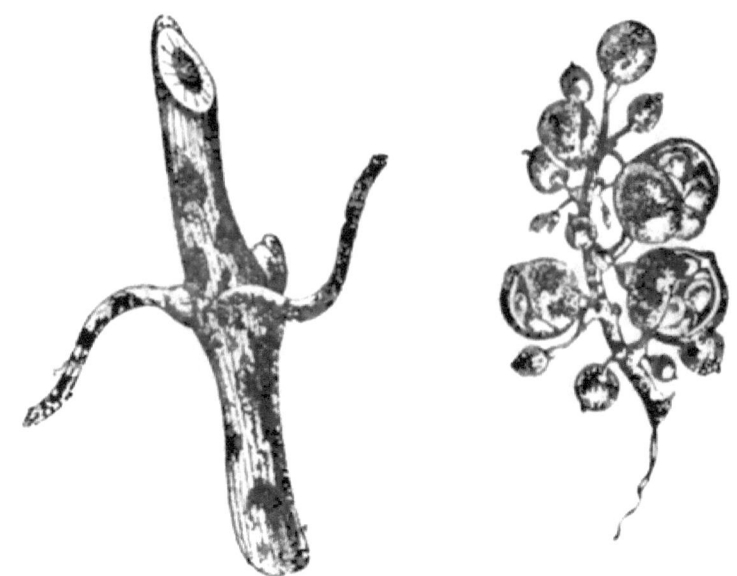

Fig. 46. A piece of vine-shoot covered with patches of oïdium.

Fig. 47. A bunch of grapes, dwarfed or fissured and burst through the agency of the oïdium.

the vines, but they are all more or less laborious or imperfect. The genius of a French gardener invented a machine for sulphuring which is at once cheap, convenient, and efficient. It consists of an inner retort filled with water, and an outer retort filled with sulphur, both fixed in a portable little stove heated with charcoal. The coal fuses the sulphur and causes it to distill; the sulphur vapour causes the water to boil, and the steam carries the sulphur

vapour with violence out of the cauldron. A man walking
with this apparatus along the vines as quickly as he can,
and keeping about a yard away from them, will cover the
plants in all their finest details with an exceedingly fine

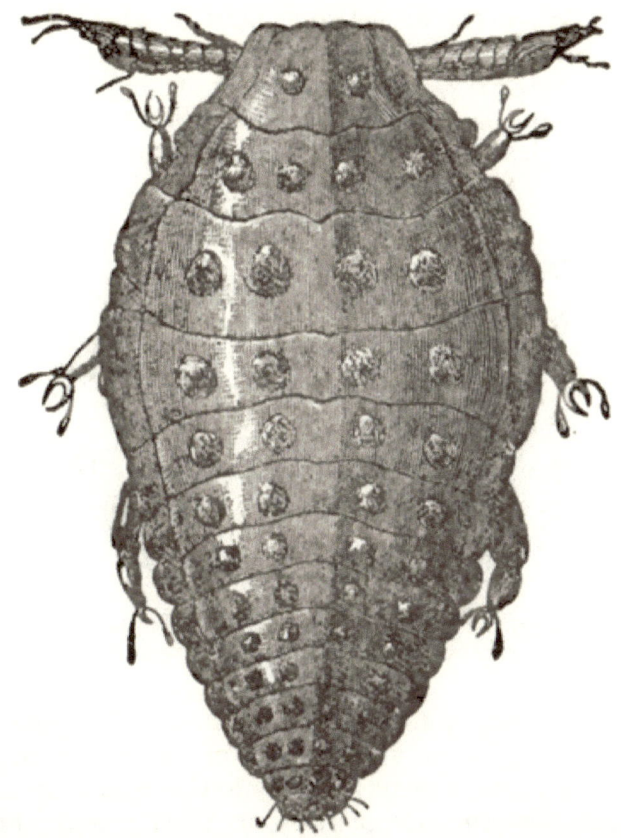

Fig. 48. Wingless female phylloxera, yellow, spotted, greatly magnified; dorsal aspect.

layer of condensed steam and sulphur. The process is
beautiful and safe, and one application is always effectual.

Of *animal parasites* affecting vines the most celebrated
and dreaded is the *Phylloxera vastatrix* (Planch.), (the
devastating leaf-dryer), an insect belonging to the *aphidia*,
genus of *green-fly*, producing galls on leaves and roots,

but damaging the vine only by the infliction upon the roots. This insect was discovered to be the cause of the most destructive vine disease by Planchon, in 1868, after it had ravaged many vineyards since 1863. Asa Fitch had previously discovered an insect which produces galls on the leaves of the vine, and which is now known to be reared out of the early egg of the winged female of the phylloxera, which does not hybernate. The life history of the phylloxera, if we start from the golden yellow, wingless female, the large spotted creature represented in Fig. 48, is the following. This female, sitting on

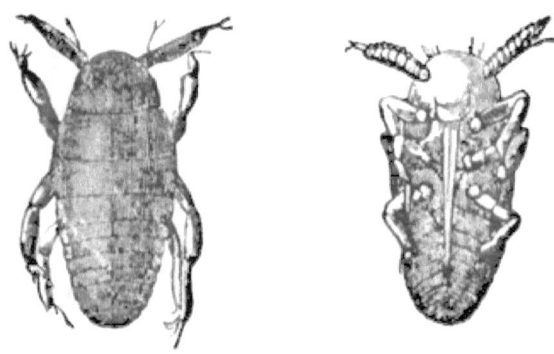

Figs. 49 and 50. Phylloxera of the roots : left specimen presents dorsal, right one ventral, side. The stinging organ is well seen.

the root, lays thirty to forty eggs, out of which the young creep in about eight days. Each of these now begins to multiply by parthenogenesis, and may produce up to eight generations in one summer. One female may therefore have a parthenogenetic progeny of thirty millions of individuals in one summer. They all remain on the roots on which they have been produced, and by stinging them and sucking their juices they produce galls and nodosities. The last brood at the end of summer, termed *nymphs*, or *pupas*, have beginnings of wings. These creep out of the earth, shed their skin several times, and become fully winged individuals. Their wings are four in number, large, and when the animals are at repose, lie flat on the body, as represented in Fig. 51. (The figures are after Oliveira, junior, of Oporto.) These winged nymphs now fly, and deposit eggs upon the leaves of vines; the eggs are four in number, and of different sizes; the larger eggs develop into wingless females, the smaller eggs into wingless males. This development ensues in little galls formed on the underside of the vine-leaf, as represented in Fig. 52. When the

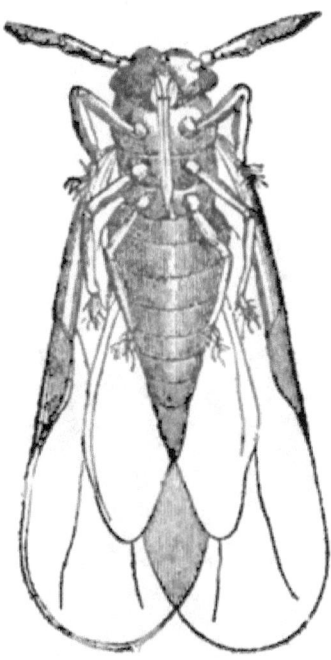

Fig. 51. Winged female Phylloxera, presenting ventral side.

wingless animals are mature, they copulate, whereupon each impregnated female puts down one large winter egg in a crevice of the bark of the vine. In spring this egg develops to a wingless female, which descends to the roots, and propagates on them within the earth by parthenogenesis as above described. The destruction effected by this parasite can be estimated by the fact that, while during the four years from 1875 to 1878, included, the average yield of the French vintage was 1,275 million gallons, the three vintages from 1882 to 1885 decreased at a greater rate than 100 million gallons a year, so that the production of wine in France fell to little more than half of what it was before the spread of the phylloxera. The animals are most certainly destroyed by inundation ; when that is impossible, sulphide of carbon

Fig. 52.   Vine-leaf, from underside, with galls of phylloxera.

is forced into the earth by an injector, and is said to produce the death of the parasites.

Of the *shield lice*, or *coccina*, a variety of which is the *Coccus cacti*, or *cochineal insect*, a species, called *vine louse*, or *vine bug*, *Coccus vitis*, is common in England on vines grown in conservatories ; it settles on old wood, covered with loose bark ; to prevent its existence and multiplication, the vine trunks have to be scraped clean of the bark and to be painted with milk of lime and tobacco infusion.

There are some *higher insects* which effect local damages, but are never epidemic One of these is the *Eumolpus*, a beetle a third of an inch in length, the larvæ of which eat the vine-leaves. Another beetle of similar size, but provided with a strong, stinging organ on its head, is the *Attelabe;* the female fixes its eggs on a vine-leaf, and by stinging it in many places, causes it to roll up spirally and house the egg; it also stings thick green branches, and causes them to shrivel and die. A third beetle noxious to vines is the *Altica oleracea* (Geoffrey), *altise* of the French, which gnaws buds and grape-stalks.

The *larva of a small moth*, French *Pyrale*, eats young leaves and grape-stalks at blossom-time, enveloping them in a fine veil of netting ; it appears a second time when the grapes are nearly ripe, covers them again with its silk, bites stalks, and eats into the grapes. This animal is much dreaded by French viticulturists. But compared to oïdium and phylloxera, all other parasites of the vine are of relatively small significance.

§ 253. Diseases of Wines, their Prevention and Cure.

Wines are liable to be spoilt by many natural causes, all being the result of the action of *fungi* which live in must or wine as their material of nutrition and medium of propagation and multiplication. They were recognized and described both as to their life-history and effects mainly by Pasteur. Some are the result of the occasional failure of human interference, such as sulphuring, plastering, and fining with albumen, as described already on p. 285.

The acetous ferment transforms alcohol into acetic acid, wine into vinegar ; for the development of its full action it requires much air, as its effect is the result of oxydation. Wine must, therefore, be protected from the access of the acetous fungi not only, but also from extensive contact with air. Even a small proportion of acetic acid will spoil the flavour of wine.

The scud or viscosity ferment multiplies with terrific energy in must, transforms it into a milky-white tasteless liquid, destroys all sugar, and completely crowds out the torula of alcoholic fermentation. It seems that sulphurous acid is the best preventive of this destructive change; the acid does not kill the fungus or spores, but paralyses them, and allows time for the true alcohol yeast to develop and transform the sugar into spirit. This is antagonistic to the scud fungus, but does not kill or prevent its development on a minor scale. When the scud or viscosity fungus attacks wine in barrel or bottle it forms in long threads, which cotton together, and give to the wine the appearance of jelly. It also develops some acetic acid, and wine which is once invaded by it, does but rarely recover. It is this dangerous ferment, mainly, which requires the addition of brandy to southern wines to preserve them. It is also not improbable that the removal of tartaric acid from wine by gypsum acts as a hindrance to the development of this fungus. But the plastering neither destroys the fungus, nor prevents its development entirely; it only modifies the growth and prevents the appearance of a little acetic acid as a decomposition product, in this case not of alcohol, but of tartaric acid. Common, low qualities of must in Spain and France require sulphurous acid, plaster and brandy, to be protected from the principal ravages of this dangerous fungus.

The bacillus muris, or mouse taste ferment, produces a peculiarly disagreeable flavour in wine, which is closely resembling to the smell of a residence of mice. It may spoil the best wines, but its ravages are mitigated by the fact that, with time and ripening, the fault may disappear in the main. But the affection always retards the usability of the wine by two years.

The fungus of bitterness attacks red wines more than white; it also causes them to shed their colour. Burgundies are most liable to its development; of white wines the Manzanillas of St. Lucar sometimes show its traces.

The mycoderma vini is a fungus which grows on the surface of wine and destroys its ethers in so remarkable a manner as to make the best wine flat to taste in a short time. By keeping the barrels always quite full, and allowing no ullage, the formation of this fungus is entirely prevented.

Flor, or *mycoderma montillanum*, is a ferment which, like the *mycoderma aceti*, requires to float on the surface of wine, and to have plenty of air for its existence; the wine must also be of a certain alcoholicity to exclude the vinegar plant, which can "crowd out," *i.e.*, overwhelm by greater numbers, the Montilla plant. When grown on the surface of good wine, as a pure cultivation, the *mycoderma montillanum* produces the flavour known as *Amontillado*, formerly rejected, but now considered as a very high development of white Spanish wines.

Agredoce is a disease of South French and Portuguese sweet red wines. It is of two kinds, one in which the acidity accompanying the sweetness is caused by acetic acid, and another in which it is caused by *lactic acid*. The latter is the most incurable, as it continues to act in the presence of sugar, a certain amount of alcoholicity notwithstanding. This disorder also afflicts many white wines of the Gironde, of Barsac and Sauternes.

The prevention of these so-called diseases is entirely in the hands of the wine makers; it is also in their power if they would only apply the teaching of science. This teaching affords the means of arresting these parasitic changes wherever they may show themselves.

THE END.

INDEX.

Greece, general remarks on, 336; quantity of wine, 338; vines, viticulture etc., 337; wines of, varieties, 336.

Greek Archipelago, islands of, 339.

Grenache noir, vine, 126.

HAMBRO black grape, 208.

Hesse, north of Maine, 195.

Hesse, Rhenish, 191; Rhenish, area of vineyards, 191; Liebfraumilch, 192; Niersteiner, 192.

Hochheim, topography of, 202; vines planted at, 202; vinification at, 203.

Holy Ghost wine, 194.

Hungary, classification of wines of, 223; cultivation in, 220; Kadarka, blue grape, 220; soil of, 220; topography of, 218; vines, varieties of, 220; vintage and vinification in, 220; white Tokay vine (Furmint), 220.

IMERITIA, wines of, 342.

Inarching, compound and simple, 27, 28.

Indigenous vines of the Algaida, 297; of America, 350; of Europe, 4; of the Rhine valley, 4, 5.

Inosite, a sugar in wine, 217.

Italy, wines of, 332.

JEREZ, vineyards and wines of, 226.

Jeropiga, of Portugal, 321.

Johannisberg, description and history, 200; vines and produce, 201.

KADARKA, blue grape of Hungary, 220.

LANGUEDOC, or Midi, 131; brandy (trois-six) of, 137; muscat wines of, 136: remarkable growths of,

134; topography of, 131; training of vines, vinification, etc, 132.

Lavradio, wines of, 324.

Layers or slips, propagation by, 26.

Lisbon wine, 322.

Loire, valley of, 181; cultivation in, 182; vines and wines of, 181.

Lombardy, wines of, 334.

MACEDONIA, wines of, 336.

Mâcon, town of, 146.

Mâconnais, the, 146; classification of growths of the, 148; cultivation in, 147; production and soil of, 147; varieties of wines of, 148.

Madeira, island of, 329; wines of, 330.

Maine, lower. See Hochheim, 202.

Majorca, wines of, 304.

Malaga, wines of, 303.

Malic acid in wine, 65.

Manuring of vines, methods of, 24.

Manzanilla, de San Lucar, wine, 295.

Maraschino, grape-vine, 216; cherry-brandy, 216.

Marcobrunn, vineyard, 200.

Marsala in Sicily, 335; vineyards and wines of, 335.

Marshes of the Gironde, 124.

Mashing of grapes, 43.

Measures, various Spanish, 226; of capacity, Rhenish; English; French; Portuguese; Spanish.

Médoc, classified growths of, 108; consumption of wines of, 112; cultivation in, 101; general statistics of, 97; methods of sale in, 112; prices of wines of, 112; topography of, 97; vines and viticulture, 98; vintage and vinification, 104.

Meran, grape-cure at, 209.

Merlot, grapevine, 99.

Mescle, the fertile and the sterile, 7.

Meunier or miller grape vine, 182.

CHISWICK PRESS:—C. WHITTINGHAM AND CO., TOOKS COURT, CHANCERY LANE.

ALPHABETICAL LIST

OF

BOHN'S LIBRARIES.

November, 1895.

'I may say in regard to all manner of books, Bohn's Publication Series is the usefullest thing I know.'—THOMAS CARLYLE.

'The respectable and sometimes excellent translations of Bohn's Library have done for literature what railroads have done for internal intercourse.'—EMERSON.

'An important body of cheap literature, for which every living worker in this country who draws strength from the past has reason to be grateful.'
Professor HENRY MORLEY.

BOHN'S LIBRARIES.

STANDARD LIBRARY	343 VOLUMES.
HISTORICAL LIBRARY	23 VOLUMES.
PHILOSOPIIICAL LIBRARY . . .	17 VOLUMES.
ECCLESIASTICAL LIBRARY . . .	15 VOLUMES.
ANTIQUARIAN LIBRARY . , . .	36 VOLUMES.
ILLUSTRATED LIBRARY	75 VOLUMES.
SPORTS AND GAMES.	16 VOLUMES.
CLASSICAL LIBRARY	108 VOLUMES.
COLLEGIATE SERIES.	10 VOLUMES.
SCIENTIFIC LIBRARY.	48 VOLUMES.
ECONOMICS AND FINANCE . . .	5 VOLUMES.
REFERENCE LIBRARY	30 VOLUMES.
NOVELISTS' LIBRARY	13 VOLUMES.
ARTISTS' LIBRARY	10 VOLUMES.
CHEAP SERIES	55 VOLUMES.
SELECT LIBRARY OF STANDARD WORKS	31 VOLUMES.

'Messrs. Bell are determined to do more than maintain the reputation of "Bohn's Libraries."'—*Guardian.*

'The imprint of Bohn's Standard Library is a guaranty of good editing.'
Critic (N.Y.)

'This new and attractive form in which the volumes of Bohn's Standard Library are being issued is not meant to hide either indifference in the selection of Books included in this well-known series, or carelessness in the editing.'
St. James's Gazette.

'Messrs. Bell & Sons are making constant additions of an eminently acceptable character to "Bohn's Libraries."'—*Athenæum.*

ALPHABETICAL LIST OF BOOKS

CONTAINED IN

BOHN'S LIBRARIES.

748 Vols., Small Post 8vo. cloth. Price £160.

Complete Detailed Catalogue will be sent on application.

Addison's Works. 6 vols. 3*s.* 6*d.* each.

Aeschylus. Verse Trans. by Anna Swanwick. 5*s.*

—— Prose Trans. by T. A. Buckley. 3*s.* 6*d.*

Agassiz & Gould's Comparative Physiology 5*s.*

Alfieri's Tragedies. Trans. by Bowring. 2 vols. 3*s.* 6*d.* each.

Alford's Queen's English. 1*s.* & 1*s.* 6*d.*

Allen's Battles of the British Navy. 2 vols. 5*s.* each.

Ammianus Marcellinus. Trans. by C. D. Yonge. 7*s.* 6*d.*

Andersen's Danish Tales. Trans. by Caroline Peachey. 5*s.*

Antoninus (Marcus Aurelius). Trans. by George Long. 3*s.* 6*d.*

Apollonius Rhodius. The Argonautica. Trans. by E. P. Coleridge. 5*s.*

Apuleius, The Works of. 5*s.*

Ariosto's Orlando Furioso. Trans. by W. S. Rose. 2 vols. 5*s.* each.

Aristophanes. Trans. by W. J. Hickie. 2 vols. 5*s.* each.

Aristotle's Works. 5 vols, 5*s.* each ; 2 vols, 3*s.* 6*d.* each.

Arrian. Trans. by E. J. Chinnock. 5*s.*

Ascham's Scholemaster. (J. E. B. Mayor.) 1*s.*

Bacon's Essays and Historical Works, 3*s.* 6*d.* ; Essays, 1*s.* and 1*s.* 6*d.*; Novum Organum, and Advancement of Learning, 5*s.*

Ballads and Songs of the Peasantry. By Robert Bell. 3*s.* 6*d.*

Bass's Lexicon to the Greek Test. 2*s.*

Bax's Manual of the History of Philosophy. 5*s.*

Beaumont & Fletcher. Leigh Hunt's Selections. 3*s.* 6*d.*

Bechstein's Cage and Chamber Birds. 5*s.*

Beckmann's History of Inventions. 2 vols. 3*s.* 6*d.* each.

Bede's Ecclesiastical History and the A. S. Chronicle. 5*s.*

Bell (Sir C.) On the Hand. 5*s.*

—— Anatomy of Expression. 5*s.*

Bentley's Phalaris. 5*s.*

Björnson's Arne and the Fisher Lassie. Trans. by W. H. Low. 3*s.* 6*d.*

Blair's Chronological Tables. 10*s.* Index of Dates. 2 vols. 5*s.* each.

Bleek's Introduction to the Old Testament. 2 vols. 5*s.* each.

Boethius' Consolation of Philosophy, &c. 5*s.*

Bohn's Dictionary of Poetical Quotations. 6*s.*

Bond's Handy-book for Verifying Dates, &c. 5*s.*

Bonomi's Nineveh. 5*s.*

Boswell's Life of Johnson, (Napier). 6 vols. 3*s.* 6*d.* each.

—— (Croker.) 5 vols. 20*s.*

Brand's Popular Antiquities. 3 vols. 5*s.* each.

Bremer's Works. Trans. by Mary Howitt. 4 vols. 3*s.* 6*d.* each.

Bridgewater Treatises. 9 vols. Various prices.

Brink (B. Ten). Early English Literature. 2 vols. 3*s.* 6*d.* each.

—— Five Lectures on Shakespeare 3*s.* 6*d.*

Browne's (Sir Thomas) Works. 3 vols. 3s. 6d. each.

Buchanan's Dictionary of Scientific Terms. 6s.

Buckland's Geology and Mineralogy. 2 vols. 15s.

Burke's Works and Speeches. 8 vols. 3s. 6d. each. The Sublime and Beautiful. 1s. & 1s. 6d. Reflections on the French Revolution. 1s.

—— Life, by Sir James Prior. 3s. 6d.

Burney's Evelina. 3s. 6d. Cecilia 2 vols. 3s. 6d. each.

Burns' Life by Lockhart. Revised by W. Scott Douglas. 3s. 6d.

Burn's Ancient Rome. 7s. 6d.

Butler's Analogy of Religion, and Sermons. 3s. 6d.

Butler's Hudibras. 5s.; or 2 vols., 5s. each.

Caesar. Trans. by W. A. M'Devitte. 5s.

Camoens' Lusiad. Mickle's Translation, revised. 3s. 6d.

Carafas (The) of Maddaloni. By Alfred de Reumont. 3s. 6d.

Carpenter's Mechanical Philosophy 5s. Vegetable Physiology. 6s. Animal Physiology. 6s.

Carrel's Counter Revolution under Charles II. and James II. 3s. 6d.

Cattermole's Evenings at Haddon Hall. 5s.

Catullus and Tibullus. Trans. by W. K. Kelly. 5s.

Cellini's Memoirs. (Roscoe.) 3s. 6d.

Cervantes' Exemplary Novels. Trans. by W. K. Kelly. 3s. 6d.

—— Don Quixote. Motteux's Trans. revised. 2 vols. 3s. 6d. each.

—— Galatea. Trans. by G. W. J. Gyll. 3s. 6d.

Chalmers On Man. 5s.

Channing's The Perfect Life. 1s. and 1s. 6d.

Chaucer's Works. Bell's Edition, revised by Skeat. 4 vols. 3s. 6d. ea.

Chess Congress of 1862 By J. Lowenthal. 5s.

Chevreul on Colour. 5s. and 7s. 6d.

Chillingworth's The Religion of Protestants. 3s. 6d.

China : Pictorial, Descriptive, and Historical. 5s.

Chronicles of the Crusades. 5s.

Cicero's Works. 7 vols. 5s. each. 1 vol., 3s. 6d.

—— Friendship and Old Age. 1s. and 1s. 6d.

Clark's Heraldry. (Planché.) 5s. and 15s.

Classic Tales. 3s. 6d.

Coleridge's Prose Works. (Ashe.) 6 vols. 3s. 6d. each.

Comte's Philosophy of the Sciences. (G. H. Lewes.) 5s.

—— Positive Philosophy. 3 vols. 5s. each.

Condé's History of the Arabs in Spain. 3 vols. 3s. 6d. each.

Cooper's Biographical Dictionary. 2 vols. 5s. each.

Cowper's Works. (Southey.) 8 vols. 3s. 6d. each.

Coxe's House of Austria. 4 vols. 3s. 6d. each. Memoirs of Marlborough. 3 vols. 3s. 6d. each. Atlas to Marlborough's Campaigns. 10s. 6d.

Craik's Pursuit of Knowledge. 5s.

Craven's Young Sportsman's Manual. 5s.

Cruikshank's Punch and Judy. 5s. Three Courses and a Dessert. 5s.

Cunningham's Lives of British Painters. 3 vols. 3s. 6d. each.

Dante. Trans. by Rev. H. F. Cary. 3s. 6d. Inferno. Separate, 1s. and 1s. 6d. Purgatorio. 1s. and 1s. 6d. Paradiso. 1s. and 1s. 6d.

—— Trans. by I. C. Wright. (Flaxman's Illustrations.) 5s.

—— Inferno. Italian Text and Trans. by Dr. Carlyle. 5s.

—— Purgatorio. Italian Text and Trans. by W. S. Dugdale. 5s.

De Commines' Memoirs. Trans. by A. R. Scoble. 2 vols. 3s. 6d. each.

Defoe's Novels and Miscel. Works. 6 vols. 3s. 6d. each. Robinson Crusoe (Vol. VII). 3s. 6d. or 5s. The Plague in London. 1s. and 1s. 6d.

Delolme on the Constitution of England. 3s. 6d.

Demmins' Arms and Armour. Trans. by C. C. Black. 7s. 6d.

Demosthenes' Orations. Trans. by C. Rann Kennedy. 4 vols. 5s., and 1 vol. 3s. 6d.
—— Orations On the Crown. 1s. and 1s. 6d.
De Stael's Corinne. Trans. by Emily Baldwin and Paulina Driver. 3s. 6d.
Devey's Logic. 5s.
Dictionary of Greek and Latin Quotations. 5s.
—— of Poetical Quotations (Bohn). 6s.
—— of Scientific Terms. (Buchanan.) 6s.
—— of Biography. (Cooper.) 2 vols. 5s. each.
—— of Noted Names of Fiction. (Wheeler.) 5s.
—— of Obsolete and Provincial English (Wright.) 2 vols. 5s. each.
Didron's Christian Iconography. 2 vols. 5s. each.
Diogenes Laertius. Trans. by C. D. Yonge. 5s.
Dobree's Adversaria. (Wagner). 2 vols. 5s. each.
Dodd's Epigrammatists. 6s.
Donaldson's Theatre of the Greeks. 5s.
Draper's History of the Intellectual Development of Europe. 2 vols. 5s. each.
Dunlop's History of Fiction. 2 vols. 5s. each.
Dyer's History of Pompeii. 7s. 6d.
—— The City of Rome. 5s.
Dyer's British Popular Customs. 5s.
Early Travels in Palestine. (Wright.) 5s.
Eaton's Waterloo Days. 1s. and 1s. 6d.
Eber's Egyptian Princess. Trans. by E. S. Buchheim. 3s. 6d.
Edgeworth's Stories for Children. 3s. 6d.
Ellis' Specimens of Early English Metrical Romances. (Halliwell.) 5s.
Elze's Life of Shakespeare. Trans. by L. Dora Schmitz. 5s.
Emerson's Works. 3 vols. 3s. 6d. each, or 5 vols. 1s. each.
Ennemoser's History of Magic. 2 vols. 5s. each.
Epictetus. Trans. by George Long. 5s.
Euripides. Trans. by E. P. Coleridge. 2 vols. 5s. each.
Eusebius' Eccl. History. Trans. by C. F. Cruse. 5s.

Evelyn's Diary and Correspondence. (Bray.) 4 vols. 5s. each.
Fairholt's Costume in England. (Dillon.) 2 vols. 5s. each.
Fielding's Joseph Andrews. 3s. 6d. Tom Jones. 2 vols. 3s. 6d. each. Amelia. 5s.
Flaxman's Lectures on Sculpture. 6s.
Florence of Worcester's Chronicle. Trans. by T. Forester. 5s.
Foster's Works. 10 vols. 3s. 6d. each.
Franklin's Autobiography. 1s.
Gesta Romanorum. Trans. by Swan & Hooper. 5s.
Gibbon's Decline and Fall. 7 vols. 3s. 6d. each.
Gilbart's Banking. 2 vols. 5s. each.
Gil Blas. Trans. by Smollett. 6s.
Giraldus Cambrensis. 5s.
Goethe's Works and Correspondence, including Autobiography and Annals, Faust, Elective affinities, Werther, Wilhelm Meister, Poems and Ballads, Dramas, Reinecke Fox, Tour in Italy and Miscellaneous Travels, Early and Miscellaneous Letters, Correspondence with Eckermann and Soret, Zelter and Schiller, &c. &c. By various translators. 16 vols. 3s. 6d. each.
—— Faust. Text with Hayward's Translation. (Buchheim.) 5s.
—— Faust. Part I. Trans. by Anna Swanwick. 1s. and 1s. 6d.
—— Boyhood. (Part I. of the Autobiography.) Trans. by J. Oxenford. 1s. and 1s. 6d.
—— Reinecke Fox. Trans. by A. Rogers. 1s. and 1s. 6d.
Goldsmith's Works. (Gibbs.) 5 vols. 3s. 6d. each.
—— Plays. 1s. and 1s. 6d. Vicar of Wakefield. 1s. and 1s. 6d.
Grammont's Memoirs and Boscobel Tracts. 5s.
Gray's Letters. (D. C. Tovey.) [*In the press.*
Greek Anthology. Trans. by E. Burges. 5s.
Greek Romances. (Theagenes and Chariclea, Daphnis and Chloe, Clitopho and Leucippe.) Trans. by Rev. R. Smith. 5s.

Greek Testament. 5*s*.

Greene, Marlowe, and Ben Jonson's Poems. (Robert Bell.) 3*s*. 6*d*.

Gregory's Evidences of the Christian Religion. 3*s*. 6*d*.

Grimm's Gammer Grethel. Trans. by E. Taylor. 3*s*. 6*d*.
—— German Tales. Trans. by Mrs. Hunt. 2 vols. 3*s*. 6*d*. each.

Grossi's Marco Visconti. 3*s*. 6*d*.

Guizot's Origin of Representative Government in Europe. Trans. by A. R. Scoble. 3*s*. 6*d*.
—— The English Revolution of 1640. Trans. by W. Hazlitt. 3*s*. 6*d*.
—— History of Civilisation. Trans. by W. Hazlitt. 3 vols. 3*s*. 6*d*. each.

Hall (Robert). Miscellaneous Works. 3*s*. 6*d*.

Handbooks of Athletic Sports. 8 vols. 3*s*. 6*d*. each.

Handbook of Card and Table Games. 2 vols. 3*s*. 6*d*. each.
—— of Proverbs. By H. G. Bohn. 5*s*.
—— of Foreign Proverbs. 5*s*.

Hardwick's History of the Thirty-nine Articles. 5*s*.

Harvey's Circulation of the Blood. (Bowie.) 1*s*. and 1*s*. 6*d*.

Hauff's Tales. Trans. by S. Mendel. 3*s*. 6*d*.
—— The Caravan and Sheik of Alexandria. 1*s*. and 1*s*. 6*d*.

Hawthorne's Novels and Tales. 4 vols. 3*s*. 6*d*. each.

Hazlitt's Lectures and Essays. 7 vols. 3*s*. 6*d*. each.

Heaton's History of Painting. (Cosmo Monkhouse.) 5*s*.

Hegel's Philosophy of History. Trans. by J. Sibree. 5*s*.

Heine's Poems. Trans. by E. A. Bowring. 3*s*. 6*d*.
—— Travel Pictures. Trans. by Francis Storr. 3*s*. 6*d*.

Helps (Sir Arthur). Life of Thomas Brassey. 1*s*. and 1*s*. 6*d*.

Henderson's Historical Documents of the Middle Ages. 5*s*.

Henfrey's English Coins. (Keary.) 6*s*.

Henry (Matthew) On the Psalms. 5*s*.

Henry of Huntingdon's History. Trans. by T. Forester. 5*s*.

Herodotus. Trans. by H. F. Cary. 3*s*. 6*d*.
—— Wheeler's Analysis and Summary of. 5*s*. Turner's Notes on. 5*s*.

Hesiod, Callimachus and Theognis. Trans. by Rev. J. Banks. 5*s*.

Hoffmann's Tales. The Serapion Brethren. Trans. by Lieut.-Colonel Ewing. 2 vols. 3*s*. 6*d*.

Hogg's Experimental and Natural Philosophy. 5*s*.

Holbein's Dance of Death and Bible Cuts. 5*s*.

Homer. Trans. by T. A. Buckley. 2 vols. 5*s*. each.
—— Pope's Translation. With Flaxman's Illustrations. 2 vols. 5*s*. each.
—— Cowper's Translation. 2 vols. 3*s*. 6*d*. each.

Hooper's Waterloo. 3*s*. 6*d*.

Horace. Smart's Translation, revised, by Buckley. 3*s*. 6*d*.

Hugo's Dramatic Works. Trans. by Mrs. Crosland and F. L. Slous. 3*s*. 6*d*.
—— Hernani. Trans. by Mrs. Crosland. 1*s*.
—— Poems. Trans. by various writers. Collected by J. H. L. Williams. 3*s*. 6*d*.

Humboldt's Cosmos. Trans. by Otté, Paul, and Dallas. 4 vols. 3*s*. 6*d*. each, and 1 vol. 5*s*.
—— Personal Narrative of his Travels. Trans. by T. Ross. 3 vols. 5*s*. each.
—— Views of Nature. Trans. by Otté and Bohn. 5*s*.

Humphreys' Coin Collector's Manual. 2 vols. 5*s*. each.

Hungary, History of. 3*s*. 6*d*.

Hunt's Poetry of Science. 5*s*.

Hutchinson's Memoirs. 3*s*. 6*d*.

India before the Sepoy Mutiny. 5*s*.

Ingulph's Chronicles. 5*s*.

Irving (Washington). Complete Works. 15 vols. 3*s*. 6*d*. each ; or in 18 vols. 1*s*. each, and 2 vols. 1*s*. 6*d*. each.
—— Life and Letters. By Pierre E. Irving. 2 vols. 3*s*. 6*d*. each.

Isocrates. Trans. by J. H. Freese. Vol. I. 5*s*.

James' Life of Richard Cœur de Lion. 2 vols. 3*s*. 6*d*. each.
—— Life and Times of Louis XIV. 2 vols. 3*s*. 6*d*. each.

Jameson (Mrs.) Shakespeare's Heroines. 3s. 6d.

Jesse (E.) Anecdotes of Dogs. 5s.

Jesse (J. H.) Memoirs of the Court of England under the Stuarts. 3 vols. 5s. each.

—— Memoirs of the Pretenders. 5s.

Johnson's Lives of the Poets. (Napier). 3 vols. 3s. 6d. each.

Josephus. Whiston's Translation, revised by Rev. A. R. Shilleto. 5 vols. 3s. 6d. each.

Joyce's Scientific Dialogues. 5s.

Jukes-Browne's Handbook of Physical Geology. 7s. 6d. Handbook of Historical Geology. 6s. The Building of the British Isles. 7s. 6d.

Julian the Emperor. Trans by Rev. C. W. King. 5s.

Junius's Letters. Woodfall's Edition, revised. 2 vols. 3s. 6d. each.

Justin, Cornelius Nepos, and Eutropius. Trans. by Rev. J. S. Watson. 5s.

Juvenal, Persius, Sulpicia, and Lucilius. Trans. by L. Evans. 5s.

Kant's Critique of Pure Reason. Trans. by J. M. D. Meiklejohn. 5s.

—— Prolegomena, &c. Trans. by E. Belfort Bax. 5s.

Keightley's Fairy Mythology. 5s. Classical Mythology. Revised by Dr. L. Schmitz. 5s.

Kidd On Man. 3s. 6d.

Kirby On Animals. 2 vols. 5s. each.

Knight's Knowledge is Power. 5s.

La Fontaine's Fables. Trans. by E. Wright. 3s. 6d.

Lamartine's History of the Girondists. Trans. by H. T. Ryde. 3 vols. 3s. 6d. each.

—— Restoration of the Monarchy in France. Trans. by Capt. Rafter. 4 vols. 3s. 6d. each.

—— French Revolution of 1848. 3s. 6d.

Lamb's Essays of Elia and Eliana. 3s. 6d., or in 3 vols. 1s. each.

—— Memorials and Letters. Talfourd's Edition, revised by W. C. Hazlitt. 2 vols. 3s. 6d. each.

—— Specimens of the English Dramatic Poets of the Time of Elizabeth. 3s. 6d.

Lanzi's History of Painting in Italy. Trans. by T. Roscoe. 3 vols. 3s. 6d. each.

Lappenberg's England under the Anglo-Saxon Kings. Trans. by B. Thorpe. 2 vols. 3s. 6d. each.

Lectures on Painting. By Barry, Opie and Fuseli. 5s.

Leonardo da Vinci's Treatise on Painting. Trans. by J. F. Rigaud. 5s.

Lepsius' Letters from Egypt, &c. Trans. by L. and J. B. Horner. 5s.

Lessing's Dramatic Works. Trans. by Ernest Bell. 2 vols. 3s. 6d. each. Nathan the Wise and Minna von Barnhelm. 1s. and 1s. 6d. Laokoon, Dramatic Notes, &c. Trans. by E. C. Beasley and Helen Zimmern. 3s. 6d. Laokoon separate. 1s. or 1s. 6d.

Lilly's Introduction to Astrology. (Zadkiel.) 5s.

Livy. Trans. by Dr. Spillan and others. 4 vols. 5s. each.

Locke's Philosophical Works. (J. A. St. John). 2 vols. 3s. 6d. each.

—— Life. By Lord King. 3s. 6d.

Lodge's Portraits. 8 vols. 5s. each.

Longfellow's Poetical and Prose Works. 2 vols. 5s. each.

Loudon's Natural History. 5s.

Lowndes' Bibliographer's Manual. 6 vols. 5s. each.

Lucan's Pharsalia. Trans. by H. T. Riley. 5s.

Lucian's Dialogues. Trans. by H. Williams. 5s.

Lucretius. Trans. by Rev. J. S. Watson. 5s.

Luther's Table Talk. Trans. by W. Hazlitt. 3s. 6d.

—— Autobiography. (Michelet). Trans. by W. Hazlitt. 3s. 6d.

Machiavelli's History of Florence, &c. Trans. 3s. 6d.

Mallet's Northern Antiquities. 5s.

Mantell's Geological Excursions through the Isle of Wight, &c. 5s. Petrifactions and their Teachings. 6s. Wonders of Geology. 2 vols. 7s. 6d. each.

Manzoni's The Betrothed. 5s.

Marco Polo's Travels. Marsden's Edition, revised by T. Wright. 5s.

Martial's Epigrams. Trans. 7s. 6d.

Martineau's History of England, 1800–15. 3s. 6d.

—— History of the Peace, 1816–46. 4 vols. 3s. 6d. each.

Matthew Paris. Trans. by Dr. Giles. 3 vols. 5s. each.

Matthew of Westminster. Trans. by C. D. Yonge. 2 vols. 5s. each.

Maxwell's Victories of Wellington. 5s.

Menzel's History of Germany. Trans. by Mrs. Horrocks. 3 vols. 3s. 6d. ea.

Michael Angelo and Raffaelle. By Duppa and Q. de Quincy. 5s.

Michelet's French Revolution. Trans. by C. Cocks. 3s. 6d.

Mignet's French Revolution. 3s. 6d.

Mill (John Stuart). Selected Essays. [In the press.

Miller's Philosophy of History. 4 vols. 3s. 6d. each.

Milton's Poetical Works. (J. Montgomery.) 2 vols. 3s. 6d. each.

—— Prose Works. (J. A. St. John.) 5 vols. 3s. 6d. each.

Mitford's Our Village. 2 vols. 3s. 6d. each.

Molière's Dramatic Works. Trans. by C. H. Wall. 3 vols. 3s. 6d. each.

—— The Miser, Tartuffe, The Shopkeeper turned Gentleman. 1s. & 1s. 6d.

Montagu's (Lady M. W.) Letters and Works. (Wharncliffe and Moy Thomas.) 2 vols. 5s. each.

Montaigne's Essays. Cotton's Trans. revised by W. C. Hazlitt. 3 vols. 3s. 6d. each.

Montesquieu's Spirit of Laws. Nugent's Trans. revised by J. V. Prichard. 2 vols. 3s. 6d. each.

Morphy's Games of Chess. (Löwenthal.) 5s.

Motley's Dutch Republic. 3 vols. 3s. 6d. each.

Mudie's British Birds. (Martin.) 2 vols. 5s. each.

Naval and Military Heroes of Great Britain, 6s.

Neander's History of the Christian Religion and Church. 10 vols. Life of Christ. 1 vol. Planting and Training of the Church by the Apostles. 2 vols. History of Christian Dogma.

2 vols. Memorials of Christian Life in the Early and Middle Ages. 16 vols. 3s. 6d. each.

Nicolini's History of the Jesuits. 5s.

North's Lives of the Norths. (Jessopp.) 3 vols. 3s. 6d. each.

Nugent's Memorials of Hampden. 5s.

Ockley's History of the Saracens. 3s. 6d.

Ordericus Vitalis. Trans. by T. Forester. 4 vols. 5s. each.

Ovid. Trans. by H. T. Riley. 3 vols. 5s. each.

Pascal's Thoughts. Trans. by C. Kegan Paul. 3s. 6d.

Pauli's Life of Alfred the Great, &c. 5s.

—— Life of Cromwell. 1s. and 1s. 6d.

Pausanias' Description of Greece. Trans. by Rev. A. R. Shilleto. 2 vols. 5s. each.

Pearson on the Creed. (Walford.) 5s.

Pepys' Diary. (Braybrooke.) 4 vols. 5s. each.

Percy's Reliques of Ancient English Poetry. (Prichard.) 2 vols. 3s. 6d. ea.

Petrarch's Sonnets. 5s.

Pettigrew's Chronicles of the Tombs. 5s.

Philo-Judæus. Trans. by C. D. Yonge. 4 vols. 5s. each.

Pickering's Races of Man. 5s.

Pindar. Trans. by D. W. Turner. 5s.

Planché's History of British Costume. 5s.

Plato. Trans. by H. Cary, G. Burges, and H. Davis. 6 vols. 5s. each.

—— Apology, Crito, Phædo, Protagoras. 1s. and 1s. 6d.

—— Day's Analysis and Index to the Dialogues. 5s.

Plautus. Trans. by H. T. Riley. 2 vols. 5s. each.

—— Trinummus, Menæchmi, Aularia, Captivi. 1s. and 1s. 6d.

Pliny's Natural History. Trans. by Dr. Bostock and H. T. Riley. 6 vols. 5s. each.

Pliny the Younger, Letters of. Melmoth's trans. revised by Rev. F. C. T. Bosanquet. 5s.

Plotinus: Select Works of. 5s.

Plutarch's Lives. Trans. by Stewart and Long. 4 vols. 3*s*. 6*d*. each.
—— Moralia. Trans. by Rev. C. W. King and Rev. A. R. Shilleto. 2 vols. 5*s*. each.

Poetry of America. (W. J. Linton.) 3*s*. 6*d*.

Political Cyclopædia. 4 vols. 3*s*. 6*d*. ea.

Polyglot of Foreign Proverbs. 5*s*.

Pope's Poetical Works. (Carruthers.) 2 vols. 5*s*. each.
—— Homer. (J. S. Watson.) 2 vols. 5*s*. each.
—— Life and Letters. (Carruthers.) 5*s*.

Pottery and Porcelain. (H. G. Bohn.) 5*s*. and 10*s*. 6*d*.

Propertius. Trans. by Rev. P. J. F. Gantillon. 3*s*. 6*d*.

Prout (Father.) Reliques. 5*s*.

Quintilian's Institutes of Oratory. Trans. by Rev. J. S. Watson. 2 vols. 5*s*. each.

Racine's Tragedies. Trans. by R. B. Boswell. 2 vols. 3*s*. 6*d*. each.

Ranke's History of the Popes. Trans. by E. Foster. 3 vols. 3*s*. 6*d*. each.
—— Latin and Teutonic Nations. Trans. by P. A. Asbworth. 3*s*. 6*d*.
—— History of Servia. Trans. by Mrs. Kerr. 3*s*. 6*d*.

Rennie's Insect Architecture. (J. G. Wood.) 5*s*.

Reynold's Discourses and Essays. (Beechy.) 2 vols. 3*s*. 6*d*. each.

Ricardo's Political Economy. (Gonner.) 5*s*.

Richter's Levana. 3*s*. 6*d*.
—— Flower Fruit and Thorn Pieces. Trans. by Lieut.-Col. Ewing. 3*s*. 6*d*.

Roger de Hovenden's Annals. Trans. by Dr. Giles. 2 vols. 5*s*. each.

Roger of Wendover. Trans. by Dr. Giles. 2 vols. 5*s*. each.

Roget's Animal and Vegetable Physiology. 2 vols. 6*s*. each.

Rome in the Nineteenth Century. (C. A. Eaton.) 2 vols. 5*s* each.

Roscoe's Leo X. 2 vols. 3*s*. 6*d*. each.
—— Lorenzo de Medici. 3*s*. 6*d*.

Russia, History of. By W. K. Kelly. 2 vols. 3*s*. 6*d*. each.

Sallust, Florus, and Velleius Paterculus. Trans. by Rev. J. S. Watson. 5*s*.

Schiller's Works. Including History of the Thirty Years' War, Revolt of the Netherlands, Wallenstein, William Tell, Don Carlos, Mary Stuart, Maid of Orleans, Bride of Messina, Robbers, Fiesco, Love and Intrigue, Demetrius, Ghost-Seer, Sport of Divinity, Poems, Aesthetical and Philosophical Essays, &c. By various translators. 7 vols. 3*s*. 6*d*. each.
—— Mary Stuart and The Maid of Orleans. Trans. by J. Mellish and Anna Swanwick. 1*s*. and 1*s*. 6*d*.

Schlegel (F.). Lectures and Miscellaneous Works. 5 vols. 3*s*. 6*d*. each.
—— (A. W.). Lectures on Dramatic Art and Literature. 3*s*. 6*d*.

Schopenhauer's Essays. Selected and Trans. by E. Belfort Bax. 5*s*.
—— On the Fourfold Root of the Principle of Sufficient Reason and on the Will in Nature. Trans. by Mdme. Hillebrand. 5*s*.

Schouw's Earth, Plants, and Man. Trans. by A. Henfrey. 5*s*.

Schumann's Early Letters. Trans. by May Herbert. 3*s*. 6*d*.
—— Reissmann's Life of. Trans. by A. L. Alger. 3*s*. 6*d*.

Seneca on Benefits. Trans. by Aubrey Stewart. 3*s*. 6*d*.
—— Minor Essays and On Clemency. Trans. by Aubrey Stewart. 5*s*.

Sharpe's History of Egypt. 2 vols. 5*s*. each.

Sheridan's Dramatic Works. 3*s*. 6*d*.
—— Plays. 1*s*. and 1*s*. 6*d*.

Sismondi's Literature of the South of Europe. Trans. by T. Roscoe. 2 vols. 3*s*. 6*d*. each.

Six Old English Chronicles. 5*s*.

Smith (Archdeacon). Synonyms and Antonyms. 5*s*.

Smith (Adam). Wealth of Nations. (Belfort Bax.) 2 vols. 3*s*. 6*d*. each.
—— Theory of Moral Sentiments. 3*s*. 6*d*.

Smith (Pye). Geology and Scripture. 5*s*.

Smollett's Novels. 4 vols. 3*s*. 6*d*. each.

Smyth's Lectures on Modern History. 2 vols. 3*s*. 6*d*. each.

Socrates' Ecclesiastical History. 5s.

Sophocles. Trans. by E. P. Coleridge, B.A. 5s.

Southey's Life of Nelson. 5s.

—— Life of Wesley. 5s.

—— Life, as told in his Letters. By J. Dennis. 3s. 6d.

Sozomen's Ecclesiastical History. 5s.

Spinoza's Chief Works. Trans. by R. H. M. Elwes. 2 vols. 5s. each.

Stanley's Dutch and Flemish Painters. 5s.

Starling's Noble Deeds of Women. 5s.

Staunton's Chess Players' Handbook. 5s. Chess Praxis. 5s. Chess Players' Companion. 5s. Chess Tournament of 1851. 5s.

Stöckhardt's Experimental Chemistry. (Heaton.) 5s.

Strabo's Geography. Trans. by Falconer and Hamilton. 3 vols. 5s. each.

Strickland's Queens of England. 6 vols. 5s. each. Mary Queen of Scots. 2 vols. 5s. each. Tudor and Stuart Princesses. 5s.

Stuart & Revett's Antiquities of Athens. 5s.

Suetonius' Lives of the Caesars and of the Grammarians. Thomson's trans. revised by T. Forester. 5s.

Sully's Memoirs. Mrs. Lennox's trans. revised. 4 vols. 3s. 6d. each.

Tacitus. The Oxford trans. revised. 2 vols. 5s. each.

Tales of the Genii. Trans. by Sir. Charles Morell. 5s.

Tasso's Jerusalem Delivered. Trans. by J. H. Wiffen. 5s.

Taylor's Holy Living and Holy Dying. 3s. 6d.

Terence and Phædrus. Trans. by H. T. Riley. 5s.

Theocritus, Bion, Moschus, and Tyrtæus. Trans. by Rev. J. Banks. 5s.

Theodoret and Evagrius. 5s.

Thierry's Norman Conquest. Trans. by W. Hazlitt. 2 vols. 3s. 6d. each.

Thucydides. Trans by Rev. H. Dale. 2 vols. 3s. 6d. each.

—— Wheeler's Analysis and Summary of. 5s.

Trevelyan's Ladies in Parliament. 1s. and 1s. 6d.

Ulrici's Shakespeare's Dramatic Art. Trans. by L. Dora Schmitz. 2 vols. 3s. 6d. each.

Uncle Tom's Cabin. 3s. 6d.

Ure's Cotton Manufacture of Great Britain. 2 vols. 5s. each.

—— Philosophy of Manufacture. 7s. 6d.

Vasari's Lives of the Painters. Trans. by Mrs. Foster. 6 vols. 3s. 6d. each.

Virgil. Trans. by A. Hamilton Bryce, LL.D. 3s. 6d.

Voltaire's Tales. Trans. by R. B. Boswell. 3s. 6d.

Walton's Angler. 5s.

—— Lives. (A. H. Bullen.) 5s.

Waterloo Days. By C. A. Eaton. 1s. and 1s. 6d.

Wellington, Life of. By 'An Old Soldier.' 5s.

Werner's Templars in Cyprus. Trans. by E. A. M. Lewis. 3s. 6d.

Westropp's Handbook of Archæology. 5s.

Wheatley. On the Book of Common Prayer. 3s. 6d.

Wheeler's Dictionary of Noted Names of Fiction. 5s.

White's Natural History of Selborne. 5s.

Wieseler's Synopsis of the Gospels. 5s.

William of Malmesbury's Chronicle. 5s.

Wright's Dictionary of Obsolete and Provincial English. 2 vols. 5s. each.

Xenophon. Trans. by Rev. J. S. Watson and Rev. H. Dale. 3 vols. 5s. ea.

Young's Travels in France, 1787-89. (M. Betham-Edwards.) 3s. 6d.

—— Tour in Ireland, 1776-9. (A. W. Hutton.) 2 vols. 3s. 6d. each.

Yule-Tide Stories (B. Thorpe.) 5s.

New Editions, fcap. 8vo. 2s. 6d. each net.

THE ALDINE EDITION

OF THE

BRITISH POETS.

'This excellent edition of the English classics, with their complete texts and scholarly introductions, are something very different from the cheap volumes of extracts which are just now so much too common.'—*St. James's Gazette.*

'An excellent series. Small, handy, and complete.'—*Saturday Review.*

Akenside. Edited by Rev. A. Dyce.

Beattie. Edited by Rev. A. Dyce.

*Blake. Edited by W. M. Rossetti.

*Burns. Edited by G. A. Aitken. 3 vols.

Butler. Edited by R. B. Johnson. 2 vols.

Campbell. Edited by His Son-in-law, the Rev. A. W. Hill. With Memoir by W. Allingham.

Chatterton. Edited by the Rev. W. W. Skeat, M.A. 2 vols.

Chaucer. Edited by Dr. R. Morris, with Memoir by Sir H. Nicolas. 6 vols.

Churchill. Edited by Jas. Hannay. 2 vols.

*Coleridge. Edited by T. Ashe, B.A. 2 vols.

Collins. Edited by W. Moy Thomas.

Dryden. Edited by the Rev. R. Hooper, M.A. 5 vols.

Goldsmith. Edited by Austin Dobson.

*Gray. Edited by J. Bradshaw, LL.D.

Herbert. Edited by the Rev. A. B. Grosart.

*Herrick. Edited by George Saintsbury. 2 vols.

*Keats. Edited by the late Lord Houghton.

Milton. Edited by Dr. Bradshaw. 3 vols.

Parnell. Edited by G. A. Aitken.

Pope. Edited by G. R. Dennis. With Memoir by John Dennis. 3 vols.

Prior. Edited by R. B. Johnson. 2 vols.

Raleigh and Wotton. With Selections from the Writings of other COURTLY POETS from 1540 to 1650. Edited by Ven. Archdeacon Hannah, D.C.L.

Rogers. Edited by Edward Bell, M.A.

Scott. Edited by John Dennis. 5 vols.

Shakespeare's Poems. Edited by Rev. A. Dyce.

Shelley. Edited by H. Buxton Forman. 5 vols.

Spenser. Edited by J. Payne Collier. 5 vols.

Surrey. Edited by J. Gregory Foster.

Swift. Edited by the Rev. R. Hooper, M.A. 3 vols.

Thomson. Edited by the Rev. D. C. Toovey. 2 vols.

Vaughan. Sacred Poems and Pious Ejaculations. Edited by the Rev. H. Lyte.

Wordsworth. Edited by Prof. Dowden. 7 vols.

Wyatt. Edited by J. Gregory Foster.

To be followed by

Cowper. Edited by John Bruce, F.S.A. 3 vols.

Kirke White. Edited by J. Potter Briscoe.

Young. 2 vols.

These volumes may also be had bound in Irish linen, with design in gold on side and back by Gleeson White, and gilt top, 3s. 6d. each net.

www.ingramcontent.com/pod-product-compliance
Lightning Source LLC
Chambersburg PA
CBHW021341110726
47900CB00005B/1563